Books by Lynn Steigleder

Rising Tide
(Volume I of the Rising Tide Series)

Eden's Wake
(Volume II of the Rising Tide Series)

Terminal Core

LYNN STEIGLEDER
TERMINAL CORE

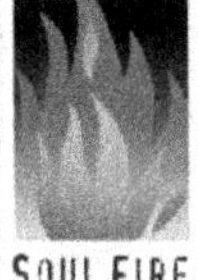

SOUL FIRE
PRESS

Boston

Terminal Core

Editor: Jeremy Soldevilla
Cover design: MJC Imageworks

ISBN 978-1938985-97-3
ebook ISBN 978-1-938985-98-0

Published by
Soul Fire Press

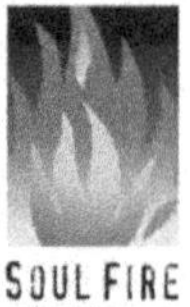

an imprint of
CHRISTOPHER MATTHEWS PUBLISHING

http://christopher matthewspub.com
Boston

Printed in the United States of America

Dedicated

to

Evelyn Holladay, a.k.a. Mom, Curly

Hazel Hale, a.k.a. Mom-in-law, Sweetheart

Donna Steigleder, a.k.a. Wife, Sweetie

Acknowledgments

Thanks go to Carol Neilan, my typist; personal assistant; tea maker extraordinaire; good-natured, skeptical person from parts north; muse; slightly opinionated nemesis and most importantly, my friend.

I would be remiss if I did not mention my buddy Suzie Martin, who could read such improper English from "Gert" (one of the book's characters) that I had to question her educational accomplishments. She soon proved herself an intelligent lass, and her ability to read totally miscued English was exactly that.

ONE

CLAY STEPPED UP onto the raised walkway.

"I hate this place," he mumbled, patting his sidearm. He grabbed the door handle and prepared to enter.

Clay was a bounty hunter. His latest skip (if you want to call him that since Clay had spent the better part of two years chasing empty leads) was Sal Ricky—a career criminal with a taste for refined women, as he would consume certain body parts of his victims after performing whatever atrocities piqued his fancy.

Clay stood tall, six foot five. He almost always wore black, except for his blue jeans. He felt it more intimidating.

He stepped into the brothel. A dozen pair of eyes turned his way. Clay removed his sidearm from its holster.

"I'm looking for Sal Ricky," he announced. After a slight pause, he repeated the phrase. "I said, I'm looking for Sal Ricky."

"If you want me, all you gotta do is ask," came a smug response. The voice emanated from a dark corner. In it stood a six foot tall figure. Instead of legs, it sported four eight foot long appendages. These members would shoot forward landing on the ground and allow the rest of the body to move over them like treads on a tank. He could move surprisingly fast when necessary.

"So?" Sal Ricky asked. "What can I do for you?"

Clay moved closer toward the corner and cocked his weapon.

"Don't play stupid, you ball of snot." He raised his free hand and pointed a finger. "I've been looking for you for almost two years now." Clay cocked the second hammer on his handgun. "This time you're all mine."

Sal Ricky was a hydrak. He lived up to his name, constantly oozing fluid and leaving a trail similar to that of a slug when he moved.

"Ya think so." The creature lit a cigarette with two human-like hands. The hydrak inhaled deeply, burning up half the smoke in one drag.

"Better men have tried," he said, finishing his cigarette with a second drag and dropping it into a puddle of slime; the butt hissed as the glowing ashes died.

Clay tightened his grip.

"We can do this the easy way or the hard way. I get just as much for you dead as alive." Clay smiled out of one corner of his mouth. "It makes no difference to me."

Sal Ricky crossed his arms which were anything but human. They were muscular with a lizard-like texture and a green color to match. His lower half was bulbous and horizontal to the ground, turning vertical at mid-thorax until it formed his head.

"Don't you tire of the same old clichés?" Sal Ricky snickered. "Easy way, hard way, alive or dead, blah, blah, blah. After two years, you should know I do nothing the easy way." His head was square with a round circle on each side. Sal Ricky could spin his neck three hundred and sixty degrees if need be. He had a set of eyes at the upper portion of each circle. One side contained an orifice with which he spoke and took in nourishment. One big tuft of green hair sprang from the center of his scalp, climbed vertically, about a foot, and then flopped over on all sides.

"Have it your way," Clay said.

Just then, two dark humanoid figures appeared on either side of the slug. The first figure made a move and then slipped on his boss' excretions, landing flat on his back.

Clay rolled to his right behind a steel column and fired one barrel, removing most of the second figure's head. The first man, still floundering in the goo, was an easy take out.

Sal Ricky moved toward Clay knocking him to the floor as he passed by.

Clay moved to one knee and steadied himself. He would have but one shot.

Sal Ricky could easily burst through the wall, and that's what he had a mind to do, Clay surmised. He made sure both hammers were cocked. Cocking them was one thing; firing both at the same time was something you didn't do unless you had to.

Clay took a deep breath and pulled both triggers.

TWO

SULLY SLAMMED HIS CARDS down hard on the wooden table. It was among six others that sat in the saloon.

"I've had just about enough of this," he grumbled.

The other five people at the table moaned.

"Will you shut up and play?" one gambler said. The rest acknowledged his sentiments.

The nineteenth century saloon was of solid construction and equipped with the fixtures of the day. Six chairs encircled each oak table. The bar was custom made from black walnut with a bronze bar running the length six inches off the ground for patrons to park their feet.

An oversized mirror graced the back of the wall surrounded by a large selection of liquors starting with the cheap and running to the best of the top shelf booze. A player piano sat in the corner to offer entertainment to the saloon patrons.

"No, I won't," Sully insisted. "That good for nothin president has got us in such a pickle we don't know which way is up." He freed his sidearm from its prison and, pulling the trigger, sent a spine cutter slug through the roof.

He began to re-holster his weapon.

"And I, for one, ain't gonna take it no more." The revolver bottomed out in its holster and snapped, confirming the finality of his statement.

Three blue whirling columns of nothing appeared in the middle of the saloon. They started at the ceiling and worked their way down to the floor. As the azure columns dissipated, three men appeared with guns drawn.

They sported cowboy garb complete with boots, Stetson hats and holstered dozen guns. The dozen gun was a hybrid of the six shooter, except it held twice the amount of ammunition; hence the name.

The shooter had the choice of releasing two bullets at one time. This was done when the possibility of deadly force confronted the shooter or on a bet when alcohol was usually involved. In either case, it was a painful choice as it rattled every bone in the gun carrier's extremity from his hand to his shoulder, occasionally fracturing smaller bones.

All three wore brass stars. The figure flanked by a man to his left and one to his right stepped forward. His badge was larger than the other two and more ornate, an oval blue stone planted in its center.

"Marshal Quincy," Sully said. He nodded and removed his revolver, placing it in the law man's outstretched hand.

"Gotta quit shootin up the town, Sully," Quincy said. "Maybe a few days in the lockup will help you realize that." He looked around. "Don't seem to be much damage," he said to the bartender. The marshal paused. "You in agreeance, Kabell?"

The bartender shrugged. "I reckon."

The marshal nodded and led Sully over to the jailhouse. He pushed the button lowering the charged cell bars.

"In with you," the marshal said.

Sully stepped into the imaginary box. The marshal pushed the button once again raising the bars and forming an inescapable electronic prison.

"Why didn't we transfer using the splitter," Sully asked, "instead of hoofing it all the way over here."

"Wasn't an emergency," the marshal replied. "Besides, you look like you could use a little exercise."

The splitter was a transfer device normally employed when one had to move from point A to point B. It would split the body into lengthwise slices both ways, turning the traveler into a tangled mass of quarter inch strips. The strips were encased in a vortex and then transferred at an immeasurable speed to its destination. It would reassemble the strips back into their original form. During the earlier days of its inception, many times the unlucky traveler would wind up resembling a large pile of spaghetti and meat sauce.

Sully smiled. "Since all the big changes, the food's gotten too good." He took both hands and pinched a large band of fat on his stomach. "Guess I can't help myself."

Quincy took a seat at his desk.

"All kidding aside, you need to watch what you say about the president." He leaned back in his chair. "You know there are eyes and ears listening to what we say and there's been some unexplained disappearances." He pulled a cigar out of his pocket, struck a match on his boot and puffed until the end glowed a bright red.

"And most of them had big mouths." He paused, straightened up in his chair and stared hard at Sully. "If you know what I mean."

He leaned back once again, blowing smoke upward and watching it meander until it spread out sliding along the ceilings rough-sawn boards.

The jailhouse was constructed much the same as the saloon, save for the lavish furniture. A single desk, chair and a bench built into the opposite wall. If need be, the marshal had four separate cells at his disposal.

"You got her set on low?" Sully asked.

Quincy nodded.

Sully leaned against the electrified bars, which could be set in intensity. Low was the setting that would cause no harm if touched. High could be instituted to turn anyone or thing into a puff of ozone.

"While we're on the subject," Sully said, "what do you think about our illustrious prez and all his new notions?"

Marshal Quincy shook his head.

"You don't listen, do you?" He stood up and walked over to the bars. "Now lie down, be quiet, and if you're a good little boy, I'll let you out of here in the morning."

"I could use a little something to eat," Sully said.

"In time," Quincy said, "keep quiet and I'll take care of it."

Sully opened his mouth to speak.

"You say one more word and I'll keep you in here for a month. After that, we'll discuss those spine cutter loads you're carrying in that sidearm of yours."

The spine cutter loads incorporate a copper disc that on impact liquefies and shoots out in a straight line shearing whatever it hits in two. The name originated because when most victims were shot at mid-thorax, the copper would travel vertically, shearing the spine and the entire body into two separate pieces. These loads were illegal, but the law seldom enforced.

Sully closed his mouth and shrank back on his cot.

THREE

SAL RICKY HAD CLEARED the saloon wall by ten feet when Clay's gun fired. The dual rounds flew true, making contact in the middle of his back. A bright light and a sonic boom of sorts ensued, splitting the creature in half. The two portions continued to run, slowing to a wobble and falling over sideways. No blood or fluid escaped the bifurcating wound as the molten copper rendered the cauterization complete.

Clay shook his head and picked himself up off the floor. A flood of pain shot from his right hand, up his arm, spidered through his shoulder and into his brain.

"Remind me not to do that again," he said to himself, as he gingerly shook his hand hoping to relieve the widespread burning.

He made his way through the hole in the saloon wall (compliments of one decimated hydrak), and upon reaching the deceased creature, he nudged it with his boot.

"Now I've got to move two large pieces that are nothing but dead weight as opposed to one larger being that could move itself." He removed his hat, lowered his head and shook it several times. After replacing his hat, he looked at the two dead halves.

"Why do they always have to choose the hard way?"

F O U R

MARSHAL QUINCY AND HIS TWO DEPUTIES walked into the jailhouse after sunrise.

"Up and at 'em Sully." He walked to the control panel and lowered the jail cell bars. "That is, unless you want to stick around and visit a while."

Sully jumped to his feet, having to overcome a light sleep.

"Much obliged for your kind offer, but I think I'll be going, if it's all the same to you." He moved to the jail entrance, tipped his hat and left.

"I don't think he's worth wasting too much time over, but keep an eye on him just the same," Quincy said.

The deputy everyone knew as Clive nodded and left the building.

Marshal Jim Quincy was known for using questionable tactics when performing his duties. This also included his process of deputy selection. No one dared speak when one of his men, to put it bluntly, beat the information they desired out of a suspect. The same was true when prying a confession out of an innocent person. There were even deaths rumored for those who opposed him and his men.

Sully stood in the middle of the potholed street. He was short, about five foot six. His smooth complexion made him look younger than his fifty-two years. He didn't sport a full beard, just a scraggly rug that looked like it belonged on a teenager.

He wore brown baggy denim jeans, plaid shirt and a corduroy vest with a watch pocket and golden chain. No timepiece was attached to the end of the chain inside of the pocket, but Sully figured that as long as no one knew, it didn't matter. And maybe folks would think a little more of him being the owner of a gold timepiece.

He took off his hat and scratched his head. Straight ahead the road led out of town.

Behind him the road led into town; it all depended on which way you were facing.

On his left, the barber shop and to his right, the saloon. He pulled on the mop atop his head and knowing how badly he needed a haircut, turned right and headed for the saloon.

Sully took one step over a puddle of water and noticed in midstride ripples forming in the center of the puddle and moving outward. He instinctively knew what was coming. He dropped to his knees as the ground slid back and forth twenty to thirty feet each time it moved.

Most planets are created with a molten core, mantle and crust. This crust comprises tectonic plates which build up pressure pushing against each other until one slips causing an earthquake.

On Aon, the crust was eighteen miles deep at its thickest point. The planet was small, barely four thousand miles in diameter. As it revolved on its axis and circled the sun, this combination caused the crust to slip against the core. This initiated a buildup of magnetized static anti-electricity. As these forces continued to build, the crust would expand, separating from the core. When the energy built to an unstable level, the crust would roll back and forth on the static cushion. Eventually, the power would be defused and the core would be in contact with the crust once again.

These instances to the scientific community are known as *endoshear*, whereas in layman's terms the name is *groundslide*. The length of the event depends on how far the core separated from the crust. Separation can be up to two feet, causing the slide to last up to thirty minutes. In this case, all was calm within forty-five seconds.

Sully picked himself up off the ground, dusting off one pant leg with one hand and scraping mud off the other leg with his free hand. He did a one-eighty and once again took a step toward the saloon.

F I V E

"THANK YOU KINDLY, MARSHAL," Clay said, as he cut free the last piece of the slimy hydrak from behind his horse.

"I'm the one that should be thanking you. We've been trying to round up this slug for quite a while now." The marshal lied.

"Well," Clay said, "Now you have one less worry."

Quincy smiled, boiling inside. One of his strongest allies lay in two pieces rotting in front of him in the noonday sun.

"Best get this one underground before he stinks up the whole town." The marshal said. His two deputies nodded and grabbing the rope tied around Sal Ricky, dragged the two pieces off to bury.

Clay counted his money as he headed toward the nearest watering hole. He pushed through the double doors of the town's saloon. He stood until his eyes adjusted to the dim light. Clay noticed a familiar figure standing at the bar swilling down the cheapest whiskey the bar offered.

"There goes the neighborhood," Clay said. "It's getting so they'll let anyone in here."

Sully placed his hand on his holster while he sucked down his drink, the shot glass already at his lips. He set his glass down on the bar, wiped his mouth with his sleeve and turned around.

"That's mighty big talk from a crosseyed bounty hunter what couldn't hunt down a dead horse if he was chained to it."

The two men squared off.

"Well," Sully said, "you going to draw or stand there looking stupid?"

Clay smiled. "As I gravitate towards what I do best, I reckon I'll stand here."

The two men faced each other for several more moments and moved close, embracing each other in a bear hug.

"Bring a bottle and two glasses," Clay said. Sully and Clay took a seat at the nearest table. A bottle soon arrived. Sully removed the cork with his teeth and poured two drinks. Both men turned their glasses up, emptying the contents.

Clay slammed his shot glass down onto the table just ahead of Sully.

"Never could keep up, could ya?"

Sully smiled. "I'm already two up on you."

"Figures," Clay said.

"So?" Sully asked, "What brings you to the bustling town of Baine?"

Clay grimaced. "A ball of snot by the name of Sal Ricky." Clay took a sip of his drink, careful not to keep up with Sully. "Know anything about him?"

"In a town this size, you couldn't eat a slice of watermelon without everyone within a fifty mile radius knowing how many seeds you spit out."

Clay nodded and took another drink.

"And" Sully added, "there's a joke already going around town."

"Which is?"

"It's bad; you sure you want to hear it?"

"Yeah, come on get it over with."

"Don't say I didn't warn you." Sully cleared his throat. "How do you make a Sal Ricky?" He paused, waiting for Clay to respond.

Clay shrugged his shoulders.

"One shot and make mine a double."

Clay cracked a smile and shook his head.

"Bad," was all he said.

"How about you?" Clay asked, changing the subject. "What brings you to a hole of a town like Baine yourself?"

"Gotta be somewhere," Sully replied, "I guess here's as good as anywhere."

Both men nodded and took a minute to pour and have another drink. An awkward lull had appeared in the middle of their conversation.

"How old are you now, Sully?" Clay asked.

Sully thought a moment.

"Somewhere around forty, I reckon." He leaned closer to Clay and whispered. "I should ask you the same thing. In fact, you're not even supposed to be here, are you?"

"To answer your second question first, no. To answer your first question, none of your business."

Sully raised his eyebrows and nodded.

"So what will you tell me about yourself?"

"Not much," Clay replied, "but I have a question for you."

"And that would be?"

"This town, Baine, what do you know about it?"

"Well, being born and raised here, not much more than what you see." Sully leaned back against his chair. "Kinda strange you'd ask though." He looked at Clay. "You remember my grandfather?"

Clay nodded. "Good man."

"He passed six years now." Sully tapped his finger on the top of his shot glass. "You remember how close we were."

Clay nodded a second time.

"Gramps used to tell me stories that came from his daddy and his daddy before him, no telling how far back they went." Sully poured himself another drink. He stretched the bottle toward Clay, who waved him off.

"Suit yourself." Sully emptied the glass and continued. "Long before this little one horse town came into being there was another Baine." He pointed a finger out the door.

"About two days ride north, there's a huge pile of rubble and ruins everywhere you look." He wrapped his thumb and index finger around his chin. Then, looking at Clay, a surprised expression crossed his face.

"Concrete," he said. "I believe they called it concrete."

Puzzled Clay looked at him.

"You know," Sully said, "what all them ruins was made of."

Clay raised his eyebrows in recognition and said,"Well, keep going, don't stop there."

"Don't think so," Sully replied, "If you want to get anything else you will have to give a little."

Sully stared at Clay from head to toe and back again. "You're an offlander, aren't you?"

"What if I am?" Clay responded. "For argument's sake mind you."

"I'd have to ask how long have you been here and how have you managed to stay?"

Sully fidgeted in his chair.

"It's been all but sixty years since anyone could enter Aon's airspace or leave the planet. And offlanders were ordered gone ten years earlier."

"Theoretically," Clay continued, "about the only way a person could stay here with authorization is to, number one; be close to, if not over, a hundred years old. Number two, said person would have had to be here before the government ordered the offlanders away."

"I'll never forget that round up," Sully said.

"A group known as the Seekers were hired and given free reign to bring in all offlanders. They used a device that allowed them to detect whether or not a person was a legitimate citizen or an offlander."

"Who's telling this story?" Clay asked. He filled Sully's glass and his own.

Sully sipped half of the contents in his shot glass.

"Then, get to tellin'." Sully emptied his glass and extended it to Clay.

Clay refilled it and set the bottle down.

"Make that last," he said. "Neither one of us will be able to walk out of here if we don't."

Sully nodded and Clay continued to speak.

"Let it be said that the Seekers themselves were mercenaries without scruples, morals or any redeeming qualities. They would take out ten natives to get to one offlander."Clay paused. "And what they would do to their captive . . ." He closed his eyes and took deep breaths until he calmed down.

Understanding Clay's anger, Sully said,"Take your time."

Clay opened his eyes and sipped from his shot glass.

"Thanks," he said. "When I think about those days . . .well, you know."

"No," Sully said, "but I've heard."

"Anyway," Clay said, "if this hypothetical person would take a notion he liked Aon and wanted to stay, steps would have to be taken to find some way around the Seekers' detection system."

Sully smiled. "I suppose you're gonna tell me how this make-believe man would accomplish this."

Clay raised his eyebrows and tossed his head sideways.

"That's the idea."He picked up the bottle and twirled it in a circle, causing a small amount of liquor to swish around the bottom.

"No need to save this."He topped off each glass, pressed the cork into the hole and drove it in with the palm of his hand.

"This locator that the Seekers used worked on a molecular level. Now, from what I understand, all a person would have to do is to travel once through a splitter. This would alter the body's makeup sufficiently and not allow the locator to define them as an offlander."

"The splitters have always been under government control," Sully said. "Not just anyone can jump on a transfer pad and take a jaunt around town."

"True, true," Clay said, "unless one has friends in high places." A mischievous smile spread across his face. "Or low places."

SIX

"HEAD OUT TO STATION POINT," Marshal Quincy said. "We need to check on how the extraction is going."

Clive nodded and headed out the door, untying his ellack from the hitching post. Two spurs dug into the six-legged animal's sides and sped off to do the marshal's bidding.

The ellack was about the size of a full grown horse and, except for the two extra rear appendages, looked almost identical to a four-legged equine. A long, smooth coat of fur covered its body along with three toes on each foot instead of the usual hoof.

* * *

"How goes it?" Clive yelled, trying to be heard over the noisy machinery. "Doesn't look like you're making much headway."

"We're not," Jake replied, already angry at the slow progress and resenting Clive's comment.

"What seems to be the hold up?"

Jake seethed, grinding his molars together. It was all he could do to keep from plowing a fist into Clive's nose. But he knew better than to sign his own death warrant. He took several deep breaths and motioned for the deputy to follow him.

They walked several hundred feet away from the rig so they were able to talk at a comfortable audio level.

Jake pulled the plugs from each ear then pulled out a rag and wiped splotches of oil from his face.

"We've already been through two shipments of crude." Jake put his hands on his hips. "Either this calladium is the hardest I've ever seen, or the quality of the crude oil is so low in distillates, that it's unable to dissolve the crystal efficiently."

"This ain't gonna set well with the boss," Clive said, pulling a makeshift toothpick out of his mouth and throwing it on the ground.

Jake stared deep into Clive's cold, dark eyes.

"Which boss would that be, the snake or the weasel?" It was a risky comment to make, but one he couldn't resist. He discovered how risky, seconds later as he picked himself off of the ground, courtesy of Clive's right fist.

"Would you like to change that answer?" Clive asked, rubbing the knuckles on his right hand in the palm of his left.

"That would seem to be the most prudent course," Jake responded, also rubbing a body part, namely his left cheek. "Are we talking about the marshal or the regional president?"

"That's better," Clive said, smugly. "And to answer your question, it's none of your business."

"Fair enough." Jake spat several times depositing blood-laced saliva on the ground. "Okay, now what?"

"You tell me what you're gonna do to remedy this situation."

"We're running tests on both the calladium and the crude to see which one is the culprit." Jake paused. "It could be both."

Clive squinted. "What then?"

"At least twice the original time projection to complete the core extraction."

Clive thought a moment and nodded twice. He poked Jake in the chest hard with his index finger.

"For your own sake, you'd best hope that ain't the case. I'll be back this way in two or three days." Clive stuck both thumbs on the inside of his belt just above his pants pockets. "I'll be looking for good news."

"It's not up to me, but I'll do the best I can."

Clive removed his thumbs from his belt and straightened his hat. "Let's hope so."

S E V E N

"WOULD YOU LIKE TO ELABORATE on that?" Sully asked.

"There's not a lot more to say."

"What do you mean?" Sully protested, "You've told me nothing at all."

"It's like I said, to get into the transfer bunker you need someone that has a key."

"Ah," Sully said. "Now I understand."

Clay sat up straight in his seat.

"Let's say, this imaginary person we brought up just happened to know the caretaker of the impenetrable fortress that housed the transfer device."

"You don't mean old Deke's, do ya?" Sully asked, the excitement evident in his voice.

"You got to remember we're speaking hypothetically."

Sully smiled, finished his drink and set down his glass.

He opened his mouth to speak as two blue vortexes deposited Marshal Quincy and a second deputy on the barroom floor. The pair walked up to Clay and Sully's table.

The marshal pulled his gun.

"Got a few questions for you, bounty hunter. Best we take our leave over to the jail."

Clay turned to look at Quincy.

"What's the charge, Marshal?"

"Not here. Now move."

"I'm having a drink and talking to an old friend," Clay said, "I don't recall doing anything that would require incarceration."

Quincy cocked his pistol.

"I'm not gonna tell you again. Let's go."

As the deputy drew his weapon, his arm and most of his shoulder disappeared in a spray of blood and minute pieces of flesh.

Marshal Quincy hit the ground as did Clay and Sully. The deputy looked numbly at the missing appendage and began to rock back and forth. A second shot rang out removing everything from the waist up, leaving a pair of legs which toppled over forward. The knees locked, causing the legs to remain leaning against the table top.

Grouped together under the table, the three men sat back on their haunches, guns drawn, not uttering a word.

Clay broke the silence.

"You still plan on taking me in?" A smug grin twisted on the corner of his mouth.

The marshal eyed Clay with distaste.

"You'd be surprised," he muttered. Quincy pushed the blue stone in the center of his badge three times.

E I G H T

JAKE STEPPED INTO the small building he used as an office and living quarters. The air conditioning was a welcome relief. During the middle of summer (in which he now found himself), the temperature could soar to well over one hundred forty degrees. It rarely dropped below a hundred at night.

"I see our buddy paid us a visit," Pops said.

Jake rubbed his cheek, and moving his jaw back and forth said, "Yeah, he was here all right."

"What was his complaint this time?"

"How do you know it was complaint?"

"Well, first off, that's all he does is moan about something when he's here." Pops threw Jake a handkerchief. "Wipe your nose; it's bleeding; which brings up my second point."

Jake caught the handkerchief and pressed it to his left nostril.

"Which is?"

"When everything's going all right the boss doesn't normally deliver a haymaker to the foreman's jaw," Pops said.

"Good point," Jake said, tossing the blood-stained rag onto his desk.

"What's the problem?"

"The crude isn't dissolving the calladium fast enough." Jake picked up the handkerchief and wiped a small stream of blood from his top lip. "Do we have any data on the tests we performed yesterday?"

Pops walked over to a small gray machine, the front covered with various buttons, switches and lights. He pushed several of the buttons, turned a knob, and the gray box came to life. It spit out a strip of paper three inches wide by eight inches long. Pops looked over the figures imprinted on the strip and then turned to Jake.

"The calladium seems to be normal as far as its makeup goes. There is evidence that one small molecule in the fifth chain of Doranite, seems to have an anomaly that should not be there."

He looked over his glasses at Jake.

"I'll have to run it again to make sure." He went back to studying the strip of paper.

"What about the coalon?" Jake asked.

"You mean the crude?"

"Whatever you want to call it." Jake picked up the handkerchief, his irritability raising his blood pressure and starting a new flow of the crimson fluid.

"It appears someone is refining at least one distillate from the crude before they're shipping it to us."

Jake furrowed his eyebrows.

"Which element is being taken out?"

Pops squinted at the paper and then looked up.

"Near as I can tell, it's something called gasoline."

"That does it," Jake said. "Fix the strip of paper. I don't want to lose the figures."

Trees were so scarce on Aon that unless printed paper had been treated in a fixing solution, the ink would automatically disappear allowing the sheet to be used again.

"So what's the verdict?"

"I'm headed to see that snake, Quincy. It's a day's ride until they get a transfer unit out here unless that was a lie as well."He left the office, the door slamming so hard that it shook the wooden frame building.

NINE

"ANY SUGGESTIONS?" Clay asked as pieces of the saloon rained down around them.

Three blue vortexes descended from the ceiling and encased the men, immediately whisking them away.

The table, chairs and part of the floor turned to so much sawdust.

Clay blinked and found himself still on his knees on the jailhouse floor.

The marshal was standing, gun drawn and ordering the two men to their feet.

Clay didn't know how it was accomplished, but his own gun had been taken from his hand. He could see the butt end of his and Sully's pistols protruding from the marshal's belt, the barrels disappearing down the inside of Quincy's pants.

Oddly enough, this gave Clay a sense of comfort. He knew that the part of his pistol he held in his hand was not dilly dallying around with any anatomical parts corralled in the marshal's shorts.

"In the cell, both of you," the marshal nodded in the direction of one of six raised platforms. He waved his gun in the same direction to reinforce his point.

"Aren't you the least bit curious who was trying to blow us to pieces in the saloon?" Clay protested.

"That's lawman's work," Quincy said. "Nothing for you to concern yourself with. Now get in the cell."

Clay and Sully stepped onto the raised area. The marshal pushed a button, and the blue energy bars that formed the cell shot from floor to ceiling with a low hum.

Clay squinted and listened.

"Tell me," he said, moving closer to the bars, causing the hum to increase. "What did we do to cause you to put us in this death trap?"

Sully moved to Clay's side. "What do you mean death trap?"

"The marshal here has these bars set so that the slightest touch will turn us into a puff of smoke."

"You gonna answer my question?" Clay asked the marshal.

Quincy was reclining in his chair with his feet on his desk.

"And what question might that be?" Quincy reared back, further placing both hands behind his neck.

"So we're playing games?" Clay asked.

"Not a clue what you're talking about."

"For the second time, why are we in here?"

"Oh," Quincy said. "Well, why didn't you say so?" He removed his feet from the desk, stood and walked over to where his newly imprisoned subjects stood. "I'll have a list for you in a little while."

"A list," Clay said., "What do you mean a list?"

Marshal Quincy raised one eyebrow.

"You wanna add resisting arrest to that list."

"Resisting arrest?" Sully stammered, "We ain't give you a bit of trouble."

"Think I can make it stick?"

Clay just stared.

"Now sit down and shut up. You're in enough trouble as it is."

Clay shook his head, turned and sat down on a wooden bench anchored to the back wall of the cell.

"What—"

"That's enough, Sully," Clay said. "Do like the man said, sit down and shut up."

T E N

JAKE TIED HIS ELLACK TO THE POST in front of the saloon. He pushed through the barroom doors and then stopped, taking in the carnage that lay before him.

"What in the world happened here?"Two thirds of the south wall was missing, along with ten feet of flooring. Tables and chairs were scattered here and there. A fine coating of sawdust covered every horizontal surface, proof that more pieces of furniture had once existed.

"Can't say for sure," the barkeep said. "It's kinda hard to see what's going on when you're laying down behind the bar."

Jake nodded in agreement, pulled off his hat and scratched his head."Reckon a fella could get a drink?"

"Sure," a shelf behind the bar fell, producing a sound of shattering glass and the fresh smell of liquor wafting through the air. The bartender looked at Jake and smiled grimly.

"Better hurry up though."

ELEVEN

THE BLUE BARS CEASED their humming and disappeared into the floor.

"I'm letting you out," the marshal said.

"What brought about this change of heart?" Clay asked.

"Heart ain't got nothing to do with it, and if I were you, I'd be doing less questioning and more moving."

Clay and Sully stood, recognizing a gift, whether real or laden with strings.

"What about our weapons?" Clay asked.

Quincy nodded toward his desk.

"Pick 'em up on your way out."

Both men obliged. Clay put his hand on the doorknob and twisted the metal ball.

"And make sure neither one of you leaves town." The marshal shut the door and eyed the two as they left the jailhouse.

"Where we headed?" Sully asked. "I could sure use a drink."

"In time," Clay said. "First, I want to get a look at the saloon wall from the outside."

Clay and Sully eyed the jagged perforation for several minutes, wondering what caused that amount of damage.

Looking through the opening, Clay noticed a lone figure pouring shots at the bar. He moved closer. The floor was about three feet off the ground. He pushed up with his hands and twisting, landed on his butt. He stood and headed toward the figure with Sully close behind.

TWELVE

RUBEN HOVERED OVER THE CURVED console, perching on a small, round pedestal. From this vantage point he could monitor the flow of crude oil during the extraction process and make any necessary adjustments to the laser drill.

This was his life in the years since he'd been projected to Earth. He learned from the ground up the new technology developed to harvest the crude oil.

"How're we doin'?" A tall, thin newcomer asked.

"Mornin', Lynch," Ruben said. He flipped a switch, turned two buttons and then scanned three separate gauges. "Looks like the best yet." He looked back at the last gauge and then up at Lynch.

"Yep, just under a hundred thousand barrels from this well alone."

Ruben ranged as far to the west as Lynch did to the east in demeanor and appearance. Lynch's disposition could change from amiable to offensive in the time it would take the average person to capture a deep breath and exhale, provided it was done quickly.

In contrast, Ruben was friendly, eager to help and always ready with a smile. He was short, clean-shaven and bald save for a horseshoe of hair stretching from ear to ear by way of the back of his head.

Lynch was tall, thin and sported a closely trimmed dark beard. His facial hair was laced with gray, which carried over into his short gray hair.

Their only similarities came by way of their dress. Both men wore jeans, cotton shirts and cowboy boots.

Lynch chose a Stetson as a crown while Ruben preferred a bowler.

At that point, a loud pulsating alarm sounded. Its buzz-like quality shook each man, belching its warning at regular intervals.

Ruben moved to the left side of the console.

"It's the carillon field." He conveyed this information to Lynch in between the audible blasts.

Lynch cupped his hands behind is ears. "Whadda we do?"

Ruben ignored what he heard of Lynch's question and continued to flip switches and turned knobs, attempting to equalize the power between oil flow and laser bit.

Lynch covered his ears, knowing that the next moments were critical, but not knowing why.

Droplets of sweat rained on the console, and the floor of the small outpost began to shake.

Lynch, having nothing to hold fast to, tumbled forward, catching himself but fracturing his chin.

Ruben spread his legs and braced against the console to continue working. A small amount of steam pushed up through the floor around the console, sending Lynch into a total panic.

Unbeknownst to the haggard man, blood pouring from the gash in his chin, the steam signaled the end of the crisis.

The shaking slowed to an almost undetectable vibration, and to both men's delight, the alarm sounded its farewell blast.

Ruben pulled a handkerchief from his back pocket, wiped his forehead, took one swipe across the top of his head and placed the rag back into its home. He made his way to Lynch, who was now sitting up with his arms across his knees.

"I see it has started to clot."

Lynch only grunted. He lowered his blood soaked handkerchief, pulling with it several strands of crimson goo. He pushed the cloth back up to his chin.

"What was all that?"

"Here," Ruben said. "Let me help you up and I'll fill you in over a cup of coffee."

CLAY AND SULLY SAUNTERED up to the bar and ordered a drink.

Jake stood, sipping his whiskey and looking forward. He didn't want to mix conversation, business, or anything else, with anyone.

Clay downed his first shot, turned toward Jake and stood silent, all but daring Jake to face him.

Jake stuck to his guns and ordered another drink.

"Well," Clay announced, "there goes the neighborhood."

With that, Jake could no longer keep his mind on his own business. The stranger had coaxed him into a position he didn't like to find himself. Jake finished his drink and slammed his shot glass down hard on the bar.

"Say again, stranger." Jake hesitated and then turned to face his heckler.

"Like I said, there goes the neighborhood." Clay faced Jake full on and tapped his sidearm with his fist.

Sully's eyes widened, and he backed away from the bar.

"How about some help over here, barkeep." Sully looked at the bartender. "Kabell, you don't want your nice establishment all torn up, do ya?"

Kabell looked at Sully and nearly dropped the glass and the rag he was drying it with.

"Have you seen this place," Kabell said, chuckling grimly. "A dozen sticks of dynamite could only be an improvement." He set the glass down and threw the rag over his shoulder. "You wanna stop 'em, then be my guest."

Sully shook his head and continued his retreat.

"Neighborhood looks like it's already gone to the dogs, far as I can see." Jake said.

Clay took a step toward his foe. Jake reciprocated. One, two, three, four.

F OURTEEN

"EVEN THOUGH IT GOES without saying, I'm going to say it anyway." Ruben continued to draw on a napkin as he talked.

"Petroleum and a flame of any kind don't mix."

Lynch nodded. "You're right, you didn't have to say it."

A waitress brought two plates, one with two eggs over easy, sausage, bacon, hash browns and a side order of pancakes and toast with butter and grape jelly. She placed this plate in front of Lynch.

"You're not going to eat that?" Ruben asked.

"Gotta feed a growing boy," Lynch replied. A glob of grape jelly hung briefly from the corner of his mouth before falling back onto his plate to be recycled in the next fork full.

The second plate was less inviting, containing a serving of cottage cheese and a half of a bagel. This she placed in front of Ruben and filled both men's cups with coffee.

Ruben took a bite of his bagel, chewed, swallowed and continued to speak.

"As I was saying, fire and oil don't mix." He put the bagel in his mouth, holding it there while he fumbled through a stack of papers. Finding the one he was searching for, he pulled it from the pile, took another bite, chewed and then swallowed.

"See here," Ruben said, sliding closer to Lynch and pointing to the diagram on the paper.

"This is how the carillon field keeps the laser and the crude from contacting each other and causing an explosion."

Lynch wiped his mouth with the back of his sleeve.

"Why in the world do we use something as hot as a laser to drill anywhere around flammable liquids?"

"A conventional bit dulls too quickly. It would take forever to reach the pools of crude; we'd spend all our time changing drill bits."

"I understand all that," Lynch said. "But the extra depth you would gain wouldn't do you any good if you're blown to pieces."

"True," Reuben agreed, "that's why we employ the carillon field."

"All right, I'll bite." Lynch slid his pocket watch out of its nesting place, checked the time and then redeposited it in the small woolen vest pouch. "We got time."

"That's about all we have." Ruben rearranged several stacks of paper on the lunchroom table. "There we go." He picked up one sheet of paper. "This is identical to the one I gave you." He paused. "You still got it?"

Lynch waved a piece of paper in the air and nodded.

"Good," Ruben said. "A visual aid will help to explain, making the process easier to understand."

Lynch nodded once again.

Ruben didn't want to come across as being condescending. He knew with Lynch's lack of education, he needed to make this as simple to understand as possible. Without another thought, he jumped into it feet first.

"I know it seems next to insanity to marry a three thousand degree fire with a flammable liquid," Ruben said. "As I told you earlier, conventional drill bits won't last. Whether in the nineteenth century on planet Earth or the best we can manufacture on our home world of Aon neither will drill through a substance as hard as calladium."

Ruben slid the paper from the back of the stack he was holding and moved it to the front.

Lynch paid no attention to the printed information he'd been given.

Pretending not to notice, Ruben continued his talk.

"The carillon field supplies a small buffer between the tip of the laser drill and the crude it seeks. It does this by supplying an area no larger than the point of a pencil void of oxygen."

His interest now piqued, Lynch spoke.

"Pray tell, what does that have to do with anything?"

"No oxygen, no fire." Ruben said.

Lynch raised his eyebrows.

Ruben leaned over placing both hands on the table to support himself.

"You must supply oxygen to support combustion no matter how large or small the fire may be."

Lynch just scratched his head.

Ruben rolled his eyes. It's going to be a long day.

FIFTEEN

A WIDE GRIN SPREAD across both men's faces. Clay and Jake embraced and quickly separated so as not to appear too chummy.

"First rounds on me," Clay said.

"Second and third too," Jake replied.

The three men took a seat at one of the few remaining tables and reminisced about the past, discussed the present and planned for the future.

"Got an opinion concerning the changes going on around here for the past fifty years?" Jake asked.

"You don't mind jumping right into it, do you now?" Clay replied. He poured himself a drink and lifted the glass to his lips. "That's gonna take a little thought, my friend." He emptied his glass and sat the receptacle on the table, "and a bit more liquid stimulation to answer."

He repeated the process and then settled in, taking small sips as he spoke.

"I remember my grandfather, on my mother's side. This is important because my paternal grandfather was an offlander." Clay rolled his empty glass back and forth on the table. "He would tell me of the real city, Baine."

"You mean that pile of rubble thirty miles north of here?" Jake asked.

"One and the same," Clay said.

"How would he know?" Sully chimed in. "He wouldn't have been old enough to remember Baine in its heyday."

"Slow down," Clay said. "Give me a chance to finish." He turned his glass upright and filled it, allowing the surface tension to hold the liquid just above the rim of the shot class.

"Waste not, want not," Jake said.

Clay leaned over and slurped enough whiskey to make the glass manageable.

"No waste here," Clay said.

"We gonna continue our conversation or talk about whiskey and shot glasses all day?" Sully asked.

"Sorry," Jake said, "just can't stand to see good whiskey wasted."

"Now, to clarify;" Clay said, "the information I received from my grandfather passed down several generations. It all began with his grandfather, which would be my great, great grandfather."

He looked at Sully.

"Satisfied?"

Sully crossed his arms and leaned back in his chair.

"Yep," Sully nodded.

"It seems," Clay began, "that eighty years ago that pile of rubble was a bustling metropolis."

"Metropolis?" Sully and Jake said together.

"A big city," Clay reiterated.

Jake and Sully both nodded.

"Now, for whatever reason, the government, in its infinite wisdom, dismantled its military."

"And the people went for that?" Jake questioned.

"There's one thing you can always bet on." Clay filled his glass, dumped the contents down his throat and slammed the glass on the table. "Everybody's got a price."

"Sounds like you're opening up another can of worms," Sully said.

Jake took his hat off and placed it on the table.

"You want to elaborate on that comment?"

"I know you've all heard of calladium."Clay looked around the table as each man nodded.

"Every weapon on this planet, no matter how large or small, used to contain a small amount of the valuable crystal."

"What in the world for?" Sully questioned.

Clay signaled to the bartender for another bottle. Once it arrived, he popped the cork and filled all three glasses.

Clay took a sip and continued to hold his glass.

"It took the place of gun powder and never wore out."

"So it was an inexhaustible power supply?" Jake said.

"Exactly," Clay acknowledged.

"This might sound like a stupid question," Sully said, with a slight slur in his speech, "but what does that have to do with anything?"

"Slack up on that fire water," Jake said. "You're garbling your words."

Sully shrugged, finished his glass, crossed his arms and sat back in his chair.

"Well, it seems our illustrious government in all its wisdom offered their constituents a piece of the pie."

"How so?" Jake asked.

"From the way my grandpa explained it," Clay said, "if they turned in all of their personal weapons and voted to have the military disbanded, the calladium reclamation would be dispersed among all the people."

"Which would make everyone rich," Jake said.

"Considering the value of a small piece of calladium you would think so," Clay said, "but in fact it levels the playing field, making everyone equal."

"Then why do it?" Sully asked, having snuck another drink and entering back into the conversation.

"Good question," Jake said, he too removed his hat and preened the crown, then placed it on the table. "Greed, pure and simple."

"Still, you'd imagine that someone would have thought the whole thing through before proceeding," Jake said.

"Grandpa said, the powers that be assured things would get better. No more war, skirmishes, or territorial conflicts. They would retain their democracy, antiquities and all things beneficial to their society, including medical advancements, the arts and recreation. The one thing they would have to relinquish was their lifestyle. The arrangement required they revert to a simpler existence and abandon the larger cities."

Jake raised his eyebrows.

"Well, I guess you could say part of it worked." He looked around surveying the building. "You couldn't get much simpler, that's for sure."

"What they failed to realize," Clay said, "when everyone has the same thing the situation breeds discontent, which leads to more crime."

"Yep," Jake agreed, "when Billy Bob has more than Johnny Mack something's gotta give."

"And give it did," Clay said. "In the past ten years the crime rate has risen thirty percent if not more."

"Which brings us to another problem," Jake said.

S IXTEEN

RUBEN LOWERED HIS HEAD, cradling it in both hands.

"How can any one person be that dense," he whispered to himself.

Ruben raised his head, dragging his face through his fingers, distorting its features as he rose to an upright position.

Lynch yawned.

"I don't care what you say, fire and oil don't mix." He brought his coffee cup underneath the table and poured it half full of bourbon from a small flask kept in his vest pocket.

"And the aye's have it," Ruben said, throwing his hands in the air. "It appears as though we've reached a new level of futility." He flung his hat across the room like a Frisbee. "Next order of business." Ruben looked hard at Lynch. "Come on, dummy, sling another one of your award winning ideas up for discussion."

Lynch downed his coffee, stood and moved toward Ruben.

Ruben snatched open the top two buttons of his shirt and rolled his sleeves up anticipating Lynch's advance.

Ruben raised his fist and began a slight shuffle sideways. Just because snow was on the roof top didn't mean there wasn't fire in the furnace.

Lynch took two steps, stumbled and rolled rear end over tea kettle, landing flat on his back.

"You're drunk," Ruben exclaimed. He pushed his way through several chairs until he reached Lynch.

"It's the only way anyone could listen to that boring drivel you spout out of your pie hole." Lynch moved to get up as Ruben pushed him back down.

"That boring drivel," Ruben said. He reached down and grabbed Lynch's shirt collar in is his left hand, belt in his right. "As you choose to call it, at the very least is why we are here." He slid Lynch across the floor, head first into a cluster of chairs. "More importantly, it's the very thing that keeps us alive."

Lynch quickly rose to his knees and clamored through the chairs in an attempt to escape his attacker. The cut on his chin had reopened and bled profusely, causing his hands to slip on the tile floor.

An enraged Ruben tossed chairs aside until he reached the beaten Lynch.

Cowering down with his hands covering his head, palms up, Lynch pleaded.

"Okay, okay I'm sorry I called your talk boring." He peeked through his fingers. "Can't ya cut a guy some slack?"

Ruben reached down and grabbed the shaky Lynch. Strands of clotting blood stretched from his chin bursting as he reached his full height.

Ruben pulled him close.

"Do you think that's what this is about?" Ruben snarled, "you sniveling little worm."

Lynch could do nothing but stare questioningly.

"This is about your life, you imbecile!" He began to escort Lynch toward the back of the restaurant. "And I've had enough of your lackadaisical attitude." He reached the back door and kicked it open. "When you kill yourself I'll be damned if you're taking me with you."

Lynch rolled into the heat, with the door slamming hard behind him. He made his way to his feet, stumbling twice.

Lynch pulled a large clot from his chin, starting the blood flow once again.

"This ain't over, mister smart guy. No sir, this ain't over by a long shot."

Ruben paid his tab, thanked the waitress and made his way the short distance back to the extraction station. He couldn't help but wonder what Lynch had on his mind, oh to be sure it was retribution, but of what type. That would be something he would have to wait for, and something he didn't relish. Lynch may possess the IQ of a lobotomized cactus, but downright meanness didn't require intelligence, just a knack to inflict pain in a personal way. Despite his fragile appearance this lanky loner had acquired more than his share of cruelty.

Ruben found the stone. He tapped it three times with the toe of his boot, causing a four foot square section of ground to drop down and slide sideways, exposing a wide metal staircase. He stepped down and once below ground, pressed a button that pushed the false piece of ground back into place. The ionized edges of the plate along with an electrostatic expulsion field would obliterate any foreign objects from preventing a tight seal. This kept the underground installation free from prying eyes.

Ruben sat down at his workstation and took another volume reading.

"Still a good flow of crude out of this one." Ruben leaned back in his chair. "This is worse than watching grass grow." He reached for his personal journal and marked down the latest figures. No matter how high tech life became, Ruben still relied on the tried-and-true method of pencil and paper. Even during his training, his peers would laugh at him for doing double the work. Ruben would begin work first on his holographic sketch pad a unique device the size of a dime. The sketch pad could be brought up in front of the user for a multitude of purposes. Then he would duplicate his assignments using pencil and paper.

Ruben would call this his, "personal failsafe."

The outpost he called home for the past eight months comprised his work area, a small restaurant and a lounge. Each of these zones was complete with a small bar and a visioneer, so that occupants could view entertainment from their home planet.

There was also the all-important extraction equipment. It along with all other amenities were underground or camouflaged. The extraction equipment, including the laser drill, sat alongside Ruben's workstation behind a twelve foot thick wall of kalvinite.

All this was fine, but it wasn't enough for Ruben. His outpost sat about thirty miles from the nearest town, the town known as Stave.

Encroachment into this town was forbidden, except in the case of an extreme emergency. Who will know? Ruben thought. I won't be there long.

They kept a small ranch house and pole barn, complete with three horses for transportation and to satisfy snoopers.

Ruben smiled as the wind ruffled through the little hair he had that protruded from underneath his bowler. The trail dust he created dissipated as he moved out of sight.

S E V E N T E E N

"OH BOY," CLAY SAID. "Just what we need—another little ditty to ponder." He raised his glass. "Lay it on me."

Sully sat snoring, his eyes shut as he nodded forward, catching himself just before his head hit the table and rising again, his eyes wide open.

He reminded Jake of one of those glass tubes with a bird's head on one end and his tail on the other. As long as you kept water in the small plastic reservoir, the bird would bob up and down. This kept the beak in the water fueling a constant motion similar to the way Sully swilled liquor.

"I see one of us is not long for this world."

"Don't worry with him," Clay said. "He's in his natural environment. Why don't you fill me in on this new development?"

"Ah yes," Jake said, "the new development." He reached for the bottle. "I'm gonna need another drink for this."

A loud dull thud reverberated through the rest of the saloon. Both men turned to see Sully's unceremonious face plant into the table. A small trickle of blood exited his nose and formed a puddle in the nearest indentation. After the thud, a steady snore emanated from Sully, now in the grasp of an alcoholic coma.

"And he's out," Clay said.

"As I was saying," Jake continued. "Are you aware of the overall plan for the removal of the planetary calladium?"

"Sure," Clay said. "Once the calladium crystals are removed from the weapons, a one foot depth of core material is harvested, stored and used at the planets' convenience."

Jake smiled.

"That's what they've conned an entire world into believing, and for the better part of a century."

Clay furrowed his brow and clenched his glass.

"I'm listening."

"I don't know everything, but what I know ain't nothing like what you've heard."

Clay shifted in his seat.

"Like I said, I'm still listening."

Jake turned his glass upside down.

"I'm gonna feel that in the morning." He turned his full attention toward Clay. "Everything you understand about this world, originated years ago and passed from generation to generation until now, correct?"

Clay nodded. "Go on . . ."

"That's because they were fed the same garbage systematically from the beginning. This information was reinforced down through the generations and still holds true today."

"I don't like your innuendo," Clay said. He sat up straight in his chair, his eyes squinted and both fists on the table. "My grandfather was no liar!"

"Hold on," Jake cautioned, both hands, palms out. "I'm not calling anyone a liar, just stating fact."

The bristles lay down on the back of Clay's neck and he harnessed the anger about to escape and pulled it back in.

Clay pulled the cork on the half empty bottle. Motioning to Jake, Jake nodded and turned his glass over. As Clay poured, Jake thought what a good idea another drink would be. When Clay finished pouring, he set the bottle down.

"Tell me more about this 'fact' you mentioned, and what do you mean by systematically." Clay took a sip and watched Jake.

"The 'fact' is that a small ionic chip was implanted in your ancestors, skipping every other generation. This also explains what I meant by systematically."

"Chip you say." Clay looked puzzled. "Why?"

"The chips," Jake said, "were a passive way to maintain control over the population."

"What need for control?" Clay said, "As far as I could see everyone seemed content."

"That's just it," Jake said, "if you keep any malcontent from arising in the first place there's never any need to quell any uprisings."

Clay shook his head and took a drink.

"Makes little sense." He set his glass down on the table.

"All I know," Jake said, "is that microcomputer chip insertion took place in every member of the population. It was manufactured under the guise of an inoculation for a bogus epidemic. These injections skipped a generation because the ones in control deemed it unnecessary. They cited that the masses were (for lack of a better word) too stupid to require mind control any more than that."

"Unless . . ." Clay said, deep in thought.

"I don't like this," Jake said, "I can see the wheels are spinning." He paused. "Dare I ask unless what?"

Clay nodded and smiled at the same time.

"They want something, pure and simple, they want something."

"Slow down a minute. Want what? And who are *they*?"

"Later," Clay said, becoming more animated. "Where did you get all this information and how can you be sure it's reliable?"

"You seem to forget," Jake said. "I recently turned my white research coat in for these snazzy duds."

He grabbed both vest lapels and shook them up and down to demonstrate his point. "To be more accurate, it's been two years four months and a handful of days since I escaped from the CR&D scientific facility of greater Baine."

"That's right," Clay said, with a hint of deviance in his voice. "You're a wanted man."

"Now I get it," Jake said. "When you say 'they' you're referring to my former employer."

"I am." Clay ran his index finger and thumb down both sides of his mustache several times

"How high did your clearance go?"

"Not high enough, if you're thinking, what I think, you think, I'm thinking."

Clay was taken aback.

"Would you mind repeating that?" He held up an opened hand. "And this time, so someone of average intelligence can comprehend."

"Sure, just pay attention to what I'm about to tell you." Jake placed both hands on the table and leaned forward, to convey his message. "Other than a few outstanding details, which are interesting in and of themselves, but have no bearing on what you seek and we will discuss later. You're mindful of everything I do."

Clay stared at Jake several moments, his expression unchanging. He nodded.

"Okay, I want to know everything you know."

EIGHTEEN

"ARE YOU SURE ABOUT THIS?" Victor asked. "I'm getting deeper and deeper, seeing no return."

"You worry too much," Clive said, "I've told you everything is under control."

"That's the problem, you're running your mouth, but you're not showing me anything."

"Is there some question about my authority?" Victor eyed the knife in Clive's boot.

Clive noticed where Victor's gaze ended and this gave him a sense of power.

"Look," Clive said, trying to keep the peace. "As soon as we get the gasoline, the calladium is ours."

"You keep saying that, but if they find that diffraction station we tapped over the pipeline, it'll take them every bit of five minutes to figure out what it's doing there. After that, I'll give them another five to figure out who's responsible."

"You've got to give it a rest," Clive said.

Victor took one of the two seats that were the furnishings in this small outpost shack. This chair was behind a beat up metal desk. He opened the top drawer and pulled out a small leather pouch and a cardboard pack. Victor nodded at Clive.

"Never had a taste for it," Clive said, shaking his head.

Victor pulled a paper from the cardboard pack, opened the leather pouch and shook an even line of tobacco across the paper. He placed the paper between both index fingers and thumbs then rolled.

"Another pregnant one," Victor said. He held the cigarette up, showing off the bulging center. Victor placed the smoke in his mouth and pulled out a small cylindrical object from his shirt pocket. He pushed a button on the side of the object producing a laser flame on one end. Victor touched the flame to the end of the cigarette and drew. He allowed his exhalation to drift toward the ceiling. Victor seemed to melt into the chair. He coughed once and then continued to speak.

"Still can't help but worrying about how effective the ruse will be."

"That station is disguised to appear just like the surrounding territory," Clive said. "There's nothing out there but desert, cactus and boulders."

Victor reached down into the bottom of the cabinet. He pulled out a bottle and two shot glasses.

"Have a seat," he said, "I need something to take the edge off."

A smile crossed Clive's face, something seldom seen on this strange man. He moved a chair to the opposite side of the desk. Pulling off his hat, he sat down."Now you're talking my language."

Clive slammed his glass down."One more time and no holding back."

Victor complied. Once the shot glass was full, he corked the bottle and pounded the cork in with the palm of his hand. He was pleased at the change in Clive's demeanor brought about by the addition of alcohol.

"How's that?" Victor asked.

"You know," Clive said, "you're not such a bad guy." He took a sip of his drink and inhaling a small amount, choked and coughed. Victor beat him on his back. Just before all the color left Clive's face and Victor knew he was about to pass out, Clive drew in a shallow breath full of unnatural garbled wheezing. Another round of coughing and wheezing ensued until he cleared the irritant. He wiped his eyes and began to breathe normally, save for an occasional cough.

Victor leaned over and picked up the empty shot glass. The whiskey it had held was now a wide splotch on the floor, soaked up by the dry floorboards. He looked at Clive. Clive nodded and bringing his right fist to his mouth coughed one last time.

Victor filled the glass and handed it to the waiting man.

"Take it easy this time, there's plenty to be had."

Clive eyed Victor with disdain over the comment, his eyes caught sight of the full glass and once again his demeanor softened. This time the drink went down without incident.

"Like I said, you're all right." Clive set his glass down on the desk. "You seem like a standup guy, one I could share . . . let's just say some . . . sensitive information with."

This could be interesting, Victor thought. *I'll play along and see where it goes.*

Clive let out a long sigh.

"Smooth," he said, as he admired the shot glass he rolled around in his hand. "This isn't sipping whiskey, its guzzling whiskey."

"By all means, have another," Victor said.

"Don't mind if I do." Clive extended his glass.

Victor filled the glass and set the bottle down. He smiled at Clive and leaned back in his chair, one arm on the table and the other hanging from the thumb shoved into his pants pocket.

"So it's doing okay for you?"

"No complaints on this end." Clive reached for the bottle and then paused, making eye contact with Victor.

"By all means, help yourself, that's what it's here for."

Clive smiled, then continued his journey toward the bottle.

"You were saying something about sensitive information earlier."

Clive filled his glass and corked the bottle. He looked at Victor.

"Yes, yes I did." His voice had taken on the demeanor of the old Clive. Lost was the jovial attitude Victor had sensed the bottle had supplied the man sitting before him.

Surprised at Clive's response he backpedaled.

"I . . . I didn't mean to imply . . ." Victor stammered.

Clive raised a hand, then finished his drink.

"No," he said calmly. "I said it, now we talk."

"So where do we start?" Victor asked.

"With that weasel, Quincy."

Victor's expression turned to one of surprise.

"Can't say I know much about the marshal, but I was always under the impression he was a respected man in these parts, at least around Baine."

"Oh them that don't know the real man fear him like a child fears an old cur dog." Clive pulled the cork. Bypassing the glass, he drank straight from the bottle. He set the container down, wiped his mouth with his sleeve. "Me, I've seen his kind before. Get him by his self, remove his little trinkets, and he's nothing more than a bug to squash underfoot."

"Trinkets?" Victor asked. "What do you mean *trinkets*?"

Clive was busy sucking down the last of the whiskey. He lifted the bottle.

"My tongues not loose enough yet." He smiled out of the corner of his mouth. "Another one of these should do. Yes, I believe one more will do nicely."

Nineteen

POPS SAT AT THE CORNER TABLE, going over the computer readout. He shook his head and banged his fist on the table top.

"That's the third sample I've run and they're all the same." Pops took off his glasses, set them on the table and leaned back in his chair wiping his eyes. "Whatever's going wrong with the crude, it's not on this end." He hooked his glasses over his ears.

"Better watch it talking to yourself, they'll be coming to pick you up before long."

A sharp humming in the opposite corner caused Pops to jerk. For a moment he thought he had uttered a self-fulfilling prophecy and someone really was coming to get him. Pops turned in the direction of the noise. A blue vortex was making its way down from the ceiling, halting when it touched the floor. It pulsed and then slowly dissipated, leaving a tall, lanky stranger in its wake.

"Lookin' for a man name of Quincy." The stranger wiped gingerly at the dried blood on his chin. "I hear I can find him around here." Lynch stood silent for only a second. "You seen him?"

Pops stared over the top of his glasses before pushing them up on his nose. He stepped from around the console.

"Who wants to know?" Though small in stature, no one encroached upon this fiery man's territory.

"Lynch is the name." He offered nothing more.

Guess I will have to fight for every piece of information I get from this clown, Pops thought.

"What do you want with Quincy?"

"Gotta talk."

"Try to understand, big mouth; we're having what you'd call a conversation. That means when I say something, you say something back in a clear coherent manner. If all you do is grunt when I ask you a question, then you might as well jump back on your blue twister and blow on outta here."

Lynch shoved both hands down into his front pockets.

"All right," was all he said.

Pops rolled his eyes and shook his head. *Why me?*

"What do you want with Quincy? And what happened to you? You look like you were caught in an ellack stampede." He paused. "Now it's your turn." Pops waited in anticipation.

"I was on my way to Baine when my ellack threw me just outside of Shell. As far as Quincy goes, he contacted me a week or so back; said he had information about my brother." Lynch scratched the side of his head. "He's been missing quite a while now."

"How were you able to transport to this building without a splitter?" Pops suspicions began to grow with this newcomer.

"Don't need one. When you're coming from a place with a transporter you can go wherever you want. The only problem is getting back again."

"So you transported from Shell?"

Lynch nodded.

"Why not transport straight to Baine?"

"The transfer office there listed several destinations." Lynch shrugged. "Guess I chose the wrong one."

You chose the wrong one, all right, he thought. *Sashay in here without a speck of dirt on you, half beat up and with a mouth full of lies.* Pops drew up a mouthful of saliva and spat on the floor. *I'll be watching you. Yes, sir, I've got my eye on you.*

Lynch fumbled with a small, blue jewel-like fob in his pocket. It was no bigger than a half dollar, but oh what power it wrought, and this slight man was one of only a few to possess one such as this.

TWENTY

QUINCY TOUCHED THE TIP OF HIS CIGAR to the small blue flame. He continuously sucked in his cheeks, pulling air through the brown tube that hung out of his mouth. Once the end glowed, he extinguished the lighter and tucked it away in his top shirt pocket.

"Things aren't right." Quincy stood, meandering around the jailhouse.

"What makes you think something's up?" Carl asked.

Quincy raised his eyebrows and shook his head.

"That's just it." He took a drag off his cigar, deeply inhaling the smoke and flicking the butt into the energized bars of the only occupied cell. "Too quiet."

A single prisoner lying on his bunk jerked so violently when the cigar touched the bar that he shattered his clavicle after landing on the floor. The remainder of the smoke, provided a small diversionary bit of amusement, popped and sizzled, turning into so much ozone.

The prisoner began to moan, grabbing his shoulder and asking for help.

"Shut up the noise," Carl said. "You'll be swinging at the end of an ionizer in a couple days and all your troubles will be over."

If Clive was Quincy's right-hand man, then Carl was his left. Not quite as odd as Clive, but every bit as dangerous.

"Quiet's only part of it," Quincy said. He sat back down at his desk. "The rest of it is just gut."

Carl took a seat on the opposite side of the desk.

"You know," he said, waving an accusatory finger at Quincy. "You're not supposed to inhale that smoke. That ain't the proper way to smoke a stogie."

Marshal Quincy diverted his attention from staring out the window to burning holes through Carl with his eyes.

"When I see a medical degree with the name Carl Stamper displayed across it hanging on the wall, you can tell me that very same thing." He paused, studying the man sitting across from him with his eyes, slowly moving from head to toe. "Until such time as that becomes a reality, shut up!"

The redness welling in Quincy's face told Carl it was time to leave.

T WENTY-ONE

"YOU KNOW," JAKE SAID, "of the government's plan to dismantle the military and collect all civilian weapons?"

Clay nodded.

"They wanted to retrieve the small amount of calladium that powered each one."

"Spot on," Jake said "calladium is such a rare mineral, and the amount collected was promised to the population. The wonderful citizenship of this planet was more interested in lining their pockets than in their own protection."

"Something I don't understand," Clay said, "why such a ludicrous program in the first place?"

Jake smiled, picked up the bottle, poured himself a shot and offered one to Clay. Clay nodded and filled his glass before corking the bottle.

"It seems our governmental buddies announced that disarming everyone would take away the threat of violence, therefore, removing the need for weapons. As I said earlier, they would allow the calladium to be distributed equally among the masses. This would make everyone if not rich, then in well enough shape so as not to want for necessities."

"Wouldn't that put everyone on an even playing field, leading to more problems?" Clay said.

Jake nodded. "Correct, and you came up with that not knowing the whole story."Jake took a sip of his drink, being careful of the amount he imbibed. "I can't believe anyone on this pea-sized planet couldn't realize how this crazy plan would play out."

"Couldn't see," Clay said, "or didn't want to see."

"Right," Jake replied. "I worked for the CR&D for seventeen years."

A low moan emanated from Sully as he came to.

"Well," Clay said, "it lives."

Jake smiled. "I'm not so sure."

"Let's get him outta here," Clay said.

Jake stood up.

"As I was saying, I don't know everything, but I'm privy to enough that will give us a good handle on what may be going on."

A screaming whistling came from outside just before an explosion obliterated the back of the already decimated building, including the bar and bartender.

Both men ducked as Sully sat up straight, all three being peppered with shards of wood and glass.

"Looks like someone doesn't like us very much," Jake yelled through the commotion.

"That's a subject for discussion anywhere but here," Clay retorted.

* * *

"Looks like someone knows as much about your time at the CR&D as you do," Clay said. He stirred the dying coals and threw several more pieces of wood on the fire. "Leastwise, that's the best I can come up with; assuming that blast this afternoon was for all three of us with a special emphasis on you."

"It was for me, all right, with high hopes for collateral damage, namely you and—"

A moan interrupted the conversation followed by a cough, with a smooth transition into the sound of watery vomit, ending with the dry heaves.

"See," Clay said, "it lives." He stood and walked to his mount. Clay removed a bundle wrapped in paper from one of his saddlebags. He walked back to the fire, knelt and opened the bundle. It contained a dozen or more dried and salted strips of meat. Clay handed a piece to Jake and removed one for himself.

"Amberean," Jake said. "Aren't we quite the connoisseur?" He took a bite. "Even better than I remember."

"It's more the technique in the curing process than in the animal itself."

"Well, whatever it is, it's quite a feast to enjoy in the middle of nowhere."

Clay nodded, then spoke loud enough for Sully to hear.

"Yep, can't get much better than a big hunk of salted fat meat."

It took a few moments, but soon another chorus of the dry heaves echoed around the camp. This time it sounded as though Sully was relieving himself of organ chunks with each abdominal contraction.

"That's cold," Jake said.

"I'll leave him be," Clay said, smiling. "I wouldn't want him to hack up something he needs." He took a bite of the succulent meat.

"Although, Sully's going to have to learn, when to say when." Clay threw the last bite into his mouth. He then re-wrapped the remaining strips. "With all we have facing us, we can't afford to have any one of us in less than one hundred percent."

"Agreed," Jake said.

"Yeah, me too." A haggard face peered over the log it had been lying behind. Sunken eyes, gray wrinkled skin and dangling strings of solidifying vomit, hung from patchy facial hair. The combined projected a notion that the old face had died, decomposed and reanimated several times to display such a look.

The face rose, revealing a thin, shaky frame covered in disheveled clothing.

Jake couldn't help but smile.

"I don't know, Clay; alive may be a stretch." He rubbed the stubble on the side of his face. "Now 'death warmed over' I just might entertain."

Clay nodded and cocked his head.

"Yeah, now that you mention it, I can see whatcha mean."

"Well, since you have already made my funeral arrangements," Sully said, "how about offering a fella . . . that is, a corpse, a cup of joe?" He wiped a grizzled hand across his face, removing the buildup of stale vomit. The interruption of hand to face caused the stench of partially digested stomach contents to waft across the area.

"Whoa," Clay barked. He poured a cup of coffee and handed it to Sully. "Check my saddlebags and you'll find a half a bar of lye soap. You won't remember, but we crossed a creek about a quarter mile back." Clay waved his hand in front of his nose.

"Wash your face and change that shirt." He gave the sickly man an empathetic grin.

"Then maybe we can stand to be around you." Clay patted Sully on the back as he turned to leave.

"Yeah, yeah, yeah," Sully muttered as he disappeared into the darkness.

"Now back to business," Clay said, "if I recall it was your turn."

* * *

"Ain't no call to treat ol' Sully that-a way." He finished his coffee and dipped the soap into the stream rubbing it briskly between his hands, producing a rich lather. Sully washed his face, hair and chest before splashing water onto the soapy parts to rinse.

Once finished, eyes burning from the harsh cleanser, Sully fumbled for the dirty shirt to use to dab his face and chest dry. A commotion in the brittle vegetation, just to Sully's right, caused him to suspend the search for his makeshift towel.

"Come back to gloat, eh?" He began to rub at his eyes. As he blinked, the tears he produced slowly washed the irritating residue away, and his sight began to clear. Sully turned in the direction of the noise. He craned his neck forward and squinted.

"You ain't Clay or Jake neither." Sully began to back away from the new arrival. "You ain't from around here." He tripped over a root and then quickly found his footing and continued his retreat. Sully fumbled for his sidearm.

"Stay back, ya hear?"

Before the barrel could clear the worn holster, a hand, many times the size of a normal man's, clamped over Sully's head. Muffled screams pushed their way around the unnaturally hardened palm until a 'pop,' like that of a coconut in a vice, brought silence. A sickening slurp was the only sound, save for the calming trickles emanating from the stream.

Unable to stand the oxygen-laden atmosphere for more than a few minutes, the being burrowed into the earth and returned to its crystalline existence.

Twenty-Two

THE BROWN AND WHITE BLAZE equine trotted down Main Street in the town known as Stave.

Well, at least it's a change of scenery, Ruben thought. He missed his home world of Aon. There wasn't much to do on this fledgling planet Earth. After all, how much could you expect a race to develop in nineteen centuries?

Ruben chuckled to himself. *I guess I answered my own question.*

He wasn't much of a drinker, but the town's watering hole provided about the only entertainment. It offered a place to catch up on the most recent gossip,and in his case, meet new people.

His next option would be the ladies of the evening. Ruben had yet to see one, but they were somewhere preparing for the night's work. It's something he may have considered if it weren't for the lack of hygiene among the locals. He shivered at the thought of curling up next to a naked woman in this desert climate who hadn't bathed in weeks.

"I s'pose the saloon will have to do." Ruben secured his horse in front of the bar. He took a moment to look over the animal.

"I guess you're all right." Ruben swatted at a group of flies on his mount's rump. "No offense, but I'd trade ten just like you for one ellack."

Seemingly understanding his master's comments, the offended equine grunted and pulled back against his mooring.

"Don't worry there, fella." Ruben scratched between the horse's ears and rubbed its muzzle. "Looks like we're together for the duration."

Ruben pushed through the double doors. For a Tuesday afternoon, the saloon held more patrons than one would've thought.

A bearded man sat in a corner playing the fiddle. Several separate groups of men sat playing five card stud or blackjack and one customer stood at the bar nursing a beer.

Ruben sauntered over to the bar, trying to make it appear as though he was a regular at the bar scene, even though this was his first time in such an establishment. He propped his foot up on the brass rod beside the beer drinker.

"Whatcha have?" The bartender asked.

"Beer," Ruben announced. Just the act of stating so "matter-of-factly" his order for such a royal beverage gave him a sense of power.

"Beer it is." The barkeep sat a cool foamy mug down on the bar.

Ruben took a sip. Fighting back his gag reflex, he smiled at the man beside him.

"How's it going?" he asked.

The stranger looked at Ruben. He was dressed in dark pants, a long dark coat, something akin to a top hat and a moderate length gray beard. He nodded ever so slightly and then grunted something inaudible. Ruben couldn't quite put his finger on it, but felt a presence in this man that did not translate to this, his outward appearance and sorely lacking demeanor.

A mug of horse pee and stimulating conversation—wow, what an afternoon.

Little did Ruben know, this scenario would soon change, and unlike Ruben had hoped, this change would not be for the better.

AS SURPRISED AS POPS WAS, he didn't show it. He had seen transfers before, but this was the first one that had almost dropped on his head.

"*Quincy*," Pops repeated. "Can't say as I recollect anybody named Quincy."

"He's the marshal in these parts," the stranger said.

Pops saw the man slide a small blue object into his pants pocket.

"Now I remember. I met the marshal once; didn't know his name was Quincy though. Anyway, you're about thirty miles off target."He paused, waiting for the newcomer to react; when he didn't, Pops continued to speak. "Like I said, you're about thirty miles off. He's north of here in a town called Baine."

"North you say?"

"Yep." Pops took a moment to evaluate the stranger. "Gotta name, friend?"

"Lynch," was all he said.

"Don't talk much, do you?"

"Ain't got much to say, leastwise not to you."

"Friendly too, I see."

"I'll be leaving now, wouldn't have an ellack I could borrow, would ya?"

"Afraid not, only got the one." It's against my better judgment, he thought, but being as I've never been accused of using judgment good or otherwise. "Why don't you stick around, have some coffee and I'll take a look at that chin of yours."

"I guess I can do that, a cup of joe would hit the spot."

Pops and Jake's quarters were modest. Two bunks, a small kitchenette and work stations to monitor inflow and output. The kitchenette boasted a small table with four chairs.

Lynch took a seat while Pops blew the dust out of two cups, put the coffee on to perk and located the first aid kit.

Lynch didn't budge as Pops cleaned the wound with alcohol wipes. Once he had worked his way through the blood and hair, he found the gash in the gaunt man's chin. He looked through the first aid kit and found what he was looking for. Unscrewing the top from the small tube, he squeezed the two ends of the wound together, and ran a line of adhesive down the length of the laceration.

Lynch moved his mouth to speak.

"No," Pops ordered. "No talking till this sets up."He held the wound together and counted to sixty, then released his fingers. "You're good to go. That glue will last long enough for your wound to heal and is stronger than your own skin."

"Much obliged," Lynch said, rubbing at the newly closed gash. The coffee pot signaled its doneness by bubbling up into the glass knob on top.

Pops poured two cups. "I take mine black, how about you?"

"Black's fine." Lynch accepted the cup.

The men sat enjoying their beverage.

Lynch spoke first.

"Sorry 'bout my gruff attitude earlier."

"Nothing to worry about. A new place will do that to you, especially when you planned to end up somewhere else."

Lynch couldn't tell his benefactor he was in fact exactly where he wanted to be. This one fact weighed heavy on his mind, but no matter—when you have a job to do, you can't afford thoughts like these to get in the way.

"So," Pops said, "what brings you to these parts?"

Lynch took a sip of his coffee and pursed his lips.

Pops' eyes grew wide, the laser blade having split him from groin to sternum.

Lynch stood and retracted the four foot long beam of light. He shoved the handle into his front pocket and then placed a hand on the older man's shoulder.

Pops continued to stare in disbelief. "Why?"

"Nothing personal, just business." He held Pops' shoulder and eased him down until his cheek lay touching the table.

Twenty-four

"AS I'VE SAID," Jake began, "I was with the CR&D for seventeen years." He looked at Clay. "You can stop counting; I was twenty-five when I started."

Clay smirked and bit the side of his cheek.

"I started off, in what you would call the mailroom, even though there was no such thing as handwritten correspondence. All information reached the facility through wireless and then traveled to its final destination in the same fashion. They used encrypted routers to split the massive ball of data into its individual bits and send it on its way."

"What does working an entry-level job have to do with anything?"

Jake sighed."If you want to hear any of it, you've got to hear all of it."

"Point taken," Clay said. "Please continue."

Jake didn't acknowledge Clay's comment, he just resumed his story.

"We'd receive digitally locked communication devices; we referred to them as COM boxes. They would arrive by special courier. The armored vehicle would back up to a secured hatch. Once the package was in the building, the grunts, meaning me, could handle the COM box. I was not allowed to possess the box no longer than to pass it on to the next individual with a higher security clearance."

"Higher security clearance?" Clay asked, "Or higher pay grade?"

"One translates into the other." Jake rubbed his thumb and index finger together.

Clay nodded. He threw several pieces of wood on the glowing embers. Both men drew back as the fire flared to life. Clay moved the fuel around, enticing the flames to subside. He then shifted his rear end to a more comfortable position on the downed tree he had been sitting on.

Sensing that Clay was ready for him to continue, Jake once again took up his tale.

"After several years I climbed out of the mailroom and far enough up the security clearance ladder to be the last one to hand off the COM box."

Clay cocked his hat back on his head.

"Don't tell me that all this went on in one of those wooden shacks like the town of Baine is built out of."

"No, no," Jake assured. "Our little world was a fortress inside of that pile of concrete and steel, known as the original Baine." Jake stared off into space for a short while. "In fact," he said, upon his return. "To keep an operation like we had going, there's no way they could have relocated."

Clay removed his hat, ran his fingers through his hair, then replaced the Stetson to its usual position.

"I'm still not grasping the pertinence of this to anything."

"There was a short time during one of those transfers I was unaccounted for. With the level of paranoia that drifted around the entire compound, they assumed that I was now privy to their secret."

"Were you?" Clay asked.

Jake stared at Clay as his mouth spread into a wide grin.

"After that, I transferred to a different part of the facility. They couldn't let me go, for I would talk. And disappearance was out of the question since my unit boasted an accident-free workplace and something of such magnitude would bring along with it unwanted inquiries." Jake shrugged. "So for the next few years, I was relegated to mundane work, hoping I would quit."

"Now for the question." Clay's interest had piqued to the point he was unaware he had removed his hat and was rolling it around in his hands. "What did you see?"

The unmistakable sensation of dread fell over both men like a falling cloud.

"Sully, where's Sully!"

Twenty-Five

RUBEN HELD HIS BREATH and downed his beer. *The way this day is going,* he thought, *if I can keep this beer down, a buzz couldn't do anything but help.* The brew welled up in the back of his throat. Summoning all the fortitude he could muster, Ruben forced the sour ale back down. It was then he noticed a strange thing begin to occur.

"I'll have another," he said, holding up his mug. Ruben furrowed his eyebrows. *Did I say that?* The bartender slid another beer in front of him. *I guess I did*, he reckoned.

A crooked smile spread across his face, the first indication that the alcohol was beginning to do its job. Ruben took another drink, this time emptying half of his mug and savoring the complex flavor. His face flushed as he embraced the warmth that spread throughout his body.

Ruben counted the number of times he had been drunk on one hand. He couldn't recall if this was number four or five.

"No matter," he mumbled to himself. "I'd have to say that this is the best yet." Ruben finished his beer. Deep within his brain, his last coherent thought told him that this time something was amiss. The notion searched for something tangible to latch onto and then slid into the desolate fog.

"Hit me again." Ruben's speech was now coming in thick slurs.

"Here ya go." Another beer landed on the bar. Ruben dug into his pocket and removed a silver coin.

The bartender waved him off.

"It's on the house."

Ruben managed to enunciate the word, "Tanks," before concentrating on replacing the coin back into his pocket. After several attempts, he seemed satisfied as the coin slid down his pant leg and onto the floor.

Ruben looked to his right. The man who had been nursing his beer was still there, only now he seemed to be frozen in time. His mouth was open; mug turned up with its rim resting on his bottom lip, but the beer, although angled toward his mouth didn't flow.

"How ya doin, handsome?" a feminine voice said.

With great effort, Ruben wove his head to the left. He craned his neck toward the woman.

"Youse smells real good." He managed to turn in her direction with his right side leaning against the bar.

"Name's Ruben," he said, with surprising clarity. "What's yours?"

She placed her index finger over his mouth.

"Shh," she said, picking up his glass and putting it to his lips. "Drink first, and then talk."

Ruben didn't protest as she turned the mug up, allowing the beer to flow down his throat. As the edge of beer began to lower, revealing the clear bottom of the mug, Ruben's eyelids mirrored this occurrence until darkness dominated his world.

Twenty-six

AFTER CARL LEFT, Quincy locked the door and pulled the shades. He walked to the energized cell, lowered the bars and stepped up onto the platform.

"Thank goodness," the prisoner said, "someone's here to help me."

"Just you stay still, son," Quincy assured, "I'm here to help."

The prisoner smiled, closed his eyes and relaxed. Quincy pulled out a round silver bar one inch in diameter that was small enough to conceal in the palm of his hand. He placed one end against his patient's chest.

"This won't hurt a bit." He applied slight pressure to the bar. The sharp blue light of the laser stiletto pierced the heart and shattered the spine of the doomed man. The wound being cauterized, there was nothing to clean. A release of bodily fluid associated with the relaxing of muscles when a living body became that of a corpse, could compromise this entire situation.

Quincy dragged the body to the edge of the cell and laid it over the holes that directed the energizer bars. Urine was just beginning to soak through the dead man's jeans. He turned the power level to high and pushed the button to activate the bars. The body within an instant evaporated into a thimble full of dust.

"No witnesses, no questions." Quincy smiled and lit another cigar.

"Technology, what in the world would us average Joe's do without it?" He laughed as he set about his next task.

Quincy coughed. He held the cigar in his mouth, needing both hands to dig a skeleton key out of his one size too small blue jeans. He fancied himself a ladies man, although his belly covered his belt buckle. But the most disturbing part of his anatomy was the pair of "B" cup-sized man boobs he was cultivating. He wore loose-fitting shirts to cover the unwanted mounds.

Once he pried the key from his pocket, Quincy pushed it into the corresponding lock on a multi-door cabinet in the back of his office. He turned the key and opened the door. Inside the simple wooden cabinet sat a plain, square, silver box. It measured twelve inches in all directions and was smooth except for an oval shaped indentation on the side facing out.

Quincy placed his right thumb and index finger on the tips of the two horizontal star points of his badge. He pulled both pieces forward as they were mounted on hinges near the center of the badge. The blue stone popped off and landed in the palm of his right hand. He placed the jewel into the depression.

The machine hummed and flashed a blue aura at regular intervals. It crackled to life as a man spoke.

"Bout time," an unattached voice said, "I was thinking you had screwed up again and bought the farm."

Quincy seized. He knew better than to say anything. The man on the other end of this communication device was not one to trifle with. He would have to bite his lip and take the abuse, lest buying the farm become a real possibility.

"I'm very sorry, Mr. Gaylen," Quincy said, "To what do I owe the pleasure of your call."

A hearty round of laughter boomed from the box.

"Pleasure of your call," the cynicism evident in Gaylen's voice, "That's real sweet." Gaylen hesitated. When he returned, his demeanor had changed. The jovial man just moments before, was now the no-nonsense cosmic mobster Quincy was used to. Gaylen didn't have to utter a word, his silence spoke volumes.

Quincy pulled out his handkerchief and wiped the sweat from his forehead. He knew the questioning would begin, but when? And would he be able to answer satisfactorily. Gaylen had killed for less and his "playtime sessions," as they were known, involved several hours of torture, ending in the demise of the subject. At least what was left of him.

Once again the box crackled to life.

"So, marshal," Gaylen said. Quincy could feel the smirk across the evil thug's face. "Why don't you fill me in on when I'll be able to see some return on my investment? And think before you answer." Gaylen's tone dropped to a whisper. "And I want to know down to the second."

T W E N T Y - S E V E N

"WELL?" VICTOR SAID.

Until now, Clive sat slouched in his chair, drinking the second bottle of whiskey. Upon Victor's comment, he sat up straight, placed the bottle on the table and leaned forward towards Victor.

Clive squinted, cocking his head to the left and then to the right, all the while strumming his fingers on the table top. He stopped.

"Well, what?"

Victor, now weary of Clive's attitude, was becoming more brazen.

"Your tongue," Victor said, "is it loose enough now?"

Clive stared at Victor and nodded.

"I suppose it is." He grabbed the bottle, took a healthy drink and tapped the cork in with the palm of his hand. "Now, where were we?"

"Quincy and trinkets," Victor said.

Clive expressed an air of recognition. "Have you ever seen the marshal?"

Victor shook his head."Can't say as I have."

"Nothing special about him," Clive said. "Just your everyday run-of-the-mill idiot." He reached for the bottle. "You know the type—short, fat and stupid."

Victor stared at Clive, a puzzled look on his face.

"I don't understand, if there's nothing special about him, then why are you going on so?"

"Well, I may have failed to mention one small detail." Clive turned the bottle bottom side up. When the last of the whiskey ran through the bottleneck and down Clive's throat, he set the bottle down and slid it towards Victor.

Victor watched the bottle slide in his direction.

"If you're asking for another, I'm sorry, but that's it, there is no more." He picked the bottle up and examined it. "How could you drink so much anyway? At the least, you should be passed out on the floor, at most, and more than likely, dead."

"As far as my drinking goes, that's a story you're not yet ready to hear. And to reiterate; as far as my drinking goes; if that's all the whiskey you have, I believe our discussion is over." Clive pushed back from the table.

"Hold on," Victor said. He stood and walked over to a small cabinet. He opened the bottom door, reached in and pulled out another bottle.

Clive smiled."Holding back on ol' Clive, eh?"

Victor handed his strange visitor his third bottle.

"Not that I blame you." He pulled the cork out with his teeth and took a good-sized drink. "I know supplies don't make it out this way often." He winked at Victor and took another big slug from the bottle. "So you kinda have to ration things so they'll last."

"You owe me an answer," Victor said, "and before you say 'an answer to what?' I'll tell you. If Quincy is such an ordinary man, what's that one special thing you've yet to reveal?"

"So you're a special thing kinda guy," Clive said. He thought for a moment. "I guess I said something like that." He took another pull from the bottle. "Okay, so here it is. Quincy wears a badge, but this badge has a little extra something to it."

"Don't tell me that I saw you kill three bottles of good liquor so I can find out a marshal wears a badge."

"Hold on there, Skippy," Clive was at last slurring his words. "The marshal considers me his right-hand man, so he wasn't that concerned when I interrupted a communication he was finishing up."

This piqued Victor's interest."What kind of communication?"

Clive fumbled the bottle, but held on. He pulled the cork out with his teeth and spit it across the room. He turned the bottle up and drained the contents, sucking on the empty container to remove every drop. The bottle fell out of his hand. It rolled to the center of the table and stopped.

"The kind of communication that requires a blue ornament from a law officer's badge," (Clive burped and pounded his chest several times with his fist) "to be inserted in a tiny hole, in a shiny box, in a raggedy old cabinet."

Victor looked at Clive like he had horned toads crawling out of his ears.

"Would you mind explaining whatever you just said?"

"Sorry, old boy, that's for another day, and by the way, bacon and eggs in the morning will be fine." Clive laid his head on the table and closed his eyes.

T WENTY-EIGHT

CLAY AND JAKE moved carefully through the thick foliage. The moon offered little assistance, but it was the only light source they had. As they made their way toward the stream in search of Sully, their vision improved as their eyes became more accustomed to the lack of light.

"What the—"

Jake tripped, falling on his hands and knees, his right hand landing on solid ground, his left falling into a puddle of viscous material.

"Be careful," he warned, "the terrain is changing." He raised his left hand and attempted to shake loose the sludge. The black colored muck continued to thicken, making it virtually impossible to remove. Jake found a patch of dry ground and raked his hand through the dirt, removing most of the gunk.

Clay, having moved some twenty feet to Jake's left to cover more ground, had encountered his own obstacles.

"Thanks for the warning; you're just a tad too late." Clay worked his way through a hanging, sticky, wet mesh, amidst gelatinous globs that threatened to trip him up with each step.

"Jake," Clay said, "we've gotten too far apart. Follow my voice and—"

Clay walked into one of the sticky strands that made up the web. A marble-sized piece landed in his mouth. Clay reacted convulsively. He spit, coughed, gagged and peeled it from his tongue with his fingers.

Jake touched Clay's shoulder. Clay was bent over with his hands on his knees. Had he not been recovering from his recent ordeal he would have attacked the hand that touched him and the body connected to it. As it stood, all he could muster was,"Bout time."

"Sorry I took so long. Had to stop and ask for directions."

Clay shook his head and stood up straight. "All the bounty hunters on this planet, and I get stuck with a comedian."

"You doing okay now?" Jake asked.

"Yeah, I'm fine," Clay answered, "but before we go another step, we have to produce some light."

"Manufacturing light is beyond our capabilities, don't you think?"

Clay didn't answer for several moments.

"Maybe not." Clay could hear the stream from where he stood. He walked in that direction until he reached its edge. He knelt down beside a gaylock bush, barely visible in the tandem moonlight. The two moons of Aon were rarely seen together as they were usually on opposite sides of the planet. On the occasion they came together, logic would dictate a brighter sky; however, the opposite would occur with the light from each canceling the other out.

Clay felt around until he pushed his hand into a clump of moss. He curled his fingers into a fist and then the ball of moss, with a sucking sound, left the hole to gurgle full of water. Clay moved back several feet from the stream and spread out his handkerchief. He squeezed the excess moisture from the clump of moss. Crawling around on his hands and knees, Clay scraped together a pile of dried vegetation.

"Now for the glue."

Jake remained quiet, watching Clay's silhouette travel in and out of the dim light. Unsure of what he was doing, Jake was fascinated all the same.

Clay slid his boot knife out of its sheath. He dug through the topsoil until he hit clay. He paused for a moment and smiled.

"How ironic—Clay digging clay." He chuckled to himself and then continued to remove the thick substance from the ground. Once he perceived the amount was sufficient, he placed the clay with the other materials he had gathered.

He pulled six spine cutter rounds from his gun belt. Clay placed the projectile end between his teeth and twisted the casing until it popped free. He then set the powder-filled casing on its end and did the same with the remaining five.

Clay divided the moss and glue into six equal parts. He placed a piece of each in the palm of his hand, then squeezed and kneaded the material together as he shook the gunpowder from the casing into the mixture. Once the shell casing was empty he crumbled pieces of dried leaves and twigs.

Clay mixed the dried vegetation with the other components to obtain the correct amount of moisture. This allowed the gunpowder to burn at a slow rate without exploding. Clay, satisfied with the consistency of his concoction, rolled the substance between his palms, forming a ball three inches in diameter. He broke a limb from the gaylock bush, sharpened one end and drilled a hole through each of the six balls. He removed six more limbs from the bush and placed them through the six drilled holes. He packed clay into the remaining space to hold each ball in place.

Clay found several good-sized stones. He fumbled around, scraping the ground until he located what he considered to be enough kindling. Clay then rubbed dry leaves between his hands to grind them into the smallest pieces possible. He removed another limb from the gaylock bush and scraped it with his knife to ensure that the scrapings would be suitable as tinder.

Clay removed another spine cutter from his gunbelt magazine. He twisted the projectile end from the casing, just as he had done before. This time he left the powder in the casing and plugged the end with a small, balled up green leaf, plucked from his benefactor, the gaylock bush.

Clay unloaded his dozen gun, he placed the modified shell into the rotating magazine and locked it into place as the next shell to fire.

Clay placed two stones side-by-side six inches apart. He layered the flammable materials accordingly. First, tinder became the base as it was the most flammable. Kindling would be the next to ignite and hold a flame long enough to start larger pieces of wood.

Last of all, he stacked the remaining stones on top of the loose kindling careful not to flatten the tinder.

Clay knelt down in front of the miniature fireplace. He pointed his gun and pulled the trigger.

The hammer struck the firing pin, causing a chain reaction that spit fire several feet out of the end of Clay's dozen gun. It kissed the edge of the tinder, starting several embers to glow. Clay shoved his gun back into its holster and began to blow, bringing the embers to life, followed by heavy smoke as the tinder burst into flames.

Jake joined Clay and snapped limbs from the beleaguered gaylock bush, which, by this point in its random deforestation, would not survive. This agricultural phenomenon had given its all. For what no one realized planet wide, was that the roots of this little bush apply pressure to the solid calladium core. This supplied stabilization to the entire world's crust. Aon could stand to lose only so many of these anchors. Due to the aesthetic value of its bark, they were already disappearing at an alarming rate.

Clay removed the stones from atop the kindled fire and stacked the broken limbs over the flames until the blaze could maintain itself.

"Impressive," Jake said. "What do you do for an encore?"

"We put two of these on the fire," Clay said. He held up two of the makeshift torches, handing one to Jake and keeping one for himself. As soon as the round flammable balls touched the flames, they came to life, hissing and spewing sparks and debris as they burned.

Clay lowered his torch, the ground, covered with shallow puddles of blood, was now almost black as it dried. The squishy blobs that had so hampered his progress were chunks of organs and muscle tissue.

Jake discovered that the netlike substance comprised veins, tendons, nerve fibers from the spinal column and pieces of shredded clothing.

The ground was littered with fingers, toes and multiple body parts strewn helter-skelter.

Something caught Clay's eye. He reached down and picked up a flap of skin. He stared at it, mesmerized by what he saw. It was half a mask of Sully's face. It had been severed vertically. He expected its half-mouth to speak at any moment.

Jake stepped up. "I guess we know where Sully is."

Clay looked right and then left."Looks like he's all over the place."

Clay noticed Sully's handgun lay in pieces next to his tattered gun belt. He knelt down and dug a shallow hole eight inches square. He removed his hat and looked at Jake, who did the same. Placing the rest of Sully's face in the hole, he covered the silent object.

"Any idea what could have done this?" Jake asked.

Clay removed the spine cutters from Sully's belt and placed them in his own. He stood and brushed off his right knee.

"Not a one," Clay shook his head, "not a single one."

"What's our next move?"

"To get outta here."

T W E N T Y - N I N E

RUBEN BLINKED TWICE and then opened his eyes. The light, even though at a comfortable intensity, caused him to slam them shut again to ease the searing pain coursing through his brain.

"Beer, never again."

He covered his face with both hands to prepare for another attempt. Ruben opened his eyes.

He slowly spread his fingers apart, stopping to allow his eyes to acclimate to the increasing light. Something continued to move his fingers further apart until they offered no protection.

Ruben forced himself to hold his eyes open. Images came into focus. What he saw caused any pain he may have been experiencing to flee posthaste.

On his chest sat what appeared to be a blue translucent globe about twice the size of his own head. Extending from each side were six legs, each with four joints and serrated pincers. The rear six legs balanced the body while the front half dozen spread his fingers apart.

It didn't have a head, but a raised area where its head would have been. Two white dots sat on top of the dome. Ruben assumed these were eyes. The ocular protrusions seemed to twist back and forth as if focusing. They could orbit three hundred and sixty degrees, giving it a one hundred and eighty degree field of vision.

"I sure hope you're not as mean as you are ugly."

Two pairs of black shiny fangs, two upper facing and two downward facing, each pair six inches apart, clicked needle sharp points together. No orifice or hole was present to serve as a mouth.

The creature released his fingers and scurried down a hole through the floorboards and into the soil underneath. Another emerged from the depths of the same hole to take its place.

A woman walked into the room.

Ruben's eyes widened.

"Ah," she said, smiling, "you *do* remember me."

"I remember you," Ruben said, pointing a finger at the woman standing beside his bed.

A single pincer clamped around the extended digit and gently pulled Ruben's finger with his hand and arm in tow back to their original static position.

"Yeah, I remember you all right."

She placed a hand on his shoulder."I do have a name."

"I'm sure you do, but before we start getting all chummy, you've got a few questions to answer."

"Fair enough." She took a seat on the bed. "Okay, shoot."

Ruben reached to scratch his nose. The arachnid type creature sitting on his chest loosened its grip and allowed him to do so. It seemed to know the difference between attending to a bodily need and an escape attempt.

Ruben eyed the creature's grip and then turned his attention back to the woman seated on his bed.

"Why are you holding me prisoner?"

"The word prisoner is a bit extreme—"

"*Extreme,*" Ruben interrupted, "Watch this." He jerked his arm in an attempt to escape.

The creature pulled Ruben's arm down and extended a serrated cutting blade from the end of one of its arms.

"Just what do you call extreme?" he asked, the blade pushed far enough into his neck to draw a trickle of blood.

This can wait, she thought. *I owe a certain marshal a quick visit back on Aon before I can conclude my business on Earth.*

THIRTY

VICTOR OPENED HIS EYES and worked his way from underneath the covers. He sat up on the edge of the bed with his bare feet landing on the floor. In between bouts of closing his eyes, Victor noticed that his toenails needed trimming. Chasing an itch, he hit the right spot, then dug his fingernails into the back of his head.

Victor froze. *Something's not right.* He took a deep breath and then sniffed the air.

His fear subsided by leaps and bounds, having already left his room and nearing the source of the enticing aroma. Victor turned the corner, and a wave of deliciousness pounded his entire body.

Clive stood at the same table he had passed out on the night before. He held a midsized frying pan in his left hand and a fork in his right. The frying pan sat on a round flat disc that Victor reckoned was supplying heat for cooking. The pan contained four thick cut strips of meat and a yellow gelatinous pile that resembled scrambled eggs.

"I thought you were kidding about the bacon and eggs," Victor said.

"I never kid about food," Clive replied, "and besides, *you're* supposed to cook." He turned the strips of meat and stirred the yellow clump. "If I remember correctly, my final words last night were 'bacon and eggs will be fine in the morning.' Which in my book," Clive tapped the fork against the edge of the frying pan several times."Means you do the cooking."

"Believe me," Victor said, "that is something you do not want."

"Not handy in the kitchen, eh?"

"Couldn't boil water."

Clive pulled the pan off the disc and doled out its contents into separate plates. He paused with a serving spoon full of food in midair.

"I'd just as soon not have to look at you half-naked while I'm eating."

Victor noticed for the first time he was scantily dressed in a pair of jeans and nothing more. He wrapped his arms around his chest and took his leave to finish dressing.

"Excellent," Victor said, "I can't remember when I've had a finer meal, and not just the food, but real silverware and plates." Victor wiped his mouth and set his napkin down.

Puzzled, he looked at Clive."Where did you get all this?"

"Do you remember several questions ago I mentioned Marshal Quincy's trinkets?"

Victor nodded.

"And said questions, were your questions I said I would answer at a later date, including the question you just asked?"

"Okay," a perplexed Victor said, "talk so I can understand you, I don't speak gibberish."

"More coffee?" Clive asked.

"I guess, and you can start by telling me where you got all this food." Victor held out his cup. "I survive on dehydrated rations, not to mention the over the top plates and utensils."

Clive filled his cup."We start with Quincy; this'll have to wait till later."

Victor nodded, "As long as I get it all."

Clive took a sip of his coffee."You've already stated that you've never seen Marshal Quincy."

Victor nodded.

"Since you've never seen him, I'll fill you in on what makes our lackluster law enforcement official so special." Clive poured himself another cup of coffee and offered the pot to Victor.

Victor waved him off."Not all that crazy about it. I must say that this is the first time I've heard of such a thing. Where'd you say it comes from?"

"I didn't."

"Suit yourself, but if you drink coffee like you down liquor we'll be finishing this conversation in the privy."

Clive smiled. "That's another story we'll get to in time, but first things first." He raised his cup as if to toast Victor and drank. Once finished, he set the cup down.

"His badge," Clive said. "That star he wears on his chest."

"That's where the conversation ended last time," Victor acknowledged. "Now I'd like to know where it's going."

"Where it's going, is right back to the badge." Clive paused a moment to allow this to sink in and continued. "In the middle of Quincy's brass star is a blue stone; at first glance, one would speculate for aesthetics, but I know better."

"What do you know that no one else does?"

"As I mentioned last night before I passed out, I walked in on the marshal while he was in the middle of communicating with an unknown he called Gaylen."

"Communicating?" Victor said. "You mean talking to?"

"No," Clive reiterated. "I mean he was talking with someone remotely. He removed the stone from his badge and placed into an indention in a small, silver colored box. The voice Quincy was conversing with emanated from the box." Clive stopped and then seemed to reach a satisfactory conclusion.

"Gaylen, that's who he was talking with?"

"Any idea who this Gaylen is, or what he may have to do with Quincy?"

Clive shook his head."No, but the way the two were talking, Gaylen was the boss, and not at all that happy with the way Quincy was running things."

"Running what?" Victor asked.

"Not a clue." Clive dug into his front pocket. "But you can bet we'll find the stone from Quincy's star and this, smack in the middle of it." He tossed a poker chip-sized blue, translucent disc onto the table. It wobbled in a circle several times before coming to a complete stop.

Victor reached down and picked up the disc."This doesn't look anything like the way you described the stone in Marshal Quincy's badge other than the color. So is it safe to assume that it's related in some way?"

Clive raised his eyebrows and nodded several times."I'm impressed. That's it exactly, and furthermore, the disc you're holding provided all the niceties, from the gourmet chow down to the cloth napkins."

"How is that possible?" Victor scratched his head and looked at Clive. "You're talking about magic or some other silly nonsense."

"Not magic—" Clive chided, "technology."

"Technology?" Victor said, "That word went out of style decades ago, when the powers that be began this wonderful trip to a simpler life."

"Speaking of trips," Clive interjected, "we need to check the diffraction station."

"When?"

"How about now?"

Victor nodded, "Let me pack a few things."

"Not necessary," Clive said, producing another disc and flipping it up in the air. "Got everything we need right here." He caught the disc and slid it in his pocket. "All we need do is saddle the ellacks."

"Then let's ride."

"I've heard quite a bit about how things used to be nearly a century ago." Clive said. He cinched the saddle tightly around his mount's belly, placed his left foot in the corresponding stirrup and threw his right leg over.

"What I don't understand is the explanation given for this change. I mean, when you think about the ramifications, it doesn't make any sense unless there's an ulterior motive."

Victor looked around in an exaggerated motion before mounting his ellack. "Ulterior motive," he said. "When I pay attention to my surroundings I see red dirt, gray and red rock outcrops and clumps of faded green and brown weeds." He turned his full attention to Clive. "And those are the exciting parts."

"Maybe you aren't looking deep enough."

Victor furrowed his eyebrows."What's that supposed to mean?"

"Just think about it a while; it'll come to you."

The two men traveled in silence as Victor used all the brainpower at his disposal in an attempt to decipher Clive's last comment.

As the sky began to darken, two figures, one deep in thought and the other seemingly just along for the ride, made their way through the only grasslands on Aon. Three rows of grass being pressed down wound their way toward the two riders.

"Why don't you lighten up?" Clive said, "There's a lot that I don't understand about this situation we found ourselves in and you're reading way too much into what I told you earlier."

"Calladium!" Victor exclaimed. "That's what you meant by going deeper, calladium."

Clive smiled. "Exactly."

Victor watched as Clive's ellack rose to a vertical position, throwing Clive from its back and into the waist-high grass. The animal was systematically dissected and eaten. The crunching of bones and slurping sounds, of what Victor perceived to be entrails being sucked down the gullet of some unseen monster, led him to kick his mount into high gear. He knew Clive must've suffered the same fate, and this weighed heavily on him, even though he had only known Clive a short time.

By now, Victor's ellack had reached seventy plus miles per hour. Once the third pair of legs synchronized with the other four, nothing other than the flying rache would be able to catch it. And this was of no consequence, as the harmless avian's wingspan is no more than eight inches.

Victor continued on for several more miles, guilt beginning to well within for not making sure of Clive's demise before exiting to save his own skin.

THIRTY-ONE

"SOMEBODY OUGHTA TO TAKE ME OUT behind the woodshed, pick out a nice piece of stove wood and beat me half to death for not charging my transition stone," Lynch said. He had been rolling the smooth, blue stone between his fingers.

Lynch stopped walking and began tossing the stone up, only to catch it and toss it up again. Then in a fit of indecisive rage, he threw the offensive item nearly out of sight.

Lynch bent over and placed his hands on his knees. He was breathing heavily, not so much from the exertion, but moreover the frustration. He stood upright and placed both hands on his hips.

"Way to go, stupid. Now you have to find the accursed thing," Lynch began to mumble to himself as he walked.

"They're gonna get me some decent equipment." He kicked at the ground causing a small dust cloud to rise and blow back against his legs.

"No, sir. No more of this charge and play mess. From now on, it's the good stuff." Lynch shook his fist in the air.

"What do they think I am—one of their second-class citizens?" They're about to find out that Lynch Craiger is nobody's lackey.

THIRTY-TWO

"COULD HE KNOW?" Quincy asked.

He had locked himself in his office, alternating between sitting, standing and pacing.

"How?" The marshal lit a cigar, downed a shot of whiskey and poured a cup of coffee. By now he had returned to pacing around the office, only this time he had added chewing his fingernails to his repertoire of nervous habits.

A knock on the door rattled the loose panes of glass in the upper half of the hinged egress. This caused Quincy to jump, tossing his empty coffee cup over his shoulder and jabbing himself in his left nostril with the lit end of his cigar. The hot embers broke off, inducing the sizzle of mucous membranes made worse by the marshal's attempt to put the agonizing inferno to rest.

The knob turned, and the door moved inward. A pretty blond pushed her head through the narrow opening. A scene that could only be described as surreal played out before her.

An out of shape, middle-aged man danced in erratic circles smacking himself in the face. He would alternate blows, first with the hat in his right hand and his open-palmed left hand. Each time the distressed man connected, he would let out a yelp and shake his head and hit himself again.

The woman watched until the spectacle ceased. The man stood still, bent over with his hand on his knees. Blood trickled from his nose, forming a small puddle on the wooden plank floor.

Against her better judgment. she spoke.

"Hello." Her voice was soft yet full of confidence.

Surprised, Quincy jerked his head toward the voice, slinging spatters of blood in her direction. He pulled a handkerchief from his pocket and covered the bleeding appendage.

"I'm sorry to have startled you," she said. "My name is Cassie. I'm the new teacher." She took a moment to look at the window and then at Quincy. "Although I noticed that the schoolhouse has yet to be completed."

Cassie brought her right hand to her mouth to appear embarrassed, when in fact, it was to hide her amusement at the situation.

"Oh, pardon me, Sheriff, I didn't mean to—"

Quincy waved her off, turned and took two steps to his dry sink. Once he'd blown the clots from his nose, he used the morning's shaving water to cleanse any leftover blood residue, doing his best to avoid his seared nostril.

Quincy turned to face his visitor, having done the best he could to clean himself up.

"Please to meet you, and that's *Marshal* Quincy."

"Pardon?"

"It's Marshal Quincy." He stared at Cassie expecting her to catch, what he deemed a horrific breach of etiquette.

She stared back.

"It's *Marshal*," he repeated, this time with all the authority a man with a bright red nose can project. "You said Sheriff."

"I am sorry. I did not intend to demean your title in any way."

Quincy softened. "What's done is done. Now, what can I do for you?"

"You'd be surprised." Cassie was no longer the timid schoolmarm, but a woman to be reckoned with and perhaps feared.

"Wait a minute," Quincy protested, "the door was locked."

Cassie smiled and motioned toward the door. "I believe you will find it still is."

Quincy sidestepped to the front entrance (keeping an eye on Cassie) and tried the doorknob. To his astonishment, it was just as she had said, locked.

"I know what you're doing," Cassie said. "Because of your greed, you are way in over your head."

"I have no idea what you're talking—"

"Save it for those idiots you call deputies."

"Now, wait just a minute—"

"No! Marshal Quincy," she said, "here's how it's gonna be. You can continue to deny your involvement in this little petroleum skimming debacle, and I'll leave you to Gaylen. Then again, you can fess up and maybe, just maybe, I can afford you protection."

Quincy found himself torn between the rage he felt for this blackmailing wench and the real fear of eradication one harbored when dealing with Gaylen.

The marshal (if only in name and even more so now) walked to his desk, flopped into his chair and began working on the bottle from his bottom drawer.

Cassie watched him fill his shot glass. She wondered, would he choose the bottle or a bullet to the brain. She had almost hoped the latter. Aside from the initial mess, it would've made things a lot cleaner in the long run.

After the third drink, Quincy set his glass down. As with most people who enjoy the occasional or the frequent libations, the first thing to leave is the inhibitions. The first thing to arrive is a high rpm motor built especially for the mouth.

"I figure you're the lesser of two evils." Quincy poured another drink. "So until you prove to be a worse employer than Gaylen, I guess I'm all yours. Now, what do you want to know?"

Cassie's stomach churned. She needed a man, not some sniveling lackey. Not much to work with, she thought, but I guess it'll have to do.

THIRTY-THREE

TWELVE THREE-TOED LEGS moved in a synchronized motion. Two furry creatures lumbered along carrying one human rider each.

"Something preying on your mind?" Clay asked.

Jake nodded, stared straight ahead and said nothing.

"Wanna talk about it?"

Jake turned toward Clay and held up a stained right hand. "Do you know what this is?"

"I'd have to say a hand, and a dirty one at that." Jake smiled grimly.

"That's Sully." He looked at his own hand. "At least what's not spread all over the ground back there."

The half facial mask had been indelibly burned into Clay's brain.

"Kinda sticks with a man."

The sky had been growing lighter for some time, no one spoke until the sun peeked over the horizon. An indistinguishable silhouette stood in the foreground.

"There it is," Jake said. "Baine."

"Not much to look at," Clay said.

"Never has been, at least as long as I've been around."

Clay pointed to a stand of foliage that resembled bonsai trees gone wild. "You see those lackaide trees a mile ahead?"

Jake nodded. "Yeah, I see them."

"Let's make for those," Clay said. "We can eat, get some rest and talk about our next move. I don't want to enter your previous place of employment without a plan."

Jake watched as the sun danced off any remaining building materials that had not succumbed to corrosion, which were quite a few. This area of

Aon was known for its dry climate. It allowed for a long period of preservation stemming the tide of decay.

"Which means," Clay continued, "I'll be picking your brain, so I hope your memory is up for the challenge?"

Jake looked at Clay and then straight ahead."The only thing you need worry yourself with is keeping up."

THIRTY-FOUR

CASSIE HAD TO SMILE when she walked into the building. Ruben sat on the floor with the spider creature lying across his lap like the family pet.

"You two been playing fetch while I was away?"

Ruben scowled. "Yeah, we're just taking a break between fetching sessions."

At that moment, the arachnid tending Ruben traded places with its identical twin and scampered back down the hole.

"Why the changing of the guard?" Ruben asked. "I can't get used to one before another takes its place?" Ruben squinted. "It's not like I can tell one from the other anyway."

"They can't survive in this oxygen-rich atmosphere for over thirty minutes at a time."

Ruben nodded, "Interesting, which brings about another question."

"Sure," Cassie replied, "let it fly."

"You know I'm not from around here."

Cassie nodded.

"I think it's safe to assume that the little blue bugs running to and fro are not from around here either."

Cassie nodded a second time. Ruben stared hard at the young girl.

"Just where are you from?"

Cassie smiled. "Unlike you, I *am* from around here."

"Maybe you owe me an explanation." Ruben tapped the creature on his lap and stroked its back several times. It reciprocated by vibrating and emitting a low pitched hum. "Yes," he reiterated, "and quite the explanation at that."

THIRTY-FIVE

ONCE AGAIN, QUINCY FOUND himself barricaded in his office.

"I can't stay here." He sat on his desk, fidgeting and gnawing away at his fingernails. Quincy stood and began to pace. "If that little girl can walk right through a locked door, what chance do I have barring anyone else who wants to get me?" He sat back down on his desk, his fingers starting to bleed from the constant assault from his teeth.

"I gotta get outta here, there's no other choice. I'm a sitting duck if I stay. Yes, sir, I gotta leave this place and now."

Quincy perceived the room beginning to darken, which meant nightfall was coming on. He praised the removal of the electric streetlights, a move he had cursed a few short years ago.

"Now I can slip out the back, make my way to the livery stable and out of town all under the cover of darkness. They won't know that I'm gone for at least twelve hours." He gathered a few personal items; anything else he needed could be had by way of the stone.

Quincy moved quietly out of town. Once at what he deemed a safe distance, he brought his ellack to a fast gallop. Soon he was miles away and increased the distance until he saw the sunrise.

He continued on for another hour or so, then stopped for a quick breakfast. As he was finishing up, he saw something move in the distance.

The sun was now high enough to cause heat waves to emanate from the ground. The further away an object, the more distorted it appeared because of these waves.

Quincy stared at the object to make sure his eyes weren't playing tricks on him. After several minutes he determined that it was not a mirage, but a living bipedal form.

He felt fairly sure that this was not an assassin sent to do him in. He tapped his sidearm with a clenched fist and decided to wait it out.

"What is he doing?" Quincy asked impatiently. "I could've walked there and back at least twice by now."

He continued to monitor the lone figure, not moving in a straight line, but zigzagging back and forth as if searching for something.

Fed up, he climbed aboard his ellack and began to ease his way toward the stranger.

At about one hundred feet away, "Slim," as Quincy had already dubbed him due to his slender build, bent over and picked up an object.

Slim seemed to recognize Quincy for the first time. He hastily slid the newly found object into his pocket.

Quincy kept a hand on his weapon as he pulled up to the stranger.

"You need help?" Quincy asked. "Or are you out in the middle of nowhere, hunting seashells."

"Could use something to drink."

"What's your name?"

"Who wants to know?"

"Quincy, *Marshal* Quincy," he said.

The stranger looked at Quincy with a scowl on his face.

"Folks call me Lynch."

"Lynch," the marshal said, "something about that name sounds familiar."

Lynch noticed the blue stone in the center of Quincy's badge.

"A High One. I've heard tell of your kind, but you're the first one I've seen." He eyed Quincy. "And I'm not that impressed."

"Have no trouble speaking your mind, now do ya?"

Lynch reached into his pocket and produced a dark blue stone.

"Ah," Quincy said, "what have we here?" He stared at the stone in Lynch's hand and smiled.

"A Low One and not just that, but one who seems to have failed to power his Racknor stone before leaving on his journey." Quincy hesitated before continuing. "That is what you're doing, journeying I mean, or are you hunting seashells?"

Since Quincy saw no weapon on Lynch, belittling the stranded man made him feel superior and in control.

Lynch never batted an eye nor changed his lackadaisical expression during Quincy's passive aggressive tirade.

"You done?" Lynch pushed both hands into his pockets and shifted his feet, awaiting an answer.

Had Quincy been a balloon, he would've fizzled through the air, ending as a pile of deflated vinyl on the ground. Lynch had deflated the swollen ego Quincy had worked so hard to inflate that all the beleaguered marshal could manage was a sullen, "Yes."

"Got anything to drink?" Lynch asked.

Quincy nodded and tossed a liquid filled container down.

As Lynch satiated his thirst, Quincy dismounted.

"Drink your fill and then we'll sup." As Quincy dug through his saddlebags, Lynch lowered the canteen. Water coursed down the corners of his mouth and soaked the front of his shirt. He replaced the cap and handed it back to Quincy.

The marshal shook his head. "Keep it, you'll need it later."

Lynch shrugged and pushed his arm through the shoulder strap.

Quincy located two small leather cases and two flat twelve inch discs in his saddle bags. He held one disc by its edges in the palm of each hand. Quincy shook the disc, causing the sides to protrude downward, forming a small round seat. He did the same with the other and then passed one of the leather packages to Lynch.

Each package held a self-contained, ready-to-eat meal. Quincy held a silver canister in his hand. He set this down between Lynch and himself and twisted the top a quarter turn. After a few seconds, the chemicals contained within mixed and produced a small fire that would last around eight hours.

The two men sat enjoying their bounty. Once finished, Quincy took the empty container from Lynch and stowed garbage in a contained compaction bag.

"Don't say much, do you?" Quincy asked.

"Ain't got much to say," Lynch replied.

"We'll pretend that you have something to say and you can start by telling me what you're doing out here in the middle of nowhere, with a Racknor stone void of power."

"Got in a tussle," Lynch said. "Thought it best to leave Earth and head back to Aon while things cooled down."

"Who are you working for? The stone you carry gives me some idea, but I'd like to hear it from you."

Lynch stared at Quincy a long while before he answered.

"Gaylen."

"I know the name but never had any dealings with him," Quincy lied.

Lynch said nothing.

"What happened on Earth to make you feel like you had to leave?"

"The so-called scientist I was working with, a giant of a man, took it upon himself to decide I was unnecessary to his agenda."

"Which was?"

Lynch was busy painting himself into a corner. He had already told one lie, when in truth, the scientist he worked with was a mild-mannered, easy-going sort. Lynch pushed this easy going coworker so far that he had to strike back. Now Lynch had to come up with another untruth to cover the first one.

"I can't be sure, but I think he had his sights set on the calladium."

"So you do know about the calladium extraction?"

Lynch nodded.

"Good," Quincy said, nodding several times. "That eases my mind somewhat. Now, tell me . . ." Quincy leaned in bringing himself closer to Lynch. "What do you think of Gaylen?"

Quincy was surprised to see something he hadn't seen before. A wide grin spread across Lynch's face.

THIRTY-SIX

JAKE BIT DOWN on the dark brown strip. He had to grind his molars against the leathery substance to pull the strip apart.

"I don't want to seem ungrateful." Jake held the remaining piece in the air. ". . . but what happened to the meat we had last night? If I keep eating this stuff, I'm going to dislocate my jaw."

"First time tasting slangermoss jerky?"

"Again, I don't want to seem ungrateful, but really, I'm eating dried mud rat?"

"Indeed you are," Clay said, "just wait till you see what's for dessert." Clay closed the knife he was using and tossed it to Jake. "Here, use this, cutting smaller pieces will save some wear and tear on those mandibles."

Jake opened the knife and went to work.

"Thanks," he said, through a mouth full of jerky.

"Doesn't make this leather any easier to chew," Clay said, "but at least it's something."

After breakfast, Clay poured two cups of coffee he had brewed over a meager fire. He handed one to Jake and then took a sip of his own.

"I need you to tell me what you saw, Jake. The survival of this world may depend on those words."

"What makes you so sure of that?"

"I didn't say sure; more of a gut feeling than anything else, that and—" he stopped, unsure of how to voice his thoughts. "It . . . it groans."

Jake looked perplexed. "Groans? What groans?"

"The planet," Clay said. "It sounds crazy, but that's the only way I can describe the sensation. Tremors have increased. It's like the world is being slowly torn to pieces."

"That would imply the planet is alive."

Clay finished his drink and set the cup down. "Crazy, right?"

"I'm not gonna touch that one."

Clay nodded. "You still owe me a story."

"So it's a story you want?"Jake said.

Clay smiled. "The one I've been trying to dig out of you for the past few days."

"Ah," Jake acknowledged, "that one."

"Yeah, that one. Now quit stalling and start talking."

"I think we ended where I had become the last stop as far as the specialized deliveries we received, and it was up to me to direct them to their final destination. As I recall, I had just conveyed to you I had been unaccounted for, prompting the powers that be, to assume I now knew their secret. This put me in the envious position (for reasons I've already stated) requiring them to take care of me instead of the opposite to shut me up."

"So you did see something," Clay asked, his patience wearing thin.

"Yes, I did."

"Well, what?"

"All the cases that transported material, no matter what the size, were molded from a mixture, combining high strength lunar steel, pure low shorn erudite, and three microns of calladium."

A puzzled Clay shook his head.

"Sounds like the crates were more expensive than the contents."

"In some situations that was the case." Jake took a sip from his cup. "These containers were vacuum sealed with a poisonous gas that would kill within seconds if opened without prior removal of the toxins."

"Those things must have weighed a ton."

"They were heavy enough that their support had to come from air casters."

"So they floated several inches off the floor?"

Jake nodded. "On this day, we had a short shipment--one container. As I guided the container through a common area where six corridors converged, the vacuum seal on the container released and the top popped open." Jake raised both hands in a calming motion. "Before you say anything, yes, I was wearing protective gear from head to toe; a requirement any time you were in that section of the compound."

"Let me guess," Clay said, "this is where your so-called 'time unaccounted for' came into play."

Jake nodded and smiled.

"Yeah, something like that. When the top cracked open, in order not to draw any attention to myself by exhibiting indecisiveness, I directed the container down an alternate corridor without breaking stride. As soon as I located a lab, which was thirty feet down the hallway, I turned into the room, not bothering to lock the door."

"With something that important," Clay asked, "why wouldn't you lock the door?"

"If a door was locked without pre-authorization, it would've thrown up so many red flags the entire compound automatically reverts to restrictive seal. Other than that, I planned to be in the lab one minute tops."

"And did you make it?"

"With fifteen seconds to spare."

"What happened during the forty-five you were there?"

"I opened the lid and looked inside, and before you ask me what it contained, the only honest answer I can give is, I don't know."

"What do you mean you don't know? When you opened the container did you forget to open your eyes?" Clay stood, pulled off his hat, ran his fingers through his hair and began to pace.

"No," Jake protested. "I saw what was inside; I just can't explain it." He glared at Clay. "If you'll sit down, maybe we can work it out together."

Clay replaced his hat and retook his seat."Sorry, I tend to get a little worked up."

Jake's nod showed his acceptance of Clay's apology.

"We all carried a portable ingestion device. That way, in case of an accidental hazardous spill, or in my case, toxic gas, we could, in simple terms, vacuum up the mess and contain it."

"Even though everyone was required to wear protective clothing?" Clay asked.

"There was always that one guy who was in too much of a hurry to suit up or just didn't think the rules applied to him." Jake shook his head. "We'd find them the next morning, having dropped dead in their tracks." Jake sighed. "What a waste." He emptied his cup and wiped his mouth. Setting the cup down, he continued to speak.

"The gas was light green and looked like fog, so removal and containment was easy. So easy, in fact, I didn't bother using the sniffer afterwards." Jake removed his hat and scratched his head.

Clay took this as just another attempt to stall, but in Jake's mind, confusion still reigned.

"Once the cloud of gas dispersed from the interior of the container, I had a few seconds to scour the contents and commit them to memory." Jake said. "Then reload the gas, reseal the top and direct it back to the common area. Once there, with no alarms having gone off, I moved down the correct corridor and delivered my parcel free and clear; or so I thought."

"Two days later, I was brought before the Council and told in no uncertain terms demotion would be the next course of action. The reason given, during my last delivery, surveillance taped me in the common area at two different times forty-five seconds apart. This meant I was somewhere other than where I should've been.

"Even though they were right with their assumptions, I argued, to no avail, ending up, as I started, in the mailroom, this time with the title Pest Control Specialist."

Jake nodded several times.

"I know what you're waiting for, and I appreciate your patience."

Clay's expression changed to one of surprise and pain. He raised his hand. In the center of his palm was a quarter inch hole. A drill bit could not have made a cleaner cut. The culprit, a slashworm, had exited on the backside of Clay's hand and wasted no time working its way up his arm.

"Ah," Clay groaned, "there's more than one." He pulled his right pant leg up in time to see a parasite exit his calf muscle.

"What are they?" Jake screamed. A worm entered his shoulder just above the clavicle connection. Both men writhed on the ground in pain. The soil seemed to move as thousands of the slashworms vied for a free meal.

Before long, Clay and Jake would be consumed alive.

THIRTY-SEVEN

"WHAT DO YOU WANT ME TO EXPLAIN?" Cassie asked.

"If this is your home world," Ruben replied, "what's with the alien bugs?"

"It's a long story."

"I've got time," Ruben said. "You've never been to Aon have you? It's a ridiculous question, but I thought it best to get it out of the way."

"Not as ridiculous as you might think," Cassie replied.

"How can that be?" Ruben stammered, "You're too primitive to get more than a few feet off the ground."

"Simmer down, and I'll tell you. About a year ago, I ran into several strangers at a local watering hole in my town of residence in the Oklahoma territory." Cassie smiled a wide mischievous smile. "It's amazing what you can get with a pretty face and a bottle of liquor.

"I soon learned of the plan to remove oil from deep within the Earth and transfer the crude to Aon. After several months, I became rather close friends with one of the men, if you know what I mean. His name was Derek, and he was primed for marriage.

Derek brought me to Aon to show me my new home. During the months on Earth with Derek, I learned much about Aon, Shell (my supposed new home) and Baine, what I considered to be my final destination. Once I landed on my new planet, all it took was a bottle of liquor, a few favors and freedom was mine." Cassie grabbed a broom and started to sweep, then stopped, and using the broom for support, spoke.

"I guess it seemed callous treating him that way?"

Ruben stared at Cassie for several moments."That's not for me to say."

"I guess not," Cassie said. "Anyway, my first order of business was to pay a visit to the good marshal. My time with Derek procured the names of all the players I would need to weave a web of extortion." She continued to sweep.

"I had poor lawman Quincy ready to cry before I left. He believed I could walk through locked doors." Cassie propped her broom against a wall and produced a long thin metal instrument. "Magical lock pick." Cassie returned to her cleaning. "The plan was moving along as I had hoped, then J. Smith shut me down cold."

"Explain," Ruben said

"I can't," Cassie said. "Somehow he got wind of the plan to deplete Aon's core, those involved, and of my little shake down. J. Smith sent his two little bug thugs up a hole in the middle of my quarters, and that's where we are up till now."

Cassie paused, "Any more questions before I finish sweeping?"

"You're kidding, right?" Ruben spread his hands out to each side. "I've got this blue ball sitting in my lap, ready to slice me open at the slightest move. Yet the cursed thing purrs like a kitten and encourages me to rub it." Ruben stared at Cassie. "I don't know how, but some way or the other this thing is inside my head.

Something caught Ruben's attention.

"Ah, right on time." An identical twelve legged super arachnid crawled from the hole and relieved the sentry sitting on Ruben's lap. He watched as the new arrival settled in and looked at Cassie.

"Any more questions?"

"I guess you deserve an explanation." She closed the door and sat down beside Ruben. "I'll tell you what I can, or at least what I believe to be true."

"That's all I'm asking." The thing in Ruben's lap wiggled back and forth as if making itself more comfortable.

"I've never seen that before," Cassie said.

Ruben noticed she had a disturbed expression on her face, but said nothing.

"In case you're wondering," Cassie began, "I have no control over these creatures."

The thing in Ruben's lap seemed to stiffen. It emanated feelings of offense, not just telepathically, but also in a fashion that made Ruben and Cassie's skin crawl.

"It doesn't like being called a creature," Cassie said, "They're a complex, crystallized, silicon-based life form."

Ruben thought for a moment, doing a few calculations in his head.

"Almost sounds like they're made of calladium. That would also explain their appearance, but this fellow here is much too soft." He demonstrated this by leaving small indentations in the back of the one sitting in his lap as he rubbed it.

"They lack one element," Cassie said. "One molecule of calladium is all it would take."

"You are correct," Ruben verified, "but that leads to an even larger conundrum and please correct me if I'm wrong. calladium and the being that rests in my lap do not exist on planet Earth."

Cassie nodded. "Noticed that, did ya?"

"Doesn't take a rocket scientist," Ruben said, "Even though that's more or less what I am."

"In case you haven't noticed," Cassie said, "the sprawling town of Stave isn't much more than an outpost."

"If that," Ruben replied.

Cassie smiled."Two months ago a stranger rode into town. Now you have to understand that when Stave gets a visitor, it's big news."

"I'd like to say I believe you," Ruben said, "but that's not something I can embrace. Do you realize that of the three people I met when I pulled into town, I was ostracized by the first, then drugged and kidnapped by you and your bartending accomplice?" Ruben rubbed the thing that sat in his lap. The creature reciprocated by emanating a low satisfied hum.

"This stranger had a very interesting story to tell," Cassie said, ignoring Ruben's last comments.

Ruben, feeling snubbed, said nothing, so as not to appear bothered by her failure to acknowledge his concerns.

"There was nothing unusual about the way he looked--vest, blue jeans, cowboy boots and a Stetson, like every other man on this rock." She stared straight ahead. "If there was anything unusual, it was the way he carried himself." She moved her gaze to Ruben. "Or the way it carried him."

"What do you mean—?"

Cassie moved her hand in a slicing motion and stood. "I've asked myself that question a thousand times."

The changing of the guard interrupted the conversation as the blue bug in Ruben's lap jumped up and scurried down the hole. A second later, the next sentry settled itself into position ready for its thirty minute shift.

"And no answer to any of those thousand questions?" Ruben asked.

"Not one that makes any sense," Cassie replied.

Ruben continued to rub the multi-legged thing, this time on its head. As he worked his fingers back and forth, wherever his fingers came in contact with the creature's outer layer, a thick, viscous, cloudy syrup oozed out, filling the indentions. It bathed Ruben's finger tips in a soothing lotion. The warmth climbed slowly through his hands, up his arms, across his shoulders, the two parts mixing in his spinal column like epoxy. It traversed his neck and entered the deepest, unknown parcels of gray matter.

"It was like the man was possessed," Cassie said, "yet the possession was of no concern. Losing the parasite that had invaded his body terrified this stranger." Cassie shook her head. "And even through all the turmoil, he still exuded an unnatural calm that pulled me close, imploring me to join."

Cassie was crying for help. Even with Ruben less than three feet away, her cries fell on deaf ears. Ruben was drowning in syrup.

THIRTY-EIGHT

CLIVE HIT HARD ON HIS BACK, knocking the wind from his lungs and sending his diaphragm into spasms. As he began to recover, taking in small breaths at first, he saw in the fading light his ellack disappearing, one bite at a time, by three ravenous Moro beasts.

The only way to describe one of these thirty foot long horrid creatures was a mouth laced with dagger like teeth and a tale. A bony ridge ran down the length of its back, and thick barbels or whiskers protruded from each side of its head and trailed back eight feet or more. These served to tell the creature whether it was above or below ground, being as it was a blind burrower.

The Moro beast used its mouth to move underground nearly as fast as it could through the air. It would use its tongue to seal the bottom of its mouth when it ate and then lift it, exposing a large hole to allow dirt and debris to exit when it was tunneling. It used powerful muscles located in its sides to propel its frame and steer as it moved.

Clive found himself on the outer edge of the carnage, having begun his escape once he hit the ground and could draw in the tiniest amount of air. He was able to make more headway as the three creatures fought each other over scraps, diverting their attention away from him.

Just as Clive was about to slip away unseen, one of the Moro beasts detected his retreat and began to slither his way. As the creature advanced and Clive continued his retreat, the ground that remained between the two began to rise, pulsate, fall and then rise again. This turned the Moro beast's attention from Clive to what was happening underground before him. He opened his mouth and dived, disappearing beneath the top layer of ground.

The other two, upon seeing the third in their party burrow underground, balanced precariously on their tails over the spot where their comrade had entered. A few seconds later, a sinkhole twenty feet in diameter suddenly developed as the ground caved in down to an indeterminable depth.

A huge form climbed from the hole with the mutilated body of the Moro beast in its right hand. As the creature emerged, holding its victim by the tail, the two remaining beasts began to howl and simultaneously lunged toward the creature.

Clive observed the large creature, in an almost comedic display, began to beat the two living beasts with the dead one he held in his hand. He would alternate, lifting a dead or dying Moro beast. Holding one in each hand it continued to wail on the third lying helpless on the ground or slam the two it held together.

This continued until there was nothing but a carpet of mutilated flesh remaining. The creature dropped the two tail stubs it was holding and turned to face Clive, who could make out no discernible details in the nearly nonexistent light, only that the creature's silhouette appeared to be that of a giant human.

"Well, dummy, I guess you should've gone while you had the chance."

"I reckon so" he answered himself.

The creature took a step toward him. Clive felt something tighten around his chest and arms. It pulled tight, jerking him off his feet and onto his back. In no time at all he was traveling through the grass at breakneck speed. A rock relieved him of his consciousness, and he faded into oblivion, thinking, *how odd, I never noticed four moons before. I thought there were only two.*

* * *

"The next thing I remember," Clive rubbed his head. "At least I think I remember . . ." He looked at Victor. "For all I know, I'm still knocked out and dreaming all this."

"I assure you you're not," Victor said.

"That's what you say," Clive replied.

"Okay, for the sake of argument, what do you remember after rolling from your ellack?"

"Bits and pieces." Clive dropped his head, grabbing his temples as pain seared through his brain.

"Clive, you okay?"

"Yeah, I've got this big knot on top of my head." He demonstrated this by touching the affected area and grimacing as he did so.

"I'm . . . ah, sorry about that rock. I couldn't see it, but I sure felt it when you two connected." Victor hesitated unsure of what to say. "Unfortunately, it was either that or leave you to play with your new friends."

"No, no, that's quite all right. Better this lump than pieces of me not big enough to stir fry."

"Are you beginning to recall more?"

Clive nodded. "Yeah." He grabbed his forehead as another wave of pain coursed through. Once it passed, he opened his eyes and continued.

"As my mount went vertical, and I slid off its back, there was enough light left to see three huge mouths tearing it to pieces."

"That's gotta be rough," Victor said.

Clive nodded and smiled grimly.

"Especially when it's coming after you next."

Victor acknowledged Clive's sentiments with a nod.

"After that is when it gets a little dicey. I remember the bottom dropping out and something huge crawling out of the hole. It turned the three mouths into so much mush and set his sights on me. Before I was able to react, I was on my back, flying through the grass. Next thing I know, I'm laying here watching you coil your rope."

"How's your head?"

"Other than the excruciating pain, dizziness and nausea, it's not too bad."

"Glad to hear you're doing better."

Clive smiled. "Something to eat would be nice, despite my queasy stomach."

Victor rubbed his stomach.

"I'm as interested in seeing where this food comes from as I am in eating it."

Clive managed to push himself up until he rested on his knees. He reached into his pocket and pulled out the round blue disc. He looked at Victor.

"What's your pleasure?"

"Surprise me."

Clive held the disc in his hand until it started to glow. He set it on the ground in front of him. A blue vortex extended from the disc, swirling to the height of about two feet. After a few seconds the vortex spun itself out, leaving two round metal plates with metal covers and a knob in the center of the top to lift by. To the side of each plate sat a white piece of linen, rolled into a tight tube.

"Go ahead," Clive said.

"I can't believe what I smell," Victor said. He swallowed hard. The aroma wafting up into his sensory glands made it difficult to contain the overflow of saliva in his mouth. Victor wrapped his fingers around the knob and lifted it from the plate. On it sat a large porterhouse steak, a half-dozen small red potatoes and a mound of green beans topped with toasted almond slivers.

Victor grabbed the linen tube and hastily unrolled it, sending flatware sprawling into the dirt.

"You can slow down," Clive said, "nobody's gonna take it from you." He looked to his left and then to the right. "Leastwise, I don't think so." Clive smiled and filled his mouth with the huge piece of meat.

Victor gathered his silverware and followed suit. Soon both men were literally licking their plates clean.

Victor sat his plate down.

"I'm at a loss for words."

"Don't lose them all, we have a lot to talk about."

THIRTY-NINE

"GAYLEN—" LYNCH SAID, " to tell you the truth, I never gave him much thought."

"Let me see that stone of yours," Quincy said.

Lynch complied, pulling the dead stone from his pocket and handing it to Quincy. The marshal took the stone and touched it to the one in the center of his badge. A bright light ensued, followed by a small shower of blue sparks. Quincy handed the fully charged racknor stone back to Lynch.

Lynch looked closely at the stone, tossed it into the air and caught it on the way down. He looked at it once again before sliding it into his pocket.

"We might get along just fine at that."

Quincy smiled. "And to start off this new relationship in good faith, you can tell me, what and how you're familiar with Gaylen."

"Strange you would say such a thing." Lynch continued to stare at Quincy. "You told me a short time ago you had heard of Gaylen, but never met him." Lynch's eyes began to burn holes through Quincy. "Now if I was a bettin' man, I'd wager you're smack dab in the middle of a lie." He paused for effect. Quincy was beginning to sweat and Lynch could sense it. "So it seems to me any gesture of good faith now becomes your burden."

The marshal shifted nervously.

"I think you know more about Gaylen than you're lettin' on. So why don't you spread a little of that good faith you've been rambling on about."

Then Lynch did something totally out of character.

"And, marshal, thanks a heap for powering up my rock."

"Since our president is appointed and not elected, there are very few people on the planet, save for his family and a few political officials, that know what he looks like." Quincy said.

"So that allows him to go pretty much anywhere he wants unmolested," Lynch said.

Quincy nodded. "Including my office."

"So that's how Gaylen got to you, eh?" Lynch grabbed a used toothpick out of his shirt pocket and shoved it into his mouth. "Waltzed right down Main Street, up to your door, turned the knob, and there he is; a ray of sunshine or your worst nightmare." Lynch pulled the toothpick from his mouth. "I guess it all depends on how you want to look at it."

Quincy frowned, "Yeah, well the jury's still out on that one."

"So what did our illustrious president have to say?"

"Not so fast," Quincy said. "Now it's your turn to tell me what you know about Gaylen."

Lynch stared at Quincy, rolling the toothpick around in his mouth.

"Fair enough." He put the toothpick back into his shirt pocket. "I was a graduate of one of the most prestigious schools in this hemisphere."

Quincy wrinkled his forehead.

"Not Thurman?"

"One and the same," Lynch said proudly. "And guess what it got me?"

Quincy shrugged.

"Well, allow me to fill you in." Lynch tilted his head back, shoving his nose into the air. "None other than the presidential handyman."

One corner of Quincy's mouth curled upward in a satisfied smirk."Was the degree a prerequisite for the job?"

"No, but you'd be surprised at the places an unassuming position such as the one I held would get you into. No matter how secretive or classified information may be, the building it's housed in will eventually need maintenance."

"So you're a fraud," Quincy said. "You're not supposed to be here, you belong back at the ranch cleaning out the crapper."

"That's pretty much it."

"No," Quincy said, "you're absolutely brilliant."

Lynch stared at Quincy. "Brilliant is an admirable word but hardly fitting in my case."

"I beg to differ," Quincy said. "You managed to work your way into Gaylen's inner circle, with Gaylen himself being none the wiser."

Lynch poured himself another cup of coffee, taking a big sip.

"This sure does beat what I'm used to drinking."

"Why don't we stick to the discussion at hand?" Quincy said, appearing a bit miffed.

"Okay," Lynch said, "I'll stick to the discussion."He set his cup down, and laying his forearms across his thighs, he interlocked his fingers. "And where this, so-called 'discussion' ends is against a wall that I am unable to penetrate."

"That's where I come in," Quincy said. "I know the who, where, how and why of what you seek." Quincy smiled like a poor man who has just received a key to the Mint. "In other words, your wall is now a pile of rubble."

"Tell me," Lynch insisted

"Now you seem more interested."

Lynch nodded, "Very much so."

Quincy stood and began to prepare another pot of coffee, speaking as he worked.

"You're right smack dab in the middle of the extraction point." He tapped the blue crystal on his badge. "All of our installations or outposts, if you prefer, are no more, and in most cases, exactly thirty miles apart."

"What's that got to do with your badge?"

"Nothing to do with the badge, everything do with the stone." Quincy filled the pot from a gray flask, then set it on the heating element and sat back down. "Unless you're traveling between worlds, thirty miles is the maximum you can transfer from point to point."

"Okay," Lynch said, "what about the rest of it?"

"Gaylen thinks I'm his second in command." Quincy filled two cups and handed one to Lynch.

"Aren't you?"

Quincy grinned. "Let's just say I got a better offer."

FORTY

RUBEN FOUND HIMSELF TUSSLED about in a jerky back and forth motion. A muffled sound began a mantra that seemed to travel into one side of his head and out the other without explaining its presence. Ruben's fingers had turned to jelly up to his wrists, and other than the sound, which he had now determined to be a voice, was the slightest inkling of a notion. A notion taking root in the farthest corner of his psyche.

With no explanation, the fog and confusion exited his head, leaving Cassie shaking him back and forth while uttering his name over and over.

"Enough already!" Ruben said, knocking her hands away. He grabbed his head, waiting for the spinning to subside.

"I'm sorry," she said. "You had spaced out, and I didn't know what else to do."

Ruben moved his hands. The dizziness was all but gone.

"No, if anyone's to blame, it's me."

He noticed his new friend shook violently and appeared to be vomiting.

His cohort skittered out of the hole, ahead of schedule this time. The sick creature rolled out of Ruben's lap and hobbled in a drunken sideways gate towards its sanctuary. Once reaching its objective, the creature fell, disappearing down the hole, save for the tip of one leg, which could be seen supporting its body. It maintained this precarious position until it could hold on no longer.

Ruben looked at Cassie and down at the new arrival in his lap, busy ingesting the small pools of regurgitation left by its comrade.

"Waste not, want not," Ruben joked.

"But waste what?" Cassie replied.

"That would be the correct question to ask, now wouldn't it?" Ruben ran his finger through a small drop of white vomit stuck to his pant leg. He smeared the substance between his thumb and index finger. It was warm and smooth and even offered a calming effect.

Ruben jerked, causing the bug in his lap to rise and sit back down.

"That's it, communication." Ruben turned to Cassie. "Tell me more about this stranger that rode into town last year."

"Like I said, nothing special about the way he looked—"

"Not that," Ruben's animation was uncharacteristic. "You mentioned possession or something that seemed to control him."

"It's not a question of possession, but more like something unseen coexisted as an essential part of his being."

"What else?"

"The relationship between the three was mutual; I emphasized this because these three separate beings were as one."

"What do you mean three? There was only one guy."

"You asked," Cassie said.

"And I'm about to do it again. You said this man had an interesting story to tell."

Cassie nodded.

"That's a good place to start," Ruben said.

"I'll do you one better," she said, "Let's start from the beginning. I arrived in Shell about two months ago under the guise of the new school teacher. The school building was still under construction and had been for some time. The way things were going, the building would never be finished, so my ruse was in no danger of being discovered."

"What did you mean when you said 'the way things were going?'" Ruben asked.

"Ever since gold took over, everyone in this grubby little town is so concerned about getting their fair share that nothing gets done."

Ruben squinted. "What is gold?"

Cassie stared at Ruben with a hint of indecisiveness before deciding. "Gold is as valuable here in Stave as calladium is to you back in Baine."

Ruben's mouth dropped open and his eyes bugged out of his head. "How could you know about Baine or calladium?" He pulled a handkerchief from his back pocket, and removing his hat, wiped the sweat from his forehead.

"Are you okay?" Cassie asked. "You're looking kind of pale."

Ruben stared at her.

"Uh-huh," was all he could muster as he shook his head in direct contradiction to his statement.

Cassie slapped Ruben gently aside his cheek.

"Come on now, if you can travel from Aon to Earth, with the proper resources, why can't I do the same thing in reverse."

Ruben turned to her."I guess so, " he said.

Cassie handed Ruben a cup of water. He accepted the container and emptied its contents, then wiped his mouth and handed the cup back to Cassie.

"More, please."

She complied, and soon both were conversing, only this time there was a different feel to the dialogue.

"Can't say why I spaced out like that," Ruben apologized. "I guess having a daughter about your age back on Aon had something to do with it."

"Ah," Cassie said. "A family man."

Ruben smiled and nodded.

Cassie was tough, petite and pretty. She kept her shoulder-length strawberry blonde hair in a bun so as not to draw attention away from the fact she was a schoolteacher. Most of the time she wore an ankle-length skirt, a light colored high-necked blouse, glasses and a pair of boot-like shoes. For now, she had dropped her ruse and donned normal clothing, including the bun.

"Tell me, Ruben, does the name Extolian Branch mean anything to you?"

Ruben thought for a moment."The name sounds familiar, but if what I understand is true, they are a collective which deserves a wide berth."

Cassie acknowledged Ruben's statement, "And unfortunately, I find myself in their employ."

"Employee? What could they want with one such as you, and why would you endanger yourself in such a way?"

"Calladium," Cassie said. "They want calladium and will stop at nothing to get it."

"What does all this have to do with you?"

"I'm the point person. It's up to me to see it gets done."

"You mean the Extolian Branch getting the calladium?"

"At any cost," Cassie said, "but I think they are more commonly known as the erratts, at least that's the name circulated by the locals."

"Erratts," Ruben repeated.

Cassie nodded. "Caladium is just the half of it. They use it to buy subjects for their sacrifices, which is their real focus."

Ruben looked at this young woman through eyes of confusion.

"What are you doing? This isn't like you."

"You don't know me," Cassie snapped, "so you can lay off the 'I pretend to care' garbage, because I'm not buying it."

"True," Ruben said. "I haven't known you that long, but I've seen enough to realize that the Cassie you described isn't you."

She raised her hand to her mouth and Ruben could see tears run down her cheeks.

"Something else is pushing this," Ruben said. "Why don't you fill me in; maybe I can help."

The bug sitting on Ruben's lap rose, twisting his head from side to side, giving the impression of increased alertness. The second bug climbed out of the hole and stood beside Ruben also moving its head from side to side.

Cassie threw a quick glance, without moving her head toward the two arachnids, then back to Ruben. She shook her head just enough for Ruben to recognize what she was attempting to convey.

Ruben nodded in the same fashion and mouthed the word "later."

FORTY-ONE

"ALL RIGHT," VICTOR SAID, "let's talk. You first. You seem to have a better command of the subject."

"First, let me explain how I came to be involved in this mess." Clive hesitated, staring at Victor. "But before I do." He leaned over and looked deep into Victor's eyes. Clive rubbed Victor's shirt collar between his thumb and index finger, then leaned back.

"As much as I hate to do this, I have no choice." Clive inched his hand closer to his sidearm.

Victor noticed the slight movement, but said nothing.

"I have to ask this," Clive said. "You are from this planet, aren't you?"

Victor stared in disbelief once Clive finished.

"Yeah, Clive, I'm from Aon, and I have to ask what brought that on."

"So you would understand what I'm about to tell you, geographically having a general knowledge of the planet."

Victor stood and retrieved a small pot, heating element, two cups and leather pouch from his saddle bag. He sat down and made a pot of coffee.

"If that was your main reason, tell me your secondary reasoning and why you felt it necessary to make ready your weapon?"

"When I became involved in this so-called 'profit-making venture,' I thought it was a quick in and out. I soon found out that its origin was alien." Clive found his hand still tense, ready to draw. He relaxed his arm and continued to speak.

"I was running low grade scratch from the seventh parallel, when a . . . we'll just call him a subject, with the personality of a mud ball, approached me. Said he was hiring and wanted to know if I'd be interested?"

"Isn't the seventh parallel closed to harvesting," Victor said. "Especially scratch."

"It is," Clive replied, "but it's a law that's never enforced."

Victor filled both cups and handed one to Clive. Both men took a sip.

"Mr. Personality said it was a short-term position, but with a much larger return than normally seen in this type of arrangement."

"Sounds a tad to the left of the legal, illegal line," Victor said.

"More like way to the left," Clive acknowledged. "If you've ever had any dealings with our esteemed legal system, you know, for the most part, the word 'illegal' does not exist in their selective vocabulary."

Victor shook his head. "It was driven into me as a young man to avoid the law at all costs, so I've made it a point to keep my nose clean."

"Until now," Clive said.

"Looks that way."

Clive tilted his cup, emptying the contents and set it back down. "What caused the change?"

"Look around," Victor said, "the whole world's going to hell." He refilled his cup and poured the rest of the coffee into Clive's. "As much as I hate to admit it, it's the only way to survive."

Clive pulled a magnetically attached cylinder, three inches tall and three inches in diameter from his belt buckle. He set it on the ground between himself and Victor. A quarter turn to the left, and the two men bathed in the glow of a simulated campfire.

"I accepted the stranger's conditions, no questions asked. Money is money, and no matter whose it is, it all spends." Clive tilted his hat back and placed his forearms on his knees. "He sent me to Baine with instructions to meet up with a Marshal Quincy, and under no circumstances was I to mention his name."

"That makes little sense," Victor said. "If he didn't want his name known he shouldn't have shared it with you."

Clive squinted, deep in thought. After several moments his eyes cleared. "He wanted me to spread his name, but why?"

"Can't answer that, but spread his name is what we will not do." Victor smiled at Clive. "You're not even gonna tell me."

F O R T Y - T W O

A LIGHTNING-LIKE PATTERNED GRID of positively charged ions, danced a few inches above the ground. It covered a region a quarter square mile, turning the area into a stunning pyrotechnic show.

In the middle of this square, lay two human figures. Both were in fetal positions, swatting at their necks and faces. The constant hum emanating from the charged grid came to an end along with the light display.

A comical scene played out as the men continued to slap themselves. Then, realizing the slashworms had ceased their attack, they stopped their flailing and sat up.

A short, slender man, barefoot and dressed in overalls walked up on Clay and Jake.

"Well, now," he said, through a scraggly mustache and beard, "'pears like you two went and sat down amongst some mighty nasty critters."

"Yeah, I guess it would appear that way," Clay said. He brushed dirt and debris from his clothes and examined himself for slashworm damage. Strangely enough, there was no pain associated with his wounds.

"I'm-a guessin' you two is fair the well stupid to be sittin' down in a slashworm nest." He pushed a strange looking pistol into a wide holster hanging from his side. The pistol was attached to a double cylinder backpack, by way of a flexible metal hose. At the top of each cylindrical tank set a cone that ended in a dull point. An electrical charge danced between the tips of the two cones.

"Reckon it's a good thing I were out and about."He stuck his finger in his right ear and dug around, pulling out a large brown lump and wiping it on his overalls.

"Yes, sir, dang good thing fer real I jest happened along."

"You . . . you killed those filthy bloodsuckers?" Jake exclaimed.

"Oh no," the little old man said, "I didn't kill' em, I jest ran' em back in the ground fer a spell."

Clay and Jake stood, continuing to brush themselves off.

The small man extended his hand.

"Names Taggert Lee." He shook Clay's and Jake's hands. "My friends call me Gert. Being you two fellers ain't what I'd exactly term as mean, I reckon it'll be fittin fer you to call me jest that."

Both men acknowledged Gert's gesture of friendship, and in the spirit of camaraderie offered their first names to be used by Gert.

"Now, I ain't sure if you two knows it or not, but them there nasty little buggers that was a gnawin' on ya is hardheaded little fellers. They ain't ones to back down from an easy meal."

Clay along with Jake looked at Gert and then at each other, not understanding what the little man was trying to say.

Gert shook his head. "Some peoples can be so dense that it jest ain't proper. Looky here, you two." He hocked up a big ball of phlegm and spat it on the ground, in front of Clay's boot. A single slashworm pushed through the soil and sucked the phlegm ball down.

Clay and Jake were mesmerized watching the parasite, push through the Earth, devour the organic Jell-O and disappear.

"Is you two stupid or is ya tryin to get et up?"

The two men broke from their reverie and jumped. They landed beside Gert as the ground boiled with thousands of slashworms in search of the meal they had tasted moments earlier.

"I guess stupid would fit best," Clay said.

"No argument there," Jake echoed.

The sky had been growing light for some time now. The uniqueness of this hemisphere included dual suns that never fully set. So there was always light even if just a small amount.

"You two dummies gets not a argment from me neither." He pulled his pistol out of its holder.

"See dis here?"

Clay and Jake both nodded.

"It got no mo left, no zap. I couldn't help. You be a pile of et up mess."

Clay's eyes widened.

"That thing he carries, that drove the slashworm back into the ground. It doesn't work anymore. I guess it needs to be charged."

Jake nodded. "If we hadn't gotten out when we did there would've been nothing he could have done to help us."

"Ever wonder if somebody's looking out for you?" Clay asked.

"Not till now," Jake replied.

Gert removed his tattered floppy hat and scratched his scalp through long gray locks. Replacing his hat, he turned to Clay and Jake.

"Good thing ya not have yer lacks close by, em worms et yer ridin critters fer sure."

Clay and Jake shook their heads.

"Where you two fellers a-headed?"

Jake nodded to a pile of rubble, ten or more miles away.

"Baine."

Gert nodded several times.

"Bad place, lotta bad things twixin here and thar." He pulled the electric pistol from its holster once again.

"We goes to my livin place and git this here workin agin. I go wit you to Baine, I'm a-thinkin you need hep."

"Lead the way, Gert," Clay said, "we're right behind you." He turned to Jake. "And don't forget, you still owe me an answer on the contents of that unit."

Jake nodded. "In time."

FORTY-THREE

"WE'VE BEEN HANGIN' pretty close to the diffraction station for a while now," Victor said, "and it looks as though we've amassed a good amount of gasoline."

Clive nodded. "We're doing a little too well. There are questions being asked, and I've even roughed up one of my best men, blaming him for a delay that wasn't his fault."

"So what now?" Victor asked.

"As of today, we cut back on the amount of gas were pulling from the crude."

"Won't that slow our extraction time down?"

"Better it takes us a little longer than we get caught skimming off the top."

Victor extended his hands and leaned in toward the simulated campfire as if to warm himself.

"You sure that's the best way to go?"

Clive, who had been staring at the fire, now looked up. "Something eatin' at you?"

Victor nodded. "Yeah, you told me about the old man who pulled you into this new career path, but something just doesn't add up."

"And that would be?"

"It's too big."

"Too big? What's too big?"

Victor spread out his arms.

"This . . . this whole operation is too big. You, me and some old fart do not have the resources to pump thousands of gallons of gasoline, twelve miles beneath the surface of this planet. Then extract tons of liquefied calladium and distribute it into the proper sized molds before it hardens again."

Clive nodded. "I'm surprised it's taken you this long to ask me that question."

Victor waited, saying nothing. Once he realized Clive was remaining silent also, he spoke.

"No answer?"

Clive shook his head.

"Not yet, but soon." He looked into Victor's eyes. "I need you to trust me on this one."

Victor nodded. "You've never given me a reason not to." He spread his sleeping bag on the ground, courtesy of Clive's disc. "Maybe it's time we take a trip into town. We need news. Whatever may be going on, we need to know."

Clive lay back, pulling his hat over his face.

"At first light we leave for Baine."

* * *

"It's not a sure thing," Clive said, "but I know for a fact that Gaylen chose Quincy to head up this operation. He, like Baine, was the only choice. The only reason Baine is in the picture . . . well . . . is for pretty much the same reason. It's where the thinnest crust exists on the planet, and therefore the easiest place to extract the calladium, hence, the only choice."

"What's not a sure thing?" Victor asked.

"Gaylen thinks Quincy is an idiot and for all intents and purposes he's right. All I need do is fan the flames, slide into Quincy's place, and we have everything we need." Clive leaned over and patted his ellack on the neck. "Of course, that's in a perfect world."

Victor nodded, "In other words, not a sure thing."

Clive returned the nod, "Exactly."

Victor pulled a silver colored bottle out of his saddlebag, removed the cap and took a drink.

"How far to Baine?"

"Not sure, but if pressed, my best guess would be twenty-five or thirty miles."

Victor slid the bottle into his saddlebag.

"Are we looking up Gaylen the first thing?"

"Not sure," Clive said.

"Fill me in on what's bouncing around in that head of yours. I can't help if I don't know what you're planning."

Clive looked at Victor.

"If it's one thing you don't lack, its persistence."

Victor smiled, "Seems to me I've heard that before."

"I think it best to look up Quincy first," Clive said. "I haven't seen him in a couple of days, and I want to make sure nothing has changed."

"Won't that take a while, especially if he's hiding something?"

Clive chuckled. "That's one man I've always been able to read like a book."

"Then we find Gaylen?"

"Not so fast. First, we find my counterpart and get the real lowdown on what's been going on."

"You holdin' back on me?"

"I guess I am," Clive admitted. "Carl, he's the other deputy. Unlike Quincy, he's got a spine."

"I could sure use a drink," Victor said. "I bet you could use a case by now."

Clive nodded. "I like your suggestion. The first place we'll hit is the saloon."

* * *

"You gotta be kidding me," Clive said. "This ain't a saloon; it's barely a pile of sticks!"

Victor nudged a shattered piece of wood to the side with his boot.

"This was nothing short of old weaponry brought into play."

Clive was busy digging through debris behind what was left of the bar. He rose."Looky here what I got." He held up three bottles of whiskey. "All top shelf hooch and plenty enough for two." He popped a cork and took a long pull, relieving the bottle of half its contents.

"Not too shabby."

Clive handed the bottle to Victor.

"I was afraid you were gonna Bogart all the whiskey." Victor took a swig and passed the bottle back to Clive, who finished it off.

"That's right," Victor said, "you were going to explain your rather dubious gift for holding copious amounts of alcohol."

Clive was spitting out a cork and drinking his second bottle. He stuck one finger in the air, signaling a pause until he lowered the bottle.

"And so I shall, my friend. I see one table and a few chairs still intact. Grab that last bottle and let's have a seat."

Victor found a shot glass amidst the rubble and joined Clive at the only table in the house.

Victor opened a third bottle.

"Figure the only way I'll get a drink is to open a bottle for myself." He blew out the shot glass and poured himself a drink.

"Don't worry, two is my limit." Clive took another healthy pull from the bottle and wiped his mouth with the back of his sleeve. "After this I need to find Quincy. It wouldn't do for a sworn officer of the law to appear before his superior in a state of drunkenness, now would it?"

"Think I'll just wait here for you," Victor said. "I'm growing rather fond of this semi-patio bar scene."

Clive finished his bottle. "Be back shortly."

"No, sir," Victor said as Clive rose to leave. He nodded toward the empty bottle. "You still owe me an explanation how you're able to swill your weight in liquor and continue to function normally."

"Ah yes, I believe I promised such an explanation, and being a man of my word, you shall now have it."

Victor poured himself another drink.

"I'm all ears."

Clive dug out another bottle from behind the bar and then returned to his seat.

"For the story," he said

"For the story," Victor raised his glass, Clive countered with his bottle. The two clinked containers together.

"For the story."

"As you can tell," Clive began, "my sunny disposition and motor mouth increase exponentially after I imbibe the elixir of life." He took another drink from the bottle. "And that's about all the effect it has on me, until I fall asleep."

"Now that you've told me, or rather reiterated what I already know, why don't you tell me what I don't know?"

"Fair enough," Clive took another drink.

"I understand why you needed another bottle to tell the story."

Clive winked. "As I was saying, I'm part of a different race, one I can discern little of, but one not of this world."

"What brought you to such a conclusion?"

"My father raised me, and even that I say loosely." Clive thought for a moment before continuing. "It's kinda fuzzy but I remember him handing me off to different individuals. I stayed sick a lot and the only relief I recall came from a nasty tasting strong liquid." Clive raised the bottle. "I eventually learned that the liquid in this bottle would be the only thing to keep me on an even keel. Unfortunately, I would be ostracized as a drunkard and menace to society."

"Rough way to be brought up," Victor said.

"I wasn't brought up," Clive replied, "I was drug up."

Victor nodded a sympathetic gesture.

"I vaguely remember an image; it was the image of one I feel as though I would recognize if I were to see it again. Other than that, my childhood, until I could get whiskey for myself, is a blur."

"What brought you from outcast to where you are now?"

"A law man in the north territory saw something in this drunken kid. I learned to hide my drinking, and he made me his deputy. Since then I've learned to play the game. Sometimes on the right side of the law," Clive finished the bottle and threw it in with the rest of the rubble on the floor, "and sometimes not."

"Now," Clive said, standing. "I've got an appointment with the sheriff."

F O R T Y - F O U R

"YOU TWO FELLERS WAIT rat here a spell. I'd vite ya in, but I tweren't ready fer company. Soon as I get ol' sparky back to spittin' far, I'll be right back wit you boys."

Neither Clay nor Jake could see a dwelling of any kind. Just then, Gert disappeared down a hole.

The old man could be heard whining away a song, while a pulsating blue light and steady shower of sparks, spat from the hole.

Men from LaMacchia sneaking underground.
Up through the blue and look what they have found.
Little men's playing a stomping on their stuff.
Smash the little melon head we'd done had enough."

Clay and Jake both looked at each other, shrugging.

"How long do you reckon that'll go on?" Jake asked.

"Don't know," Clay said. "Not much longer is what I'm hoping for."

Jake nodded. "Something's been eatin' at me ever since we hightailed it out of Baine, due to the untimely deconstruction of the saloon."

Clay chuckled. "Deconstruction, is that what you call a building being blown to pieces while you're still in it?"

"What," Jake answered, "a little too anti-climactic?"

"Just a tad. Why, what's eaten atcha?"

"Simple—who and why?"

Clay dropped his reins and rubbed his ellack behind the ears. The exotic equine accepted the attention gratefully. Clay picked up his reins, but continued to rub his mount on the side of its neck.

"Can't say with a hundred percent surety, but I think I'm close." Clay moved his free hand to his reins as both ellacks became restless while a string of cuss words poured out of the hole. Before long, all was calm again with the same song emanating from the underground cavity over and over again.

"As I was saying, even though I can't be sure, I'd bet a straight flush it's tied in with that worm Gaylen."

"President Gaylen?" a surprised Jake said.

"One and the same."

"Any idea who's doing the deed?"

"Gaylen surrounds himself with low life's. There is one, an older, scrawny fella who takes care of most of his dirty work." Clay turned to Jake. "He already knows who you are."

"That's enough to get us killed," Jake said.

"After your days at CR&D that's enough to get you, me and half the people we know taking a dirt nap."

"How are we gonna fight what we can't see?"

"First, you're gonna answer my question so we don't end up dead. Now, what did you see in that container?"

"Howdy again, young fellers. I done got ol' sparky a firin to beat the band." Gert did a reverse snort through his nose and hocked up a phlegm ball that all but filled his mouth. He inhaled through his nose and blew the ball a good ten feet through the air.

"That dad gum sparky gonna choke me plumb to death. Okey dokey, fellers, times a-wastin'."

For the first time, Clay and Jake noticed the little old man was riding on the back of a miniature ellack, and riding he was. It took a good deal to catch up with Gert and slow him down.

"Where's the fire, Gert?"

"Taint seen no far, I'm a-headed . . . huh . . . I'm a-headed."He brought his ellack to a halt, Clay and Jake pulled beside him. Gert looked Clay square in the eyes. "Where am I a-headed?"

Clay patted him on the shoulder. "Kinda getting ahead of yourself there, aren't ya, old timer?"

"I lit outta there like a tassy wit its tail on far." The old man pulled off his hat and beat it against his knee. "Dang old fool. Sorry I dent wait fer you fellers."

The sides along the trail Gert had led them, had risen to twelve feet or more above the road. Fortunately the roadway was twenty feet wide at its narrowest point.

"Don't worry about that now," Jake said "We need to sit down and plan our next move."

"No, siree," Gert protested, "I done telled ya afore. We gotta take care if'n we take a notion to camp." He looked around then back at his traveling companions. "Maybe I ain't zackly sure where I's post to be, but I knows I's close and dere's meanness all round us."

Gert's ellack became erratic and backed across the road. Both Clay's and Jake's mounts could feel the tension as their restlessness increased in intensity.

"Let's ride!" Clay yelled. Eighteen legs dug into the packed Earth. Gert, getting a late start, lagged behind. A stalagmite-like formation broke through the ground, entering through the ellack's abdomen and exiting just to the left of its spine, narrowly missing Gert.

"Clay," Jake screamed. Clay pulled back on his reins and turned in time to see a stalagmite, drenched in ellack blood still pushing upward with beast and rider in tow.

A root-like tentacle pushed through the embankment, snatching Gert from the back of his lifeless mount.

Clay moaned and then pulled his sidearm from its holster. Remembering the painful experience he endured the last time he fired this weapon, Clay cocked both triggers and took aim.

A bright blue flash severed the root, obliterating Gert from sight. The outer end of the root fell to Earth with the white-hot fireball still burning on one end. As the light subsided, a small gray man could be seen pushing a pistol-like implement into the holster on his side.

Gert was beating his hat against his thigh, extinguishing the last of the flames around its edges, when Clay and Jake pulled up.

"Consarn zapper. Evey time I shoot et close range I ketch somethin' on far." He placed his hat on his head, wisps of smoke still curling upward from its charred edges. "And that somethin' is usually me."

"Are you okay?" Jake asked.

"Fair-thee-well, I reckon." He tugged at his beard. "Wishin' I cud say the same fer my old Lackey Belle. She weren't a bad gal a-tall. Dad burned old cuss, done and got herself stuck plum through."

"Sorry about your ellack," Clay said, "but I think it best we get to moving. Gert, you ride with Jake. I don't doubt he's fifty pounds lighter than me."

Gert threw his saddlebags over his shoulder and then shook his head.

"No siree bobcat tail; I ain't doin no such a mess. I'm quite the faster then I appears, so you boys jest get a movin' and let me worry bout me . . . Go on now, I keep up."

"It's on you," Clay said.

Gert nodded. "Be it so."

The three men took one last look at the stone and organic monument before turning to leave.

"What was that back there, Gert?" Jake asked.

"That were one o dem—"

The ground shattered as stalagmites pushed their way upward. Clay missed losing his ellack to a sharp conical stone, moving seconds before it entered the animal's chest.

Jake sidestepped one stone to have another push into his mounts rear foot. It exited halfway up the leg, cutting a trench through its hip as the stone point passed.

The monoliths rose to a height of thirty feet or more, trapping the men in a stone cage. What looked like hundreds of flesh covered roots pushed their way out of the embankments. Each side of the path thrust underground foliage making a beeline for ellack and man alike.

FORTY-FIVE

RUBEN OPENED HIS EYES.

Must have fallen asleep, he thought. The blue creature continued its vigil, perched atop his lap. Cassie lay curled in the corner closest to Ruben, snoring softly.

Ruben rolled his eyes. "Here we go again."

The arachnid in his lap stood and skittered toward the hole. At the halfway point the second creature emerged from the hole and moved toward its humanoid throne.

As the bug pressed itself into Ruben's flesh, it brought back memories of his fingers turning to goo as he massaged the thing's head. The ensuing transfer of thoughts that left him dizzy and the creature sick, seemingly near-death.

"That might be the answer," Ruben said. Even so the monstrosity in his lap jerked, almost as if it knew his host's thoughts.

Until Cassie awoke, Ruben sat in a dim light planning.

* * *

Cassie stirred. She yawned, extended her arms, then yawned again. An expression of disdain crossed her face as she realized the taste of rampant bacteria flooding her mouth. She noticed Ruben's gaze and mouthed, "Good morning."

He smiled back.

Cassie rose, stretched and yawned one last time.

"You hungry," she asked while passing Ruben on her way to the kitchenette.

"Starving," he replied. "What's on the menu?"

"Not much I'm afraid, but there is coffee."

Much to Ruben's surprise, the arachnid in his lap stood and stepped to the side, allowing Ruben to stand for the first time since he had arrived. He moved to the privy to relieve himself. The aroma of roasted coffee beans wafted through the air upon his return.

Cassie had already poured two cups and bade him sit down. Ruben joined her, picked up a brown hard square and examined it. He placed a corner of it in his mouth and bit down. The processed nutrition bar disintegrated, mixing with his saliva, making it easy to swallow.

"You were wrong when you said not much," Ruben touted. "Nothing could be closer to the truth."

Cassie smiled and took a bite of a resin cake.

"It's not much on flavor, but it supplies the nutrients we need each day."

Ruben took another bite. "It's obvious they want to take good care of us." Ruben remembered his first encounter with these creatures. "As long as we don't get out of line, at least what they perceive as the line to be towed."

Ruben and Cassie finished their breakfast and attempted to communicate without attracting attention.

"We may be better off taking the approach of hiding in plain sight," Ruben said. "It seems they become more aware when we talk quietly or attempt to hide what we're doing from them."

"I don't think that they understand the words we use," Cassie noted. "They sense whether we are acting with malice or with no malicious intent." She polished off her coffee. "While I wouldn't recommend blurting out what we're planning to do, I believe we can convey to each other what we want to do. This will muddy it up enough to keep it between ourselves." Cassie nestled her chin into one end of an open fist. "That is, assuming we have a plan."

"Yeah, there's a plan," Ruben said. "But first, I feel a need to share something with you."

"Sure," Cassie said.

"When I was massaging one of the bugs and you had to bring me back from whatever type of trance I slid into—"

"I remember," Cassie interrupted. "I had to shake you awake."

Ruben nodded. "While I was out, I was in its thoughts and it was in mine."

"You mean you could read its mind?"

Ruben propped his elbow on the table and nestled his chin into his palm.

Cassie rose and filled two coffee cups. Sitting down again, she handed one to Ruben.

Ruben smiled and accepted the gift.

"No, it was more like our consciousness switched places." Ruben took a moment to consider his thoughts. "Even though most of what I took away from the exchange is shrouded in fog, the one constant is that having taken the place of the bug had one purpose. That purpose was to prevent the disruption of the planet's calladium core at all costs."

"What do you think he learned from you?"

Ruben took a sip of coffee and shook his head.

"Not a clue, but I don't think their intelligence level is very advanced. I would wager their comprehension is limited to basic emotions and instinct." Ruben looked at the current sentry. "Our biggest obstacle will be their curiosity."

Cassie nodded. "We must keep our emotional responses on an even keel."

"Agreed," Ruben said, "and attempt to quell their curiosity if they get too close to something we're trying to conceal."

The twelve-legged guard pushed itself up and turned its head from side to side as if aware of the content in Ruben and Cassie's conversation.

"That one move speaks volumes," Ruben said.

Cassie took her coffee cup and splashed what was left on the floor a few feet from the bug. The creature eyed the wet stain on the plank flooring and then cocking its head, stared at Cassie.

"Why?" Ruben asked.

"If we act irrationally then possibly they will mistake it for rational behavior and that may suppress their curiosity."

"Brilliant," Ruben said. He threw his coffee to the opposite side of the creature and as hoped, the arachnid, lackadaisically dismissed the event and settled back down.

Ruben and Cassie sat at the table devising a plan amidst laughs and giggles one minute and temper tantrums the next. For two days the pair inverted the meager furnishings, slept on the floor, played patty cake and ate off the floor. They smeared a mixture of flour and water on each other's face along with numerous other absurdities. Soon the bugs paid little attention to the couple's antics.

The time had now come.

"WHAT DO YOU MEAN, you got a better offer?" Lynch asked.

"What do you think it means?"

"All right, stupid question, I'll give ya that one and start over again." Lynch cleared his throat. "Now, what was this better offer you received?"

"I'm not comfortable giving too many details; let's just say it's a better deal than Gaylen laid on the table, with protection to boot."

Lynch pulled the old toothpick out of his shirt pocket and shoved it in his mouth.

"Sounds like a good deal. When are you going to cut me in?"

"As soon as I'm sure that you've come clean with me."

"Have it your way," Lynch said. "Just remember, I can hold back too."

"You can hardly blame me," Quincy said, "I don't know you from dirt."

Lynch nodded, "I guess we'll see, won't we?"

"I guess we will."

A shadow passed over both men.

Quincy looked up and caught a face full of sunshine. He brought his head down and covered his eyes.

"What was that?"

"That quite possibly may be one of those things I failed to mention."

"Don't forget you're in this too."

Lynch smiled. "Like I said, I guess we'll see, won't we."

The shadow returned, but this time remained over the men. Quincy swore he felt hot breath on the back of his neck, as a massive wing movement stirred the dirt and debris around his feet.

AS THE ROOTS MOVED CLOSER, Jake noticed hundreds of thousands of tiny serrated projections that lined one side of each of the tentacles. They moved back and forth against one another ripping into whatever they came in contact with.

"Looks like a nasty way to go, don't ya think?"

One corner of Clay's mouth turned upward in a sarcastic grin. He slid his gun from its holster.

"If we sit here gabbin', we're liable to find out." Clay fired. Each hit shattered a tentacle, covering the immediate area with a fine blue mist.

Jake joined in, doubling the count as the roots fell. For each tentacle destroyed, a replacement pushed its way out of the embankment.

The foliage gained ground until it touched the combatants.

Jake wrapped his left hand around a sawed-off scattergun, removing it from its saddle holster. He fired twice, creating a large hole in the system of roots which quickly filled in. A rogue tentacle swung around, touching the shotgun barrel, slicing clean through the metal, rendering the gun useless.

Clay was forced to cock both triggers on his dozen gun. Holding the weapon with both hands as he fired, the shrapnel tore massive holes in the advancing system of roots, while fracturing smaller bones in the gun wielders hands.

Both ellacks were losing fur and chunks of flesh as the roots wildly slashed around.

Clay fired another shot. "Didn't think it would end like this."

Jake held a revolver in both hands."Gotta go sometime."

A tentacle whipped over Jake's right shoulder, opening a wound down through his pectoral muscle. Another tore through his upper right thigh.

Clay hunched down as his ellack's ears were removed and the dismantling of its head had begun with random swipes from the roots, which now covered everything.

A blinding flash of light followed by another removed a huge section of the flesh eating foliage. As new tentacles took its place they were obliterated along with sections of the existing system.

Clay and Jake looked toward the top of the canopy that had formed over them. They saw a small man nimbly jumping and slipping through the tangled maze of animated vines.

Gert fired pulses of light, destroying root after root, cauterizing the ends, rendering them powerless to reproduce.

Two bare feet landed carrying a large smile and a larger gun, debris raining down, covering man and beast alike. He slid the weapon back into its holster.

"How in tarnation did you twos git yerselves in such a pardicament?" Gert gave no chance for either to answer. "You fellers git offin them thar lackys You'ns need tendin' to."

Clay slid off his ellack. Amazingly, his beast had survived the barrage of tentacles with superficial wounds. He himself came through unscathed.

The same could not be said for Jake. Clay looked in his friend's direction in time to see Jake slide into Gert's arms. Clay could distinguish nothing else as he made his way around stalagmites and ellack legs. Once he emerged, he saw Jake on the ground and Gert gathering herbs and clay.

"Is he gonna be okay?" Clay asked.

"Too soon," was all Gert would say. He busily picked herbs, using only what he deemed appropriate. Gert did the same with the clay, making several trips to the embankment to get the correct type. He then packed both wounds with what he had gathered.

Gert looked into Clay's eyes."Bad. Much blood gone. Bad."

FORTY-EIGHT

"WELL, SPEAK OF THE DEVIL, and look who shows up," Carl said.

"I could speak of a lot of things," Clive said, "but I'd just as soon keep my mouth shut for a change."

"You saying I've got a big mouth?"

Clive smiled. "I think that speaks for itself."

The two men locked in a firm handshake.

"Good to see ya," Clive said.

"Same here," Carl replied, "And where have you been? Two and from station point translates to a day, no more than a day and a half. You were gone closer to four. So what gives?"

"First tell me where Quincy is; we need to talk."

Carl shrugged.

"He slipped out in the middle of the night near as anyone can tell, and hasn't been seen since."

"If I didn't know better," Clive said, "I'd swear he was running from something."

"But seeing as how you know better, who do you think it is?"

"Why, our illustrious president, of course."

"Gaylen?"

"One and the same," Clive said. "Obviously you haven't been privy to the information I gleaned by being in the right place at the right time."

Carl crossed his arms and leaned back against the office desk.

"Enlighten me."

"It seems our sheriff has been sleeping with the enemy, in a manner of speaking. I walked in on Quincy during a conversation with Gaylen." Clive pointed a finger at a small wooden cabinet.

"Inside that cabinet is a metal box, and on the surface of that metal box is an indentation." Clive took a seat behind the desk and nosed through a couple of drawers before continuing.

"If you've ever paid attention to Quincy's badge, you will have noticed a blue stone at its center. This blue stone fits perfectly into the indentation on the metal box and allows communication between Gaylen and Quincy. And from what I heard, Gaylen is not at all happy with Quincy's performance."

"Performance," Carl said. "What performance? He does nothing."

"True," Clive agreed, "but as incompetent as he is, the buck stops with him." Clive walked over to the door and stared out the window. "Maybe that's why he's not here,"

"What do you mean?"

Clive turned his attention from the window.

"Simple, either he left of his own volition or he had help."

"And by help you mean . . .?"

"He was forced," Clive said. "I think it's a safe bet he's got an enemy or two floating around out there."

"Speaking of floating around," Carl said, "what's going on out at Station Point?"

Clive gnawed on the inside of his cheek and stared at Carl.

"Since it looks like Quincy could be out of the picture, at least on this end, and you've been a standup guy for the years I've known you, I don't suppose it'll do any harm to fill you in on my latest venture."

Carl's interest piqued; he took a seat and listened.

* * *

Clive and Carl walked into the decimated saloon. Victor sat where Clive had left him, happily nursing the bottle of whiskey.

"Well, well," Victor said. "Either you've brought someone back with you or I've swilled enough rotgut till I'm seeing double." He closed one eye and reopened it. "There are still two of you when I close my eye and one of you is a might uglier than the other, so I believe I'll opt for my first notion."

Clive and Carl took a seat at the table with Victor. Introductions were short as Clive pulled the cork on two more bottles and poured drinks before a word was spoken.

Victor reached down and picked up a chipped shot glass. He blew the dust out and slid the vessel to Clive. He filled the glass with an amber liquid and passed it on to Carl.

After the bottle made several rounds, the conversation began.

"So tell me about your meeting with the sheriff," Victor said.

"Never happened," Clive said.

"Out of town?" Victor asked.

Clive nodded. "Not just out of town, but it appears he's gone for good."

Victor took a drink and wiped his mouth, a mischievous smirk on his face.

"You didn't kill him, did you?"

"No," Clive said, a bit perturbed. "I didn't kill him."

"How do you know he's gone for good?"

"When you leave in the middle of the night, telling no one," he nodded toward Carl "even your deputy, it's a pretty sure thing you're running from someone or something and you won't be back in the neighborhood anytime soon."

"Reasonable assessment," Victor said. "So, tell me about your friend here."

"You know his name. As far as friends . . . Let's say it's more of a working relationship. With Quincy out of the picture, it makes our jobs that much easier."

Carl broke his silence.

"You said the very same thing earlier, but I still don't understand how Quincy's absence will make extracting the gasoline from the crude and ultimately collecting calladium any easier."

"The act of retrieving the calladium hasn't changed; the break comes from not having an idiot like Quincy heading up the project." Clive picked up a bottle and pulled half of the liquid out of it. He swallowed hard. "You've gotta admit that 'inept' in his case is a compliment."

Carl caught with his glass to his lips, only nodded.

"We've got a good supply of gasoline stockpiled," Victor said. "Why can't we start now?"

Clive looked around the table.

"It's impossible to start right now because of our location. The gasoline is stored at station point. To retrieve the calladium we need to transport it as close to the old city of Baine as possible." He finished up the bottle he held in his hand and tossed it aside.

"Unfortunately, that's where the main governmental calladium collection is taking place."

"Why can't we move further away from Baine?" Carl asked. "It makes no sense to perform an illegal operation right in the middle of where the authorities have set up shop."

"We don't have a choice," Clive said. "Baine holds the secret. That's where the thinnest crust on the planet exists." Clive leaned back in his chair and cocked his hat forward. "If it's a no go there, then it's a no go period."

"We'll do what we have to do," Victor said, "the payouts are too good not to."

Carl nodded in agreement.

"There is one thing. We've lost close to thirty townsfolk in the last few days and I know that at least half of those were headed toward old Baine." He leaned forward in his seat placing his elbows on the table. "I've also been getting some strange reports from travelers coming from that direction."

"What kind of reports?" Clive asked.

"Didn't think too much about the first couple. People claimed the ground was rumbling, cracking and moving. After that, there were stories of holes that didn't seem to have bottoms; creatures popping in and out. Of course the eyewitnesses were too far away to make out any details."

"Sounds like the whiskey was flowing unabated," Victor said, slurring his words.

"No," Carl said. "That's when things really got weird. Folks were complaining about bloodstains and body parts tossed around as much as thirty yards from the openings."

"Did you check it out?" Clive asked.

"Sure did, but by the time I got there (and you know how difficult that can be with the government's projection protocol in force) every little scavenger and nibbler in the area had taken a bite and there wasn't much left. I managed to find a few fingertips and pieces of skin. Even though the area had been picked clean, you could tell something heinous had happened there."

"What do you mean *projection protocol*?"Victor asked.

"If you're traveling toward Baine, it's constantly changing, so you can never tell how far away you are. This gives the government an edge and dissuades many would-be travelers from attempting to make the trip."

"Well, boys," Clive said, "looks like we've got us one more thing to contend with. Carl, you get us a team of ellacks, two will do. Victor, hunt us up a wagon; the blacksmith should have one." Clive stood, removed his hat and ran his hand through his hair. He preened his hat and placed it back on his head.

"Either of you run into any trouble, just tell him the sheriff needs them. We'll meet at the jailhouse in one hour."

Three men went three separate ways each wondering what the next day would bring.

FORTY-NINE

QUINCY FELT HIMSELF being drawn backward, through a slit and into a fur-lined pouch. The soft sides closed in around him. The pleasant texture of his cocoon along with an unusual aroma, kept the sensation of claustrophobia at bay. What threw him was the sense that something seemed right and yet wrong with this scenario. It was as if a betrayal contrary to his own mission coexisted around him, yet he remained powerless to intervene.

Quincy's head swam as he thought he sensed traveling through the air, similar to the interplanetary travel attainable with his stone. He couldn't be sure if that was the case, or if it might be the intoxicating fragrance that filled his nostrils with each breath. The aroma sent his mind deeper within itself until unconsciousness on a plateau, higher than what would be considered sleep, was attained.

* * *

"Greyshod's got 'em," Lynch said. "He'll be ready whenever you are."

The part reptile/part avian Greyshod, stood patiently with his wings folded close to his body. His head resembled an Earth's bald eagle except encased in a leathery covering in place of its contrasting white feathers. Greyshod stood twenty feet tall with a forty foot wing span.

"Good," Gaylen said, "he'll keep." Gaylen had a three room mobile unit furnished to the nines. He took a seat on his leather easy chair, packed his pipe and put fire to tobacco. The soothing aroma of cherries drifted through the room as miniature cirrus clouds.

Lynch moved to take a seat on the living room sofa.

"Halt!" Gaylen ordered. "You're not to sit anywhere, including the floor." Gaylen paused, drawing on his pipe until the tobacco in the bowl glowed. "You look as though you've been dragged through the mud and that's being kind."

Lynch frowned, "Been a rough couple of days."

Gaylen shook his head.

"Head out back and find Raif; he'll show you where you can hose down and find a clean set of clothes." Gaylen wrinkled his nose. "Now get on outta here, you're smelling up my home."

Lynch left, seemingly unshaken by Gaylen's harassing treatment.

Gaylen tapped the tobacco from his pipe into a blue calladium ashtray and stood.

"I believe it's time I welcome my good friend Quincy home." He followed the same path Lynch had taken out the back door. Where Lynch had turned left, Gaylen made his way right and into a large metal building with a circular opening cut into its top. A panel mounted on tracks could be slid into place in case of inclement weather. Tonight the outlet was open.

Gaylen entered the building through a small door made for human traffic.

"Good boy, Greyshod," Gaylen said.

A satisfied, "squawk," was the reply.

Gaylen smiled. "Now open up for daddy." Greyshod took three steps in place, each one with more force than its predecessor. He squawked again, signifying compliance, then Gaylen moved close and spread apart the slit in the creature's abdomen.

Several feet into the compartment Gaylen met a smiling dumbfounded face. He led Quincy into the fresh air and his head began to clear.

"What happened," Quincy said, rubbing his head. He looked to his right and jumped when he saw Gaylen.

"Well, marshal," Gaylen said "how are you doing? You're looking a little uneasy. Are you feeling all right?"

Quincy stared blankly, unsure of what to say, or even if he should speak at all. The perception of betrayal welled within. The unusual bit of this overwhelming sensation is that it had nothing to do with him, at least not the betrayal itself. In some strange way, his was all inclusive, and this scared him to death.

Gaylen tapped his lips with an index finger.

"Could it be that something is bothering you?"

Quincy opened his mouth, but nothing came out.

"No need to answer, in actuality that was a rhetorical question." A wide grin spread across Gaylen's face, "although I would be interested in hearing your thoughts on . . . I don't know . . . let's just pick a word out of the air . . . hmm . . . how about Cassie?"

Quincy turned white as a ghost and his knees buckled.

"Ah, I see we've struck a chord of familiarity."

The expression on Quincy's face pleaded for forgiveness.

Gaylen held up a finger, wagging it from side to side.

"No need, my friend, all is forgiven."

The tension flowed from Quincy's body as the corners of his mouth turned upward.

Before his smile was completed, his head along with a "v" shaped chunk of his chest from sternum to spine disappeared. Before a drop of blood hit the floor, Greyshod inhaled the rest of the corpse as it tilted forward.

Gaylen rubbed the creature's forehead as it leaned down to accept the attention.

FIFTY

JAKE'S EYELIDS TWITCHED, flickered several times and began to open.

"I don't know how long I've been out." He rubbed his eyes and blinked several more times. "But you're as ugly as you were when I went out."

"Ugly?" Clay said. "Try looking in a mirror."

Jake chuckled and then winced. "Well, I guess that answers that."

"Yep," Jake nodded. "I've been better."

Clay laid a hand on Jake's shoulder. "Sit tight, I'm going to locate our eleventh hour savior/M.D./overall wild man and see what he's got on that seedy little mind of his. If I'm not here when you get back, don't forget to keep my supper warm."

"You got it," Clay said.

Truth be told, Clay wanted to get an idea of Jake's condition out of the injured man's earshot.

He caught up with the little man tinkering with his weapon.

"I want to thank you for saving our hides earlier today."

"Ah, twern't nothin'," Gert said, "I jest see what needs a-doin' and then I takes to doin' it."

Clay smiled. "Well, thanks just the same."

Gert looked up from his work. "It were all my pleasure." He swatted an insect on his neck. "I done and growed rat fond o you two fellers and I 'spect I'll be a sticking wit y'all till we gits to Baine."

"Can't thank you enough," Clay said. "Which brings me to my next question—how's Jake doin'?"

"Can't say fer sure, but by the morrow yer good partner, he'll be ready to travel or we'll be diggin' a hole."

FIFTY-ONE

JAKE'S EYELIDS BLINKED several times and then opened.

"Well, lazy bones," Clay said, "you gonna sleep all day?"

"To tell you the truth," Jake replied, "I'm not feeling so well."

"At least you're not a corpse," Clay said softly, though not softly enough.

"What do you mean by that?"

"I'll tell you later. Right now I need to know if you're able to travel."

Jake rolled out of his bunk.

"If we're going to Baine, I don't know of any other way to get there."

"Well, looky here," Gert said, "'pears yer partner's perked up and ready to ride."

"Yeah," Clay said, "He gets beat down and then right back up again." Clay shook his head."Don't know how we're ever gonna get rid of him."

"Why in tarnation would ye ever wanna git rid of a good hand like Jake thar?"

Clay furrowed his eyebrows and stared at Gert.

"Don't have much in the way of humor in these parts, do ya?"

"I knowed what you'ns is a gabbin on. Now let's get one thang straight, Gert ain't no dummy, and I didn't laugh at what ye said cause it twern't funny." The short little man turned and stomped off. "You two funny boys git a move on." He stopped and turned around. "I'm a leavin' in two shakes of an ellack's tail. If in youse is a-comin wit me, git a move on, I taint waitin."

"Way to go, P. T. Barnum," Jake said. "You sure handled that one in rare comedic fashion."

Clay looked puzzled.

"Who or what is a P.T. Barnum?"

"I'm not real sure," Jake said. "I ran into this offlander not too long ago back in Shell."

"Shell!" Clay echoed. "Been slumming, huh?"

"I'll ignore that last comment." Jake began to roll up his bedding. "I think his name was Ruben; yeah, that's it, Ruben."

"Who's Ruben?"

"How soon we forget." Jake hoisted his bedroll on to the back of his ellack. "You remember asking about P.T. Barnum.?"

"Yeah."

"Well, Ruben was the offlander who'd raved about this character P.T. Barnum. Claimed he was a real huckster, his famous saying was 'there's a sucker born every minute.'"

Clay finished lashing his bedroll to his saddle.

"I'm not finding the humor."

Jake shrugged. "I guess you had to be there."

Clay and Jake finished their packing and caught up with Gert.

"Gert," Clay began, "I want to apologize—"

"Now you jest hold on one minute. I had no call to git on you like I did. So you jest keep any 'I'm sorrowful' to yerself, we got too much aheada us to worry bout the past."

The three men traveled without a word for the better part of an hour.

Jake broke the silence. "Just what was the material that you pushed into my and the ellack's wounds?" He laid his hand on his right shoulder and painlessly worked the arm back and forth.

"Twern't nutting' but a poultice my pappy taught me to make. He did all the doctorin' when I was a-comin' up."

"He taught you well," Jake said, "and I want to tell you I'm mighty grateful."

"Nuff said." Gert pointed to the rubble that was the old Baine. "That thar's what we'd best be a-fixin' our attention on."

"Doesn't look like we've gotten a bit closer," Jake said.

Clay tilted his hat back and wiped his forehead. "We'll get there soon enough, maybe sooner than we'll want to."

FIFTY-TWO

CASSIE DANCED AROUND THE FLOOR using a broom as her partner. At the same time, Ruben flipped the kitchen table over and over, on its legs one moment and its top the next. Cassie danced several times around the bug, and then, holding the broom stick by its end, she allowed it to lay at a forty-five degree angle.

With the bristles touching the floor, she danced provocatively in a circle and then jumped, landing on the end of the stick nearest the floor. The broomstick split along its grain, leaving a wad of bristles still bound together on the floor. The piece Cassie still held in her hands showed a sharp, jagged end deadly to human and insect alike.

The bug rose as if alarmed. Cassie continued to dance, pretending to pay no attention. The bug settled down to a more relaxed posture.

She moved until she was in front of her blue guardian, knowing that soon the creature would be at its weakest and the changing of the guard would commence. No sooner had the thought passed through her mind, the scratching of twelve pairs of pincers on a deliberate mission echoed from out of the hole.

The table that Ruben had been flipping was larger than the hole itself.

Cassie winked at Ruben and he positioned the table. It was upside down as if he were going to cover the hole, leaving plenty of space for the bug to exit.

Cassie raised her right arm into the air, her right hand firmly wrapped around the broken broomstick. She brought her left hand up, curling her fingers around the makeshift spear. Cassie performed a single pirouette before driving the ragged edge of the stick through the bug's head and an inch or more through a crack between two floor planks.

The creature exuded a high pitched squeal as each one of its legs tapped furiously on the wooden floor. A gusher of fluorescent blue fluid shot upward from the lethal strike. The body melted into a blue puddle of goo.

An increasing sense of urgency was perceived as the second arachnid made its way toward the surface.

Cassie opened her mouth to speak.

Ruben placed a finger over his mouth.

She closed her mouth and nodded.

Ruben stood behind the table. First the tips of the creature's legs and then head appeared from its lair. It paused, seeing its dissolved brother and Cassie removing the makeshift spear from where its head use to be.

The bug's hesitation proved to be the last move it would make.

Holding the top two legs of the table, and his foot in the center of the top, Ruben released the legs and pushed down hard with his foot. He added his full weight by placing his other foot on the underside of the table top.

No sound was heard save for the whoosh of the wood as it displaced air and the pop and blue splatters that traveled in all directions. Ruben's attack flattened the bulbous portion of the creature's thorax.

A second later, Cassie drove the broomstick into the creature's head, ending their jailer's last link of control over the two humanoids.

Cassie moved to a small corner cabinet. She removed two pairs of socks and threw one pair to Ruben.

"They're gonna be kinda small, but take yours off, put those on and leave your shoes off."

Ruben sat down, removed his shoes and pulled the ill-fitting socks on to his feet, ripping both at the top, his fingers bursting through the material.

"Be sure not to get any of the blue slime on the bottom of your shoes."

"Why?" Ruben questioned.

"They won't be able to track us."

"Who won't be able to track us?"

"No time to explain."

A dull thud reverberated through the cabin floor.

"Gotcha," Ruben said.

"Put both feet in the blue slime and let's go."

Ruben looked at her and almost asked a question. Thinking better of it, he nodded and followed her out of the door.

* * *

Cassie and Ruben exited the small utility building that had been their prison.

"Listen carefully," Cassie said. She pointed east. "Run in that direction one hundred steps. Pick a single point to focus on so you'll travel in a straight line. Then turn to the left at a ninety degree angle and run another hundred steps. Repeat the left turn and hundred steps a third time. Once you reach that point, turn left but stop at fifty steps. Remove your socks and put on your shoes and make sure you bring your socks back here. You should be fifty steps from this spot."

Ruben nodded."Got it."

"Good," Cassie said. "I'll be doing the same thing in the opposite direction. We'll meet back here. Now, go!"

The two traversed their incomplete squares and then rendezvoused at the utility building.

"You wanna explain what we just did?" Ruben asked.

"No time," Cassie answered. "Follow."

Ruben, barely able to keep up with his female counterpart, maneuvered his way through wooded areas, thickets and fields of tall grass. After what he perceived to be about an hour, Cassie stopped.

"Now," Ruben said, his breath coming in shallow gasps "we make time."

"Okay," Cassie conceded, "we've bought a few minutes."

"Same question. What was that all about?"

"In the short time I've been exposed to these creatures," she began, "I've been able to glean a certain amount of information." She hesitated with a puzzled expression entrenched on her face. "I know they can't speak." Cassie paused once again, her eyes widened, and she stared at Ruben. "I've wracked my brain, and as crazy as it sounds, I keep coming back to the same conclusion."

Ruben placed a hand on the visibly upset young woman's shoulder. Now she was free, the emotions Cassie had suppressed during her capture, containment and release were now surfacing.

"Take all the time you need," Ruben said.

"That's one thing we don't have." she placed a hand over his and rose to her feet.

Ruben admired the way she maintained her composure. He removed his hand from her shoulder.

"Okay, let's have it."

"Well," she said, wiping her eyes. The bugs communicate two ways, with taps and clicks when they're together and telepathy when apart.

"Which they were most of the time," Ruben added.

She acknowledged Ruben's comment and then continued.

"Somehow I could intercept this telepathic communication and unscramble it to where it became a conscious and meaningful part of my thought process."

"I don't quite understand," Ruben said, "these creatures obviously didn't speak English so how could you understand anything you intercepted."

"It wasn't like that at all. What language they used to communicate was immaterial."She put a hand on either side of her head and moved them out and back to her scalp repetitively, mimicking the transference of brain waves. "I knew what they were thinking; there was no conversing of any type. In fact, if they knew I could read their thoughts, it's possible I wouldn't be standing here right now."

"What were you able to learn?"

"As their thought waves infiltrated my brain, there was no cognitive recognition until enough information gathered to form a complete concept. Once that happened, I learned they were Azurians from a planet named Aon, there to prevent crude oil from being extracted via the ground. There were three beings sent to Earth."Cassie looked at Ruben. "We've already disposed of two."

"What about the third?" Ruben asked.

A large shock wave shook the ground, creating a loud boom.

"There's your answer," she said, "We'd better get moving, I'll explain the rest later."

"ANY TROUBLE?" Clive asked.

"Nah," Carl said. "Cullen over to the livery had a fine pair. I told him he'd get them back just as soon as we finished."

"And he was okay with that?"

"I didn't even have to push him to give them up," Carl replied. "He said to keep them as long as you need."

"Good," Clive said, "with that gutless Quincy out of the picture, it's time the people in this town knew who the real marshal is."

Clive turned his attention to Victor. "Any trouble with the wagon?"

"No." Victor said. "Only . . ." He paused, an embarrassed expression on his face.

"What's wrong?" Clive asked.

"Well," Victor said, "no one mentioned exactly how we were to procure the items, so I—"

"Don't tell me you held him up," Clive bellowed.

"No!" Victor exclaimed, he then became quiet and uttered something inaudible.

"Speak up," Clive urged. "We can't hear you."

"I said that I bought the buckboard outright."

Clive and Carl both chuckled.

"I don't guess you did have any trouble," Clive said. "I didn't mean to buy the thing; the blacksmith wouldn't have had any qualms about lending the wagon, knowing they were for Quincy."

"Now you tell me," Victor said. "That was my last forty dollars."

"What's done is done," Clive said. "I imagine we can get your money back; at least most of it."

"So what's our next move?" Carl asked.

Clive sat down in Quincy's old chair, placing his feet on the desk. "The way I see it, a changing of the guard."

Carl and Victor both stood staring at Clive with quizzical looks on their faces.

"Work with me here," Clive said. "We'll be shifting the mantle of leadership."

"How about giving it to us in plain language," Carl said.

"I guess that's the only way I'll get my point across," Clive said.

"Just get on with it," Victor said.

Clive smirked. Something as small as annoying his subordinates gave him a sense of power.

"Try to pay attention this time." He removed his hat and tossed it onto the desk.

Quincy governed with an iron fist, but it wasn't his own. The good marshal was superb at using intimidation and any other tactic he deemed necessary to achieve his desired results, provided he had backup. Clive stood and paced behind Quincy's old desk. He used the length of the furniture as his turnaround point to guide him in the opposite direction.

"By himself, Quincy was a self-indulgent, sniveling coward, afraid of his own shadow. But with muscle behind him, he converted into that nasty little sadistic weasel we all knew and loved."

Carl sighed. "At the risk of sounding dense, what's your point?"

"As you may remember," Clive said curtly, having detected the sarcasm in Carl's question. "I mentioned Quincy ruled with an iron fist." He stopped pacing, made two fists, placed his knuckles on the table top and leaned toward Carl. "He didn't have the guts to use his own." Clive leaned closer, lifted one hand and opened and closed his fist. "Those steel fingers belong to me"

"Point taken," Carl said. "But for the sake of argument, let's say the good marshal comes back and finds things not as he left them." He sat down on the edge of Clive's desk. "Quincy couldn't beat his way out of a wet paper bag; I'm also fairly certain he has chipmunks dancing the foxtrot in his head. Don't forget, I've worked for him near about as long as you have."

"I appreciate your concern," Clive said, "but I can handle the marshal. Allow me to correct that . . . *ex*-marshal."

"Just watch yourself," Carl reiterated. "I'd rather face a mad dog than deal with a crazy rat nipping at my heels."

"Hmm," Victor grunted, "if you two are finished consoling one another, I believe there is that bit of business that requires our attention."

"Where'd you get this one from?" Carl asked, throwing a nod in Victor's direction.

"That's another story," Clive said. "Right now he's got a point. You two pick up the horses at the livery and then head over to the blacksmith. Make sure we have barrels and everything we need to hitch the team to the buckboard. And Carl, see about getting Victor's money back."

"Don't worry," Carl said, as he patted Victor on the back, "I'll see that our financial whiz kid gets reimbursed."

FIFTY-FOUR

LYNCH LEFT THE KNEE-HIGH GRASS in favor of the cover offered by the forest.

"I don't get it. Gaylen sends me to Baine, and instead of transferring, I have to hoof it all the way. He says he don't want anybody to see me." Lynch picked his way through a patch of briars. "There's a perfectly good splitter in Baine." He pounded his thigh with his free hand he had clenched into a fist. "If ya got technology and don't use it, what's the use of having it?"

Lynch still held the brass lawman's badge firmly in his hand. *At least I don't have to worry about this stone losing power*, he thought. He chuckled out loud and pushed his hand into his pocket, pulling out his old stone.

"I'll keep this one as a spare." Lynch touched the stone in his left hand to the one still attached to Quincy's badge he held in his right. A bright flash ensued, causing him to stop abruptly. The single stone slipped out of his hand and onto the ground. He slid the badge into his pocket and dropped to his knees. Lynch had to fight the temporary blindness afforded him by the flash of light as he fumbled on the ground searching for his lost possession.

"Can't see a blame thing." He opened his eyes as wide as possible, distorting his facial muscles and squeezed them, attempting to blast through the fog that clouded his vision.

After several minutes of squeezing dead vegetation and dirt between his fingers, the opaque white ball that floated in front of his eye's faded to translucent. Nothing but wisps of white remained around the outer edges of his field of vision.

Lynch moved his right hand in an arc in front of himself as he crawled. He hit a small round object, knocking it further away.

"No, you don't." He advanced forward and to the right. "You can't hide from me, you little booger." Lynch tapped something lightly with his pinky finger. Even in the dim light, he knew and immediately slammed his hand over his now recovered stone.

The instant his flesh contacted the blue jewel, a split, as if someone had opened a zipper appeared in the ground under his hand. As the illusion of the zipper was being tugged further and further, the split lengthened and widen at a slower rate. It swallowed the stone, leaving Lynch suspended over a bottomless crevasse with no evident sides, only an endless blue expanse of nothing.

A sudden, excruciating pain, something akin to a large brick slamming into both sides of your head, hit Lynch. He moved his hands toward his head, but the intense pain was gone before his fingers could reach their target and had been replaced by a voice doling out instructions.

Lynch levitated over the crack in the ground, listening intently.

FIFTY-FIVE

"MY BELLY'S A-TELLIN' ME it's pert near time to rustle up some vittles," Gert said. "What say ye, fellers?"

"To tell the truth," Clay said, "that's been on my mind for quite a while now."

"I'm game," Jake said.

"Then let 'er be so." Gert let the saddlebag he carried over his shoulder slide to the ground.

The first thing he did was gather a small pile of wood, remove his gun from its holster and zap the kindling with a short electrical charge. The dry tinder immediately burst into flames. Gert fed the fire with a few larger pieces he found close by, while Clay and Jake gathered enough wood to last for several hours.

"Anytime you be a-stoppin' fer a while," Gert said, shaking his finger at the two men as if there were children., "always be tenderin' up a far, cuz ya never kin tell what mite be a lookin' at ya." The old man scratched the back of his neck and chuckled. "Course, they is them times when you ain't gonna want to be a-sightin' what's out there eyeballin' ya, cuz it be bout to et ya!"

Jake looked at Clay, managing a grim smile. "We'll keep that in mind."

"You two got a hankerin' fer anythin ticular to break this here evenin' fast?"

"Wouldn't have any learsack, would ya?" Clay asked. The mere thought of the dried delicacy caused his salivary glands to double their production.

"You and your bugs," Jake said, with a look of disgust.

"Crunchy and delicious," Clay replied. "Long as you don't mind a leg or a wing stuck between your teeth."

Jake just shook his head. "Gert, I'll just have what you're having."

Gert was busy digging through his saddlebags, muttering as he dug into the treasure trove of goods.

"There ya are." He shoved his hand into the bag several times. "Gotcha." Gert looked at Jake. "If yer suppin' wit me, you is in fer some kinda good eatin'."

The little man pulled something from the bag and held it tight to his chest. Jake could see what appeared to be a foot sticking out between Gert's fingers. A muffled squeaking could be heard, indicating the displeasure of whatever Gert held in his hands.

"Now you bite me, you little consarn vittle snatcher, and old Gert'll bite ya back." He reached back into his saddlebag, removed a package and tossed it to Clay. "Them's my last ones. I be full of the hope they put a likin' on yer tasty buds."

"Thank you kindly," Clay said and unwrapped the bundle.

"Whatcha got there, Gert?" Jake asked.

"Jest never you mind." He placed his other hand over his chest to further conceal the evening entrée. "I'll be back directly." Gert took a deep breath and sighed. "They tends to make a mess," he said, solemnly. Gert turned and disappeared into the dim light of evening.

Clay sat happily munching away, producing a loud cracking sound with each compressive movement of his mandibles.

"How can you eat those—"

A deafening roar followed by a whimper moved along the forest floor, leaving even the smallest crevice vibrating, having been violated by the unnatural audio. Clay and Jake both interpreted it as a plea for life.

"That came from the same direction Gert set out," Jake said. After one final heinous squall, all was quiet.

Clay swallowed hard. "I think that's one place we don't want to be right now."

Jake nodded and then furrowed his eyebrows. The crunch of footfalls on the brittle ground cover, with what appeared to be whistling, grew steadily until Gert appeared; carrying what looked to be ten pounds of meat or better.

Gert held up a hand. "Not nary a sound outtin' either of ya. I gots to get cookin', so leave me be."

Gert continued on another thirty feet and then came to a halt. He continued to whistle as he kindled a second fire. Soon the inviting smell of roasted meat wafted through the air.

Clay and Jake stood, watching the little man, both men too leery to approach the melodic cook at this point.

Clay dug at the spaces between his teeth.

"Why don't you eat a few more bugs," Jake said.

"They're all gone," Clay replied. He made several sucking sounds and then spit an assortment of hard brown chunks into the fire.

Once again the musical stylings of Gert on the move caused Clay and Jake to whirl around, drawing their attention from the fire. Gert walked into the light carrying three sticks with meat wrapped around the end of each one.

"Let's get to her, boys. She's more the tasty when she's hot." He handed each man a skewer. "Looky here," Gert said, "doer jest dis a-way." Each skewer held a piece of meat rolled around the end of a stick. The grain of the meat ran crossways to the makeshift skewer that held it. This allowed strips of any width desired to be torn off at the diner's leisure.

Gert had already torn off several strips of the medium rare flesh and crammed them into his mouth. A piece of meat hung from his mouth, and juice ran from each corner, meeting at his chin and dripping on the ground. As he chewed, he attempted to speak, using muffled bursts in between breathing and swallowing.

"Goot tuff, huh?" Gert garbled.

Clay and Jake wasted no time and followed suit. The more they ate, the more they craved. The three men ingested the chewy substance until satiated and beyond, not stopping until Gert snatched the skewers from their hands.

Two surprised men stared at Gert, chewing what remained in their mouths.

"No mo!" Gert demanded. He held up the three skewers. "Dis here meat cause ya to et yerself plumb to deaf." He paused for several seconds. "Youse understand what I is a-tryin' to tell ya?"

Clay shook his head, clearing away the clouds left by his meal."Gotcha."

Jake nodded.

"We gotta git dis here mess cleant up afore—"

A low pitched growl wound its way from the dimly lit forest to three pairs of human ears.

Jake placed his hand over his holster. "Where is it, I can't tell." He turned in a slow circle.

"There's more than one," Clay said "We're surrounded."

"This wouldn't be one of those sounds we don't want to see what it's coming from, would it?" Jake asked.

Gert ran his hand through his beard and then looked at Jake. "I'm a-feared to tell ya."

FIFTY-SIX

WHERE ARE WE HEADED?" Ruben asked. He grabbed a sapling and then another to pull himself up a steep embankment.

Cassie lost her grip and slid down several feet before catching herself. "Baine." She paused several moments waiting for a reply. One came just as she had expected, and she used it as her cue to resume her movement upward.

"Baine," he protested. "Why don't you pick a spot in the middle of the desert? One's just about as interesting as the other."

Cassie stopped moving, turned around and looked at Ruben.

"Baine was the only location I could glean from the bugs they gave any importance to. In fact, I got the impression that their presence here on Earth centered around the cozy little town of which we speak."

"I stand corrected," Ruben said, "Please excuse me while I pull this size twelve out of my mouth."

"You didn't know," Cassie said, as she pulled herself to the top of the incline and sat down.

Moments later Ruben plopped down beside her.

"Sorry about the presumption," Ruben said, "I tend to speak before I think."

"Just like everyone else, including yours truly," Cassie said. "Let me explain to you 'why' Baine."

"First things first." Ruben removed his bowler and ran his fingers through his graying hair. "What was all that, shoes off, shoes on, run a million steps in my stocking feet about?"

Cassie sat with arms spanning across both knees and her chin planted on her forearms. She was smiling.

"I guess that seemed ridiculous."

Ruben returned the smile. "A bit."

Cassie raised her head. "I told you I could assimilate communications between the bugs."

Ruben nodded.

"I also mentioned a third creature."

"You did," Ruben said.

"Reading the thoughts between the bugs was pretty much automatic, but I found myself lured toward the relationship between the bugs and whatever resided underground."

Ruben leaned toward Cassie, eager to hear more.

"It took a while," she continued, "but I could finally piece together most of what was going on."

The ground she was sitting on was damp and extremely hard. She shifted her weight and rolled onto her knees, resting back on her haunches.

"The two bugs were temporary to begin with. They wouldn't have lasted much longer had we not taken matters into our own hands."

"Doesn't seem like much of a purpose."

"The bugs were there to protect their other. Each time one of them would skitter down the hole during their frequent exchanges, their host, who was much larger, became their haven. This allowed the bugs to begin the process of acclimation."

"You mind revisiting what you just said, only this time with a little more detail?"

"Sorry, I'll try to be a little more explicit." Cassie rolled to her right and returned to sitting on her rear.

"Ground's kinda hard, isn't it?" Ruben reinforced his point by shifting to a different sitting position.

"I'll say. That's the second time I've had to move."

"Okay, let's have it."

Cassie nodded, as she rubbed both knees, her jeans stained by the damp ground.

"As I said, the host was much larger and protected from the detrimental effects of the oxygen-laden atmosphere in its temporary underground tomb. Even the bottom of the hole the bugs used to enter and exit had been sealed with a gas that would prevent any seepage of unwanted toxins." She shifted once again, putting more weight on one butt cheek than the other.

"It was about this time I learned the bugs, as we knew them, were the twins. And their host's name, of all things, J. Smith." Cassie stopped talking. She squinted and chewed on her thumbnail as if pondering the question of the ages.

"Cassie?" Ruben prompted. "Are you okay?"

She nodded. "Yeah, but it doesn't make any sense."

"What?" Ruben questioned. "What doesn't make any sense?"

"It's like I'm going through the timeline of events with the twins and J. Smith all over again."

"I don't understand."

Cassie rolled to her knees. Ruben shifted his position as well.

"When I first began telling this story I should have referred to our visitors as, the twins and J. Smith. Instead, I used the same terms I used when I first encountered them." Her hands balled into shaking fists and her arms drawn in tight to her sides in frustration as she talked.

"I didn't use their proper titles until the same point in the story as I did in real time as it happened."

"I can imagine how maddening that must be," Ruben said, "unsure of your own thoughts, but right now I need you to concentrate and finish the story."

Cassie nodded. "As far as our running around in our stocking feet escapades go, after we killed the bugs . . . or rather the twins, I knew J. Smith would soon follow. We needed to lay a trail to keep him busy while we made our getaway."

"Good idea," Ruben said, "but what would keep him from coming after us, especially with the limited time he could survive in this atmosphere."

"He wouldn't come after us if there were a viable distraction close by. They're a methodical and driven species who will stop at nothing to achieve their objective. J. Smith would follow the trails we made to nowhere and then check the shelter before leaving to find us." Cassie shifted her position once again. "Their unwavering resolve is certainly to our detriment, but they're not too bright. As far as being able to survive in this atmosphere, that's where the twins come in."

Ruben sighed. "The more I listen, the less I like what I'm hearing."

"Hang in there, I'm almost done."

"Go on, get it over with."

"Each time one twin made their trip down the hole they would enter the body of J. Smith."

Ruben smiled and shook his head. "I can't get over that name— 'J. Smith.' It sounds like somebody's uncle."

Cassie waved him off. "As I was saying, this symbiotic relationship would afford the twins protection from the environment. This would allow the twins to release the oxygen they had gathered into the body of their host. This would act as a vaccination over time, allowing J. Smith to build a resistance to our atmosphere, allowing him to function in the open."

"So we haven't seen the last of him," Ruben said.

"Not by a long shot," Cassie replied. "Only--" she stopped her sentence.

"Only?" Ruben prompted. "Only what?"

"Well," Cassie replied with a hint of reluctance, "at the risk of sounding clichéd, I've got good news and bad news."

"Let's have it."

"When we eliminated the twins, it cut short their effort to complete the acclimation of J. Smith to our world."

"And that's a good thing?" Ruben asked.

Cassie nodded. "It means it's only a matter of time before J. Smith succumbs to our atmosphere, how much time I don't know, but at least his days are numbered. The problem being is that the last communication between the twins and J. Smith is incomplete. The small amount I deduced from their last communiqué led me to believe that there may be others."

"Others!" Ruben snorted. "Like reinforcements?"

Cassie nodded. "And that's where it ended."

"So what kind of insane message is that?" The irritation evident in Ruben's voice. "You must have heard something wrong."

"I heard nothing," Cassie said. "All I learned were captured thoughts from simple minds."

"What does it all mean?"

Cassie shook her head.

"Maybe nothing, then again, maybe everything."

She shifted her weight one last time. "I've had about enough of this." She stood, rubbing her knees. She hadn't noticed that the moisture she felt covered her from the waist down. What was once a clear liquid was now turning into a thick slime.

Ruben jumped to his feet and slipped, landing hard on his right hip. He made it to his feet by grabbing one of the many saplings that shot from the ground.

How odd, he thought. *It's not possible for something so supple to push through something so hard.* Then the thought was lost as the ground began to vibrate.

Ruben limped the few steps to Cassie by grabbing the slender handholds. Cassie had the same idea and stood with her hands firmly grasping one of the round protrusions.

"Any ideas?" Ruben asked.

"Not a one," Cassie replied.

The vibration subsided.

"We should consider crawling down off this rock," Ruben suggested.

Before Cassie could answer, the vibration returned, followed by a violent earthquake. The rock formation pushed itself free from the ground and lumbered away with its two human riders.

FIFTY-SEVEN

"HOW FAR IS THIS STATION POINT?" Carl asked, "Quincy always left that piece of real estate up to you."

"Yeah," Clive said with a sarcastic chuckle, "he was always good that way. We're not going to Station Point. That was Quincy's deal."

"And I suppose that we're now in the middle of a new deal?" Carl said.

Clive nodded.

"Clive's new deal?" Carl asked.

Clive smiled. "Give that man a cigar."

"Well," Carl said, "fill me in."

"Hold on," a voice from the back of the buckboard said. Victor rolled from his butt to his knees as the wagon hit a rut. It threw him into the air and caught him again as his knees plowed into the floor boards.

"Ahh!"Victor squalled.

Clive and Carl sat up front, Carl driving the team and Clive riding shotgun. Victor had agreed to ride in the back with the barrels.

Clive turned around. "Victor! I wondered where you'd gotten off to."

"Aren't we hilarious," Victor said. "Keep a close watch out; you might get lucky and find a few more ruts to bounce into." He made his way to his feet, using the back of the driver's seat to pull up and then steady himself with one hand and rub his knees with the other.

"Nice of you to join us," Carl said.

"Great, two comedians." Victor grabbed the iron bar behind the seated men with his free hand for more stability.

"As I was saying before you tried to break me in half, you've got a few questions to answer."

"And what might they be?" Clive asked.

"They might be, what's your sister doing Saturday night, but they're not." Victor leaned over the rail to get closer to Clive. "What I want from you is you."

Clive looked a bit perplexed. "That's a mighty strange request."

"No stranger than watching you drink bottle after bottle of liquor with no real effect."

"What kind of effect were you looking for?"

"Oh, I don't know. With that much alcohol in your system, death comes to mind."

Clive tapped Carl on the arm. "Shut 'em down."

Carl pulled the team to a halt. Clive jumped into the back and made himself comfortable on one of the barrels. Carl watched and then followed. Victor turned around and, facing the two men, crossed his arms. "I guess it's your turn."

Clive sighed. "I guess it is." He removed a small leather drawstring pouch from his shirt pocket, along with a cardboard sleeve containing rolling papers. Clive slipped a paper from the sleeve and folding the paper a third of the way, created a trough. He pushed two fingers into the top of the leather pouch and spread them apart creating an opening. Clive filled the trough half way from the contents of the pouch, and clinching the drawstring in his teeth, closed the opening. He rolled the paper into a tight cylinder, and licking the adhesive, he sealed the smoke. Clive placed the homemade cigarette in his mouth and removed a small black rectangle from his pants pocket. He pushed a button on the device and touched the end of his cigarette to the blue laser flame.

He pulled hard on the stick, then released the inhalant. It was as if his entire body slumped as the smoke expelled.

"I'm an offlander," Clive said.

"From where?" Victor asked.

Clive took another drag. "Does it really matter where you've been or where you're going?"

"Depends on what you do in between." Victor kept shifting his weight to keep pressure off his pounding knees. "So tell us, Clive, what did you do in between?"

Clive took one last pull from his cigarette. He allowed the smoke to drift from his mouth and nose, momentarily concealing his features as it made its way upward.

"I always enjoyed working for a living," Clive said, "even if my chosen vocation was on the outside of certain preset boundaries."

"Just out of curiosity," Victor said, "how far outside of these boundaries did you allow yourself to drift?"

"Nothing like that," Clive said, making calming motions with his hands. "Taking another's life wasn't for me, but then again, neither was manual labor. I excelled in what I liked to call creative allocation."

"Scams," Carl said.

"I suppose that's another way to put it," Clive said, "but things run a little deeper than that."

"The floor's all yours."

Clive nodded. "I'm not sure where I was born, only that I left before I was ten years old. It was one of those magical times in a young adolescent's life he never forgets." Clive rolled and lit another cigarette.

"You know those things are going to kill you," Victor said.

"You wanna take bets on smoke or my occupation?" Clive asked.

"Never mind," Victor replied.

Clive took a drag and blew several smoke rings to taunt Victor.

"I don't know who my father was and don't remember my mother. In fact, it was one of my mother's many male friends who placed me on an off-world transport. He assured me that a grandparent I had never met would meet me when I landed." Clive pulled long and hard, causing him to drop what remained of his smoke before it burned his fingers. "Needless to say, there was no grandparent, and I've been on my own since I was nine."

"Looks like you've done pretty well for yourself," Carl said.

Victor's opinion of Clive was softening somewhat as he learned of his storied past.

"I stumbled around; keeping to myself, eating from trash cans and fell in with another street urchin." A wide smile spread across Clive's face. "His name was Skank, and that wasn't a nickname, it was his given name. Kinda gives you an idea of the first place I called home."

"Did this little slice of heaven have a name?" Carl asked.

Clive shook his head. "I didn't know at the time, but I was dumped on a no name planet that housed every piece of bipedal refuse that had the means to get there."

* * *

"C'mon man, what else is there to do?" The preteen waved a plasma-cell handgun, pretending to fire at imaginary targets in the back alley. "Bang . . . Bang . . . Pow."

"I've got a name, Skank," Clive protested, "and it ain't 'Man.' You got that?"

"Yeah, I got it, ain't no need to get so bent."

"And put that gun away before you shoot somebody, namely me."

"Well, what about Brantford? We're going to hit him again, aren't we?" Skank slid his handgun back into its holster.

"We've nailed Brantford four times in the last three weeks," Clive said, "Now we leave him alone."

"Alone?" Skank said. "His little shop is such an easy mark, why in the world would you back off now?"

"That's why. He's trying to eke out a living and support a family on the income we're stealing to buy crap with."

Skank wrapped his hand around his holstered handgun. "You wait, I'll be twelve real soon now and I'll show you, you just wait. I'll show you how things are gonna be."

"Calm down Skank, everybody's got—"

Clive heard a whistling sound that Skank did not. The eleven-year-old's head, along with the upper four inches of his shoulders, disappeared, allowing his arms to hit the ground moments before his body.

Clive backed into the shadows upon hearing footsteps heading in his direction. A tall, slender man with a tightly trimmed black beard appeared.

All Clive could think, was how well this man was groomed. Every other being he had encountered made disheveled a look to attain. Even he and Skank were filthy, wearing ripped clothing and Mohawks they had fashioned themselves.

The man knelt over the boy's lifeless body and checked his pockets. He shoved his hand into Skank's left pant pocket and pulled out the blue marble that the two boys had found several days earlier. At least Clive had thought it to be a marble until it glowed and pulsated in the stranger's hand. The tall man stood and pushed the still glowing stone into his pocket. He left the alley as calmly as he had entered . . .

* * *

"Roll me a smoke," Victor said.

Clive complied and held the white stick up. "You know these things are gonna kill you, don't you?"

"After what you told me, I think I'd prefer it."

Clive chuckled, lit the smoke and handed it to Victor.

Victor accepted the cigarette, took an awkward drag and coughed.

"Tha . . .hat's Smoo . . .oo . . .th."

"I'm glad you're enjoying it," Clive said

"Hold your ellack's," Carl said. "You can't stop your story right there. I wanna know more. Now come on. You don't start a story like that and leave a fella hanging."

"How about you, Victor?" Clive said, "Are you ready for more story time?"

Victor was leaning over the side of the buckboard. He held up a single finger until his stomach spasm pushed out another round of contents.

"Say the word, and I'll roll you another one," Clive said. A mischievous grin spread across his face. "I know how much you love to smoke."

Victor wiped his mouth and spit. He slipped back over the edge of the buckboard, landing on his butt.

"Nice shade of green," Carl said. "It really brings out your eyes."

"Just get on with it," Victor said. "I asked for a cigarette. Not a stick filled with garbage."

"Hang in there," Clive said. "The first time is always the worst."

"First and last," Victor assured. "I ain't never rolled anything that tasted like that. I'll retrieve my stash once I can touch my saddlebags."

"Enough of smokestacks here," Carl said, "get back to the story."

"There's not that much to tell," Clive began. "I was eleven when the incident with Skank occurred. From then on, I kept to myself, stealing what I needed. There were plenty of rats for food and always a meal to be had in the trash."

"Nice diet," Carl said.

Clive raised his eyebrows and nodded. "Ya do what ya gotta do."

Victor heaved twice and managed to swallow the vomit that had risen in the back of his throat. The idea of rats clawing their way back up his esophagus to avoid the acid bath stuck in his mind, ordering him to empty his stomach.

"After a while, I'd tire of being a loner and join a gang, but that wouldn't last long. It was safer, and you ate much better, but I couldn't stomach the killing." Clive withdrew deep inside himself. For a moment he was back, the hunger, the loneliness and the constant stench of death.

"Clive."

Hearing his name brought him back from his reverie.

"Clive," Carl said, "you okay?"

"Yeah, I'm okay." Clive rubbed his face and shook his head.

"Figured we'd lost you," Carl said. "Even Victor dropped a couple shades of green."

"Tell the story," Victor said, "I've had enough dramatics for one day."

So have I, Clive thought. "I couldn't stand the killing. Life was cheap and cannibalism an everyday food source for some. Oh, my hands weren't clean; I had taken my share of lives, but only in self-defense or to save another."

Clive looked at Carl and then at Victor.

"I made myself look downright noble, don't you think? Truth is I'm as dirty as any piece of trash that ever walked across that planet." Clive slid off the barrel and onto his feet. "I stayed in that cesspool until I was somewhere around twenty. In a place like that, you lose track of time. Years run together. I was beginning to believe I would die there, having already beaten the odds of survival by five years. Then things got worse.

"As bad as this lawless planet had become, throw civil war into the mix and you have a world with an almost zero chance of survivability." Clive rolled another cigarette and offered it to Victor.

Victor having recovered from his first bout with the lethal white stick just stared, eyes ablaze. Clive smiled, lit the cigarette, took a deep drag and let the smoke roll out of his mouth and nose as he continued to speak.

"I had come to terms with my death, but someone else had a different idea." Clive finished his cigarette and smashed it underfoot on the floor of the wagon.

"Well, come on," Victor said, "did you make it or not?"

"I liked you better hanging over the edge of the buckboard puking your guts out. And to answer your question, where am I now?"

Victor grinned sheepishly. "Stupid question, huh?"

"You two finish your spat later," Carl said. "Right now Clive's got the floor."

Clive sat down, this time on the edge of the buckboard.

"He looked to be about thirty. I was at the end of a blind alley, four men covered in blood, moving my way. It wasn't anything personal, a normal little nightly activity. I would only be out a minute, no need to strap on a weapon. The small four-shot handgun I carried in my front pocket would be enough." Clive cocked his hat back on his head.

"What a coincidence—four men, four shots. What I didn't count on was four flak jackets."

FIFTY-EIGHT

LYNCH WALKED PURPOSEFULLY in more or less a straight line, wavering only to circumnavigate trees, rock formations and anything that blocked his passage until he could resume his intended path.

"Baine," he said to himself. "So it's back to that two-by-four town. Quincy wanted this, Gaylen wanted that and this new guy wants something else." He kicked at the ground, sending a cloud of dust into the air. "And Lynch wants everybody to leave him alone."

"Sounds like a reasonable request to me," a young man said.

Lynch jerked and dropped to a squat position. The voice had originated from his left. There was a small plateau about six feet high, thirty feet wide and over the length of about sixty feet tapered down until it was flush with the ground. He looked up into a blinding sun and saw the silhouette of a man sitting on an ellack.

"Who's there?" Lynch placed a hand over his eyebrows in an attempt to cut the sun's glare.

"No one you need worry about," the stranger said.

"Ought not be sneakin' up on folks."

The man backtracked until he was at a point he easily moved down to Lynch's level.

The stranger dismounted and extended a hand to Lynch.

"Jason," he said. "Jason Carter."

Lynch eyed the hand jutting towards him and then eyed the man. "Not till I know why you're following me."

Jason smiled. "What gives you the impression I'm following you?"

"What other reason would you have for being out here?"

"I could say the same about you." Jason squatted and picked up a handful of dirt before standing again. "Seems kinda odd when you think about it." He allowed the dirt to trickle from his hand while staring at Lynch. "Two men following each other wouldn't get very far, now would they?" Once again, Jason extended his hand.

Lynch gnawed on the inside of his cheek and then placed his hand into Jason's.

"I reckon not."

"Truth be told," Jason said, "I saw you about a mile out, and being on foot, imagined you might like a ride into Baine."

The relaxed feeling that had begun to settle around Lynch about this newcomer suddenly dissipated. "How'd you know where I was going?"

"Look around," Jason said, "Where else would you be going?"

Lynch mulled this over, but said nothing.

Jason remounted his ellack.

"There is nowhere else. Now climb aboard. I want to make Baine by twilight."

* * *

"Young fella," Lynch said, "I believe you got your directions crossed up." He pointed left and slightly back. "Baine is southwest; we're headed northwest."

"You know there's more than one Baine." Jason said.

"And we're headed to the ruins," Lynch replied.

Jason nodded.

"Mind if I ask why?"

"Seems like the place to be."

"The new Baine has a lot more to offer," Lynch said, hoping to entice the young man away from what was hidden in the rubble of the old city.

"Is that a fact?"

"Oh yeah," Lynch bragged, "'Bout anything you want, if you get my meaning."

"Anything?"

"Like I said . . ." Lynch assured. "Anything."

"Except what you've destroyed," Jason added.

"What!" Lynch said. "Best be sure you have your facts straight before you start accusing."

"Certainly," Jason agreed, "like the time you blew up the saloon."

"Of course I'm speaking of the first time. If I'm not mistaken, there was a second assault on the structure shortly after the first."

"Stop this ellack now," Lynch ordered. Jason complied, and both men dismounted. Lynch was too skittish to confront this formidable mystery man. There was nothing unusual about the way Jason dressed--boots, jeans, vest, cotton shirt and hat. He rode tall in the saddle, six foot four and two hundred forty pounds. But there was something about him. It was more than the way he carried himself. Lynch found it beyond his comprehension, and it terrified him.

"Who are you?" Lynch demanded.

"A friend," Jason replied.

"I know," Lynch said, pointing a shaking bony finger at Jason. "You're in with Gaylen, aren't you?"

Jason rubbed his ellack's neck. He shook his head. "No,"

His answer unnerved Lynch that much more.

"You must be with that new fella; the one that offered me more of the take, but wouldn't let on to who he was or give me a name."

"No," Jason said, "I serve one far above the two you have mentioned."

Lynch's mind raced. *What do I do,* he thought. *I ain't no loser. Maybe . . . Just maybe.*

"How about I hook up with you and your boys? I'm sure you could use a good man."

"You'd abandoned the ones you serve now to follow me?"

Sensing himself a shoo-in, Lynch relaxed. "Sure, I'm your man."

Jason brushed his hat against his thigh, knocking off several days' worth of dust. He placed it back on his head.

"You lack loyalty and are driven by personal gain; qualities that are of no use. Now mount up, we're still heading to Baine." Jason placed his left foot into the stirrup and threw his right leg over the saddle. Jason extended his hand and helped the deflated Lynch aboard.

"Take heart, Lynch. All men can change."

FIFTY-NINE

"I APPRECIATE YOU WANTING to spare our feelings," Clay said. His voice was laden with anxiety and a bit of sarcasm. "But if it's all the same to you, I'd like to know what we're facing."

Jake nodded. "At least I think so."

"I guess it would be fer the best," Gert said. "They used to was packs o doggy type critters. We called 'em canny's. I'd say they was more like a wolveses, 'ceptin' a heap bigger and lots more nasty lookin." Gert ran his hand underneath his hat and scratched. "Only thems were near 'bout tame. You could dang near git close 'nough to pat 'em on they head."

"Just so I'm clear," Clay said, "we don't want to pet them."

The three men now stood back to back, weapons drawn.

"Jest soon stick yer head in a warcat's mouth," Gert warned. "Them there canny's they done and turnt mean." He paused, listening to the low ominous growls. "Now they hunt n packs, and near as I can figure, there be 'bout seven of 'em out there."

"It's starting to lighten up a bit," Jake said "I can barely see shadows, but they seem to be keeping their distance."

"Twon't be much longer now," Gert said, "Them canny's be makin' a move soon, you can bet fer sure. Them critters is slick. Only one'll come in first off to see what they's up agin."

"Uh, Gert old buddy," Clay said. "I think they heard you. I've got two yellow eyes movin' my way and they appear to be at about the same level as mine."

"You got 'em, or you think you need a hand?" Jake asked.

Clay shook his head, sighed and then cocked both hammers on his handgun.

"I got it." He hesitated. "Man, this is going to hurt."

"I'd hep ya if'n I could," Gert said, "but this here crunchy popper don't do nuthin' but spit out a little fired up tricity. It'll put the fear and runned off slash worms as such, but I'm a-feared I'd jest make them dadburn canny's more madder than they already is."

Clay nodded and slowly raised his dozen gun. He waited until he could barely begin to pick out the beast's features. Two eight inch canine teeth told him it was time.

The ensuing blast turned the advancing creature into chunks of meat that rained down over a forty foot radius.

"Ah!" Clay moaned. He knelt, clutching his right hand. Jake fired his fifty-eight revolver until empty. He pulled his second handgun from its holster and continued to fire. Clay did little more than drive the creatures at their flank around, joining their brothers to engage in a full frontal assault.

"Consarn canny's," Gert yelled. "I'll fry yer nards, dad blast yer hide."

Jake continued to reload and fire. Clay rejoined the assault, firing with his left hand and a smaller caliber pistol.

The stench of these vile creatures permeated the air well ahead of their arrival.

The trio ceased firing in the hope of forming a last second plan.

"Looks like we's 'bout to git et up," Gert said.

Clay nodded. "Looks like." He continued to reload his gun.

"Ain't going down without a fight," Jake said, smiling, "even if it is like peeing on a bonfire."

With that, the three men continued what they believed to be their last battle.

A huge boulder slammed down, as two of the beasts lunged forward, smashing the stationary four and catching the two on the move by the hindquarters. The boulder rose again and fell to Earth one hundred feet away. The light was sufficient enough to see four smaller stones, two on each side of the larger, acting as legs and what appeared to be two human figures riding on top. Within moments, the walking stone was out of sight.

Jake walked up to one of the remaining creatures. Its rear end crushed, it clawed at the ground and snarled.

"Eat this." Jake emptied his revolver, putting all eight shots into the thing's head.

Clay took a more primitive approach. He located a proper-sized stone and dropping to his knees, crushed the last remaining creature's skull into a muddy liquid.

Jake took one of Clay's arms and helped him to his feet.

"You sure do make a mess," Jake said.

Clay looked at his benefactor, almost giddy. "It's a lot more fun. One might even say cathartic."

"Well, now," Gert said, "it sure is good to see that you two fellers is a-doin' okee dokee. I thunked fer a bit that we was all et up and turnt to canny poop."

"Wadda you suppose the boulder was all about?" Jake asked.

"Don't know," Clay said. "A rock 'n roll rodeo, I suppose." He cocked his head and thought about his last statement. One corner of his mouth curled upward and then spread across his face into a wide grin. "Pretty good, huh? A rock 'n roll rodeo." He shook his head and chuckled.

"That there was a good 'n," Gert said, "You betcha fer sure it twere."

"Great," Jake said. "If we manage to live another hour we can take it on the road." Jake tried to stifle a grin, but couldn't. "It'll be our farewell tour."

The three men enjoyed a much-needed round of laughter.

Clay wiped a tear from his eye. He held up a hand to bring everyone under control.

"We all needed that, but now it's back to business. Baine still waits, and we have to find a way around these constant death traps to get there. From the looks of the vegetation, there's water nearby. We'll water both mounts, fill our canteens and get a bite to eat."

Jake nodded. "Something's been gnawing at me for a while now."

"What's that?" Clay asked.

"Until we find water, Gert, why don't you tell us how you came to be."

"Why, it would pleasure me somethin' fierce to converse with a couple fine young fellers about ol' Gert." He began to stroke his beard. "So many beginnings," he said softly, but not so softly that his two comrades couldn't hear.

Clay and Jake looked at each other, eyebrows furrowed and an air of concern firmly planted on each man's face.

Gert continued to fret "Where to start, where to start." The little man's eyes widened. "All righty, boys. I got 'er all figured out."

* * *

"Taggert! Taggert Lee . . ." Papa said, "We is about to sit down and sup. Now I down telled ya, if you was late nary nuther time, then you'ns is bout to go hungry."

"You better git up to the house," Pogo said, "I know you heerd your Pappy a-callin' you to et."

"Tain't no time," Gert said, "I gots to git these here sparkies out'n the ground and into the bater afore they agin to hibernatin'." Gert wiped at a wad of black dirt on his face, smearing it across his left cheek, and most of his nose. "Dad blasted sparkies. I ain't waitin' no nuther hunderd year for them no account cusses to pop they ugly mugs out so's I kin use 'em for powerin' up my necessary's."

Pogo shook his head.

"What kinda fool contraption is you workin' on now? I member that last thing near about done and kilt you."

Gert picked up a handful of the black mud and threw it at his friend.

"Ain't no such a mess. I got ten, maybe twelve feets off'n the ground afore she commenced to broke up on me." The ebony sludge flew true, catching Pogo mid-thorax and spread out, covering the front of his light colored shirt.

"Dad burn yer hide. This here's a brand-new store-bought shirt that my daddy paid good money fer. Now you gonna pay." Pogo ran down the hillside, plowing headlong into his friend. The two boys squared off. Once locked together, the pair began a barrel roll downhill coming to an abrupt halt, as Pogo's pelvis cushioned the blow against the Salem tree.

His buttocks made first contact, shattering both femoral sockets and blowing his hips outward. His body continued to curl around the tree, crushing his lower spine, exploding his chest and bringing his feet and head within a foot of touching one another.

Gert found himself face to face with the corpse of his friend. He himself was uninjured, save for several cracked ribs where Pogo's body was so crushed. It flattened out, allowing Gert's chest to impact the tree hard enough to cause the fractures.

Terrified, Gert looked into unfamiliar eyes that protruded two inches from their sockets. The teeth and gums pushed out of the mouth as the back of the head gave way, forcing everything forward. Blood trickled from each orifice in such a way it resembled the work of some maniacal makeup artist. The resulting rearrangement of facial features, left, an almost comical expression too surreal to be real.

Gert pushed away from his former friend, narrowly missing a root as it burst through the ground in search of nourishment.

"Papa," Gert yelled, "come quick. Poor ol' Pogo's done and squished up agin a Salem tree."

Gert sensed footfalls as his father made his way down the embankment.

"Gert boy!" Papa, screamed at the top of his lungs. "Gerty! You stay back from that thar tree. Now you get back, ya heard me?"

Gert froze as he watched pointed root after root push through the surface and curl around Pogo's lifeless body. The roots were uniform in every way. Each one was four inches apart from the one beside it and encircled the tree and corpse alike.

He saw his childhood friend of one hundred thirty years, pulled beneath the ground. It left a trench around the tree that filled in like an earthen mouth closing around its meal.

Gurgles and wisps of smoke were visible as the network of roots digested its grizzly meal. The ground expanded, sealing the trench tightly to the tree, and all was silent again.

Gert realized that he had been standing in his position too long, but was powerless to move as he watched Pogo's fate unfold before him.

The next thing he knew, Papa was screaming, "Move your feet!"

He looked down as a hatchet severed a root that held his right foot fast to the ground. Two more came up in its place. Gert sidestepped the new growth, the roots grazing his foot while crossing in midair, curling over and pushing down into the ground, expecting to ensnare more sustenance.

His left foot released, courtesy of the last swing the razor-sharp hatchet would make

"Run!" Papa cried, "Run!" He choked as his mouth filled with dirt.

Gert took two steps and then froze. No less than a dozen roots tangled around various parts of his father's body. His hands, feet and head were already underground and separating from his extremities.

Gert searched for the hatchet that no doubt had traveled underground firmly in the grasp of Papa's hand. All he saw was an increasing number of roots, piercing the ground looking for the tree's next meal.

Gert took one last look at the few pieces of his father's body that remained and then ran.

* * *

"I still miss my Papa," Gert said, "He went to his re-ward a-savin' his boy." Gert wiped a tear away. "From that day till this very time we is gabbin', I done and been on my own. Not nary another soul would take up with old Gert till I met you fellers."

"Why?" Jake asked.

"It's cause of that dad blame mess everbody's lookin' fer. That blue stuff-callicum—or however you say it. Ever since I was a youngun, they's been cravin' to get rich, and I done and tried to told 'em they's more to this here life then just a-buyin' and a-spendin'." Gert shook his head several times. "Didn't want to hear it, so they stayed away from old Gert, and I was happy for it to be just thata way."

"If you don't mind me asking," Clay said, "how old are you?"

"Sure, for not a bit," Gert replied. He squinted, crossed his arms and raised one hand to stroke his beard as a thought. "Let me see now . . . I was . . . No . . . That was before . . . Then we . . . Mama were gone . . . That took quite a spell . . . No, no Gerty . . . hmm. Yep." He looked at Clay and Jake. "I'm pert near four hunderd year old, near as I can figure. You know how things began to be not as good as they used to was when you hit that halfway point of your days on this here rock."

Clay interwove his fingers, pushing, palms facing outward and cracked eight knuckles in chorus. "I know exactly how you feel."

Jake cringed. "You sure you didn't break those things, old man?"

Clay looked at his fingers and then at Jake. He nodded and gave a thumbs-up.

"Good. Now maybe you can keep the noise down."

Clay nodded. Not so many years ago, Jake would've been dead where he stood, even if he was kidding. Clay smiled. But that was the old Clay. He didn't know why the change, only he liked the new Clay much better.

"Well, now," Gert said, "Looky here--jest what we done and been waitin' fer."

Clay and Jake were already filling their canteens, and the ellacks their stomachs.

"We might as well take a rest and get a bite since we stopped."

Jake was digging through his saddlebags.

"No complaints here."

Clay and Jake dined on dried meat and coffee. Gert, refusing the meat, ate what appeared to be live worms with legs. He did, however, take part in the coffee.

"I've been pondering something you said for quite a while now," Clay said to Gert.

"Well, spit 'er on out there. Don't do no good to be a-holdin' in what needs to be out. Now, go on."

"Okay. When we asked you to tell us about yourself, you were unsure of which beginning to use. Now everybody I know has one beginning and one end. How could you be any different?"

"I kin see where that might be a bit frettin' to ya now." Gert put a knuckle to his mouth and tapped his front teeth. "Let ol' Gert see can he splain it to ya so's you git zactly what I'm tryin' to told ya." He leaned closer to Clay. "Ah . . . whilst I'm a telling ya, spose I could git me another slug o that there cafer?"

Clay stared at Gert with a puzzled look on his face, and then he got it.

"You mean coffee?"

"I reckon so," Gert replied.

Clay filled a cup and handed it to Gert.

"Thank ye kindly." he took a sip and winked at Clay. "I'm part of these here folks called Rangers. Now it's kinda strange how we came to be like we is. I ain't sure zactly how that happened, but I does got me an idea of what's going on now. I'm a-startin' this here tale from whence my Papa commenced to havin' younguns."

Gert took a big gulp from his cup. "Sakes alive, that's good." He shook his head several times and let out a satisfied sigh.

"As I was saying, my Papa . . . Well if'n the truth be told, it were Ma, Ma what did the havin', and she had three boys."

"You and your brothers," Jason surmised.

"That be one mighty fine piece of figurin', cuz you is right as rain. Ya see, me an a tother was what ya'd call twain's; that means they was two of us. Now we was pert near dentical ceptin' fer my brother's (his name be Scratch) last two fingers of his left hand, had done and growed together."

"Where are your brothers now?" Clay asked.

"Don't rightly know. After Papa got pulled neath the dirt, Scratch lit out to find work. He said he twernt spectin' he'd be gone long, but since I ain't seen him in quite a spell, I reckon he were wrong." Gert's jovial expression was gone. In its place, memories, now empty, swirled lost in a sea of melancholy. "As fer zzz, well, I guess that's nother story."

"I didn't know," Clay said,

"Tweren't yer job to know," Gert said. "I thank you much for caring, but that's ol' Gert's to fret with." He pushed his cup out for a refill.

"When a ranger has twain's, that there's somethin' mighty special. Each one of them there little ones, even though he be one, little people's has seven roads to be a-travelin' down."

"I don't understand," Jake said, "one person and seven roads."

"Seven lives," Clay said. "Each child has seven lives."

"You has hit that thar nail slap on the head, but what I'm a-fearin' that you ain't knowin' 'bout is that a twain lives all seven at the same time."

BOTH CASSIE AND RUBEN DROPPED to their knees as the boulder plowed forward.

"Any idea where it's taking us," Ruben asked.

Cassie nodded. "Maybe."

"I don't follow you."

"Think," she said. "Is there any place that J. Smith has an interest in on this planet?"

"Well, the only ties he has between Earth and his planet, Aon, would be my extraction outpost. Of course, there is that pesky little fact that our home worlds are one and the same."

"I don't know why that comes as no surprise, but that's it," Cassie said. "I felt that the twins and J. Smith's purpose for being here was to save their world. That made no sense until now, and I still have reservations about J. Smith's intent." Cassie tried to stand, but the syrup had hardened and held her fast. "That figures."

She turned her attention back to Ruben. "So you're from another planet?"

Ruben smiled. "Since it doesn't look like we're going anywhere anytime soon, other than where this overgrown rock takes us, the answer to your question is affirmative."

"So tell me, what exactly do you do in this extraction outpost of yours?"

"Extract." He replied.

Cassie frowned. "I appreciate your ability to find humor in this situation, however, now is neither the time nor the place."

"My timing's not always the best." Ruben attempted to remove a coat of slime by rubbing it on his shirt. This resulted in a hand still covered with slime and a shiny stripe down the front of his shirt. He shook his hand as he spoke. "I simply drill for crude oil, store it and once I reach my quota, ship it to Aon."

"Why?"

Ruben thought for a moment."I don't know, just doing what I'm told."

"Following orders like a good little soldier, eh?"

Ruben sighed. "Allow me to fill you in concerning a little planet called Aon. First off,and let me make this clear, the government controls anything of importance. Here in your fledgling society, your governing body is not yet large enough to become oppressively obnoxious." Ruben placed his hand on the rock and realized what he was doing. Unable to stop himself, he secured yet another appendage to the surface of their traveling prison.

Cassie's mouth spread into a wide grin.

"That's enough of that," Ruben warned.

She managed to bring her reaction to his predicament somewhat under control, at least enough for him to resume.

"When it does," Ruben continued, attempting to divert attention from his faux pas, "and you can rest assured it will, that's when everything from health care to toilet paper will become screwed up as a chicken noodle soup sandwich."

"I guess your society is quite a bit more advanced," Cassie said, her interest now piqued.

"You'd be surprised," Ruben answered, "how a civilization can move forward while its people digress."

"Explain,"

Ruben furrowed his eyebrows, deep in thought.

"I've been here off and on for ten years, readying my drilling station to extract, store and export crude oil. I have learned from older friends and relatives through previous generations that eighty years ago the cities of Aon were to be abandoned to begin a simpler life. The military was dismantled and all personal weapons confiscated. Each of these weapons contained a small amount of calladium which is very rare and extremely valuable. The population agreed to this simpler way of life when the government promised all inhabitants an equal amount of calladium once it was removed from military and surrendered arms."

"People had no problem being unable to protect themselves or hunt for food?" Cassie asked.

"No," Ruben said. "The weapons that contained calladium were high-tech and specialized pieces of equipment. People still kept their conventional pieces, which are not unlike your rifles and revolvers. Unfortunately, some carry weapons that are almost as dangerous for the shooter as they are for the target."

Cassie nodded as if an answer to the question of the ages had come to her. "You've brought a lot to light. So many piecemeal thoughts I received from the twins and J. Smith are finally coming together and making sense. They are here to save their planet." She attempted to move and found that she too had one free hand, the other being stuck to her own leg. Cassie looked at Ruben and shrugged.

The sky was growing lighter, shaking off the dim twilight of night.

"Don't stop there," an excited Ruben urged.

Cassie nodded. "Your home planet has a solid core of that element you say is so valuable, Calla something or other."

Ruben's eyes widened and his mouth dropped wide open. "Calladium!"

"Yes," Cassie said, "and that's not all. The crude oil you're shipping back to Aon is being used to dissolve the core and remove it."

"By who?" Ruben asked.

"Not a clue," Cassie said.

"One thing I can't understand," Ruben said, "if J. Smith, the twins and I are all from the same planet, why can't they stand an oxygen-rich environment? Aon's atmosphere is almost identical to Earth's."

"They don't live on the surface of the planet;" Cassie said, "they live in the calladium core itself."

"How long?" Ruben asked.

"How long for what?" Cassie replied.

"Aon," Ruben said. "I've been doing some rough calculations in my head and as near as I can tell, before half the core is removed, the planet will implode, killing millions."

"Wish I could help you."

"Wish you could, too," Ruben said. His eyes projected a solemn loss yet to be understood.

"Where do you suppose this chunk of rock is taking us?" Cassie asked.

Ruben took off his bowler and rubbed the sweat off of his balding head. He pushed the handkerchief into his pocket and his hat back on his head.

"If we were on Aon, I'd say Baine, but I have a hunch our first stop will be my extraction station."

Cassie looked curiously at Ruben. "What is Baine and why your extraction station?"

"Baine will have to wait," Ruben said, "It looks like we've arrived."

The boulder stopped in front of a small mountain-like outcrop. The sticky fluid which bound the two humans to the boulder thinned to the consistency of water.

"It sure feels good to stand," Cassie said.

"Indeed," Ruben echoed. He attempted to stretch, causing his body to stiffen almost convulsively. "Let's go, I'm anxious to check my equipment." Ruben and Cassie scaled-down the side of the boulder using the protrusions they had confused for saplings on their initial ascent.

Upon reaching the entrance, Ruben pushed his hand into an inconspicuous hole at the base of the rock formation. A slab of stone slid to the right, exposing a hinged metal door. A backlit numerical pad was attached at the midpoint of the left-hand side of the door. Ruben entered his code, and the door hissed as its seal released.

Before Ruben entered, Cassie pushed him to the side and planted her shoulder firmly against the door. She strained using her weight to close it again.

"Say nothing," she whispered. "We're being watched."

"Where?" he whispered, "I don't see anyone."

"It's J. Smith; he's in the boulder."

Ruben turned to look.

"No," she whispered. "Act as though nothing is different." She smiled at Ruben and talked through her teeth. "He's sending out mixed messages. He's a little upset. Something went wrong with the acclamation process."

Ruben opened his mouth, mimicking Cassie's smile. The smiling humans looked like two idiots, attempting to communicate with their teeth.

"What could have gone wrong? We knew the twins hadn't finished preparing J. Smith for survival in our atmosphere."

"I didn't understand; much less interpret all of their communications." Her lips partially closed, expressing her disappointment. Realizing her mistake, she resumed her exaggerated smile. "My assumption J. Smith could survive outside his confines for limited amounts of time proved to be wrong."

"So, the twins would have had to complete J. Smith's acclamation, regardless."

Cassie nodded. She wobbled back and forth, grabbing Ruben's arm to steady herself.

"Whoa, there; it's a little early for that yet."

"It's J. Smith. He wants you to remove the radial link."

"Impressive," Ruben said. "The radial link is the only top secret part in the entire installation. It's what makes laser penetration with a flammable liquid possible."

Ruben activated the door latch sequence, waited for the telltale hiss and then entered his control room.

"Where is it?" Cassie asked.

"Where's what?"

"The piece of equipment J. Smith asked for."

Ruben reached into a refrigerator, removed two bottles of water, uncapped one and tossed the other to Cassie.

Ruben downed half the bottle, then wiped a sleeve across his mouth.

"He can keep on asking," Ruben finished his water. "In fact, he can yell. With Mr. Smith stuck out there in that rock, what's he gonna do?"

Cassie set her water down. "I don't think you understand."

Ruben was already busy at his main console. He paused long enough to glance at Cassie. "How's that?"

"It's true that J. Smith can't survive for any length of time outside the haven the boulder offers, but make no mistake, he'll last long enough to hunt you down and break you in half."

Ruben stood, nodding. "I think I'll get that part now."

S IXTY-ONE

CLIVE BEGAN STEPPING BACKWARD.

"You fellas are out on the town tonight?"

The four men uttered not a sound, but continued at a steady pace toward Clive. Each held a knife, conceived in the depths of a deranged mind to inflict maximum damage with minimum effort. The curved front of the forged razor-sharp blades contained offset notches, designed to remove chunks of flesh, whether being inserted or extracted. Inch long spikes protruded from the back and the curved portion of a "D" shaped handle.

All but one man wore brass knuckles on the opposite hand. The one without, owned an appendage void of digits, save for a half thumb that twitched uncontrollably.

"I hope you don't think I was trying to hurt you." Clive smiled. "I could see you had the vests on, and knowing how tough you are, I thought you might appreciate a test of your equipment." Clive's back smacked into a masonry wall that screamed, "Go no further," without a word.

The four men continued their advance, certain of at least one more kill to complete their night.

Clive had shoved the pistol back into his pocket. During his retreat, he reloaded the archaic fifty-eight caliber handgun with two scatter loads.

The group stopped four feet from their intended target.

"This one's in good shape for a Squelcher," the tallest of the four said.

"No matter," another replied, "he still looks pretty stupid to me."

"No need to put it off," the tall one said.

Clive pulled the gun from his pocket, causing the four to flinch.

"Look, I'll give this to you; it's a good shootin' iron."

"Oh, you can bet part of that's true," the tall one said, "but you won't be doing so much giving as we will be taking."

"Then come and get it," Clive said. Being the perfect distance away, Clive raised both arms and cradling the pistol took one shot and then the other.

Four bodies less, four faces crumpled to the ground.

"Well, you listened to me after all. You came and you got it." Clive turned and searched for the nights' dinner.

* * *

"I was digging through the trash," Clive said, continuing his story, "looking for something to eat, when a voice behind me said, 'If you're hungry, maybe I can help.' I didn't say a word, but wrapped my fingers around the butt of my pistol I had stashed in the front of my pants."

"Name's Jason," the stranger said.

"Since I have no friends and plenty of enemies, I guess it doesn't much matter what you call me." I spun around and drew my firearm. My finger tightened against the trigger, fully intending to fire, then I saw his eyes. Never had I seen such peace in the midst of such hate and misery. "I couldn't have pulled the trigger if I wanted to." Clive stood and leaned against the back of the driver's seat.

"I had no choice but to go with him. He fed me and we talked for hours."

"About what?" Victor asked.

"Life, I guess," Clive replied. "Of all the things we discussed, what I remember most is his insistence that there was a better way."

"Better way?" Carl asked. "Better way to what?"

"It's something I don't want to talk about. As good as he was to me, the fact remains, he's a few bricks shy of a load. He lived in some kind of fantasy world where . . . I'm not going into this; he's a nut job and that's that."

"Ah c'mon," Victor said, "you can't leave us hanging like that."

"He fed me, told me some stories and put me on a transport off that rock. That, my friends, is the end of the story. Victor, I want you in the driver's seat, Carl, you're riding shotgun. Now drive on, driver; you know the way."

Victor snapped the reins, the ellacks obeyed, and the wagon jerked forward.

Just behind the buckboard, the ground rose and then collapsed into a deep crater, three times wider than the buckboard itself. Had the wagon not moved when it did, it would lay at the bottom of a two hundred foot, growing sinkhole. Only this was no ordinary chasm. This carnivorous crater came endowed with intelligence. Hungry, but patient and knowing what was on the menu.

S I X T Y - T W O

THE ELEVATOR DOORS OPENED, and Ruben stepped out, carrying the radial link. The piece he held was cylindrical, eight inches long and varied in diameter. The first four inches of the unit comprised heat sink fins at half-inch intervals with a radius of one and half-inches. This end held the four-hole base for mounting on the drilling unit.

The rest of the radial link was smooth, with a one inch radius, the last inch tapering to a point.

"Well, here it is. What now?"

On closer observation, Cassie noticed that Ruben wasn't touching the device. It was floating several inches above his flattened palms, supported by two blue, spherical auras, one in each hand.

"Since our chauffeur seems to be on the inpatient side, it's back to the Boulder."

As soon as Ruben and Cassie exited the drilling station's utility building, the boulder vibrated and then stopped. A thin line burned itself into the rock, rotating around until it reached its point of origin. A round plug disappeared inside of the stone, leaving a smooth four inch diameter hole.

"There you go," Cassie said.

Ruben looked at the hole, the piece in his hands and at Cassie.

"Do you realize this small chunk of metal shuts my entire operation down?"

The boulder rumbled.

"There's your answer," she said. "It's up to you, but either way, J. Smith gets what he wants. The only difference is the easy way means you and I can still carry on a conversation. The alternative . . . Well, it's kinda hard to talk with a mouthful of dirt."

Ruben smiled halfheartedly.

"You do have a way with words." He took the radial link, and as soon as he neared the entrance, the device was sucked from his hands into the hole and the plug replaced. The circular cut sealed before either one noticed what had happened.

Cassie looked at Ruben. "All aboard."

The two beleaguered humans scaled the side of the boulder and took their seats on top. Tears filled Cassie's eyes as the moisture permeated her clothes, fusing both passengers to the rock before it moved toward its next destination.

"Wherever we're going, it feels more deliberate this time," Ruben said. "If nothing else, at the rate we're moving, we'll get there a lot faster."

Cassie wiped her eyes. Her last trip had taught her to keep at least one arm free.

"It is more deliberate. Why, I don't know, just that, J. Smith is determined to get there."

It didn't take long for the question to be answered. Thirty minutes from the time they boarded until the boulder came to a halt, they reached their destination.

"I'm not sure what it is," Cassie said, "but it sure is out of place in the middle of a forest."

"It's a transfer pad and the biggest one I've ever seen." Ruben craned his neck trying to see as the boulder positioned itself over the transfer pad.

"What is a transfer pad?" Cassie questioned.

"Well, I think you're about —"

The bottom dropped out as her head caved in on itself. She felt all four limbs being pulled from her body and suddenly jerked back with a sucking sound. Twilight caused both travelers momentary blindness until their eyes adjusted to the diminished light.

"To see it," Ruben finished. He put a hand over each ear and worked his mandible up and down.

Cassie covered her face with both hands waiting for the dizziness to subside.

"Mind telling me where we are?"

"I thought I did. Of course, I started the sentence on Earth and finished it once we arrived."

"So I'm not on Earth?"

"Not anymore."

The climate was more desert like in the area they had arrived, and even though it was warm, the lack of humidity made it fairly comfortable.

Aon, even though a small planet, changed in climate over the distance of as little as ten miles.

Only a few seconds lapsed once they reached Aon before they were underway again.

"Looks like our boy's in a hurry," Ruben said.

Cassie began to shake her head.

"I lost any communication with J. Smith when we landed. Either he's done with us or if that's the case, we just became expendable." Cassie stopped speaking.

"And the alternative?" Ruben asked.

"Well," Cassie said hesitantly, "he's definitely done with us, and we are most assuredly on the expendable list."

"You don't know how much I appreciate you clearing that up."

She smiled. "I'm here to please."

Ruben held a hand up to silence Cassie.

She nodded and soon sensed a disturbance up ahead. Ruben strained to see through the dim light, but the path they traveled obscured anything directly below.

"Shh," Ruben said. "Listen."

A mixed garble of human voices and deep growls were heard just ahead. When they reached the location, the growls turned into yelps of pain and the voices stopped for a moment, soon beginning again. Seconds later eight shots rang out and dull thumps seemed to echo along the ground.

They were unable to witness the foray as they were glued to the boulder in a forward facing position. The rock moved quickly over the participants, leaving the noise in its wake and a moment later, a memory.

"What was all that commotion?" Cassie asked.

"Not real sure," Ruben replied. "I made out human voices and I recognized animal sounds, but other than that I haven't a clue."

"Just as well, it didn't concern us anyway."

"I hope you're right."

"WHAT SAY WE STOP, get a bite to eat and rest a while?" Jason said.

"Sure," Lynch replied, with as much sarcasm as he could muster. "You're the boss."

"You still holding on to that little spat we had a while back?"

Lynch was incensed.

"You so much as ride in here, take over and cut me to ribbons after all I've done and you call it a spat."

"Hold on Lynch, seems you've mistakenly given me ownership to this venture you're involved in and on top of that, put yourself in my employ. Now listen and listen carefully. I want no part of your scheme to purge Aon of its calladium and no desire to hire one such as you in any situation."

Jason brought his ellack to a halt and dismounted. Lynch, dumbfounded remained seated on the animal. Jason chuckled to himself and gathered a supply of firewood. By the time he returned Lynch had seated himself on the ground, several feet from where they'd stopped. He stood.

"I would have helped had I known what you were up to."

"You can grab my saddlebags."

Lynch nodded and moved in that direction.

Jason tendered the fire with a flat piece of steel and a flint stone.

"Talk about the old-fashioned way," Lynch said, "My grandfather told me of people kindling a fire with a piece of metal and a rock back in the day. I never gave much thought to it being true."

"Your grandfather told you right." Jason reached into his saddlebag pulling out a pot and a metal cylinder sealed on both ends. Into one end of the cylinder he pushed a small odd shaped blade with a wooden handle. Jason rocked the instrument back and forth, removing a slice of metal with each pass. Once he had circumnavigated the top of the metal object, Jason removed the thin cylindrical cutaway, inverted the cylinder over the pot and dumped a thick brown, chunky liquid. As soon as the liquid hit the bottom of the warm cooking vessel, it exuded an enticing aroma that caused an immediate reaction to Lynch's saliva glands.

"I don't know what it is you're doing . . . but whatever it is, when can I have some?"

Jason tipped the pot, filling a bowl he handed to Lynch. Lynch brought the bowl to his nose and smiled. As he poured the contents of the bowl into his mouth, Jason produced a spoon.

Lynch lowered the bowl. Embarrassed, he smiled awkwardly and took the spoon. After eating his fill, Lynch sighed.

"I believe that was some of the finest grub I've ever wrapped my gums around." He raked his upper teeth over his lower lip and swallowed hard. "What did I eat and where can I get it?"

Jason sat his bowl down.

"It's a can of beef stew and where I get it depends on who has it." Jason poured two cups of coffee and handed one to Lynch. "Wish I could be more specific about the stew, but that's about all I can offer."

"I'll keep an eye out for it," Lynch said, "but I don't think there's much use. I heard tell of food being stored in what they called cans long before my time, but I ain't seen such a thing, in all my years on this rock." Lynch took a sip of coffee. "There is one thing that bears asking."

Jason nodded as if to say, "I'm waiting."

Lynch had a newfound respect for this stranger and asking something of someone you feel to be superior isn't easy for anyone. He finished his coffee, grunted a few times, clearing his throat and spoke.

"How could you possibly know about the calladium and more importantly the plan to remove it?"

"Lynch, what I told you before remains unchanged. I serve one that has no superior, no more or no less than that."

A small dot in the sky caught Lynch's attention. He dismissed it just as quickly.

"Then you'll let me join up with you? I've got all the inside information."

"I can't offer you riches, power or fame," Jason said.

"Then what, Mr. Superior? What is it that Mr., I'm bigger and better than everybody else offers?" Lynch demanded.

"Peace," Jason said, "simply peace."

Lynch once again noticed the dot in the sky, only this time it was much larger and recognizable.

"Okay, Mr. Big man," Lynch said to himself, "let's see you get outta this one."

Jason continued to talk. Lynch heard the words, but with no coherent retention. All his attention focused on the winged creature hovering above the young man.

"Now we'll see what's what." Lynch mumbled to himself.

Greyshod folded his wings and dove.

Lynch smiled as the creature neared the ground. A second later, to his astonishment, Greyshod extended his wings and landed behind Jason. Instead of a slowly digesting corpse in the stomach of a maniacal winged monster, Jason and Greyshod conversed. Twenty minutes later, Greyshod took to the air, leaving Lynch stunned and unknowingly backing away from Jason.

"I'll be leaving you for a while," Jason said.

"Who are you?" Lynch stammered.

Jason took Lynch by the upper arms.

"As I said before, a friend."

Lynch nodded, his mind so muddled by confusion, he would agree with anything.

Jason gathered the opener and trash from their earlier meal. He buried the waste and returned the tool to his saddlebag. Mounting his ellack, Jason spoke to Lynch, a final time.

"Your blue stone will supply all of your needs. I'll see you in Baine."

Lynch watched Jason grow smaller as he dealt with the final blow delivered by Jason when he revealed his knowledge of the blue stones.

Lynch could do nothing more than shake his head and mutter.

"Oh, my!"

SIXTY-FOUR

"GERT," JAKE SAID, "you ever heard of a tall tale?"

The little man stood, his emblazoned eyes focused on Jake.

"Let me tell you something, young feller. I know'd some, what every time they flap they gums they's a-spreadin' things all about what ain't nuthin' but lies." Gert curled his bony fingers into fists.

Clay reckoned that Jake might underestimate the strength in this little gray man.

"Now," Gert said, "are you a-callin' me a liar?"

"I'll admit," Jake said, "that one man living seven different lives at the same time seems a little far-fetched. And I apologize if I insulted or questioned your integrity in any way, but it's still kind of hard to swallow."

Jake finished his coffee and rose to his feet. "I've come to think quite a lot of you over the past few days, but if you're calling me out over my opinion, I guess we'll have to settle things a different way."

Gert said not a word, but stepped briskly toward Jake. He moved with such intensity that Jake nearly drew his gun. He let it slide back into its holster when the withered old man presented himself. Jake smiled and placed his hand into Gert's.

Clay holstered his gun and breathed a sigh of relief. He didn't like interfering in another man's disagreement, but felt compelled to do whatever he could to resolve this one in an amicable manner.

"I'm mighty sorrowful bout how ol' Gert's been a-treating ya." He sniffed and wiped his nose. "It's jest when I think back, I gits powerful sad and I wants to take 'er out on somebody. I sure would be mighty beholden if you ya could find 'er in yer heart to forgive old Gert?"

"Why don't we forget about what happened," Jake said. "Sit down, pour a cup of coffee and finish your tale."

"I'd like that a heap," Gert said. He wrapped his free hand around Jake's and began an exaggerated shaking until Jake put a stop to the little man's gesture of gratitude.

"You're welcome."

Both men took their respective seats. Gert downed a cup of coffee and returned to his younger years.

"Yessiree, me and ol' Scratch, why we was tight as a tick, maybe even tighter."

Both Clay and Jake could see Gert's anguish as he spoke.

The old man removed a soiled rag from within his hat. He blew his nose and replaced the rag.

"With Scratch gone, what did you do, how did you live?" Clay asked.

"I didn't wanna leave my birthin' home, but I was a feelin a hankerin to clear the cobwebs what done and set up housekeepin' inside ma head. So's I set out fer a spell."

"How'd you make it by yourself?" Jake asked.

"Assuming you were alone," Clay added.

"Oh, I were alone, you kin betcha, and as fer as makin' it on my lonesome, Papa learned me everythin' from buildin me a spot to live to huntin' me up some grub to et."

By now Gert had learned to pour himself a cup of coffee, only this time, he emptied the container. A look somewhere between sorrow and panic spread across the little man's face.

"Calm yourself," Clay said, "I'll make another pot."

"I'm mighty sorrowful fer drinkin all yer cafer."

"It's just coffee," Jake said. "Please continue."

"If you be a-thinkin' it's okee dokee."

Jake smiled and nodded.

Gert returned the smile, followed by a sip of coffee and the story.

"Territory Rangers don't take much to other folk. We keeps to us selves." Gert stared at Jake. "Not you two fellers. You is more like Rangers than most,"

"Thank you kindly," Jake said.

Gert nodded. "I were gone pert near two year, and that there Baine were bein' built whence I gets back."

Clay perked up at the mention of Baine.

"Gert, you've been around since the conception of Baine. What can you tell me about it before and now?"

Jake leaned in so as not to miss any pertinent information.

"It were huge. A might surprisin' site to gander at once'd ya git home after bein away fer a spell. "

"Do you remember the layout of the city?" Jake asked.

"Tain't never been thar," Gert replied. "They's too much noise and commotion fer me."

"So in the three hundred or so years Baine has existed, you've never been there?" Clay asked.

"Not if'n my foot were to git plumb chopped off would I be steppin the foot I had left into that thar Baine. I seen it from the time it were built and loaded with folks, till it were wearin out to nothin but a pile o rubbish. It's just like ya see 'er today and never got closer then we is now."

"What about the new Baine?" Jake asked, "It's built simpler, and I question why the original city was abandoned and replaced with a bunch of shacks?"

"I got's to tell ya I don't know no more bout them thar shacks then I did bout that pile o rubbish. Thar was this one feller what said he was gonna git his share of calladium." Gert shook his head. "Ain't never heard tell o such a thing. How bout you two—ever hear bout this seldom, callad, or whatever you call it."

"Can't say as we have Gert," Clay said. "Can't say as we have."

"May be trouble up ahead," Jake said. "Nothing but tall grass, and tall grass means places to hide."

Clay nodded, "Lots of places to hide."

* * *

Clay, Jake and Gert moved steadily toward Baine. As they traveled through the field of waist-high, brown grass, Clay detected something about the size of a grown man. It was paralleling them on the right, only this being was on all fours, and moving fast in timed bursts.

He leaned over to Jake and nodded toward Gert.

"Watch him."

"What," Jake said with surprise.

Clay signaled with his hand to keep the noise down.

Jake nodded.

"Just watch him," Clay harshly whispered, "Watch him like you never have before."

No sooner did Clay get the words from his mouth.

"Ahh!" Came the cry from the front of the pack. Gert was writhing on the ground holding his ankle.

"I thunk I done and broked my leg."

Clay and Jake both dismounted. Just before they reached Gert, Clay looked at Jake and gave a slight nod, Jake returned the gesture.

"What's the matter, ol' timer?"Clay asked.

"Are ya blind?" Gert grumbled. "Didn't ya see me twist ma leg? I was rat thar in front ya?"

"Sorry there, Gert," Clay said, "I was too busy flapping my gums."

"I'm afraid it was my fault," Jake said. "I kept Clay's attention from where it should be."

"That ought to learn you a lesson," Gert groaned. "I'll betcha done an crippled up a poor ol' man. You know'd I'm a-gonna hafta hitch a ride with one of you two?"

"Sure thing, Gert," Jake said, "You can ride along with me."

Clay and Jake carried Gert and placed him on Jake's ellack. That's when Clay glimpsed the little man's upper left arm. He couldn't be sure because the area was packed with dirt. That's it, Clay thought. He wallowed in the dirt on his left side to cover what he had done.

"Make yourself comfortable," Jake said, "I'll be right back."

He met with Clay out of Gert's earshot.

"That's not Gert," Clay said.

"What makes you think so?"

"He keeps his left hand shoved into his pocket, something he's never done before."

Jake shook his head, "So?"

"Gert told us about his twin brother, Scratch."

"That's right," Jake acknowledged, "and the two smallest fingers on his left hand were fused together."

Did you notice when he first mentioned calladium he pronounced it correctly. Then he made as though it hardly registered with him."

"So what do we do?" Jake asked.

"Like I said, watch him."

S I X T Y - F I V E

"WHAT'S THAT?" Cassie asked, pointing toward a several mile long mountain range. At second look, she decided it was too deliberate and ugly to be a mountain.

"That, my dear, is the sprawling metropolis of Baine," Ruben said.

"You sure have a strange way of building cities. I see you start by throwing all aesthetics out the window."

"I guess I should add that the city has been abandoned for over one hundred years. What you're seeing are the ruins."

Cassie squinted, deep in thought. She raised her eyebrows and looked at Ruben. "It seems we'll get a first-hand gander at Baine."

Ruben looked surprised. "How so?"

"I don't know if it was done intentionally, but our buddy, J. Smith just sent out a telepathic memo." Cassie said. "We're heading to Baine."

"More questions," Ruben said. "When are we going to get answers?"

Cassie shook her head and shrugged. "How far would you guess we are?"

"It's hard to say. Baine was a huge city, and visible from a longer distance than any other city or landmark on Aon."

"I guess we'll get there when we get——"

Once again Cassie paused and wrinkled her forehead. The boulder moved forward at a faster pace, disregarding obstacles as it toppled trees and crawled over what it could not destroy.

The sticky substance that held Ruben and Cassie fast to the stone turned into a blessing, keeping them from being tossed from their perch.

"What's happening?" Ruben exclaimed.

Cassie shrugged. "Other than J. Smith is terrified of something and using everything at his disposable to get away."

The boulder, along with its two passengers, continued to gain speed and follow its reckless course, destroying everything in its wake.

"This rock can't take much more," Ruben said.

Cassie nodded. "You read my mind."

The boulder twisted in a circle as it continued to travel forward. Ruben and Cassie closed their eyes to ward off the dizziness. Suddenly the boulder stopped, digging several feet into the ground and cracking in half.

The sticky gel liquefied, releasing its two captives. The crack was several inches wide and of no consequence. Ruben made his way to the edge to begin his descent.

"Stop!" Cassie urged. She extended an arm as if reaching for something that wasn't there.

Ruben returned. "What is it?"

"He's gone," she said, "J. Smith, he's gone."

Ruben took her by the arm. "Let's get off this rock."

"Not soon enough for me."

Ruben and Cassie stepped onto solid ground for what seemed like the first time.

"I think we should move in the opposite direction," Cassie said, "away from Baine."

"That might not be the best idea," a voice behind them said. "It's something we should talk about."

Ruben and Cassie whirled around.

"Didn't mean to startle you, but I don't see many folks who have fought so hard to get this close to Baine, then make plans to turn tail and run."

"And who might you be?" Cassie asked.

"Jason's the name." He extended his hand. "Pleased to make your acquaintance."

Cassie placed her hand into the stranger's. She removed it as if some unknown contagion may lurk there.

"And just to make you aware," she said, "we were forced this close to Baine."

"Things aren't always as they seem," Jason said. "Just the same, you'll need provisions, and with the Barren zone less than a mile away, travel by foot is not recommended."

"We can't ride with you," Ruben said. "Three on an ellack wouldn't be a recommendation I'd make either."

"Follow me," Jason said. He led the two visitors through a sparse stand of sickly wicker trees, to an oasis on the border of the barren zone. Within the perimeter of healthy shade trees, an underground stream surfaced, formed a pool and disappeared again.

Facing the stream stood two ellack's, each laden with sufficient supplies to last its owner about a week.

"There is one for each of you," Jason said.

Cassie, having already picked one out, was busy getting to know her new friend.

Ruben, being a bit more standoffish toward his new ride, found himself enamored with this young benefactor.

"You just happen to carry around a couple extra beasts of burden wherever you go?"

Jason smiled, raising his eyebrows.

"Ya keep something around long enough and it's bound to come in useful sooner or later . . . Don't you think?"

Ruben looked at the ground, kicked up a small cloud of dust and chuckled.

"Yeah, I guess that would stand to reason."

Jason walked with Ruben to meet his new mode of transportation.

"We should get moving," Jason said. "Your mounts are watered, drink your fill, and make sure each of your canteens is topped off."

"So," Cassie said. She leaned against her ellack and crossed her legs, allowing one foot to remain flat and the other to rest on its toe. "Even though our plans were to head away from Baine, somehow you're convinced that we want to ride toward Baine." Cassie stared at Jason, shook her head and climbed aboard her newly acquired steed.

"Okay, let's go. Why, I don't know, but I guess I'll find out."

"I suppose I have no say in the matter," Ruben said. "Oh well, everybody's got to be somewhere. I might as well be with you two."

Cassie extended her hand.

"We're following you."

Jason nodded, then nudged his mount forward.

LYNCH STUMBLED ALONG, unaware that his surroundings were changing. The events of the day had taken a toll. On a compact planet like Aon, ecosystems change quickly. Lynch was losing fluid, due to the arid climate. Barren earth and little or no vegetation, coupled with high temperatures and low humidity insured dehydration.

"Now there's Gaylen, and that new fella, Jason. Oh, and that ugly, whatever it was that had no name, or at least wouldn't give me one." Lynch tripped and nearly fell, unaware that his body would soon begin to shut down.

"Who do I follow? I wanna make sure that I join up with the strongest man. It wouldn't do for someone of my stature to be hanging around with weak guys." He began to march about. His lips were dry and cracked, his eyes beginning to sink deeper into their sockets. Then a thought crossed his mind. It said:

"Sit and drink."

Lynch stopped in his tracks and sat down. He reached into his pocket, and pulling out the blue stone, waited for it to glow. Within several minutes, water began to flow from the stone. Lynch gorged himself, then saturated his clothing. He stood, and after a quick search, found a depression in a rock formation that he fit into, providing shade from the relentless sun.

Lynch dropped onto all fours and crawled partially into the depression. Once out of the sun, he saw it was more than he initially reckoned. A cave extended deeper into the outcrop than appeared possible from the outside. The lure of the cool air drew him in, oblivious to anything but his own comfort.

Lynch rolled onto his back and closed his eyes, allowing what seemed to be a steady breeze to wash over him. The breeze slowed and rose in temperature.

The smile left his face as he opened his eyes. What he failed to check before entering the cave could now cost him everything. The huge eyes staring back at him along with the shallow breath crawling across his face and ruffling his hair were unmistakable.

Had the lancet not scraped the ceiling on its arc toward the ground, Lynch would have never again seen the light of day. As it played out, he rolled to his left, causing the weapon to plunge deep into the ground.

The groundskeeper, as it was known, was a hateful creature with a nasty disposition on a good day.

Lynch dodged another attack as the creature repeated its first assault, failing to take the height of the ceiling into consideration a second time.

The groundskeeper, when grown, measured about eight feet in length. Its tail was flat and segmented like that of a lobster. There was no thorax to speak of. The body rounded off, forming a simple head with huge raised eyes that absorbed more light, allowing better sight in the dimly lit cave. There were four whip-like weapons that attached to the top center of the body. Each of the four whips held a razor-sharp, hollow lancet. The entire unit lay along a channel at the top of the shell. There were two pointing forward and two rearward. These whips could be expelled up to thirty feet away.

Lynch dove behind a stone column, blocking the groundskeeper's blow. The hollow ends on the creature's tentacles would inject a substance that would dissolve the organs and musculature. This dissolution would take place almost instantaneously allowing injection of the solution and extraction of the meal with one insertion of the whip.

Lynch reached into his pocket and removed his blue stone. He drew a deep breath and then placed the stone between his front teeth. He stepped from behind the column and blew hard toward the advancing creature.

A blue beam emanated from the stone and zapped the groundskeeper in its left eye. The eyeball exploded and rained down in leathery pieces and thick globules of rubbery fluid.

"How about that, you gut sucking slug?"

The groundskeeper responded with a high-pitched squall that made Lynch cram a finger in each ear.

"I'll take that as a no."

Now at a disadvantage, the creature spun around and released its two rear whips sideways. One caught Lynch high and one low, taking his feet out from under him and to the ground. The groundskeeper pushed with its short multiple legs (unseen beneath its shell) and turned one hundred eighty degrees in the air, once again facing Lynch.

He sent two tentacles toward Lynch. Its depth perception compromised with just one eye, they both missed their target and penetrated the cave wall behind him. Thinking it had hit its target, it released the compound. Steam poured from the wall as the solution dissolved the rock it touched.

"Good shootin' there, Tex." Lynch smiled. "See if this won't take you out of your misery." He removed the stone from between his teeth, inhaled, replaced the stone and blew into the creature's other eye.

Its blindness now complete, the groundskeeper attacked in all directions including his own. The final blow was a lancet into its own brain.

As the creature gurgled and dissolved, Lynch laughed.

He first dropped to his knees and then to his back, dislodging the stone that had rolled down his throat. He coughed and gagged until his oxygen deprived body could do no more. As he lay on the cave floor, he thought, *how ironic, the instrument that saved my life will now take it.*

A thump on his chest that brought a sledge hammer to mind dislodged the stone up into his mouth. He turned sideways, spit the offending object out and began to cough.

The last thing he saw was the shadow of a man dressed as a cowboy leaving the cave. Then all went black.

S I X T Y - S E V E N

"SPEED 'EM UP, VICTOR," Clive barked. "We're barely keeping ahead of this thing."

"Ha'yah!" Victor cried, accompanied by the crack of his whip. The wagon bolted forward, leaving the ominous hole behind for now.

"What in Bill's bald head was that?" Carl questioned.

Clive looked at his comrades.

"The more pertinent question is how long can we out run it?"

"That's impossible to tell," Victor managed to communicate from the front of the buckboard.

As the wagon rounded a curve, Carl extended a finger and voiced an observation.

"Looks like we've kinda got a handle on that question of time you had earlier."

A three foot high wall of stone stood across the entire width of the road. Any attempt to circumnavigate the obstacle meant an impossible forty-five degree climb to the right and a deadly forty-five degree plummet to the left.

"Victor," Clive barked, "left turn now!"

Victor looked to the left and eyed his options. He turned to find Clive.

"It's too—"

"Now!" Clive roared.

The buckboard veered off the road. They found that the steep embankment was a small part of the problem. Hidden beneath the waist high grasses were potholes, ruts and rocks, large enough to destroy an ellack-drawn wagon.

"When I get to the station," Carl yelled, "somebody's gonna get an earful."

Clive nodded. "Give 'em one for me too,"

Clive and Carl sat on the floor of the buckboard with their backs plastered to the front of the wagon. Each man had one hand grasping the iron bar at the bottom of the driver's seat and the other hand looped through the back of Victor's belt. They wedged themselves in place by pressing their boots against the barrels in the back of the wagon.

"Thanks for the hand hold," Victor said, knowing he wouldn't be heard if he voiced it any louder. Even so, he felt the need to express the sentiment. He was doing nothing more than holding on himself. His boots were locked underneath a flat plate normally used for the driver and passenger to rest their feet on.

The ellacks bore the brunt of the punishment. The muscles in their rear pair of legs contracted, lifting them off the ground, allowing the second pair, ahead of the rear legs to carry the load. Enzymes in the animals' muscles stiffened the second set of legs to near unbreakable, allowing the joints to remain movable.

Much of the animal's weight would be shifted to the flanks, causing the front legs to tread lightly, sparing them irreparable damage. Once the crisis was over, the rear legs would relax and lower to the ground and the second pair would contract to the abdomen to heal.

"How much more of this can we take?" Carl shouted.

Clive took a deep breath. "The buckboard can't last much longer and then we're next."

Victor strained to see thirty feet in front of him.

"What is that?" He craned his neck to see, and in an instant was rolling over top of it, "A ramp?" He held his breath until the wagon landed on flat ground. "And, man, am I glad it was there."

The buckboard came to a slow rolling stop. Victor applied what remained of the parking brake. He dropped the reins, removed his hat and fanned his face.

"All passengers may disembark in an orderly fashion."

"Just get me out of this death wagon," Carl said, falling over the side before catching himself.

Clive jumped to the ground.

"Victor, I don't know how you did it, but you did it good."

Victor climbed down last, said nothing and made for the anomaly he knew he had seen.

Sixty feet from the buckboard's final resting place, was a man-made depression. It was more than large enough to hold both ellacks and the wagon. The alarming part of this scenario was the rows of sharpened, six-inch thick wooden spears that lined the bottom of the depression, protruding up some four feet.

"Ya think someone might have it in for us?" Carl asked.

Victor nodded toward a curved structure.

"I think somebody's doing a stellar job of looking out for us."

The three men moved as close as they could to the mound of clay that saved their lives. It was placed to carry both vehicle and occupants over the hazard and deposit them with minimal damage.

"Let's check the buckboard," Clive said, "then I think it best we get outta here."

* * *

"How many barrels did we lose?" Clive asked.

Victor continued to drive, Clive rode shotgun, which left Carl to count. They were traveling at a slow, but steady pace. Carl could stand and make a quick count.

"I count seventeen. We started with twenty-four. Seven lost."

"Not bad for what we've been through," Victor said.

"I guess not," Clive replied, "I can't help wondering what's next."

"What do you mean next?" Victor asked.

This piqued Carl's attention, and a third joined in the conversation. "Yeah, next doesn't sound so good back here either."

"In case you two haven't noticed," Clive said, "the closer we get to where we're going, the more trouble we run into." He ran a hand over his stubbly face. "It's making a fella feel like he ain't welcome in these parts."

"I hear ya," Victor said.

"Where are we going?" Carl asked.

"Whoa," Victor said. He turned around and looked at Carl . . . "Right here."

"Where is here?" Carl asked. "I don't see anything but dirt and rocks."

Clive hopped down from his perch.

"That's a very astute observation," he said to Carl, "Let me see if I can shed a little more light on the situation for you."

Clive walked up to a rock formation the size of a three bedroom house. He pushed his hand into a small depression that no one save for Victor would have noticed. Clive removed his hand, then turned and smiled. A muffled click then a steady hum signaled movement.

"What the . . ." Carl mumbled, as a panel slid back into the rock, leaving an open doorway.

"After you," Clive said.

Victor slipped in; to him this was home. Carl stumbled through slowly; his head moving up one side, across the top, then down the other.

A short walk down a dim hallway opened into a single round room with a dome ceiling. A large pipeline entered from the east wall, continued through the building, and exited out the west wall. Three quarters of the pipe was covered with a square shroud that reached the floor. Three steps led to a small elevated control center.

"So, close your mouth and tell me what you think," Clive said. He adjusted several switches on the wall, bringing up the lights and adjusting the temperature down a few degrees.

Carl lowered his head from gawking at the ceiling and looked at Clive.

"I want you to tell me what all this is. Quincy mentioned his involvement in an operation, but indicated nothing like this."

Victor had climbed the stairs and was working at the power console.

"What this amounts to," Clive said, "is a big siphon. Crude oil extracted from Earth is pumped through this pipeline and into the storage facility at Baine."

"I've seen nothing in Baine that would show any liquids other than liquor and urine," Carl said.

Clive chuckled, "The other Baine."

"I'll let you finish before I bring that up again."

"Good enough. As I was saying, the oil is pumped through this pipeline. The covered area you see is a miniature refinery, in part, at least. As the crude travels through this area, forty percent of one of its components, called gasoline, is extracted and pumped into an underground storage tank beneath our feet. The liquid is extremely flammable and volatile if confined without a means of pressure relief."

"All that stuff is fine, well and good, so let's talk about the old city of Baine." Carl tipped his hat back and placed both hands on his hips. "From what I've gathered, and I believe these to be reliable sources, that place is just as lethal now as it was when people occupied its hallowed halls. And feel free to ignore the hallowed halls reference."

"Calm down," Clive said, "what you've heard has brought about the exact response it was intended to. That way people would stay away from the old Baine, allowing us to work unabated by sightseers and crooks alike."

"Hey, boss man," Victor said, "we've got a problem. When we first arrived, our underground tanks were topped off. Since then, we've lost a third of our product out of tanks one and two, and it looks like tank three is gone."

"You mean empty?"

"No, I mean gone."

A barely perceptible groan could be felt.

"Now what?" Victor said.

"Well, I guess you got your answer," Carl said.

Clive looked at him. "Allow me to refresh your memory and I quote, 'I can't help wondering what's next."

The floor buckled, the slight groan now a full-fledged symphony of twisting tanks, floor plates and girders being ripped in two.

"I believe that's our signal," Clive yelled over the ear splitting chaos.

Three men exited the doorway as the faux building collapsed. Loading once again into the buckboard, they relived a scene that had played out hours earlier and would play out again.

S IXTY-EIGHT

CLAY MOUNTED HIS ELLACK. This was the longest he had been able to view the tiny brand on Scratch's arm. It was weeping through the dirt, revealing the unmistakable shape, and the fact that the wound was fresh, would aid in finding Gert.

Jake managed to get Scratch as comfortable as possible, or at least in a position he would keep his mouth shut for any length of time.

"Can't you do anythin' right?" Scratch moaned.

"Sorry, Gert," Jake said, "What seems to be the problem?"

"What ain't the problem, ya consarn devil? I been puttin' up with you two for way too long now, and I just about done and had it."

"Click."

Scratch turned his head. His eyes grew as big the gun barrel he was facing.

"I've taken about all I'm going to take from you, you big mouth sniveling little runt," Clay growled.

"Wh . . . what you got agin' ol' Gert—"

Clay's eyes turned into slits.

"Call yourself Gert one more time, Scratch, and I'll splatter your big mouth along with that tiny brain all over the countryside." Clay cocked the second trigger on his dozen gun.

"All right, you got me, but tain't no need in shovin' a thing like what you got in that thar hand of yours up into a feller's face."

"Tie his hands together, Jake."

"Now ain't no call—"

"Shut up," Clay roared, "answer when I ask and answer what I ask." Clay paused a few seconds to allow his last comment to sink in. "Got it?"

Scratch nodded.

"Where's Gert?"

"I don't know, I ain't—"

A hand clamped around Scratch's neck, severing his connection between life and oxygen.

Clay lifted the little man from Jake's horse and pressed the gun into his nose.

"You got one more chance to answer you filthy little imp." Clay swung Scratch to the other side of his ellack away from Jake. He eased his grip on Scratch's throat. "Now, answer me, where is Gert?"

Scratched took a wheeze filled breath and coughed several times. After several more breaths he could speak.

"I done and told ya, I don't— "

Scratch heard no more than a millisecond of the click that would send the upper portion of his head, as a fine gray mist, spraying in all directions. The lower jaw, still attached to the neck, jiggled up and down. It dripped its true dark teal color while getting in the all-important silent last words before flopping over sideways.

"Uh, ya think that was a little over the top?" Jake asked.

Clay ignored the excruciating pain in his hand which made it easier to ignore Jake's question. Instead, he threw Scratch's body across his ellack and twisted his left arm until it was in plain view. He tapped the arm several times with an open hand to remove the impacted material.

"See that?" Clay said, pointing to a small "U" shaped brand on the lifeless arm.

Jake nodded.

"It's called a death trap. It means you've agreed to sell a member of your family to the erratt for one of their sacrifices."

"*Sacrifices?*" Jake said. "Since when were sacrifices allowed?"

"Not allowed, tolerated. You'd be surprised at all the nuts on this rock. We've got 'em worshiping everything from the sun to ellack turds. What we have to do now is get to Gert before they do."

"Why the brand?" Jake asked.

"It would allow the seller to do it once, keeping the practice from becoming a business." He took a long hard look at Jake. "I guess even the erratt's have standards."

Clay tensed. "Don't move, Jake. Your life depends on it." Clay had twisted around and was now holding the gun on Jake, or so it appeared. "Something has been following us and its now behind you. I don't think it knows we've made it, but I believe it may be ready to spring."

"Please point that cannon of yours in a different direction."

"Sorry, I can't let whatever is stalking us see what it's up against."

"Okay, just be careful."

"Don't worry, if something happens, you'll never know it."

"Thanks."

"When I give the word, first duck and roll off your ellack toward me and hit the ground . . . Got it?"

"Yeah, I got —"

"Now!" Clay bellowed. As Jake's head moved downward, Clay's hand moved up knocking Jake's hat off as he did. An instant later he fired three times, blowing two huge holes in the thing's abdomen with the third shot removing half its head. It landed on Jake's mount, sliding off the other side.

Jake was up before the beast hit the ground. Clay slid down to his feet and joined Jake, already examining the carcass.

"One more thing out looking for a free meal," Jake said.

"Not this one," Clay replied. "Grab that leg, and let's roll it over." They turned the creature over where the head was intact.

"What do you mean, not this one?" Jake asked.

"It's called a widow, and you're right, we would have made a fine dinner, but far from free. It was sent to kill us, courtesy of our headless little friend over there."

"I'm hearing everything you're saying, but I'm real short on understanding."

"Scratch promises to turn over his brother for an agreed sum of money. Since the traitor and the betrayed are both close to two others not involved in the transaction (namely you and me) we would have to be eliminated to make sure no secrets are divulged."

"Secrets?" Jake said. "What secrets?"

"Do you remember when I told you the erratt's rituals are not permitted but tolerated?"

Jake nodded.

"Supposedly they don't exist; so to keep the peace among the status quo, they rid themselves of anything that could jeopardize their sect, no matter how small."

"It doesn't appear such a pleasant way to go," Jake said, kicking at one of the widow's paws.

The animal was about twelve feet long with black coarse hair and a ridge of bone covered in skin running down the center of its back. Each paw donned huge claws which resembled a raptor's talons. The front paws had two extra digits that could only be called opposable thumbs. These also held a nasty talon with barbs for extra holding power.

"Look here," Clay said, pulling out a huge knife from a boot sheath and knelt down over the widow's head. He pushed his knife in between the jaws in a mouth full of long curled fangs. Clay twisted his knife opening the mouth wide enough to wedge the toe of his boot against the upper jaw. He dug the knife into the ground at such an angle he could pry the lower mandible open.

Jake just shook his head.

"This thing's got fangs on its tongue, talk about a killing machine."

"We'll backtrack this widow and hopefully pick up Gert's trail," Clay said.

"How long do you think he has?"

"Don't know. He may already be dead."

"Guess we best be at it."

"What do we do with this?" Jake asked, touching the widow with the tip of his boot.

"Let it rot," Clay said, a look of disgust plastered firmly on his face. He pulled his ellack into the tall grass that ran beside the road. He waded through the sea of green until he found the trail of broken stalks made by the widow.

"Jake, over here." The two men came together.

"Our road map," Clay said, pointing out the impressions in the grass.

Jake eyed the trail until it faded from sight.

"What exactly are we looking for; the animal that made this is dead?"

Clay's eyes cut toward Jake.

"We've got a score to settle." He spat on the ground. "And if those diseased, cave crawling erratts have harmed that little one, make no mistake, there will be hell to pay."

After several miles of backtracking the deceased widow's trail, Clay stopped, then quickly turned to Jake with an index finger across his lips.

Jake nodded and returned the gesture.

Both men dismounted, Jake following Clay's lead. Clay reached into his saddlebag and removed two, one foot long black colored rods. Holding a bar in each hand, he lifted both over his shoulders and down into a black leather sheath built into Clay's coat that Jake hadn't noticed before.

"From here on out," Clay whispered directly into Jake's ear, "we must be quiet."

Jake nodded.

Clay returned the nod, avoiding any unnecessary speech.

"They're small and don't carry weapons, but don't let that fool you, they're vicious in their own right. Once we're in, we split up. When it starts, kill anything that moves." He laid a hand on Jake's shoulder. "Don't worry, you'll know."

Clay pulled a black rod from his boot, identical to the two he now carried on his back. He handed it to Jake.

"Hold the rod by the knurled end, when things get nasty, squeeze the handle. When it's over," Clay hesitated momentarily. "If you're still standing, squeezing the rod again will bring it back to the original configuration"

Jake nodded, only this time with a look of puzzlement and dark finality.

"We're going in. Just remember, nothing leaves this place alive."

S I X T Y - N I N E

"SO, THIS IS THE BARREN ZONE," Ruben said. He removed his hat and wiped the sweat from his forehead. "Just like you said, don't want to be out here on two legs."

Jason nodded, opened his canteen and took a sip.

"I want you both to be mindful, stay hydrated, but force yourself to self-ration. Sip, don't gulp."

"Beautiful piece of land you have here," Cassie said, "It must be the vivid colors and striking landscape that pull you in."

"Taken to sarcasm, I see," Jason said.

"Is that a problem?" she asked.

"It has its place."

Sarcasm was the most convenient defense she could muster against this man who terrified her and at the same time drew her close in a way she didn't understand.

In all truth, the scenery lived up to its name. The ground was barren and a dull hue of dirt gray. There were many other less interesting hills and rock formations bearing the same drab color. This included sporadic tufts of light brown vegetation that pushed their way through random cracks in the rock.

"I guess it's always this hot? "Cassie asked, her line of questioning nothing more than an attempt to hide her insecurity.

Jason smiled. He was enjoying the banter between himself and this feisty woman.

"Depends, Aon has such an unusual ecosystem, it may be hot here and ten miles east grasslands or an area of forestation." He awaited her response, which came as a masculine voice invading their conversation.

"If you two are finished with the niceties," Ruben said, "I believe we have company."

What appeared as a dot on the horizon became a massive beast overhead. Its enormous wings blotted out the sun as it circumnavigated the three tiny dots below.

Jason came to a halt and turned his anxious ellack around to face his traveling companions.

"Stand fast, I will return." He galloped to a point fifty yards away as the winged giant dropped from the sky to meet him.

Even with the distance between them, Ruben and Cassie were forced to shield their eyes from the cloud of airborne debris stirred by Greyshod's landing.

Jason stayed close to Greyshod, resting in the calm air of a vortex created near the creature's chest.

The two conversed for some time before Jason rejoined a stunned Ruben and Cassie.

"What was that?" Ruben asked.

"A friend," Jason said.

"A friend?" Cassie retorted. "Sure, and I have a pack of man eating timberwolves back at my place waiting for dinner."

Ruben looked at Cassie. "You have a what?"

"Oh, they're Earth creatures," an incensed Cassie said. "That's not the point; it's the ridiculousness of calling that thing, a friend."

"What should I call a friend other than a friend?" Jason asked.

"I give up." Cassie said.

"Are you actually able to converse with a being like that?" Ruben asked. "It makes a man wonder."

"This being, as you refer to him, is an invaluable participant in our cause," Jason said. "Even with his great size, he can infiltrate and gather much needed reconnaissance in areas others cannot trod. Greyshod (his proper name) may also gain access to and mislead those who would destroy us."

"There is no need for concern," Jason said. "What I do is for your safety. If you knew all I know, there are those who would do you great harm for even the smallest amount of that information."

Cassie found herself in the same position. She believed everything this man said, and now searched for any reason to quell that belief.

"Well, I'm not buying it," she said.

"If I had wanted to do you harm," Jason said, "I could've easily done so."

"He's right," Ruben said.

Cassie stared at both men and then sighed. "Where else am I gonna go?"

"We should leave now," Jason said.

"To Baine," Cassie said.

Jason nodded. "To Baine."

"Just as a point of conversation," Ruben said, "If this is such a dangerous area, and I gather from your previous statements that it is, why don't you carry a weapon?"

"I never gave it much thought," Jason said. "If I had to give an answer, I've never found being armed necessary."

"Fair enough," Ruben said, "although I can't see what good that does us."

"Can you at least tell us what to expect when we get to Baine?" Cassie asked.

"I fear turmoil and chaos, those being the most pleasant, " Jason said.

"Sorry I asked. "

SEVENTY

"YOU CAN SLOW DOWN," Clive said, trying to make himself understood over the thundering ellack.

"And soon!" came a voice amidst grunts and bumps from the back of the buckboard. Victor caught a pothole, tossing Carl and half of the barrels over the side of the wagon and down an embankment.

Victor, driving like a mad man on a mission, heard no one's request to slow down for another two miles. Clive's hoarse voice and constant pounding on Victor's shoulder cut through the tunnel vision that had encapsulated the frantic man.

"What got into you back there?" Clive demanded.

Victor, still clutching the reins turned to face his friend. Even in the twilight, Clive saw his sweat-drenched face and the terror in his eyes. He faced forward, shaking his head. "I never thought this would happen again."

"Again?" Clive stammered. "What do you mean, again?"

"We were working a claim at the base of Gainer's Ridge." Victor paused a moment. "It's been close to ten years now. Just a small operation, mining for surface caladium . . ."

"Carl," Clive blurted out. He turned. "Carl, are you okay? Clive climbed over his seat and into the back of the wagon. He pushed through the remaining barrels."

"Victor, Carl's not here." Clive made his way back to his seat. "Turn this thing around, we've got to find him before something else does."

Victor shook his head. "I can't go back there."

Clive wrapped a hand around the nape of Victor's neck.

"Carl needs you and I need you, now get it together or get out!"

Victor looked into Clive's steely gaze, knowing he couldn't bring himself to get out of the wagon after dark. No, not after dark, that's when it always came.

Victor threw the reins into Clive's lap.

"Okay, but you drive."

* * *

Carl heard moans. He opened his eyes and listened carefully. They seemed closer than he believed them to be. He opened his eyes again.

Must have dozed off, he thought.

The moaning was back. No time for that now, his shoulder throbbing. Carl touched his upper arm. Searing pain coursed through the offending joint. He now reckoned where the moaning had originated.

Carl made it to his feet. He pressed his injured arm tight to his body, pushing his wrist under his gun belt to help hold it there. The last thing he remembered was bouncing around in the back of the buckboard.

Carl stared up the embankment.

"Too steep to scale." He rubbed his chin. "Guess I'll move parallel to the road until I can climb back up."

Carl pushed through a patch of briars and then into more of an open area, the light too dim to tell what he was walking on. From what he could see, it appeared to be fist sized river rock, but with a pink hue. Something touched the underside of his boot causing him to slip and hit the deck.

Stars are such funny things, he thought. *Normally they're so beautiful, but these are exquisitely painful.* Carl slammed down hard into the real world, clutching his shoulder. He lay there until the pain subsided, allowing him to sit up

What looked like river rock was hard sponge-like formations fused together.

"Everywhere I touch secretes this slime." Carl lifted his hand and spread his fingers, stretching clear ooze between them, "Guess that's why I'm on my rear end."

He made it back to his feet, dodging several close calls. He noticed there was none of the offensive substance on his clothes; why, he didn't know.

There was one who knew all too well and would show Carl when the time was right.

Carl picked up his pace to avoid the slime underfoot from the pressure of each step. After another hundred feet, the slime ended, and he found himself wading through a field of tall grass.

"Ow!" His right knee slammed into something hard. The object tipped forward and then returned the favor, this time falling back into his left knee. Fortunately for Carl, there was more pain and less injury with this event. He placed his good hand on the object, a barrel from the back of the wagon. He leaned against the container until the pain eased. He did several knee bends. They were sore, but no permanent damage.

Carl found that if he stared straight ahead, he could pick out the barrels in the dim light. From where he stood, he counted six. No way to tell how many until sunrise.

A wave of nausea hit him. Carl bent double and emptied the contents of his stomach and then continued with the dry heaves.

"Ah, that smell," Carl said between sessions of dry gagging. The sound of wood being turned to splinters brought him around. He crouched behind the barrel and managed to slow his stomach spasms. The sound of destruction was moving closer. Feeling no other choice, sore knees and all, Carl ran.

* * *

Clive turned the wagon around on the narrow roadway. He raced back to where he thought Carl had most likely been tossed from the buckboard.

From here it was all going to be footwork. Luckily the sun was beginning to rise, exchanging the dim light for a brighter version of the same thing.

"All right, Victor," Clive said, "You want to tell me what's got you so spooked." Clive pulled two bottles of whiskey from his saddlebag. He handed one to Victor and popped the cork on the second. He turned the bottle up and didn't bring it down until empty.

"Well?"

Victor took a slug from his bottle. "In answer to your question, no."

"Give it to me anyway."Clive grabbed Victor's bottle and polished it off. "You were drinking so slow I figured you didn't want it anyway, now what gives?"

Victor pulled out a handkerchief, removed his hat and wiped his forehead. He replaced his hat and looked at Clive.

"I told you we worked a small claim picking up what surface calladium we could find. We'd shut down for the day. I was taking the buckboard from our camp on top of the ridge to our mining area that ran along the Raines River when something hit me and hit me hard."

"Okay," Clive said, "this is where I'm compelled to ask you, what does that have to do with anything?"

"Nothing," Victor replied, "and everything."

"I'm gonna need a little more to go on."

Victor nodded. "I know, but you ain't gonna like it."

Clive pressed closer. "Try me."

"Okay, other than losing Carl, did anything else seem unusual?"

"You'll have to do better than that. The only unusual happening was your insane driving and my stomach trying to hold down lunch."

"You sure about that?" Victor asked.

Clive smiled and his expression changed to one of puzzlement. "There was something else . . . I remember it now."

"An odor?" Victor prompted.

"The odor was sickening sweet. It was all I could do to hold it down. If it hadn't been for all the excitement, everything around me, including you, would have been covered in puke." Clive looked at Victor. "What was it?"

Victor shook his head. "The same thing that tore my wagon to pieces and ripped two ellack's to shreds nineteen years ago." One corner of his mouth curled up in a forced smirk. "The only difference being, I threw up."

The sun was now up, broadcasting enough light to make out objects in the tall grass beside the road.

"Look," Victor said, "about twenty yards further up, may be what we're looking for."

Clive snapped the reins, and the buckboard moved forward. They dismounted and continued on foot. Both men waded through the sea of grass toward a single barrel.

"Any guesses why this ground is so hard to walk on?" Clive asked.

"Yeah, I do," Victor said, "I'd just as soon not talk about it."

Clive stopped in the waist deep grass. Kneeling, he ran his hands between the stalks and picked up wood debris, ranging in size from splinters to complete barrel staves. He caught up with Victor examining the only intact barrel.

"I saw you check out the ground," Victor said, "so you have a good idea of what we're up against."

"Yeah, it seems to have real anger issues."

Victor pointed to an area of broken grass behind the barrel.

"I think this may be where Carl knelt watching the other barrels being destroyed before he lit out. You can see the path that was recently made."

Clive stared down the supposed trail.

"That's where we start. Unhitch the ellacks; I want to check something out."

Victor unstrapped the animals, and Clive followed the path, stopping at a tree line.

As Victor cinched the last mount's saddle, he saw Clive running like a madman waving his hands over his head. Once he had Victor's attention, Clive dropped his arms and concentrated on running.

Victor stepped around his ellack.

"What's got him all worked up?" Victor wrinkled his forehead and grabbed his stomach. The sickening sweet smell met Victor, surrounding him in its prophetic embrace.

S E V E N T Y - O N E

LYNCH'S EYES FLEW OPEN, and at the same time, he rolled to all fours, ready to spring. It was almost comical seeing a man of his years move so nimbly. The threat was reduced to a bubbling mass of sludge that spit errant particles in harmless arcs, as it melted into the cave's sandy floor.

Lynch felt a renewed sense of urgency to make Baine before the next twilight. He reached into his pants pocket and remembered what had transpired a short time earlier. Looking down he saw it almost immediately.

He dropped to his knees and picked up the blue stone. Holding it in the center of his open palm, the stone began to glow. Lynch moved his hand, allowing the artifact to hover in place. Straight line directional beams began to disperse from four distinct points denoting north, south, east and west.

In the lower southwestern quadrant a relief map showing rock formations and any other obstacles such as water, appeared being constructed from lines of light. A single line traced its way from the stone, weaving through the southwest portion of the holographic map to a point labeled Baine.

Lynch studied the map and pushed the stone into his pocket and left the cave.

Deep within the belly of the grotto, guttural rumblings gave way to a newborn, lapping the remains of the groundskeeper's puddle. With each mouthful of slime imbibed, the creature increased in size. Even though Lynch was now on the outside, he could detect the faint sounds working from within. Not wanting to discover their origin, he increased his gait to a jog.

* * *

I can't breathe, Carl thought. *And I'm too afraid to stop . . . Maybe I can jog for a while.*

His body approved as he slowed his pace to a brisk walk.

Carl wasn't sure how long he'd been running, or for that matter, how far he'd come. His stomach calmed down, and for that he was grateful. His immediate worry, other than being beaten into tiny pieces, was dehydration.

Carl felt as though he had thrown up every drop of water in his body and then some. His head pounded, and he began to stumble as he moved.

From the knees down Carl's pants dripped wet from the dew-soaked grass. He licked his lips at the thought of water gathering around his calves. Forgetting his recent encounter with a wooden barrel until it was too late; he dropped to his knees. Carl laid his forehead against his clenched fists waiting for the pain to subside.

Moments later he ripped handfuls of the green ribbons from the ground and slurped the moisture from their surface. After he'd gorged himself, the exhausted man with chlorophyll stained lips tipped onto his side and closed his eyes.

* * *

Lynch walked through a wooded area that soon gave way to grass and an occasional tree line.

"If you don't like the scenery, give it a couple of minutes." He leaned over and plucked a handful of grass, tossing it over his shoulder. "Don't worry, it'll change." Three more steps brought him face-to-face with the ground. The mound that put him there lay moaning at his feet.

Carl stirred and sat up.

"Why are you sleeping in the middle of nowhere?" Lynch demanded, "And in a place where no one can see you?"

By this time the sun had risen. Carl rubbed the back of his neck and holding a hand like a salute over his eyes, he looked up at Lynch, attempting to blink back the assault of light.

"Thrown out of a wagon," he said. "Thirsty, exhausted and had to rest."

Carl cradled his face with both hands, paying little attention to this new arrival.

Lynch removed something similar to a saddle bag from his shoulder. Out of Carl's sight, he reached into the bag and pulled out an empty water container and a small wooden plate. Removing the blue stone from his left front pants pocket, he waved the glowing blue orb over the plate producing dried meat, bread and a mixture of dehydrated vegetables. The container filled with water.

"Here," Lynch said, "Eat it all; it will make you feel better."

Carl snatched the offered plate and devoured its contents. He polished off the water, then handed both back to Lynch.

"Much obliged."He wiped a sleeve across his mouth, removing any remaining particles.

Lynch dropped to a squat position in front of Carl.

"Now, you want to tell me one more time what you're doing out here? And this time, try to fill in the holes."

Carl sat in the grass, legs bent at the knees, his good arm resting across one knee, the arm that hung from his injured shoulder still wedged underneath his gun belt.

"Myself and two other men I was traveling with . . . well, let's just say we were in a hurry. I was riding in the back of our buckboard along with a load of barrels. We hit a rough stretch of road and before I and the other two knew it, half the load, including me, were sprawled out in this field." He nodded toward his arm. "That's when I injured my shoulder." Carl remembered the creature. *Maybe none of that had been real*, he thought. *I'll file that away for now.*

Lynch stood and looked around.

"Are you sure you hadn't been hitting the sauce, because I don't see a road, barrels or your two friends you claim you were with, organizing a search."

"I got spooked," Carl said, "and took off running." He took off his hat and ran his fingers through his hair. "Don't know how long or how far, I kept going until I couldn't go any further. I was so thirsty that I licked the dew off the grass and passed out."He placed his hat back on his head. "And that's about it."

"Clear something up for me," Lynch said, "You said you got spooked . . . by what?"

"Not sure. There's something that got into our driver, Victor. That's why we were moving so fast. Once I was thrown from the wagon, they kept on moving. I guess with all the turmoil, they hadn't noticed I was missing."

"Maybe not the best of friends to have when you're in a pinch."

Carl ignored the comment. "Fortunately, I wasn't hurt too bad, so I walked parallel to the road. It was still twilight, so I didn't see the barrel before I ran into it." Then the thought of what had happened became a reality.

"I heard the other barrels being destroyed and sensed an uncontrollable rage. I vomited until there was nothing left. The dry heaves took over, and I felt like I'd be throwing up my stomach anytime now. Then it hit me. A sickening sweet smell unlike any —"

"Stop right there," a wide eyed Lynch insisted. "Did you say sweet smell?"

"How long would you say it's been since you noticed that odor?" Lynch asked.

"Can't say for sure, I don't know how long I was out."

"We should get out of here now." Lynch looked at Carl's arm. "Think you can move any faster? I can imagine it's tough enough trying to walk through grass like this with two good arms, let alone having your balance thrown off with one injured."

"I can try, but you're gonna spend more time picking me off the ground than we would make up by moving faster."

"If ya can't, ya can't," Lynch echoed. "I'm doing my best to save our butts. We best keep moving." Lynch took a step and ended up on his back. He jumped to his feet.

"I ran into those slime balls when I was thrown from the wagon," Carl said. "If you walk across them quickly they don't have time to secrete the slime that tripped you up." Carl scratched his face. "I don't understand why they release the clear gel on uncovered parts of your body, never on your clothes."

"I'll tell you why when there's more time, right now we've got to get out of here." Lynch grabbed Carl by the belt buckle. Any time Carl would fall Lynch would shore him up while still moving if possible.

The round, rock-like pads they were running on began to vibrate, and slowly lifted out of the ground. The pads were connected and it seemed to Lynch and Carl they were running on a rolling cobblestone walkway. A deep growl, combined with a squall, stopped the two men dead in their tracks. Lynch was unsure whether to run from the slime, or the screaming banshee a short distance away.

Something is familiar about that cry, Lynch thought. He mulled the sound around in his head, then he knew. The cave, it was that cave, the one with the groundskeeper I killed. There was something else there, and now it's followed me all this way to finish the job.

"Well, big boy," Lynch challenged, "I've had about enough of you and your ugly cousins. If you've got something for me, bring it, but you best make sure you bring a lunch, cause if I go down, I ain't going down easy."

They could feel heavy footfalls accompanied by grunts as the creature moved away. Both men, having acquired their sea legs in record time, stood on the still-moving cobblestone walkway.

"Good job dealing with that thing," Carl said. "I guess that's one less problem we'll have to deal with."

"Don't bet on it," Lynch said. "That was just a test."

"A test, what do you mean a test?"

"It has something planned for us; we won't get off that easy."

"How can you be so sure? Maybe it's—"

The section of walkway Lynch and Carl were standing on rose into the air. It snapped in two, knocking the men down. The walkway rolled up like a carpet with Lynch and Carl firmly held inside.

SEVENTY-TWO

"AT FIRST, I DISMISSED IT as just seeing things," Cassie said, "but every time I look at Baine, its distance has changed too erratically. I'm beginning to believe we'll never get there . . . Not that that would be such a bad thing," she added under her breath.

"The one's that would do us harm," Jason said, "are the same who wish to keep us out of Baine. In fact, they want no one near this crumbling city. They are able to emit an inaudible sound wave that confuses the mind. Until you can actually touch the city walls you can't be sure of your spatial relationship to the structure. "

"What reason could they possibly have for wanting to hurt us in the first place?"

"To keep us from entering Baine."

"Then let's turn around," Cassie pleaded. "There's nothing there for us."

"Know that Baine is essential and that other factions outside of the city and its interests would also take our lives if given the chance."

Cassie turned to her left, looking for any support she could garner from Ruben.

"He's gone, Jason, Ruben's gone!"

They came to a halt and began to turn in a circle, looking for their lost companion.

"There he is," Jason said, "several hundred yards back. He can't do that."

Ruben was kneeling, using his knife to dig at something in the hard packed soil.

A small tremor shook the ground as it rolled through.

"Ruben," Cassie yelled at the top of her lungs.

"No time," Jason said. He jabbed his heels into the side of his ellack and began a mad sprint toward Ruben. Another tremor caused Jason's mount to veer left.

Cassie hesitated, before she pulled herself together and followed Jason, the groundslide stopped. She saw Ruben disappear beneath the surface, and as if on cue, the tremor resumed its trek leaving the remaining two encased in a deafening silence.

Cassie dismounted before her ellack came to a stop. She hit the ground full stride, stumbled and fell, crawling the rest of the way to where Jason was examining the fissure that had swallowed Ruben.

"Where is he?" A frantic and breathless Cassie demanded.

He placed a hand on the back of her neck.

"You've got to calm down. Until you do, we're no good to anyone."

A sense of peace began to grow within her. She took a deep breath and sighed. Raising her head, she looked at Jason, her face streaked with tears. Cassie reared back on her haunches, sniffed and wiped her eyes.

"Okay, what's next?"

"Nothing takes the place of getting your hands dirty."

"You mean?"

Jason nodded, "Yep, down the hole."

Jason removed the rope from his ellack.

"Down, Agapè."

The animal folded six legs underneath its body and lowered itself onto the ground.

Cassie froze. "Agapè, what a beautiful name." It was as if something held her for a moment and then released her. "What does it mean?"

Jason smiled. "Unconditional love." He finished lashing the rope to Agapè's saddle. "Better get a move on. Grab yours and Ruben's rope; we don't know how deep the fissure might be."

Cassie brought both ropes and handed them to Jason. He tied the three together and dropped them down the crevasse.

"Follow me," Jason said, "we'll take it slow," he paused. "And please try not to fall on top of me."

Terror streamed from her eyes as she looked at him.

Jason smiled and tapped her on the shoulder.

"Lighten up. If you're going to be this serious the entire trip, no one will have any fun." With that, he placed his feet on the edge of the fissure, leaned backward and began a horizontal walk down the vertical surface.

Stunned, unsure of what to do, Cassie shrugged, grasped the rope and followed.

Is this guy legitimate or a first class nut case? she thought. *Guess I'll tag along until I find out.*

"How's it going up there?" Jason asked.

"Okay, I guess. At least I haven't landed on top of your head yet."

"Not so sure I'm crazy about the 'yet' part of your statement."

"No more than I am," she said.

"I'm down to the second knot already. There's about thirty feet left before we run out of rope."

"I could have gone all day without hearing that."

"Stop your descent," Jason said.

"What's wrong?"

"There's a tunnel cut into the side of the shaft we're in. I can swing over without too much trouble." Jason took a few minutes to size up his situation. Above him was Cassie; below him was anybody's guess, ten feet away, at an awkward fifteen degree angle, his quarry.

"Cassie," Jason said, "I'll need you to climb up another ten feet."

"Are you trying to wear me out, or just having fun watching me go up and down?"

"Once we begin swinging, if you're not far enough from me, you'll slam into the wall above when I'm close enough to reach the tunnel entrance."

"I'm glad you're paying attention, I can't get over how far down it may be if I lose my grip on this rope."

"Don't worry, you'll be fine. The problem arises in our timing as we swing. Since you're above me, as I swing out you're going have to watch and push off the wall a second after I do . . . Got it?"

"Have you ever played a board game without reading the directions first?"

"And your point is?"

"That's about how much I've got it."

"Ok then, we're playing it by ear."

"If we're both playing the same game, it's safe to say, I've got it."

"It'll take us a few times to get in sync, but we'll get it."

"At least one of us thinks this will work," Cassie said to herself. "All right I'm ten feet higher and waiting on you."

"Here we go," Jason said. He bent his knees and pushed hard. His body moved away from the wall. Cassie's attempt came too late and her static body weight jerked Jason back toward his starting point. He tapped the wall and positioned himself for another try.

"I will count off this time. One . . . two . . . three." Jason pushed off. Cassie followed, late, but better than the previous attempt. The result however was the same; this time it nearly wrenched Jason from the rope.

"Sorry," Cassie said.

Jason looked up and smiled. "Third time's the charm, try not to kill me this time."

"Okay," she said.

"One more time, One . . . two . . . three." Jason left the wall and this time Cassie timed it almost perfectly. They swung out halfway toward their goal.

"Watch me!" Jason yelled. He touched the wall just long enough to load his quadriceps for another push. This time their swing was poetry in motion and they came within two feet of the tunnel entrance.

The next swing was as perfect as the last. Jason's feet touched down more than a foot inside the tunnel. He held onto the rope so that Cassie could shimmy down and join him in the cave.

"Okay, slide down the rope and I'll hold my end until you're safe with me."

He heard a muffled, "Okay, on my way." He braced himself to make sure he didn't lose his hold on the rope. Jason sensed the vibration of Cassie climbing down the rope, then felt two subtle jerks. Seconds later, the rope was ripped from his hands, and before he could react, Cassie fell by the tunnel opening.

Their eyes met for a split second, but he saw the plea for help. He stepped to the edge and looked over to see an explosion of debris twenty feet below him. An insect like arm shot from the blast hole, ensnaring Cassie, pulling her into the newly opened abyss.

Jason didn't hesitate, but grasped the rope and began his downward climb into what was now a double rescue.

Jason reached the opening, so similar to the one he vacated. He was relatively sure they were made by the same means. Whether or not that meant animal, he couldn't be sure, but feared the worst.

He made his way deep into the tunnel and realized he had not plunged into darkness. Jason was far enough from the opening that the daylight was no longer a viable light source. He studied the tunnel walls themselves and found, to his amazement, tiny yellow phosphorescent particle's no larger than a grain of sand. They were so numerous that they lit the passageway almost to the point of being too bright.

After several hundred more yards into the lair, he came upon a fork. *To the right or to the left*, he wondered. He stared down each one looking for a sign. After a few minutes, he noticed four shallow gouges about half way up the side of the right-hand tunnel. Upon closer examination of the grooves, they ended about twenty feet into the tunnel with the last six inches dark red.

Jason ran his fingers into the scratches.

This material is pretty hard. Cassie must have dug her fingers into the wall until they bled.

Jason now had a direction. He hurried down the burrow, stopping briefly when he noticed blood smudges where her fingers had touched the wall. As he continued to move, he perceived what sounded like voices. The closer he got, he realized it was one voice, a male voice. He came to the end of the tunnel. It was a hub like the center of a wagon wheel and each tunnel a spoke which led in different directions. He counted twelve separate tunnels before he heard the voice again.

"Come out, come out," the voice said, "No need to linger, I know who you are, and you must remember me. So come and we will converse."

Jason walked confidently from the tunnel and into the hub. The man beckoned him to a polished stone table surrounded with six stone chairs. The chairs were placed at a comfortable distance from the table as they were too heavy to move.

"Gaylen, at your service, please have a seat."

"I am well aware of who you are, and I will stand."

Gaylen took a seat himself and poured two glasses of water.

"Please, may I offer you some refreshment?"

"I require nothing more from you than the whereabouts of my friends." Jason stared at Gaylen. "Tell me now or I will find them myself."

"They are being well taken care of; there is no need for your concern."

"Then our business is finished."Jason looked around the circular room deciding which tunnel to take. He spied what he was looking for, the four small smudges of blood several inches into the tunnel.

"This will not end here," Gaylen said.

Jason's eyes met Gaylen's. "But it will end."Jason walked toward the tunnel entrance.

"And how can you be so sure?"

Jason turned toward Gaylen one last time. "As I have said, our time is over." Jason disappeared down the tunnel.

Gaylen slammed his water glass down on the table.

"We will see, yes, we will see."

SEVENTY-THREE

CLAY PARTED THE CURTAIN of dangling foliage. He stepped through with Jake on his heels. They found themselves at a cave opening. One narrow tunnel led to the left, another to the right.

"You take the left and I'll take the right," Clay said. "You can bet they lead to the same place."

A low muffled mantra could be heard radiating from each tunnel.

"If we're not already too late, we don't have much time."

Jake nodded, "Meet you inside."

Both men disappeared down separate tunnels. Clay had to move slowly until his eyes became more accustomed to the darkness. He found the further in he moved, the louder the chant became, and a flickering light had worked its way up the tunnel.

Fifty more feet brought him to a space where the cave widened out into a room one hundred feet square and forty feet high, the ceiling shaped as a dome. There were fires in each corner. They danced off the various rock formations imparting an eerie glow to the entire area.

"I count thirty of the slime balls on the floor dressed in black robes that cover their heads."

What he saw next caused his blood to boil. On a raised platform Gert was lashed to an upright wooden frame, arms and legs in the shape of an "X."

The thirty bodies on the floor were chanting as a single form on the platform, with Gert dressed in the same type black robe.

Standing in front of him, another figure's garment was different, trimmed in gold. He held a knife and would slice a small piece of Gert's flesh off at a time.

"Why you wanna hurt ol' Gert? I ain't done nothing to ya. But you kin betcha if'n I git loose, you gonna wish you had never seen this little man."

With that, another slice of skin was removed.

The space Clay occupied was elevated about six feet above the chamber floor. Clay looked over and saw Jake waiting in the other tunnel. Clay nodded and Jake returned the gesture.

Clay knelt down, slipped over the edge and held on with his fingertips, dangling for several seconds so that his drop to the floor would be silent.

Jake watched and repeated the maneuver.

Clay turned and, no longer seeing Jake, assumed that he was down and awaiting a signal to begin the confrontation.

Another yelp from Gert and a string of curses, aimed at his antagonist as he cut another strip of flesh from the little man's body.

Clay seethed at Gert's predicament.

"Jake I hope you're paying attention," Clay whispered. "Here comes your signal."

Clay reached over his shoulders and removed the two metal black rods. Squeezing both handles, a black metal blade shot out of the end of each one. The blade was three feet long. It widened and curved along the leading edge until reaching its point. The back of the blade was serrated and strong enough to cut stone. Its hilt circled around the top of Clay's hand, emitting six inch spikes at a forty-five degree angle around its entire circumference.

The erratt's head, along with its cloth covering, fell cleanly away, followed by its upper thorax and legs before the head hit the ground. Body parts fell in such a way they eerily resembled an intact figure, oozing a thick green viscous material that puddled around the body. Before anyone realized the onslaught Clay had dispatched seven of the erratts.

Jake saw the first victim fall and sliced erratt bodies. He wasn't as proficient as Clay, but for a first timer, held his own.

The cloaked figure atop the pedestal was the first to notice the carnage moving through the crowd. He leaned his head back, letting out a primeval high-pitched scream. The hood dropped away from his face exposing a hairless, fanged entity. Its skin was wrinkled and a leathery brown color with large, somewhat human shaped ears that protruded several inches from the head and sunken orange eyes.

Rocking back and forth, Gert fell backward, destroying the frame that bound him. He attempted to stand when the erratt priest turned to finish his grizzly work.

Gert made it to his feet and squinted his eyes.

"You sure nuff an ugly cuss, but I done an telled ya what would happen if'n I got loose. Now I'm gonna show ya."

The priest bared his teeth and moved toward the little man.

Gert pulled a small silver cylinder attached to his hip. He pushed the button and a two foot conical shaped blade appeared. It was covered with hundreds of curved nodules. He brought the weapon up in front of his face. It began to spin.

The priest stopped. It would be the last move he ever made.

Gert somersaulted into the air, bringing his sword straight down through the top of the surprised priest's head. While Gert was still in the air he removed the sword, and on his way down, cut the already deceased body into one inch cubes, leaving a pair of feet when he hit the ground.

Gert stowed his weapon and watched as the body slowly at first, then quickly, became a heap, spewing fluid in all directions.

"I reckon you won't be a-messin with me no mo." He jumped from the pedestal and joined the fray. Soon the three men met as the last of the erratt, as Clay put it, "Bit the dust."

"If'n you two ain't some kinda sight for these poor ol' sore eyes, then I don't know what is."

"It's good to see you too, Gert," Clay said.

"Same here," Jake said, "What caused you to get separated from us in the first place?"

"Taint quite sure," Gert said, "Got snatched up by this here big black critter and hauled off to them dad burn erratt's one of them thar sacri . . . sucri . . . seekrafuzal—"

"Sacrificial," Clay said.

"Yeah, one o them things."

"We ran into your brother, Scratch," Jake said.

"Do tell," Gert said, "I ain't seen him in a month of Ritchdays. Now tell me ,and don't leave out nary a thin. How's he a-doin? What's he been up to?"

Clay looked at Jake. They both knew what the other was thinking. *We can't tell him his brother tried to sell him and we spread his brains over half the countryside.*

"Well, to tell you the truth," Clay said, "He was in such a hurry, we didn't have time to talk, but from what I could tell, he was doing just fine. He also said to make sure and to tell you hello and he'd catch up with you soon."

"Hee, hee, hee," Gert chuckled, "That's jest like that Scratch. He were always the one what liked to work a heap more than any of us younguns."

Clay laid his hand on Gert's shoulder.

"I'm glad we had time to see him on your behalf."

Gert nodded, sniffed and wiped back a tear.

"I be much obliged to you 'n Jake fer all you done for ol' Gert."

"I'm thinking it best we get out of here," Jake said, "Something doesn't feel right."

"Then 'go' it is," Clay echoed. "Reckon I'm with you two fellers."

Before they took the first step, the three men turned toward the back of the cave. A group of flying creatures filled the makeshift auditorium. The first thing they saw were the huge feet equipped with deadly talons and wings that fired barbed projectiles. Clay could attest to this as he had one in each leg and another that had pierced the palm of his left hand, stopping halfway through.

"We've got to get out of here," Jake said.

Clay turned toward Jake "Agreed, I don't think these things are the welcoming committee."

As Clay whirled around to face the enemy, he froze. A projectile several feet from his head would impact in milliseconds. There was no time for him to move; there was just no time.

Seventy-Four

AS CLIVE REACHED THE WAGON, Victor snapped the reins, and they were off again.

Clive worked his way up to the driver's seat and plopped down breathless beside Victor.

"How many . . . more times . . . are we gonna . . . have to run from this thing?" Clive asked in short huffs.

Victor shook his head.

"What about Carl?"

"If Carl is still alive, I'm afraid he's on his own." Clive removed his hat and set it in his lap. Holding it down with his elbows, he placed his face in his hands and rubbed as if he was washing his face with water. Once finished, he rubbed a hand through his hair and replaced his hat.

"Uh . . . you okay?" Victor asked.

Clive glanced sideways at the driver. "I ran through the woods screaming like a baboon . . . What do you think?"

"I guess you're right."

"When do we get to Baine?"

"Your guess is as good as mine," Victor said, "I look at Baine one minute and it's almost in my face; blink, and Baine appears five miles away. I guess when we run into it, we'll be there."

The two men rode on in relative silence for several miles. Victor slowed the ellack team to a trot. "No sign of Carl at all?"

"Nah, didn't see him," Clive replied. "No arms, legs, bits, pieces, blood trail, armpit hair, not so much as a little toenail."

"Well, I guess it's a safe bet to say you didn't see him."

"Ahhh," Clive yawned. "Get us to Baine. I have a feeling that's where our answers are waiting. Some we'll want to know, but more that we don't."

* * *

"Look out!" Clive yelled.

Victor veered, just missing the small man who stood in the middle of the road.

Rushing to make sure the stranger was unharmed, the two men met in front of the ellacks.

"Where'd he go?" Victor asked. "I'm sure I didn't run him down."

"I don't know, the way you drive sometimes." Clive was already in a squat position checking the underside of the ellacks and the buckboard.

"Whadda ya see? Anything under there?"

Clive stood up."Naw, looks like you lucked out this time."

Before Victor opened his mouth to defend his driving skills.

"Would you two herks be looking for I?" The top of a bowler could be seen against the far side of the wagon moving up and down, keeping cadence with its owner's stride.

"Say what?" Clay answered.

Legs appeared walking beside one of ellacks until they turned the corner. Standing before Clive and Victor was a slender little man, about four feet tall with a bowler hat. He wore a monocle over his right eye and sported a long, bushy mustache. He was dressed in a dark suit, white shirt and an oversized red bowtie. Spats covered his shoes, and in the crook of his arm, hung a black cane with a decorative brass handle.

"Hatch Lee, at my service, enough said."

Victor cocked his hat back on his head, placed both hands on his hips and leaned toward Hatch.

"I'm almost afraid to ask you to repeat whatever it is you said. So if you wouldn't mind, turn some of them words right side up?"

"Hatch is I, who you?"

Victor's mouth dropped open. He turned to Clive and shrugged. "Your turn."

"I think what we see is what we get," Clive said. "So you'd better put your deciphering hat on." He walked up to Hatch, who seemed to have a perplexed look on his face.

Clive looked back at Victor, turned, took a deep breath and sighed.

"Here goes." He spoke slowly as if it would make his words more understandable. "Me Clive, is you Hatch?"

The little man smiled, grabbed Clive's hand with both of his and shook with an exaggerated up and down movement.

"No is yes, no is yes, Hatch be me, Hatch be me."

Clive looked at Victor once again. This time he was smiling, his whole body jiggling from the forceful handshake he was receiving from Hatch.

"That's good enough," Clive said. He patted Hatch on the hands to stop the relentless onslaught of niceties. Clive motioned for Victor to join him.

"He Victor," Clive said, "Victor, this be Hatch."

Hatch grabbed Victor's hand and shook until the cane that hung on his arm fell to the ground. The little man lurched for the cane with blinding speed. Hatch hooked the cane over his arm and was shaking Victor's hand again before Victor even sensed his hands were missing.

"I'm not gonna ask you if you saw that," Victor said, "because I didn't, but could you give me an inkling of what happened."

Victor had to pry his hand away from the overzealous Hatch.

"We need to keep moving," Clive said, "why don't you ask mush mouth if he wants to tag along with us."

Victor rolled his eyes. "Okay." Victor looked at Hatch, wondering how to phrase his question. "You go with us?"

Hatch looked perplexed.

Victor scratched his head. "How like go you Clive and Victor?"

Hatch grabbed Victor's hand and nodded excessively.

"Well, that wasn't so hard. Looks like we've got another passenger," Victor said loud enough for Clive to hear.

"Get him on board," Clive said, "and let's get out of here."

Hatch was small enough to fit between Clyde and Victor on the driver's seat.

Several miles into their journey, the ruins of Baine came in and out of sight. This depended on the foliage that would block its view and open areas that would allow an unobstructed aspect.

Hatch bounced up and down on his seat each time the city came into view.

"Baine is to be, Baine is to be," he would shout, eyes wide with excitement.

"What do you suppose that means?" Victor asked.

"From the looks of things, I'd say he wants to go to Baine."

Victor once again attempted to communicate with Hatch.

"You want to go to Baine?" Victor said, realizing he had phrased the question incorrectly.

Hatch sat patiently, hands folded in between his legs. Victor rephrased the question.

"Baine go you?"

Hatch smiled and clapped his hands together in a rhythmic fashion, all the while singing.

"Baine go me is, Baine go me is, Baine go me is." He stopped, and with a concerned expression, looked at Victor.

"Baine go me is how when."

Victor sat perplexed.

"He wants to know when we're going to Baine."

"Ah," Victor said. He turned back to Hatch and shrugged. "Me not is to know."

Hatch smiled. "New two friends, so okay, okay. Travel reached till Baine is we there."

"Did you get all that?" Clive chuckled.

"Did reckon I maybe," Victor replied.

Hatch tapped Victor on the leg and did the same with Clive. "Friends forever best got."

Both men smiled at their new passenger.

S E V E N T Y - F I V E

THE WALKWAY UNROLLED, spilling Lynch and Carl underneath the surface of the ground. They slid down a steep incline, landing in an open area that at first glance appeared to be the ending point for numerous tunnels.

"Well, well," a familiar voice said.

Lynch jumped to his feet.

"Gaylen, you two-faced snake. You finally crawled out from underneath that rock."

"What a kind greeting for someone you haven't seen in such a long time."

"Not long enough, if you ask me," Lynch said.

"Are you not going to introduce your new friend?"

"I hadn't planned to," Lynch replied, "but since you're asking, his name is Carl."

"Something seems different," Gaylen said. "The Lynch I remember couldn't stand himself, and now I see you befriended another."

"And what business is that of yours?"

"Oh, none. I suppose; just making conversation. And you . . . Carl is it?"

Carl nodded.

"How is it you find yourself with this one," Gaylen said, motioning toward Lynch.

"Since that question has already been answered," Lynch said, "I have a question for you."

Gaylen nodded. "Proceed; I've got nothing to hide."

"What's the idea of rolling us up in your slime covered rubber wrap and dumping us off in this hole."

"I merely wanted to see an old acquaintance and perhaps converse a while."

"Sure you did. You've got some kind of half-baked scheme you needed a crony to take the fall for you in case things didn't work out."

"Hardly that at all," Gaylen said.

"To avoid wasting any more time, would you kindly show me the way out?"

"Certainly," Gaylen said, raising his hand and pointing toward a particular tunnel, "and please come again, won't you? This has been a particularly nice visit."

As Lynch and Carl walked into the tunnel entrance, Carl pointed towards four red streaks gouged into the wall.

Lynch shook his head. "Don't know, could be about anything."

After quite a while of moving deeper into the underground lair, Lynch and Carl noticed the glowing particles embedded in the wall that gave the tunnel its daylight-like quality.

"I'm not feeling so confident about the directions your friend gave us to get out of here," Carl said.

"Yeah, it looks like my buddy sent us the wrong way," Lynch said, "by mistake of course. He always was good that way."

The tunnel widened and spread in different directions. At one point it became a large room supported by erratic rock formations before narrowing back down into a single tunnel.

Lynch stopped, throwing out his arm in front of Carl.

"Shh," Lynch said.

Both men stood listening. Between the occasional drop of water, they heard muffled voices, and it didn't sound like things were going so well.

As the men moved closer, they detected a man and woman's voice and another sound they were unable to discern. Lynch and Carl located a vantage point where they could see the individuals without being seen.

A middle-aged man and a young woman sat on the sandy floor with their hands bound in front of them. To their right was a large round ball covered in drab green scales. Two eye stalks protruded several feet down from the top of the ball. Nothing visible to indicate a nose, but a wide mouth with what looked like thousands of tightly packed needle-like teeth. Four legs extended upward to its first joint, then down to the cave floor.

It seemed to talk to the two humans, but without using sound. The creature would look at its two captives as if using telepathic communication. The couple would answer back in their regular voices.

"It doesn't appear as though that thing is getting the answers it wants," Carl said. "Watch it stomp around after they give an answer."

As soon as the man finished talking, the creature would bound around in a circle by throwing its front two legs forward and dragging its back two the same distance.

The creature had had enough. It shot several steel like spears at the two humans missing them by inches with the spears embedding themselves into the wall behind the captives.

"I think he missed on purpose," Lynch said, "I don't think he'll go so easy on them next time."

"We have no weapons," Carl said. "Any suggestions?"

"Only one," Lynch said. He stood and walked into the chamber. "You folks seem to be in a heap of trouble here. Name's Lynch."

Carl stepped in and stood beside Lynch. "Didn't think I would let you hog all the fun, did you?" He looked at Ruben and Cassie. "You can call me Carl."

The creature noticed the newcomers. It opened its mouth as if to let out a squall, but there was no sound. Lynch and Carl knew it meant business when two spears headed their way.

Lynch pushed Carl to the ground and ducked as the projectile shot over his back, putting a dark horizontal streak on his shirt.

"Stay down," Lynch barked, "You'll get us both killed." Lynch reached into his pants pocket and pulled out his blue stone. He held it in the palm of his hand and extended it toward the beast. It glowed and rose above Lynch's hand. The creature focused on the floating blue stone. Lynch dropped to the floor as the blue stone took off near the speed of light.

It punched a hole about a half inch in diameter through the beast from head to tail. The creature wobbled several times and rolled toward one side. Its eyestalks became flaccid and flopped over. What served as a tongue slid into the sand as a puddle developed around the creature. Three jerks from its legs and it would move no more.

Lynch and Carl rushed to Ruben and Cassie, loosed their bindings and continued to search for a way out of the cave.

"I guess that way is as good as any other way," Carl said. "With the tunnels, passageways and burrows in this place, there's no clear way out."

"Okay," Cassie said, "let's get moving before we change our minds again." She pulled her coat tight around her and buttoned up the last three buttons. "At this rate, we'll never get to Baine."

"Baine," Lynch said. "What do you know about Baine?"

"That we're headed there," Cassie said' "Other than that, not a lot."

Lynch pushed his face tight to Cassie's ear.

"Who all here knows about Baine?"

Cassie turned toward Lynch with a surprised look. "Everyone here knows about Baine, that's where we're all headed. I'm leaving out you and your traveling companion since I don't have a clue where you two are going."

"My best guess would be Baine also," a familiar voice said. Just then Jason appeared through a narrow warren.

Ruben grabbed one of Jason's hands in both of his.

"Good to see you, stranger, I wasn't so sure I ever would again."

Cassie reached around Ruben and gave him a hug.

"How about not doing that again."

Jason smiled, "I'll try my best." He looked at the expansion in personnel. "Practicing your addition since we were separated, I see."

"Kind of ran into each other by mistake," Cassie said. "If it hadn't been for Lynch and Carl, we would have been smeared all over the inside of this cave."

"Thank you for taking such good care of my friends in my stead," Jason said.

"My pleasure," Carl said.

Lynch let out a small grunt and nodded.

"While everything seems to be clear," Jason said, "we should make our way out of here."

"That's what we've been trying to do for several hours now," Cassie said, "But it hasn't worked out as yet."

Jason chuckled, "Follow me, I think I can find a way."

Lynch threw a leery eye Jason's way. "Lead on; we're following you."

Within thirty minutes, they were on the outside breathing fresh air once again.

"Ah," Cassie said, luxuriating in the sunshine and the large gulps of fresh air she could draw in. She stopped long enough to scratch a spot on her Achilles heel and then returned to her revelry. A few seconds later, she paused again, but this time she dug into both ankles until they bled.

She raised her head. Before her appeared a surreal scene of jumping, scratching, bleeding and a sense of warped reveling.

The four were trapped in a narrow glade about thirty feet wide. Jason had made his way to the other side and stood on an elevated area with his eyes closed. Another minute and the would-be partyers came to realize that they must escape the glade or die.

"This way," Jason urged.

"I thought the Hemonati was some kind of myth." Lynch said. "In all my years, I've never seen or heard of one doing any damage. They were reserved for children and their scary nighttime stories."

Cassie, Carl and Ruben dug at their ankles, causing irreparable damage if not stopped before they reached the muscle tissue. Lynch moved close to Jason keeping his question away from the others.

"Is it true what I've gathered about these Hemonati?"

Jason nodded, "They'll dig every piece of flesh just above the ankle in a swath four inches wide right down to the bone."

"Is there any way to stop it?"

"The larva digs their way into their carrier's skin. They take one bite, explode and produce two more of their kind. These explosions create more Hemonati. They use their human hosts as machinery to do their excavation work."

"How can we kill them," Lynch asked.

"We must pair them off," Jason said. "Once a Hemonati chooses a host to imbibe, blood from another will cause an instant death without the explosion, thereby nullifying their continued creation."

Lynch nodded several times. "Sounds doable."

"Doable is not the problem. Doable while digging large enough chunks of flesh from the donor/recipient and at the same time from the recipient/donor is the challenge. The cross muscle transplant must take place before the pieces disintegrate from the constant reproductive explosions."

"Hold on there, doc," Lynch said, "When we were conversing about all the hereto and wherefores, you said, the explosions did nothing to destroy the muscle tissue. Would you like to clarify that?"

"You're correct," Jason said, "but with pieces as small as I'm talking, we'll be lucky if they don't fall off by themselves."

"Understood," Lynch said, "I'll keep my mouth shut from here on out."

Jason noticed a tear roll over the corner of Lynch's eyelid and run down his face. "How are you holding up?"

Lynch held his fingers up.

"In a few minutes you will see all ten of these and anything else sharp I can find tearing my legs to pieces. If we're going to do anything, let's do it now or you'll be on your own."

Ruben and Cassie seemed to be the worse, so Jason paired the two together, while Lynch would stand by Carl when his turn came.

"Let me have your knife," Jason said, "and I hope it's good and sharp."

Lynch looked at Jason, tears rolling down his face. "I don't have anything to cut with." His left hand lifted his pant leg, thousands of tiny Hemonati just waiting for his nails to let them in.

"Let me have it Lynch."

"Let you have what?" Lynch snarled.

"It can't do in your hands what it can do in mine."

"No, you can't have it."

"I won't take it," Jason said, "But you won't be alive to use it, and I'd like to give these others a chance to live."

Lynch dug down into his pants pocket and pulled out the round blue stone. He handed it to Jason, and it began to glow as if it was reuniting with an old friend. It was then Lynch passed out. He would awaken for short blurry spurts only to allow his friend of unconsciousness to wash back over him.

"Lynch," a voice would call accompanied by vigorous shaking. This would happen every so often. This pattern went on for hours, weeks, months or years--he didn't know. Then, during one of these sessions, he continued to the elusive state of consciousness.

It was Cassie, and she was moving around as if nothing had happened.

"Well, it's good to see you up, sleepyhead," she said

"How long?" Lynch asked. He rolled to his side and sat up on his knees. He slid his right hand down into his pants pocket. It was there, it was still there.

"Almost three days."

Jason walked by. "You seem well; I'll be by later to discuss our plans for departure."

Lynch nodded, his mind attempting to sort through the lost three day period.

SOMETHING CROSSED JAKE'S LINE OF SIGHT, blocking his view for a fraction of a second. His left hand moved instinctively to his right shoulder. Jake could not ignore the searing pain. He saw the barbed dart protruding from his upper right arm. Whatever blocked Jake's vision had diverted the deadly projectile away from his brain and into his arm.

Jake looked up and noticed that Gert had been snatched up by both shoulders. The little man began to hoot and holler, pulling his rotating weapon out once again. He removed the right leg of the flying creature, allowing it to dangle from his shirt. Gert wrapped a hand around the left leg, close to the thing's body. Gert sliced off the left foot, leaving enough stump to retain a good hand hold.

Gert carved chunks of meat from the monster, stopping just before it would hit the cave floor. He would grab another of the flying beasts, diving into the air to do so.

Meanwhile, Clay had begun to disembowel the creatures, if that was possible. He soon found that their bodies retained no anus. And even more unusual, the long pointed head contained no mouth, one small orifice to breathe and two eyes.

Clay felt an emotional tug for the animal flailing against his grip. Raised in a body designed to exist for hours. *It knows no pleasure, not even pain, living to kill and ultimately to die.*

Clay smiled, "Maybe next time." He pushed the creature to the cave floor, drew his sword, and split the beast in two, lengthwise.

Gert's whirling sword made quick work of the barbed dart piercing Clay's hand. After trimming off one side, the other side could be pulled through against the barbs.

"Kinda funny being able to see all the way through your hand," Clay said, as he watched the pinky finger size hole slowly close in his palm.

Gert made his rounds, cutting darts flush to the bodily areas the projectiles had violated.

"How do you get the rest of this thing out?" Jake asked.

"Let it get infected, fester up good and tight, put a finger on both sides and squeeze," Clay said. "If you're lucky enough and the infection doesn't kill ya, you can pop that plug of pus thirty feet or more."

"How long before that little slice of heaven takes place," Jake asked.

Gert produced a leather bag. He opened the drawstring and reached in, closing his thumb and index finger around a pinch of powder. He lifted his hand from the bag and allowed the particles to fall back into their container as he rubbed his digits together.

""I done and put that there powder on ya pert near five minute ago, so I reckon —"

"Thar she blows," Clay shouted. Seven purulent geysers exploded within thirty seconds of each other.

"How's that fer an answer, Jake boy?" Gert asked.

"Not bad," Jake said.

"And that thar powder'll close that hole up tighter than a tick." Gert pulled the drawstring tight and pushed the pouch into his coat pocket. "And you can betcha she'll keep the 'fection away."

"I assume you mean infection," Clay said.

"Six a one half dozen 'nother," Gert replied.

"All right, enough of the warm and fuzzy feelings," Jake said, "Where do we go from here?"

"With all the commotion, I plumb near forgot," Gert said, "I gots me a bone to be a-pickin with you two."

"Spit it out," Clay said, "We don't keep any secrets around here."

"Good," Gert said, "Cause I aim to lite into ya."The little man walked up to the larger cowboys. He squinted and began to speak. "You done an lied to me, and ol' Gert don't take too well to lying, but I realize you was a-doin it to spare ol' Gert's feelings. Now I know ya know what I'm a-gabbing bout when you blowed my dang fool brother's head plumb off'n his body."

"You got us dead to rights," Clay said, "But that—"

"You bet I do," Gert said, "That sidewinder done an sold me to the erratts so they could have a killin'." Gert paused a moment thinking about his brother. He wiped away a sniffle. "Dad burn mangy rat always had to do things the hard way."

"You gonna be okay?" Clay asked.

"Fine as frog hair," Gert replied, "and to answer your question Jake, we're going to Baine. My older brother 'Hatch' is there. He's spectin us so get a move on. Foller me, boys. I got me a bead on Baine, and it twon't be long afore we is there."

"That may be," Clay said, "But I believe we have company."

A quarter mile to the east three men in a buckboard wagon paralleled Clay, Jake and Gert.

"Apparently, we're not the only ones going to Baine," Clay said.

Gert shook his head several times.

"Yep, this here place is bout to get busier than Splitter Pass durin' the great Tascher migration."

"You want to bet?" Jake asked

"Sure would," Gert replied, "Matter factly, I be willin' to give you two to one odds."

Clay and Jake both took notice at Gert's words.

"How could you know?" Jake asked. "No one can tell how many people will pass through Baine." Jake thought a minute. "Unless you have information you're not passing on."

Gert came to a halt. "Let me tell you something, young feller, Gert don't bow to no man. I tell folks what I know, I tell it straight and I tell it true." He brought out a finger and pointed it towards Jake. "Think bout what ya say a-fer ya say it." He drew his hand back. "And that's all there is to say bout that."

"Gert," Clay said "slow down. You have to admit the claim you made was a little outlandish. Shouldn't you give your friends the benefit of the doubt?"

Gert closed his eyes and lowered his head, raising it a short time later covered with a sullen expression.

"I shouldn't treat you boys that a-way. You been good to ol' Gert, and I'm here to tell ya so. I'm wantin' you to know I've been appreciatin' every bit of it, but sometimes you don't pay enough attention to your pal Gert."

"Don't take this the wrong way," Clay said, "But how can you be so sure?"

"I done an been around a long time, a lot longer than you. I've seen more, including things that'll curl your hair. I've done more, which usually had something to do with getting away from everythin' I'd seen."

Clay cracked a smile which became contagious spreading to Jake and lastly to Gert where he paused a moment before finishing. "And been a lot more places."

"Good enough for me," Clay said.

"Same here," Jake echoed.

SEVENTY-SEVEN

"BAINE CLOSE. WE IS CLOSE?"

"Yeah, we are closer," Victor said, "Hatch, ol' buddy."

"What do you think?"Clive asked, "Are we any closer at all?"

Victor threw his hands up in the air. "Take your pick; when I see it close, you see it far and vice versa. Like I said earlier, we'll know we're there when we trip over ruins or bump into buildings."

"Hatch say now."

Clive and Victor both looked at the little man.

"Now what?"

The right-hand rear of the buckboard slammed into something hard. Every head turned in that direction, but, there was nothing to be seen.

Victor stopped the wagon and met Clive on the other side. The two men spread their arms and walked. Hatch sat patiently on the driver's seat, as the two men searched.

Clive was the first to scrape his fingertips across an eroded concrete block filled with rusted rebar. Each time a piece was touched; it would become visible in a ghostly fashion and return to invisibility.

Victor tripped over something that caused a nasty gash in his boot. He met back up with Clive.

"We're going to need something to make this search a little safer." Victor displayed his boot. "No doubt there are booby traps all over this place."

"Any suggestions?" Clive asked.

By this time, Hatch had made his way over to the two men. He smiled and turned toward the ruins. Hatch took his cane in his hand midway up its length. He held the staff straight out in front of where he stood. Heat waves exuded for an area of several square miles. Different formations began to fade from invisibility, leaving a city in all its ruin.

Clive smiled, "Or we could use Hatch."

"Door no see," Hatch said, "Must cleft in wall push hand, twist, door see."

"Near as I can tell," Victor said, "there's a door that's kept out of sight by a panel, which we will assume is camouflaged. It's opened by a mechanism hidden from view in a cleft close or right beside of the door."

"If you say so," Clive said. "The whole thing confounds me."

"Hatch, do you know where this door is?" Victor asked.

"Aye, however Taggert Lee must wait."

"Taggert Lee?" Victor asked. "What is Taggert Lee?"

"Aye, is Gert."

"Okay," Victor said, "what is Gert?"

"You exactly is Taggert Lee, here is good."

Clive sat on a boulder several yards away. It was all he could do to contain himself for as long as he had.

As Victor, totally frustrated, gave up his line of questioning, Clive burst into a round of laughter that soon become contagious and filtered down to Victor, and even Hatch.

After the outburst and calm was restored, Hatch stood and poked with his cane around the ruins.

"I'm gonna follow him," Clive said. "Why don't you rustle up something to eat?"

"I'm on it," Victor said.

Hatch walked an undetermined distance and then, depending on the area of interest, tapped, poked, prodded or whatever it would take to examine the object with the end of his cane. Sometimes this would bring an interested response, but most often no reaction at all.

Clive was just about ready to retreat back to Victor's home cooking (which brought a subtle blah with it), when Hatch jumped backwards three times, covering about a foot with each springy step.

Hatch tilted his head from side to side and then, grasping the handle of his cane, in one smooth pull, he removed as deadly a blade from its sheath as Clive had ever seen. It wasn't the look of the blade itself, but what could be accomplished with it. This weapon had been purposely placed in the hands of the small man who now wielded it centuries before.

Clive thought it best to leave Hatch on his own. It was about time for a couple bottles of rotgut, maybe three.

SEVENTY-EIGHT

"YOU SEEM TO BE DOING BETTER," Jason said. "Feel like talking?"

Lynch held up a finger, swallowed. "Sure, what's on your mind?"

"We've been here too long; we've got to get on the move. Are you up to traveling?"

Lynch nodded, his mouth once again full of food. He swallowed the last of it and then wiped his mouth with a sleeve.

"That's not what you wanted to ask," Lynch said. "There's no need to sidestep me. If there's something you want to inquire, all you have to do is say the word."

"Then tell me what you know about Baine, and I mean everything. Not just anyone carries what you carry. So give it to me. I want it all and I want it straight."

"Something tells me you're privy to the plan to relieve Aon of its core," Lynch said. "Tell me if I'm wrong, but I'm gonna skip that part."

Jason nodded, "We'll go along with that for now."

"I'm not sure who's at the top of this thing, only that I was to be the number three man. Gaylen number one, Quincy number two. The plan has been in operation for the past eighty years, most of that being prep work. This included building a platform that could transport crude oil from a planet called Earth to Aon. It took seventy of those years to build the platform. An oil extraction unit was constructed and camouflaged on the surface of Earth. As the oil was removed, it shipped to Aon for refinement. The chemical compound we were searching for carried the name of gasoline."

"That's not all," Jason said.

"No," Lynch replied "Early on, there had to be a way to sway the masses from a violent civilization to a more cooperative population. Everyone knows that calladium is the most sought after mineral in the universe. Anyone who owned a firearm, including the military and civilians, possessed a small amount of the mineral."

"The first phase of the plan included injecting chemicals in the food and water sources that would have a sedating effect on the people. This program continued for twenty years before phase two kicked in. Phase two included separating the citizens from their weapons. Alone, this small piece of calladium that powered their weapons was impossible for the individual owner to access. So the government offered to remove the marble sized gem in exchange for the weapon and give the power source to its owner, which would effectively make the owner wealthy."

"This plan was accepted unanimously and the population of Aon wealthy but on the downside, defenseless. And if the entire population now had calladium, they would once again be on an even playing field and all citizens equal financially."

"The military was dismantled. During this process operatives were placed in key positions to oversee the transition. Any opposition would be dealt with by aggressive and permanent measures."

"The population, to further weaken their resolve, were forced to abandon their cities and construct towns modeled after the mid-nineteenth century America. Their obsolete cities now destroyed to a point where they would no longer be safe to occupy."

"The problem as far as the upper echelon began when the program kicked into full gear. This brought oil transports from Earth and began dissolution of Aon's core. Baine, the most logical choice since that's where the planet's thinnest core lies became the withdrawal location."

"The amount of gasoline refined from the crude was much lower than initial testing had shown. Either the crude had been mistakenly tested or thirty percent of the gasoline removed before it reached the Baine refinery."

Lynch looked at Jason. "I know one thing and that's they're hell bent for leather to find out."

"Thanks," Jason said, "We're out of here in an hour."

Lynch held his hand up for everyone to halt and then turned around to face them. Jason turned also and pulled up beside Lynch.

"I've heard some of you speaking about the way Baine appears close and then far away, I understand this may be disconcerting. Lynch will give a simplified explanation of this phenomenon."

"The short of it is there's nothing to be afraid of. To keep people away from the ruins, a spatial generator was placed. The generator will confuse anyone who attempts to reach the city from the time it first comes into view. So your guess is as good as mine when we will reach it, but rest assured, you're not going nuts."

Cassie looked toward the crumbling metropolis. She couldn't tell for sure, but she thought she detected movement. She would have to get closer to determine for sure. Cassie moved to the head of the pack.

"Jason?" she asked.

"Yes, ma'am. What can I do for you?"

"Well, it may be nothing at all, but on our last pass to Baine, which up to this point was our closest, there were people moving toward the city. One wagon and the rest riding ellacks . . . maybe a half-dozen altogether."

"Thanks, Cassie," Jason said, "and don't hesitate to tell me of anything you notice that seems out of the ordinary, no matter how small it may seem."

Cassie dropped back and settled in beside Ruben.

"Well, what did he say?" Ruben asked.

"Keep our eyes open and tell him of anything unusual."

Ruben frowned, "Do you think we can trust him?"

Cassie shrugged and shook her head. "That's the problem he's too hard to read."

"We'll see how things go," Ruben said. "At the first sign of trouble, we're gone."

Lynch and Carl rode silently side by side. Carl's mind pretty much empty, with no stimulus to bring it to life. Lynch wedged deep within himself, a feisty little man called Pops, consuming his thoughts.

SEVENTY-NINE

"WHAT DO YOU THINK" Clive asked.

"Huh, no idea," Victor replied. "Appears to be two men and one stumpy little fella on foot."

"Reckon they're headed to Baine?"

Victor looked at Clive. "Looks like everybody's headed to Baine. I've heard the name so often that I'm not sure that there is any other place than Baine."

"Well, that may be, but it doesn't get us any closer to knowing what they're doing here."

"Why don't we ask?"

"Not yet," Clive said, "but we will start moving to our west which will put us right in their laps in short order."

"I think wer're close enough," Clive said, "I could throw a rock and hit one."

"What do you think, Hatch?" Victor asked.

"Meet is good, I very excited. See brother."

"Whatever that means," Victor said, "We're going in."

Victor steered the wagon toward the two men on ellacks and the small one on foot.

"Well, now, if it isn't my ol' buddy Jake," Clive said. Jake clinched his teeth and nodded. All five men dismounted, and all six came together for the first time.

"Victor this is Jake; we used to work together not so long ago. Jake, shake hands with my man Victor."

A handshake ensued, as did the same courtesy between Victor and Clay and Clay and Clive.

"Looks like you and me are the only two left, Jake boy," Clive said. He extended his hand. "Put 'er there."

Jake placed his right hand into Clive's right hand and plowed his left fist into Clive's right jaw. Clive would have hit the ground had Jake not held him up.

Clive dropped to one knee. Jake leaned over, making sure Clive could understand.

"Now, Clivey boy, does that seem a little familiar?"

Clive held his jaw and nodded.

Jake knelt. "Last time you sucker punched me, so now I figure we're even."

Clive nodded once again, but said not a word.

Jake stood and helped Clive to his feet. "We'll consider this the end of it?"

Clive worked his jaw back and forth. "Yeah."

Clay and Victor walked over to the two combatants.

"Some new form of greeting?" Clay asked.

"Just getting old business out of the way," Jake said.

"What about the two little guys?"

"They've been off by themselves talking since we all met," Clay said.

"You okay?" Victor asked. "He took you down like a sack of doorknobs."

"Yeah, I'll make it and that's the last I expect to hear about it."

Clive walked over to his saddlebags and pulled out two bottles of whiskey.

"Let's have a seat and try to figure out what we're all doing here, provided Jake didn't dislocate my jaw enough to keep it from flapping."

Gert and Hatch conversed for a good thirty minutes. Gert handed Hatch two small pieces of brass. He moved closer to the four men drinking while Hatch left the makeshift camp altogether.

EIGHTY

A SMALL MASCULINE HAND wrapped its fingers around the metal handle and pulled the glass door open. On the side of the building, carved into the stone far above the pavement, were the words "Grand Central Terminal."

Hatch made his way through the grand hall down a set of steps to a bank of lockers. These were tucked away and seemed to be more or less unused. He stood, cane in hand, reading the brass tags.

"Ah, thirteen is number tag." He dug into his pocket and pulled out one key that Gert had supplied before he left. The locker was at a lower level and easily reached by the short man. Of course, this was by design.

He inserted the key into the lock and turned. A hiss indicated that an airlock seal had been broken. Hatch reached into the locker and pulled out a wooden box four inches square and two inches thick. He placed the box in his inner coat pocket. A reverse hiss sealed the compartment, never to be opened again.

Hatch located the signage which would tell him where to board his train to the Trenton Station, boarding time and platform. Hatch took a seat, and within thirty minutes was boarding his train.

"Ticket please," the conductor said.

Hatch removed a stiff rectangular piece of paper from the wooden box he had recovered from the Grand Central Station locker. He handed the ticket to the conductor who punched the proper spaces and then returned the voucher to Hatch.

Hatch removed his hat and sat it along with his cane in the adjacent seat. The blue upholstered seating was pleasing to the eye and rather comfortable. He smiled and giggled to himself as he nestled his balding head into the head rest.

There were three others in this car along with Hatch. Three young men wearing baggy jeans and hooded sweatshirts.

Hatch wondered why they were wearing cold weather clothes on such a nice warm day. *No matter*, he thought. *One own to his each.*

He began to nod off. He closed his eyes for several minutes, then, feeling a presence, he fought back his drowsiness and opened his eyes.

Three young black men hovered over him, one in the aisle and two standing on the seats in front of him facing backwards.

"What we got here?"The kid called Junie said. "Look like a pint-sized Mr. Belvedere." Junie reached over, copped Hatch's bowler and put it on his own head.

"Hat is not you, belong me!" Hatch rose from his seat when one of the other young men, named Babra forced him back down.

"Man, where you learn how to talk? 'Belong me—' what does that mess mean? Hey, J, you hear how this little dude talk?"

"I think he must have mush in his mouth." J drove a fist into the little man's cheek, causing blood to dribble out the corner of his mouth. "Maybe that knock some of that mush out that mouth of yours."

Babra snatched up his cane and wielded it like a sword.

"No, no," Hatch protested.

"Yes, yes sound better to me," as he plowed his fist into Hatch's face two more times. As Hatch caught his breath, he was jerked into the aisle where the three men began to savagely kick and punch him without mercy.

Babra detected the wooden case with an errant punch.

"Hold it, stop." He pulled back Hatch's coat. The little man was bleeding from his mouth and nose with numerous contusions spread around his face and his eyes were swelling.

"What we got here?"He placed his hand into the interior pocket.

"Ah!" Babra screamed. A constant succession of snapping bones, starting at the fingers and worked its way through the radius and ulna. The onslaught ended at the humerus with a clean break on each end. Hatch jumped to his feet and springing toward Junie wrapped his arm around the top of Junie's head. The little man dug three fingers into the skull of the surprised youth. His forward momentum caused him to circle three complete times, leaving just a small amount of Junie's spine attached to his brain stem.

J backed up both hands out.

"No, little man, hurtin' me won't get you nowhere. If you remember, I told them to leave you alone. You remember that, don't you?"

There was no quenching the fire that burned in Hatch's eyes.

"You lie, now you die." Hatch grabbed him by the back of the neck, squeezing until his hand wrapped around his spine. He then pressed his free hand into J's crotch and removed any hint that J was ever a man. With a firm grip around his spine and his other hand grasping the bloody denim, he placed J's back across the top of his feet and pulled down breaking him in half.

Hatch picked his cane off the floor. He turned toward the sobbing Babra and unsheathed a glistening sword. He thrust the blade through Babra's head up to the hilt. It penetrated the floor and scraped against the gravel in the tie beds slowing the train ever so slightly.

Hatch gathered his things, moved to a new car and awaited his call.

"Next stop Trenton."

EIGHTY-ONE

CARL YELPED AS HIS KNEE RAMMED an invisible piece of concrete. The building it was attached to, became visible in outline only, wavered for a moment, then disappeared once again.

"Did you see that?" Carl asked Ruben.

"We all saw it," Lynch said from the front of the small group.

"Remember the talk we had less than a day ago?" Jason said. "How the city appears to move to confuse those who would seek Baine?"

"So what I ran into," Carl said, "was it the real Baine or a manifestation they're bouncing around this desert for idiots to run into?"

"Did it hurt," Lynch asked.

"Yeah, it did," Carl replied.

"Then it was real."

Carl kept silent until his embarrassment; evident in his red face subsided.

"I guess that means we're here," Jason said.

Everyone heard hammers cock, at least one of them a dozen gun.

"Now we all know where here is," Clay said, "But what we don't know is who you are?"

"Kind of hard to talk to a man with any certainty," Jason said, "having a gun in his back."

"That may be," Clay said, "but if you've been through everything we have to get here, you're not willing to relinquish what you had to fight so hard to gain."

"Also true," Jason said. "What do you propose?"

"Drop your sidearms," Clay said, "and that'll give us a chance to check you out."

Clay felt something hard press into his back.

"Ain't droppin' no gun," a strange voice said. "I reckon you best get to droppin'."

"You know what this thing can do that I've got aimed at your people?" Clay asked.

"Don't make me no never mind," the unknown said. "Just you get to droppin' it and twon't nary a one worry bout what that monstrous thing'll do."

"Katie," Jason said. "Is that you?"

"In the flesh."

"That gun he's got pointing our way," Jason said, "will take out at least three including ellacks, and that's with one shot."

"I say that's some mighty fierce sidearm to be totin' around."

"So what do you say?" Jason asked "You going to drop your weapon?"

"I'll do you one better," Katie said.

"And what might that be?" Jason queried.

"Guess it best I be a showin' ya." Katie whirled around and swept her rod low taking Clay down and knocking his gun loose before he hit the ground. Before anyone could react, Jake, Clive and Victor were unarmed and on the ground with Clay.

"Stop! Give it back; ain't got no right to take my staff," Katie yelled.

"You sure nuff ought'n to put a lid on it, little lady," Gert said "All that squallin' makin' my head to bout bust."

"Let me loose and I'll show ya how to bust something. I'll put the pain all over ya."

Everyone in Jason's party dismounted. Clay, Clive, Jake and Victor re-holstered their guns.

Jason eyed Katie with the sternness of a father chastising his child.

"I left you back in Shell; how in the world did you get this far out?"

"Ain't nobody keep Katie stopped up where she don't wanna be."

"You calm down and Gert will let you go," Jason said, "And you can bet we'll be talking about this later, young lady."

Katie slunk back, allowing her lower lip to drop in a pouting fashion.

Clay walked up to Jason and extended his hand.

"I didn't want to bear down on you like that, but I couldn't take any chances?"

"That's okay," Jason said "I'd have done the same thing. At any rate, looks like we've a lot to talk about. If you'll round everyone together, my attention is required elsewhere and I will return shortly."

"Sure," Clay said.

Jason turned to confront Katie. She was sitting on a rock, elbows on her knees and her chin cradled in both hands. Gert stood beside her, ready to pounce if she became unruly.

"Now," Jason said, "tell me what you're doing here and leave nothing out."

"You left me with that old bat Mrs. Carson." Katie said, "And she ain't got no kids my age. She spects me to eat her slimy green stuff and to go to bed afore it gets dark." Katie stood, moved as close as possible to Jason and stared up into his face. "I done and had all I was gonna take, so's I left." She returned to the rock she was sitting on. "And you can't make me go back, no sir, you can't."

Jason shook his head and frowned. He found a place to sit beside the distraught child.

"Sorry, Katie. I thought it best you stay with a proper family after finding you roaming by yourself in the barren zone. As near as we can tell, you're somewhere around thirteen years old. Someone has trained you with various weapons and taught you to survive on your own."

"Then why can't I stay with you?" she pleaded.

"You have what you need to survive in the wild," Jason said, "But you don't possess what you need to exist within a civilization."

Katie sniffled and shuddered as her tears flowed.

Jason wrapped his arms around her.

"Don't worry, for now you can stay with me." Jason sighed. "I must find out what's on everyone's mind. You stay here; we'll figure this out later."

Katie sniffed and wiped her eyes.

"Okay," she said.

Jason passed Ruben and Lynch on his way to address the crowd.

"We never finished what we started at the drilling bed," Ruben said.

"You got an attitude for finishing?" Lynch inquired.

"Nah, just saying."

EIGHTY-TWO

"THE HUE MANS HAVE GATHERED in Caze, the place they call Baine," the core creature Ell said. The crest which was his head resembled a Triceratops less the three bony daggers, the sides of the crest sweeping back for more of an angle than its prehistoric counterpart. A vertical slit in the center of its head served as a mouth, opening and closing sideways when it spoke.

"This is of no concern," Alzar replied. "We shall face them all once the forces of death are released and pave the way for the hue man's eradication."

"How long before this can happen?" Ickta asked.

"They will begin their emergence when they are ready. Until then, we wait."

Ickta paced, moving through the calladium as a human through air.

"I am concerned with the large number of our kind who make up such an integral part of Aon's inner structure. Once they leave to battle the hue mans, if merely for a few minutes, I fear enough of the core will not remain to support the planet."

"It is not your place to question," Alzar chastised, "J. Smith has checked and approved this scenario. You will do what you are told when you are told."

Ickta bowed, using his large, smooth reptilian-shaped rear legs. A long, also smooth tail, thick and stout at its base, feathering to a whip provided stability.

"Yes, your lordship, it will be as you say." The crust slipped against the unstable calladium. It was absorbed by the underground dwellers, but not so much for those above ground.

RUBEN, VICTOR, CLAY AND JAKE were caught by surprise and with nothing to steady themselves save for the ground.

Jason, Cassie, Katie and Gert huddled together steadying each other enough to remain upright.

The rest were close enough to rocks or ellacks (who remain steady with something akin to an internal gyroscope) to prevent falling until the slide ended. Once the initial slide was over, four weaker events at fifteen minute intervals followed until the whole episode concluded.

"I haven't been back on this planet that long," Ruben said, "but I've experienced nothing like that."

"I done an been callin' this here rock home for nigh on ta four hunderd year," Gert said, "and I ain't never seen nuthin' like that neither."

"That's the aim of this discussion," Jason said. "Don't hold back on anything, no matter how small you feel it to be."

"I've got a question for that older fella, the one who spoke right after the slide." Jake said.

A hand went up. "That would be me, the name's Ruben. What can I do for you?"

"You said you've been here a short time. Where are you from?"

"I'm from Aon, but transferred to a planet called Earth." Ruben's nerves were on edge, he proved this by constantly rubbing the stubble on his face.

"So what are you doing here?"

"Believe it or not I had too much drink in a town called Stave—"

"Excuse me," Jake said, "Where is this town . . . Stave is it?"

"It's on Earth," Ruben assured.

"Earth," Jake said. "Please continue, I can't wait to hear this."

"I was in Stave." He raised his eyebrows and gave Jake a stern look. "On a planet called Earth. I stopped in a saloon, had too much to drink and ended up back here."

"Why were you on Earth in the first place?"

"I relocated there to construct a laser drilling platform to extract crude oil from the ground. The crude would be stored, tested and shipped to Aon."

"For what purpose?" Clay asked, beating Jake to the punch.

Ruben shook his head. "Whatever project was going on, (and I assume it was perpetuated by the government) ; each phase was hidden from its sister. Violators were silenced with extreme prejudice."

"Is that it?" Jake asked.

"For now," Ruben replied.

"Fair enough."

"Anyone else—"

"I didn't say I was finished," Ruben interjected, "only that I had nothing else to say."

Jake nodded and stepped back.

"Please," Ruben said, "Stay out front where we can talk."

Jake took a step forward and spread both hands out to the side."I'm all yours."

"Would you mind telling us what you've been up to; oh . . . I don't know. . . the past thirty years?"

Jake shrugged. "I said I was all yours. Until two and a half years ago, I was working for the government."

"And?"Ruben said. "Or are you going to make me work for it?"

"Every letter," Jake said. "So if you please, another question."

"What did you do in your governmental position?"

"Don't like that question; oh, I'll answer it, but at a later date. Next question, please."

Ruben threw his hands in the air."Somebody else take over. I've had enough."

Clay cleared his throat. He took off his hat, preened the feather and placed the Stetson back on his head. "Mr. Lynch, there's a question or two I'd like to ask of you."

By now everyone had found a place to sit, lean, stand or lounge that suited them. Except for the content of their discussion, a passerby would have guessed them to be an outdoor study group.

Lynch sat with his left leg higher than the right. His left forearm rested across the higher leg.

"Just Lynch, you can drop the Mr., and as far as your questions, go ahead and ask. Doesn't mean I'll answer, but you're more than welcome to ask . . . In fact, let me start off by giving you an answer to the first question." Lynch smiled, "no." He laughed until he noticed that he was the only one doing so, and his laughter quickly subsided. Lynch glanced at Clay.

"I've heard the name Lynch before," Clay said. "Never gave it much thought; no reason to until now."

Lynch stared at Clay threw two eye slits.

"When I considered the name, 'Lynch,' it became synonymous with a rumored government-backed plot that would circulate from time to time." Clay was standing against a large boulder. He laughed, looked at the ground, shifted his weight and raised his head, all evidence of his previous jovial behavior gone.

"Yeah," Clay continued, "Every few years a more fantastic version of that same rumor would resurface. There are two things this story always had in common. The first being the enormous stockpile of calladium obtained through extortion, fraud, theft, murder and even genocide; secondly . . . the name Lynch."

Clay pushed the four fingers of each hand into his two front pants pockets up to his thumbs. "Now why do you suppose that is?"

"Don't know," Lynch replied. "Maybe on a planet this size someone else might carry the name, 'Lynch.'"

"Could be, I suppose," Clay said, "That's something worth checking out."

"Why don't you get on that right away?"

Clay smiled and nodded.

"I have a question," Cassie said. "I'm speaking to you three." She pointed at Clay, Jake and Gert.

"What you a-wantin' us fer, lil missy?" Gert said.

"Several evenings ago, did a large boulder move through your camp nearly crushing you?"

"With two people riding on it?" Jake added.

Cassie nodded. "Two very scared people, I might add."

Ruben looked at Cassie, smiling his approval at her comment. "To say that your boulder was moving through our camp is an understatement," Clay said, "unless your idea of moving translates to thirty tons of rock bounding a hundred feet with each stride."

"I'll tell you what you did," Jake began.

Cassie's face dropped, her smile replaced with worry.

Jake smiled. "You saved our lives."

"I'll say fer sure, and dad burn tootin ya did. Them cursed canny's dang near had us fer supper till you smashed four of'em outright and the other two you caught their hind parts. We had a fine time crashing them there varmints' skulls to mush. I'm here to tell ya we did."

"I'll take it from here, Gert," Clay said.

"Ya betcha."

"What were you, and Ruben doing on top of that rock?"

"We thought we were getting away from J. Smith—" Cassie slammed on the brakes.

Clay had to fight to maintain his composure. "I'm guessing you didn't mean to say that?"

"You'd be guessing right." Cassie covered her face with both hands and lowered her head.

"You know my next question?"

Cassie raised her head and nodded.

"There's a race of beings that live within the calladium core. They're being threatened, by whom or why, I haven't a clue. They cannot survive in this atmosphere. Ruben and I were held captive by two of their parasitic creatures.

"They were spider-like. One would stay topside, guarding us and absorbing our atmosphere, while the other would be below ground acclimating J. Smith to our climate. They didn't communicate verbally, but through thoughts, and not to me directly. Any information I gleaned came from what I was able to intercept during their conversations."

"Who is J. Smith?" Clay asked.

"My best guess is what we would call a marshal or the head of security. By watching the parasite's each day, we determined they followed the same regimen. We eliminated the parasites before J. Smith's acclamation was completed. As we made our escape, we learned that J. Smith moved through the ground as fast we could above it."

"That's when we sought shelter atop the boulder."

"We hoped the rock would stop him," Ruben said, "but we were wrong. He bored inside that boulder and caused it to release this tacky fluid that held us fast while the boulder was in motion."

"That wasn't the rock," Victor said, "it was, 'sticky' twitter.'

"Sticky what?" Cassie asked.

"Twitter," Victor repeated. "It's a carnivorous plant that likes to root itself into stone. It's not particular about what it eats, and large prey can uproot it if not firmly anchored. Once something touches its stalks it oozes a clear, sticky fluid (hence the name) that binds whatever has had the misfortune to touch the plant."

"The fluid was uncomfortable," Cassie said, "but as you can see, we weren't eaten."

"That's the strange part," Victor said, "the sticky twitters fluid not only binds what it touches, it dissolves or digests it completely." Victor reached into his pocket, pulled out a small leather pouch and rolled a cigarette. "Ought to count yourself lucky, seems like an agonizing way to go."

"I've seen things that tangled with that bush and gotten away," Jake said.

"What sort of things?" Clay asked.

"That's the problem," Jake said, "I don't know, just things, but I wouldn't want to get too close to one."

"Must have wanted to keep you two around for something," Clay said. "Guess we'll find out soon enough."

"Thanks for the encouragement," Cassie said. "The next time I'm feeling down, maybe I can get you to kick me."

"Sorry," Clay said, "that's the way things are."

"Looks like it's your turn, Vic ol' buddy," Clive said a, noticeable slur in his words. "Why don't you tell everyone about you?"

Victor glared at his compadre.

"Why don't you share that bottle? I see a few faces that could use it."

"This here's purely medicinal." Clive said. He finished the bottle and tossed it into a pile among three others with a clink.

"Guess there's no choice now," Victor said.

"There's always a choice," Jason said. "You don't have to talk, but if you don't, there'll be no trusting you. And considering the position we're in, if you don't have trust, you've got nothing."

"Believe it or not, I used to be a school teacher. After this nonsense with the planet's disarming for a pittance in calladium, no one came to school. And what these fools didn't realize is that they weren't rich. Everyone on the planet received the same portion of calladium, which brought everyone to the same economic status." Victor pulled out his pouch and rolled a smoke. He took a drag, inhaled deeply and released the smoke allowing it to drift upward, kissing his face as it did so.

"A social status of this kind is fine if you're a dust mite, but for humans it is a totally different animal. You see , when everyone has the same as you do, this can cause friction. Depending on how you look at it, you're just as poor or just as rich as the next fella." He took a final drag and crushed the butt under his heel.

"Since we're all human, which inherently makes us greedy, you can bet someone's gonna try to take your stuff. At the same time, you'll be trying to take someone else's stuff, which is why I'm here today. After any need for school teachers went bust, I strapped on my gun belt and joined the fray. I wasn't out to hurt anyone, only to keep my share and get as many of your shares of calladium as possible."

"Go ahead and tell 'em 'bout me and you," Clive said.

"I was getting to that," Victor said. "I met up with Clive here during a small heist. We got to talking, and he made me an offer I couldn't refuse."

"Which was?" Jason asked.

"He had taken up with Marshal Quincy," Victor said, "and although one of Quincy's deputies, he spent most of his time out at Station Point. Before you ask, Station Point was the facility where the oil was refined and the gasoline stored."

This started a barrage of questions.

Jake let out a whistle that would near bout bust your eardrums, and the place quieted down.

"Now if you'll keep quiet and let the man talk, Victor will answer any questions you may have." Jake nodded to Victor.

Victor nodded his appreciation. "What it boils down to is that we're all being duped," Victor said. "A substance called crude oil is being transported from another planet to Aon. The government is refining this oil to remove a chemical that will for a short time dissolve our core's calladium so it can be extracted. What myself and Clive had done was to build a substation so we could intercept the oil before it reached Station Point. That way, we'd do minimal refining, pull off a small amount of gasoline and remove enough calladium to leave this rock and start a better life somewhere else."

"That took courage," Jason said, "however, there will be retaliation if your scheme is discovered." Jason paused, to make sure Victor was finished. "Okay, who's next?"

Jake sighed. "I guess there's no way around it." He stood up and placed a hand on each hip. "I worked for the government seventeen years, in the same place we're standing . . . That's right, Baine."

A slight murmur sifted through the crowd.

"I escaped a little over two years ago. My security clearance wasn't at a level that made me privy to the goings on in the upper echelon. I do, however, have seventeen years' worth of knowledge as to the interior layout, in case we had to go in. Along with that, I've seen many things I feel we could piece together to help plan what we're up against."

"Go ahead," Clay said, "tell them."

"Tell them what?" Jake answered, looking perplexed.

"Remember the night the slash worms nearly devoured us?" Clay asked. "You were about to tell me then what you saw in the case when the worms attacked."

Jake nodded. "There is a restricted area within the complex that required special full body containment attire. This attire included respirators with oxygen and xenon, a secondary containment system that will encase the wearer in a xenon bubble."

"Sounds like high level material," Victor said.

"Dead before you hit the ground," Jake said.

"So get on with it," Clay said. "I'm tired of waiting."

E IGHTY-FOUR

HATCH STEPPED OFF THE TRAIN. He heard sirens unrelated to his incident three cars down. Glancing to the left, he saw police, EMTs and body bags on stretchers. He hastened his pace, slowing when he reached the lobby. Hatch looked around until he found what he was searching for. Just past the ticket counter on the left was a bank of small lockers.

He searched through the numbers. A smile crossed his face.

"Thirteen we is again." Hatch pushed in the key, and just as before, the hermetically sealed door hissed, releasing air that was older than the ages themselves. Hatch removed an article wrapped in a purple silken fabric. He stored this along with the wooden box obtained from the previous locker in his inner coat pocket. He set the key on the floor of the locker and closed the door.

He waited several seconds until he heard the familiar hiss, telling him the door had sealed, before he took off for the ticket counter. He pulled the last ticket from the wooden purse and waited in line.

"There he is!" A large bearded man said. "He's the only one I noticed leaving the car where the dead were found."

Hatch saw four men dressed in blue, carrying handguns. These weren't revolvers, but something called an aw-tow-matic. Hatch wasn't sure what that meant, but he knew he didn't like being on the business end of that aw-tow-matic.

"Send two more units—one from the north and one from platform A. Leave two men up top and send the other two down, we'll converge in the lobby."

"Roger that."

"Suspect is five feet tall, dressed in a dark suit, bow tie, derby, spats and carrying a cane. Over."

"You ain't been drinking, have you there, Chief? Over."

"Look sharp or you'll wish I had been. Over."

Ten men entered the lobby covering all possible exits.

They surrounded the area, making sure no one could leave without being checked by an officer.

After the last person left:

"Kind of hard to miss someone dressed like you described," Bryant said.

"This is Kimble, anything on the platform? Over."

"All quiet up here. Over."

"Now I want somebody to tell me," Kimble began, "how a midget in a clown suit got past a dozen of New Jersey's best?" The sergeant stood there awaiting an answer. When none came: "Not everybody at once, ladies, we got plenty of room."

The small figure crawled nimbly through the bar joists in New Jersey's Trenton train station. He dropped out of the ceiling in a remote corner over a handicapped bathroom stall. Hatch stopped long enough to straighten his tie in the mirror, then made the platform and boarded the train returning to Grand Central Station.

After eluding police a second time, Hatch stood before a solid door with a long narrow rectangular shaped sign. It was mounted just above eye level. The sign read "Janitor's Closet."

He removed his hat and inserted his fingers along the top edge of the sweatband where the hat size had been sewn in. Hatch pulled out an irregular shaped piece of brass similar to those given to him by Gert. He slid it into a corresponding void in the center of the doorknob and turned. The latch released, allowing the door to swing free. He returned the implement to its original holding place, set his hat on his head and slipped through the opening, pulling the door closed as he did so. The door latched and faded until a masonry wall remained.

E I G H T Y - F I V E

"ONCE THE TOXIC FOG HAD CLEARED, I committed what was in the case to memory; the problem being, I wasn't sure what I was memorizing. I've had several years to determine what I was looking at, and I'm still not sure, although I have settled on one viable theory. After careful consideration, I determined that they must be weapons. I couldn't tell you what they look like other than they're about the same length as one of our rifles."

"Can't you be a little more specific?" Clive asked.

"Just hold your ellacks, I'm getting there. It's hard to tell which end is which. They're different from each other, but neither come right out and say 'I'm the barrel' or 'I'm the stock.' What I assume to be the trigger is off center, which makes me believe the long side is the barrel and the short side the stock."

"Do you have any idea what it does?" Carl asked, not understanding any part of what was said, but wanting to appear knowledgeable.

Can't these idiots hear? Jake thought. *I only had a few seconds to access the crate.*

"No, I don't," Jake said, "But they weren't made for humans to use."

"You sure?" Victor asked.

Jake nodded. "Yes, I am."

"How?" Carl replied.

"There was no place to accommodate a human hand. The entire unit was straight with flowing curved trenches, notches, some short and some long carved throughout the weapon. It was smooth with a matte black finish and no visible means to load or fire. And to answer your question, it was wider than what a human could comfortably handle.

"After that, I sealed the case and returned to my work. I thought I had gotten by with it until two days later I was called in, read the riot act and demoted. They couldn't prove anything, but they had a good idea. The reason for the demotion was one: they made the rules, and two: they hoped the grunt work that came with the demotion would encourage me to quit. If they made conditions so deplorable as to push me out of there, I would be eliminated without any questions. I was sure of what they were trying to do, so I stayed on to prove; not only to my employers, but to myself they'd never break me. It took several more years, but I felt the paranoia was at such a high level, extermination was imminent. Since we all lived in the facility, I had to wait until one of our few outdoor exercise breaks. I feigned sickness to get away from the crowd, then never looked back."

Jason quelled any questions in favor of new information. He zeroed in on Lynch.

"How about it, Lynch, odds are you've got something to add."

"I reckon," Lynch said, "but what's in it for me?"

"You've got the wrong attitude," Clay said, "What's in it for you, is telling us what you know so we can combine our information and stay alive. Or you can keep quiet and hope you make it out in one piece."

Clay removed his gun from its holster. "Now, depending on your answer, you'll either stay or go, and I mean now. I'm not doing this for retribution, I've just got a strong hunch you're privy to information we can use." He stared at Lynch for a moment. "If you solely possess information that we all should know, it's likely to get everyone here killed, so start talking or get stepping."

"And just in case you need more incentive," Jason said, "President Gaylen's dead."

Lynch's eyes widened and his mouth dropped open.

"We don't have the luxury of time," Jason said, "What's it going to be?"

Lynch sighed. "Looks like I'm your new best friend."

Clay holstered his gun. "Let's hear it."

"What a lot of you don't know is that a plot to remove all or most of Aon's core was conceived close to a century ago. A race of offlanders called Triveks contacted the government officials of that time, concocted the plan and set it into motion. They're a benevolent race and shy away from conflict. They knew if they disarmed the planet and plied them with the illusion of wealth the Triveks would be free to remove the very ground beneath their feet."

Lynch looked at Jason. "Before I say anything else, you have to promise me I won't be hurt or even worse."

Jason looked at Clay.

Clay nodded. "Consider yourself lucky, old man. Had you not caught me on a good day, you'd be splattered all over these great outdoors."

"Okay," Jason said, "The floor is yours."

"Grr," Lynch grunted. "The hopes of the Triveks turned out to be true as the population, so enamored with their little blue stones, spent most of their time acquiring additional blue stones. Not to mention a microchip and a compound distributed to every other generation, helped the population lean toward the passive side. They kept the appropriate politicians bribed down through the years so their plan didn't take an unnecessary turn. I was more or less second in command underneath Gaylen, with Quincy under me. Specific persons were to be eliminated to avoid having to divide the calladium more ways than necessary."

"Just upper echelon government types, I hope," Clay said.

"No," Lynch said, "You'd be surprised; in fact this process has already begun. The old man, Pops,was one of the first."

"You killed Pops, you filthy snake," Jake said.

"Nothing personal, just business," Lynch replied.

"Whadda ya mean, 'just business?'" Jake said. He reached for his sidearm.

A large arm swung around his neck from behind and relieved him of both revolvers.

"You'll get these back when you calm down," Clay said. He looked at Lynch. "Keep flapping those gums, I'm beginning to like you."

"Hold on to that sentiment, you're gonna need it after this next confession. Gaylen sent down orders to destroy the saloon with you and Jake in it."

"And the arms Jake discovered at the facility in Baine?"

"As far as the weapons," Lynch said, "Gaylen mentioned a subplot that would allow the creatures that reside within the calladium to acclimate to this atmosphere. They would destroy the human population, and as they did, the weapons they used would drain the life from them."

"Why didn't you mention this?" Jason asked.

"I thought it too extreme to be believable."

"With everything that's going on, how dare you dismiss anything that would prove so devastating," Clay snarled. He shook his head. "You'll be lucky if I'm able to maintain the promise I made before you started flapping your gums."

"Anything else you got to say that may further endear us to you?" Clay asked.

"I want to know why Lynch is talking like he's got an education and not using that trail talk he normally does?" Ruben asked.

"When confronting anyone outside of our headquarters protocol was to speak as the residents of the area to avoid suspicion."

"Jason," Clay said, "shut him up before I blow his head off. I'm sure his body could use a vacation from his mouth."

"Okay, Lynch," Jason said, "you're done."

Clive raised his hand. "Reckon I got something to say."

"Have at it," Jason said.

"Most of you know me as a deputy here in Baine," Clive said, "Looks like we've got a mess that'll take all of us to straighten out. What I've got to say may help. I was working along the seventh parallel about three years ago. A businessperson approached me with a proposal I chose not to refuse. I signed on for a small job with a quick turnover and lucrative compensation. I didn't realize it was this big and once you got in; there was one way out."

Clive fidgeted. He removed a rather large flask, from a sewn pocket inside his vest, drank half, replaced the top and pushed it back into his vest.

"I was told to make Baine as fast as possible, look up Marshal Quincy, and he would fill me in and get us started. Being a deputy was just a cover. I spent more time at Station Point and running ludicrous errands for the marshal, there was no time to be a deputy." Clive sighed.

"This is gonna take forever," he muttered to himself. "There's only one of you who has heard of Station Point. To the rest I'll have to explain. When I would travel to Station Point, I would transfer by splitter or by ellack if I wanted transportation while there. On one trip by ellack, I ran into Victor." Clive nodded in Victor's direction. Victor pinched the front edge of his hat with his index finger and thumb, acknowledging his presence.

"We talked over a bottle of fine rot gut. I sized him up and I guess he did the same. About the time we stared at the bottom of an empty bottle, we came to the same conclusion. Since we were moving down the same road it would be made easier with a partner to share the load." Clive stood and leaned back against several large flat rocks stacked one on top the other.

"To make a long story short, we pilfered enough material from Station Point to construct a small extraction station. We placed it between Station Point and the off-loading platform accepting the crude from Earth. Victor and I intercepted the viscous liquid and using a cold refining process siphoned off a third of the gasoline it contained. We left to check with Quincy in Baine to make sure he hadn't caught on to what we were doing. He was nowhere to be found, and the word circulated he'd left town for good." Clive shrugged. "And that's, give or take, why we're here." He turned his attention toward Lynch.

Lynch looked at Clive."Is there some reason you need to focus your thoughts on me?"

"You don't remember me, do you," Clive said, "No, I don't guess you would, you didn't see me that night, but you can bet I remember you."

"It would help if you would be a little more specific."

"I'm not sure what you call it, but do you still carry that weapon?"

"Again," Lynch said, "specificity would be nice."

"Let me clear things up for you then," Clive said. "About thirty years ago on a planet without a name that held every piece of human refuse imaginable; you walk into one of a thousand dark alleys."

"Get to the point," Lynch said, "You're headed nowhere fast."

"In this particular alley you chose to slice an eleven year old friend of mine in half with that handy little weapon of yours." Clive turned to face Lynch, his hand inching toward his sidearm. "And all for a little blue marble."

"Who are you?" Lynch demanded, "There's no way you can prove it was me."

"We both know it, and that's all that matters."

Clive felt a hand on his wrist.

"He ain't worth it," Clay said, "and I think he may be of some use later on."

Clive nodded. "Okay, I'll give it a while longer."

"Anything you want to add to Clive's statement." Jason asked, looking at Victor.

Victor shook his head.

"Nothing that's pertinent to this situation."

To this situation, Jason thought. He filed the comment in the recesses of his mind.

"We haven't heard from Cassie," Jason said. He looked in her direction. "How about it, young lady? I bet you got plenty to say."

"To start off," said Cassie, "I'm an offlander from the very planet the powers that be are stealing the crude oil from. As the men were constructing the drilling platform not far from where I lived, I happened upon the uncompleted facility before they could finish the camouflage."

Cassie recalled that time in her life and it brought a smile to her face. "To make a long story short, I became involved with Derek, who was the foreman. In the months that ensued, I led him to believe that I was interested in marriage and would move to his planet. He trusted me completely and naturally shared what he could about the operation. When we finally made it to Aon, I moved into his house in Shell. I got him drunk the first night and off I went. I wanted my share of caladium, which made Baine my destination." Cassie perceived a dozen pairs of eyes burning through her.

"Don't any of you judge me, I still feel regret over what I did to Derek, but not a single one of you understands what my life was like before I moved to Aon." Cassie paused several minutes allowing what she said to not only sink into her audience but into herself as well.

"Knowing that a schoolhouse in Baine had yet to be built, I presented yours truly as the new schoolmarm, waiting for the building to be completed. I introduced myself to Quincy, and right away I recognized he would be a pushover. I threw around some names that would plant fear into him. Even though I didn't know these men, I now had the good marshal in the palm of my hand."

"How did you come to be in the company of the beings that lived in the calladium core?" Jason asked.

"In the wrong place at the wrong time, I guess," she said. "I was able to communicate telepathically with these creatures. They kept me there to assist with undertakings they were unable to accomplish due to their lack of hands. Even though I was allowed to leave, the mind control they held over me assured that I would always return. I think the reason I brought Ruben into the fold was purely for human companionship."Cassie looked at Ruben, her expression filled with remorse. Ruben just smiled and nodded, reassuring Cassie that he harbored no malice.

"We were able to escape, and once again to make a long story short, we ended up here."

EIGHTY-SIX

HATCH WALKED IN-BETWEEN THE ELLACKS and slid into the camp unnoticed, save for his brother Gert.

"Did ya git 'er?" Gert asked.

"Got is get," Hatch replied.

"Lemme see," Gert said.

Hatch removed the wooden box and the wrapped article from his inner coat pocket. He pushed an inlaid square that ran the length of the box one half inch from top to bottom. Next he slid another insert that ran from left to right. The box hissed.

"Thar she go," Gert exclaimed.

"What are is?" Hatch inquired.

"Jest what we be needin' to get this here party started."Gert removed the top and let it fall away. Inside there was a black cross shaped piece of pure carbon. The cross was four inches tall and the horizontal piece two inches wide.

"Looky thar," Gert said. "Ain't she 'bout the prettiest thin ya ever did see?"

A small white dot of light in the center of where the two pieces joined grew. It formed two points of light near each end of the horizontal member and a single point an inch up from the bottom of the vertical member.

"Beauty, pretty, good stuff," Hatch said.

Gert handed the cross to Hatch.

"Here ya be," Gert said, "You hold onto that whilst I fish out what's wrapped up in this here cloth." He removed something he held between his right index finger and thumb. The object was so small that his finger and thumb touched.

"I can't hardly believe it," Gert said.

The object was so bright that even in the noonday sun, they had to shield their eyes.

"Bring that cross you is a-holdin', Hatch," Gert said.

Hatch swung around, giving his brother access to the artifact. Gert lifted a door on the top of the cross. He dropped the tiny piece he held in his right hand through the narrow opening and shut the small door. The seams sealed, removing any sign that an opening ever existed. Gert and Hatch both rubbed their eyes, waiting for the spots to disappear.

"Gert," Clay said, "where are you?"

"Over this a here way," Gert replied. He waved a hand, which came above the ellack's back.

Clay heard Gert's voice, but had to scan the area until he saw the fingers wiggling above the animal's back.

"Come on up here Gert," Clay said "I'm sure you got plenty you could add to what's been said so far."

Gert took the cross and shoved it into the base of his sword. The horizontal member of the cross was longer than the thickness of the sword handle. To his amazement, he watched the cross push, unhindered through the metal and fold into the already withdrawn hilt. The blade being retracted, he slipped the neutral looking weapon back into his belt.

"You best be believin' ol' Gert's got things plenty enough to tell ya. When ya done and lived in one spot fer pert near three hunderd and fifty year, you gits to knowin' thins. Don't matter if you was to live in a hole in the ground with a sack over your head. Thar jest ain't no way you can hep it." Gert paced back and forth, keeping one hand on his blade.

"Now you'ns listen close to what I got to say cause it might be the only time ya git." He'd take three steps then reverse course. "First off, we got to watch out for them goonies down under this here ground. That's something that's gonna take us all to look after. Then we gotta get us up a posse to head into this here place where Jake worked. You kin betcha we'll get us some good info down yonder in that place. We gonna do away with this here gasoline and get this rock that we been a-livin' on for quite a few year back to where she belong. And that be my hands and all your hands."

Gert's speech caused an upwelling within the crowd and an urgency to move.

A small vibration began in Aon's crust, intensifying quickly. Cracks appeared opening into caverns. Everyone, including ellacks ,slid beneath the surface. The ground groaned as it moved back into place, uniting above and below dwellers together for the first time.

EIGHTY-SEVEN

"EVERYONE ALL RIGHT?" Jason asked. He heard a flood of yeses and assorted moans and groans. Once they came together and assessed the situation, they found minor injuries among the humans and one ellack with a broken leg.

"Look at that ceiling," Clay said. "It's almost as if it's one huge trap door."

"How ya figger?" Gert asked.

"Very little debris came in with us, and look how flat the entire ceiling is, not to mention the visible seams."

"You think someone planned this interaction with whatever lives down here?"

"I'll be glad to answer that for you," a new voice said.

Ruben recognized him instantly. "You were in the bar that day I came in and ordered a beer," Ruben said, his excitement having worked him into a frenzy. "Remember that bar in Stave? I asked you how you were doing." Ruben paused, took a deep breath and then continued. "All you did was grunt; but I knew there was something about you I could read, but you refused to let go."

"Ruben," Cassie said, "Calm down, I saw him there too. He didn't impress me then and I see no difference, other than he's here now."

"Allow me to interrupt if I may," the stranger said. "Folks call me Zachariah. I apologize for the rude entrance into this underground cavern. I'm afraid had I waited any longer each of you would have been eliminated by an Azurian death squad."

"That's a new one on me," Clay said, "what's an Azurian death squad?"

"The underground dwellers who live within the calladium, have been acclimating several thousand of their brethren for many years. Once they leave the underworld they will branch out into parties of six. These small groups can live in our above ground atmosphere for three days, and then they must return to their subterranean existence for a minimum of twelve hours. The ground slide you felt and your ultimate ending here directly resulted from the death squads being loosed. They will quell any uprisings (beginning with you) and pave the way for human annihilation courtesy of the Azurian warriors."

"Azurian warriors?" Clive questioned.

"The Azurians are a warrior race," Zachariah said. "They do not eat, drink nor reproduce. They exist for one thing, and that, my friends, is war. To mention the name Azurian is to imply all."

"So we'll be facing the entire population," Clive said. He finished the contents of his flask. "Could be fun, I suppose." He pushed himself away from the rock he'd been leaning against.

"Any suggestions?" Jason asked.

"Yes," Zachariah responded, "Use this area as somewhat of a home base. It still contains enough of your atmosphere to support life and yet allows travel above ground and deeper toward the core."

Jason nodded.

"This place you have us cooped up in?" Clay asked. He reached down, grabbed a small stone and tossed it into the air, catching it as it fell toward the ground. "You want to shed a little more light on how and why it's here. I'll admit it's convenient, but just a little too convenient, if you know what I mean; and who are you? Talk about the right place at the right time, this whole situation smells."

"I understand your suspicion," Zachariah said, "Please allow me to begin with your last question. I belong to a group of believers. We have existed two thousand years. Since our conception we have taken the name Rex Regum."

Jake nudged Clay.

"Sun worshipers."

"Ah," Clay said, while tilting his head backward.

"As for this place," Zachariah continued, "its construction dates back many centuries. My people, through prophetic teachings learned how, where, and why it must be built. The day of its initial usage has been heavily guarded so as not to be missed, for if this were to happen, all would be lost." Zachariah looked upon the face of each person present. "How unfortunate that today has become that day."

"Good answer," Clay said. "That does it for me. I don't go in for nonsense like gods, worship and such, but that's for another day."

"Clay Deveau," Zachariah said. "Take care when you utter a phrase that suggests finality and contempt for what you do not understand. Such words are not so easily ingested once released."

"I done kept my mouth shut long enough," Katie said. "Since Zachariah is here now, I figure it be safe to talk up some of my fears."

"It's all yours," Jason said.

"Zachariah here was the one what trained me to take care of myself. If it weren't fer him I doubt I'd be here talkin' at ya now."

"Katie," Jason said, "it's about time you headed home."

"Too dangerous," Zachariah said. "They'd do her in before she could get twenty steps from here."

"I guess you got what you wanted," Jason said to Katie. "Stay close, keep your eyes open and listen."

Katie smiled and nodded.

"One thing I can't seem to shake," Cassie said. "If the Azurians have concocted a plan this detailed, then why not send one of the elite air breathers after me and Ruben. It makes no sense, risking the commander of the entire race."

"What makes you think he is the Azurian leader?"

"I was able to glean that much from the two bugs that incessantly wiped his nose."

Zachariah nodded with an ever so subtle smile on his face.

"Ahh!" Carl screamed, "What are you trying to do, pull my arm off?"

"Now good is?" Hatch asked.

Carl raised his eyebrows as he worked his shoulder in a circular fashion. "Hey, it hardly hurts at all. What did you do?"

"Found shoulder, good eh," Hatch answered.

"Found shoulder?" Carl asked.

"He means relocate," Victor said.

"Yeah," Carl said. "Thanks, thanks a lot."

"I can see the wheels spinning," Jake said, "But nothing's coming out of your mouth."

"It's hard to know where to begin," Zachariah said. "This is purely conjecture; however, it is within the operational parameters of the Azurians. We can be sure that J. Smith would not be used as one of the death squad. If this were the case, his people would have no leader, since the acclimation process requires a form of suspended animation where the subject is unconscious for the entire process."

"Why not appoint someone to take his place?"

"This would never happen," Zachariah said, "The Azurians are a petty race, unwilling to relinquish anything they have attained. By the same token, they are always on the lookout to seize power by using any means."

"But why did J. Smith go to the extremes of living underground to become acclimated to our atmosphere for short periods of time? Employ two goons to watch after him, use the same to kidnap me, use me to procure Ruben, bore into a rock to follow and ultimately capture us. Then take us to Ruben's drilling platform to get a chunk of metal."

"You have answered your own question," Zachariah said.

Cassie sat on the floor, her arms wrapped around folded legs, her chin resting on her knees. With Zachariah's statement, she rolled onto her haunches, her hands firmly against her thighs bearing her upper body weight.

"Boy, I can't wait to hear this explanation."

"The reason J. Smith went to such lengths," Zachariah said, "was to obtain, as you refer to it, 'that chunk of metal.' With this piece, he could single-handedly shut down the operation the humans had devised to liquefy the calladium to deplete the core. This also tells us that the Azurians are aware of the humans' plans. This knowledge may have caused them to expedite their takeover, or have been the singular cause for their action against the humans." Zachariah removed his hat and let his arm fall to his side. He pushed his empty hand through his long salt and pepper hair, shaking his head in deep sorrow. He seemed to talk to someone unseen yet there. Several minutes later his head rose, a tear-streaked face confirming his sorrow.

"How many lives will be given in loss, the greed of man never fails to disappoint."

"You mentioned an effective way to fight these freaks," Clay said.

"Yes," Zachariah said. "I have noticed your—"

BAM!

A concussive noise echoed throughout, sending shock waves to all points of the underground den.

"What was—"

Another tremor along with a deafening blow ensued, this time shaking the den, throwing bodies to the floor.

"Is there another way out of here that will accommodate the wagon?" Clay asked.

"Yes," Zachariah replied, "Follow me."

"On your ellacks and the rest in the buckboard," Clay barked.

As all forms of transportation loaded, Zachariah began his trek toward the rear entrance.

The buckboard was the last to leave the open area and enter the tunnel which led to the exit. As Zachariah pushed through the rear exit, the six strong, death squad crashed through the dense ceiling. One glance told the pursuers the way to go.

The wagon cleared the small doorway. Moments later the death squad followed suit.

Victor was once again piloting the wagon with Clive riding shotgun. Zachariah, Clay, Jake, Cassie, Ruben and Jason along with Katie were aback ellacks. Carl, Lynch, Gert and Hatch were passengers on the buckboard.

Clive nudged Victor. "Looks like we got company."

"Do I need to ask what?"

"Don't ask, just drive."

The six assassins were a smooth azure color, and gave the impression of a reptilian background. Powerful rear legs propelled the creatures at speeds consistent with an ellack.

The drag of the wagon on the ellack engines made the four wheeled cart the slowest of the caravan. The death squad anticipated this and zeroed in on their first victim.

As the first creature reached the rear of the buckboard, the end of its left arm took on the shape of a hook, its right a double-edged sword, resembling a claymore. The creature dug the hook into the wooden tailgate and the wagon slowed. As the five other creatures moved alongside the buckboard, the humans riding ellacks turned, desperate to help their own kind in this impossible situation.

Shots bounced off the creature without leaving a mark. Victor and Clive both emptied and reloaded their weapons to no avail.

Passengers in the back pressed tight against the driver's seat, it being the farthest point from the Azurians.

The seven humans aboard ellacks watched, unable to assist their comrades.

Jason moved alone toward the wagon. Gert knelt down, back toward the aggressors. The Azurian with the left handed hook and massive blade on the right raised his arm to strike.

Hatch jumped to the middle of the buckboard.

"Brother, be sorry die you is now!" Hatch dropped onto all fours.

Gert rose and whirled in one smooth motion. His face decorated with double stripes (one red and one black) starting at the bottom of his eyes and ending at his jawline. His right foot landed on Hatch's back. Using it as a springboard, his left foot landed on the middle creature's head. Gert's momentum put him in the perfect position to strike. He removed the plain silver cylinder from his belt. He wrapped both hands around the weapon. A blinding white light shot from the cylinder. He brought the deadly blade through the raised arm of the first Azurian attacker, severing his appendage at the shoulder.

"Let's move!" Clay barked. "It's our turn."

The ellack riders charged the wagon.

Hatch followed Gert closely behind. He jammed his walking stick through the hook embedded in the tailgate. As he jumped off the wagon, Hatch wrenched the hook free. He brought the arm down, causing the hook to wrap itself around the Azurian's leg.

Gert removed the creature's head as its grappled leg tugged it to the ground, the hook severing the leg at the knee as it bounced along the road.

Surprised, the other five slowed unsure of what to do. Seconds later they were after the wagon again. They seemed to pay no attention to their fallen comrade, who with half a leg, no head and one arm still attempted to complete his mission.

The wagon came to a stop, now joined by the rest of the party. Clay, Jake, Clive, Victor and Carl continued to fire and reload for distraction.

"At their feet," Clay said. "Fire at their feet."

The slugs tore into the earth, sending up a curtain of dust and debris.

"Down, ya cursed consarn buzzard," Gert said. He was busy chopping one of the death squad members down, removing slice after slice until the creature's head was on the ground.

Hatch sped around the three remaining Azurians, presenting a target they could not hit.

"You too."

Gert brought his weapon down, removing the tail of another Azurian, causing it to tumble backward.

Gert was the first to notice the remaining two creatures retreating.

Moments later, Jason passed by with his eyes fixed on what remained of the death squad. He extended a hand, motioning for all hostilities to cease.

The creatures continued to back away, not taking their eyes off of Jason. They increased their speed, turning around and fleeing, hoping to avoid him.

Jason didn't pursue, but turned and joined his group.

Eighty-Eight

"HOW LONG HAS THE FLOW OF GASOLINE been off?" Raymond Petimore asked. His voice echoed through the three story metal enclosure that was the last vestige of the CR&D. A minimum of four guards manned the two tiers of catwalks at all times.

"Ever since the operation started several weeks ago," Nate said. "The first run was so low grade it was unusable. That shipment ran out about a week ago." He rechecked the incoming tanks just in case a shipment had slipped by. None had. "Since then, the tanks have been dry, nothing in, nothing out."

"Why, that simply won't do," Petimore said, "I refuse to accept such incompetence."

Nate chuckled to himself. *The old man is so far behind the times,* he thought. *He doesn't realize that this project doesn't revolve around him, even if he is the senior tech.*

"Time to razz the old coot."

The two men were stationed ten feet across from one another. Each man's workstation was six feet long and covered with controls, gauges and warning lights. These consoles would look more at home in the cockpit of a star cruiser than the workstation of a glorified roughneck.

Nate whistled as he sauntered from behind his console, around the end and into Raymond Petimore territory. He wore a gray flannel shirt, sleeves rolled up, the collar, and pocket flaps having never seen an iron were permanently curled and wrinkled. His blue jeans were normal among his age group (twenty-five to thirty) as were his decades-old, decrepit tennis shoes. Nate placed his hand on the shoulder of a man forty years his senior.

"How goes it, Ray, didn't that dingy lab coat you're wearing used to be white?"

Raymond Petimore was gray-haired and clean-shaven whereas his counterpart, Nate chose the more laid-back, unkempt, never cut, never shave persona.

Petimore knocked the hand from his shoulder. He rose and whirled, backing Nate against the wall. The older man stood several inches taller than the boy. This, along with Petimore's reaction, both surprised and intimidated Nate.

The tide now turned, the aggressor removed his glasses and began to shake them in Nate's face.

"My name is Mr. Petimore to you. I do not know where you received your training or your manners; however, I am unimpressed with both. Count yourself fortunate to be working in Baine, the last scientific laboratory on Aon. Do your job and nothing more, understand?"

Nate nodded.

"Good. Are there questions?"

"Why are you the only one who has a last name?"

"The answer is simple. They felt last names were no longer necessary, which is beyond me." Petimore shook his head and shrugged. "I've stopped trying to figure them out and am sticking with my last conclusion."

"Which is?" Nate asked, now cultivating a newfound respect for this man.

"They are all idiots. And since I have no way off this wretched rock, I shall stay here and do my job to the best of my ability." He glanced at Nate from head to toe. "And I expect the same from you."

"I'll give you my best."

"Back to monitoring the incoming tanks; the next shipment could be any time now."

EIGHTY-NINE

"THE FIRST GROUP OF ENFORCERS encountered the Hue Mans with disastrous results," Alzar said. "Three rendered unusable and the remaining two forced to retreat."

"How is this possible?" Ickta asked. "Calladium is indestructible."

"This may no longer be the case, or are you unable to deduce that for yourself?"

"There are no words," Ickta said.

"Just as well, I hold audience with J. Smith. Send word that all enforcers within two days travel of Baine shall converge upon the ruins and eradicate all life—Hue Man and otherwise."

"Alzar," Ickta said, "if I may?"

"Then speak, I mustn't tarry."

"The three Azurians dissected in Baine. . ." Ickta paused, fearing retribution, and then continued. "Could it be—"

"Speak not of this again," Alzar roared. "The three destroyed by a tiny Hue Man wielding a weapon never before seen, is not a prophetic fairy tale." Alzar pushed through the calladium until his face touched Ickta's. "Do you understand?"

Ickta nodded.

Alzar turned to leave.

"Do not be so hasty to discard the old notions," Ickta muttered. "Such things have ways of creeping up and severing one's tail."

NINETY

"NATE," PETIMORE SAID, "check the incoming lines and the three aft tanks for any sign of product."

Nate entered four separate codes and then tapped the Enter button on his keyboard. The screen flashed to life. He scanned the information.

"No, sir—nothing in or out." Nate finished rolling the joint away from prying eyes. The modesty panel on the front of his station saw to that.

"Keep checking," Petimore said, "I've sent a message to Ruben at the drilling station on Earth, but as yet have heard nothing."

"Uh, Mr. Petimore, I'm going to step outside for some fresh air."

"Very well. Take care not to wander outside of the compound."

"Back in a sec." The young man sprang from his seat, passing one guard on his way out. "Don't wait up."

The guard grunted.

Nate had to wait for three separate doors. For each he would have to swipe his I.D. card, endure a retina scan and finish with his thumb print. He burst out of a small door in the back of the building. Removing the doobie from his sock, he placed one end in his mouth and lit the other. Nate leaned against the wall, his right leg bent at the knee with his foot flat to the wall.

He pulled hard on the stick and breathed deeply, holding the smoke in until he was forced to cough.

"Man, I'd go through a hundred doors for just one hit of this."

Nate was the sole occupant of an outdoor compound designed to hold several hundred in Baine's heyday, when the city was a sprawling metropolis and not the pile of rubble it had become. The chain-link fence had been replaced with an Armor Guard brand "Rifle 2000" barrier. The loosely woven strands allowed an onlooker to see through, no matter which side they were on. Touch the fence from the inside and treat yourself to a warm tingly feeling meant to interact with the brain's synapses to produce a calming effect.

Touch the same fence on the outside and prepare to wake-up thirty feet or more away, smoldering and smelling of burnt hair, if you were fortunate enough to wake-up at all.

Nate hit his smoke a second time.

"Man, I don't know what's in this stuff I'm smoking, but there's some big, funny looking blue things walking through the fence and headed my way." He took another drag, closed his eyes and then opened them again. "They're still coming, I best be getting inside."

Nate put the joint in his mouth and turned to open the door. The color drained from his face and his heart began to palpitate wildly. Entrance through this doorway was strictly forbidden. He had forgotten to prop the door open to reenter the facility. Nate sensed a presence behind him, he continued to face the door and brought his cheeks together sucking hard on what would be his last stoner. He turned around.

"Wow, you are big." Nate stood looking up at the ten foot giant. The young man offered the last of his smoke to the Azurian. Out of curiosity, the blunt end of a blue arm grew two long, fingerlike pincers. The arm moved toward Nate's hand.

Nate smiled at the thought of his gift being accepted. The giant pincers close in on the smoking roach. It grasped the end of Nate's thumb and index finger. Now surrounded by Azurian's, Nate dropped to his knees, eyes and mouth wide open as his fingers were removed along with the ashes of the dying joint. A large blue hand, still sprouting fingers as it lay atop the young man's head and curved down each side applied pressure. A dull pop signaled the end.

NINETY-ONE

SINCE THE JAILHOUSE where Carl worked and Cassie's flat were both in Baine, that's where they started.

Cassie produced a sawed-off double barrel twelve gauge with a modest amount of ammunition.

"Six shells," Carl complained. "Is that the best you can do?"

"I know I should have been better prepared to blast walking chunks of calladium," Cassie said, "but it slipped my mind." She stared at Carl until she brought herself under control. Cassie pushed a lever, and the gun broke in half at its hinged point. She removed two more shells and tossed them to Carl.

"That makes eight." She snapped the gun closed with an air of proficiency. "Any more comments like that and there'll be seven."

Carl looked at this pretty young lady, unsure what to think, other than she wouldn't hesitate to fulfill her last statement. He turned away, setting his thoughts on the arsenal Quincy's distrust had amassed in a very short time.

As the group pulled up to the jailhouse, Carl was the first off of his ellack. The front door had been kicked in. One of the detention cell's energy bars was on, but void of any prisoners. Upon further inspection, the majority of the incident seemed to be centered on vandalism. Although any visible weapons were missing, this was the first time Carl could remember being thankful for Quincy's paranoia.

Clay nudged a broken oak desk leg with his boot. It traveled a foot or so across the floor.

"Well, so much for that. Where's our next stop."

"Not so fast," Carl said, "I've got something to show you."

"Hold on," Clive said, "you might want to see this." He was kneeling over a solitary boot. The top edges were seared and jagged, the heel blown completely off. "Doesn't look like one of our vandals made it out in a usable piece." Clive picked up the boot and turned it upside down. Four toes rolled out.

"I'd say you're right," Victor chimed in. "Looks more like four pieces."

"Ah, you're sick," Cassie said.

A wave of snickers filtered through the room.

"Taint rite," Gert said. He looked down at what remained of the vandal. "Ain't nobody got any business snickerin' at a feller what done and run into bad luck like this here one has, I don't care what he done done and done."

The few faces that had displayed amusement moments before now expressed remorse.

Katie moved closer to Jason.

"It's okay, sweetheart. Everything's going to be all right."

Clay let out a piercing whistle.

"If you gentlemen are finished with the comic relief, Carl has something he'd like to show us."

The group gathered around Carl fiddling with something on the back wall of one of the detention cells. He pulled a notched metal rod, twelve inches long and one half inch in diameter out of his boot. He removed a smaller rod from his vest pocket. Carl pushed the smaller rod through a hole in the larger one, forming a T that could be used as a handle to turn the notched piece.

"Our good friend Quincy," Carl said, "thankfully for us, was afraid of his own shadow." Carl pushed the rod into a corresponding sized hole. He turned the oversized key three full revolutions to the right.

A hush fell over the small gathering.

After a series of clicks, the entire section of wall slid to the left, revealing a brightly lit room containing enough hardware and ammunition to wage war against half the planet.

Gert and Hatch walked through the small room, eyeing weapons mounted on the walls forming a U shaped display. They stopped about halfway around and began a dialogue filled with excited chatter.

"What are you two going on about?" Jake asked.

His curiosity piqued by the commotion, Zachariah joined the three men.

"I never woulda thunked it in a cardovian flatbusher's lifetime that I ever could see my grandpappy's shootin' stick," Gert said.

"You say this belonged to your grandfather?" Jake asked.

"May the mush fill my bony mouth til I can't take another breath if'n I'm a-lyin'."

"How can you tell?"

A single bony finger pointed to a set of initials etched into the stock.

"Right thar." Gert tapped the neatly carved letters, nestled within a carved circle. "DC." Gert announced with pride, "Dalon Con."

Jake plucked the weapon from its holder. He looked it over and then handed it to Gert.

"All yours."

"Thank ye much," Gert said. He settled into a conversation with his brother, reliving a happier time until interrupted.

"All right," Clay said, "load everything, we'll figure out what it does later."

Ninety-two

"WHERE'S THAT KID?" Petimore grumbled. "He said he'd be back in a few minutes. If a shipment comes through, he knows I can't handle it alone."

A whining noise echoed through the enclosure, followed by a loud pop. This progression repeated two more times, the last pop followed by three four inch thick steel panels hitting the floor where four technicians had been working moments before.

Petimore looked up at the gaping twelve foot square hole as blue creatures flooded the opening. At that same moment, machine gun fire and then rocket-powered grenades, having no effect on the invasion, signaled the demise of the security force.

The Azurians made their way (each stride an awkward progression) down three flights of steps. Amidst groans, their great weight taxed the metal to the point of failure.

What appeared to be six separate death squads had come together for this assault. This left thirty-six Azurian's on a stairway that peeled from its moorings, landing in a heap on the floor.

Petimore had moved to a vantage point that afforded a view, yet kept him at a safe distance from the commotion. He was not a brave man, but made it a point to speak loudly. He felt this would elevate his position in the eyes of his peers. Sadly, he was the only one left. That of course depended on Nate and how he fared, Petimore thought.

He lifted his tall, slender frame just enough to move further back into the installation. His white lab coat was torn, and the left lens of his glasses missing. His lips cracked a sideways smile.

"What a mess." Among the twisted metal lay what appeared to be a pile of calladium shards. The Azurians, in their zeal to reach the bottom, had caused a chain reaction. As the stairway ripped from the wall, the outside supports held a fraction of a second longer, causing the structure to collapse in on itself. It started at the top, throwing Azurian into Azurian as it toppled.

No creature was spared substantial damage. Some totally destroyed, others were missing limbs, heads and broken in half. Several had lost their tail, compromising their balance. It would take a step and fall. If it landed on another creature, then more damage would ensue.

"Ah!" Petimore yelped. An Azurian with one arm, partial shoulder and half of its head, grasped the terrified scientist's lab coat. Petimore kicked at the shattered remains until he slid out of the tattered clothing.

Petimore jumped up and hit the ground running. He stopped at a hub that was the ending point for numerous hallways, like spokes on a wheel. Petimore chose a tunnel and room about halfway down. He entered the room, closed and locked the door. The space he had chosen was stacked floor to ceiling with sealed cases.

Little did he know the much-needed time the events of that day had bought for the next wave of humans to descend on Baine.

Ninety-three

VICTOR PULLED THE BUCKBOARD up to the front of the camouflaged building he and Clive called home.

Clive jumped down and searched for the keypad that would allow the party to enter.

"Strange how you can forget the location of something in such a short time," Clive said. He continued to run his fingers over the boulder. By accident, his fingernail caught the lip of that which could only be felt, not seen. Clive moved his index finger over the area. A small decoder under the surface of the fake boulder read his fingerprint. Seconds later, the door seal broke, and a panel slid sideways, allowing entrance to the facility.

"Clive, Victor," Jason said, "you need to show us where we can set up workstations. You two, along with Clay and Jake know more about munitions than anyone else. I want you disassembling and reassembling. Have the others gather materials and teach them how to cast new slugs."

"Now you jest hold on a ding dang minit," Gert said, "Some of them thar shootin' sticks we took is older then all you younguns put together."

"You mean to tell me you have over a hundred years of experience with firearms between the two of you?" Clive protested.

"Twixin' me 'n Hatch here, we gots pert near eight hunderd year sperience."

"True many is eight," Hatch said. "More is me, less Gert."

"Eight hundred years!" Cassie exclaimed.

"Yes'm," Gert said, "Course I can't lay claim to more than three hunderd myself, cause Hatch here's my older brother."

"There you have it," Jason said. "Let's get to work."

Zachariah pulled Jason to the side.

"I think it best I work with Gert and Hatch. I remember a time when no firearm existed."

"That would be fine."

NINETY-FOUR

"THE FIRST WAVE HAS BEEN RELEASED," Alzar said. "As more become acclimated to the Hue Man's atmosphere, they will be loosed as their number reaches six."

"Alzar," Ell said, "there has been a minute increase in the volume of the calladium core."

Alzar joined Ell to confirm what he had seen in the critical information display. This required one of many small round floating units used to gather Intel in the core or crust above.

"The signal is familiar," Alzar said.

"Yet how is it possible?" Ickta questioned.

"Only calladium may enter—"

Another Azurian emerged within their midst. Although of the same appearance, this one was larger and carried himself with an air of formidability.

"J. Smith," Alzar said, "you honor us with your presence." He knelt, as did Ickta and Ell.

"Up," J. Smith said. "We have many things to consider."

Ninety-five

CLIVE AND VICTOR TOOK CHARGE of softening the calladium. Shards of the mineral were placed in a nonreactive pan and then covered in gasoline. After about an hour, the calladium would be the consistency of thick molasses.

From this point on, speed became of the utmost importance.

"Make it quick," Clay said. "You let the last batch lay too long, and it setup before I could get it into the molds."

"Calm down, boss man," Jake replied. "It's the first time I've worked with this stuff."

Clay took the piece from Jake, opened the mold he used for the spine cutter loads and pushed a plug of calladium into each hole. He made sure that the substance measured twice what each receptacle would hold. Then slammed the top down, forcing the blue material into the shape of the slug he fabricated.

Carl and Lynch had the envious task of removing the lead from the brass casings.

"How about being a little more careful," Carl said. "One slip and we'll both be called Lefty."

Gert, Hatch and Zachariah controlled the removal of the artifacts from the jailhouse in Baine.

Gert stood there scratching his head.

"Can't say as I ever seen a contraption like that'n thar you gotten in yer hand."

"No see sure," Hatch added.

"I am not surprised," Zachariah said. "This 'seine' in its day remains a formidable weapon. I should think the surprise it will bring will cause it to be an exceptional device." He examined the weapon closely. "Each of these explosive pieces will have to be formed by hand."

"That be usin' up time we ain't xactly got," Gert said.

"I agree," Zachariah said, "but time we'll need nonetheless. Even a Gatling gun will be pulled into service once a special slug mold can be constructed to conform to its specifications."

* * *

After six days of near around the clock work, the changes were complete.

Clay and Jake approached Jason.

"Ready to leave?" Clay asked.

Jason shook his head. "We don't know what's waiting for us once we get to Baine. That's why every contingency we're able to handle with the personnel and the armament we have available must be considered before we leave. Not to mention our main objective."

"To save this worthless piece of rock?" Jake asked.

"Aon's value is of no consequence," Clay said. "This rock is home."

Jason nodded.

"Gather everyone together, we parlay, load the wagon and then head for Baine."

Ninety-six

"HAVING BEEN AWAY SO LONG from my natural surroundings," J. Smith said, "I am emaciated, both body and mind."

"What can your servants do— "

"Do not speak," J. Smith commanded. "Listen."

Alzar, Ickta and Ell telepathically relayed their compliance.

"My senses would betray me if I pressed for more than they are offering," J. Smith continued. "Something goes wrong in Baine. Our first death force was loosed there, and I fear they are no more." He waved his arm from left to right. "You may now speak."

"What are we to do?" Alzar asked. "We have yet to receive the promised weapons, and without them our limited time above ground will at best reinforce a lesson in futility."

"A new wave of acclimated warriors will soon surface and converge on Baine. Until then,we will wait."

NINETY-SEVEN

TWO HANDS TOUCHED HER HIPS. Cassie breathed a sigh of relief when both feet hit solid ground. She turned to see Ruben. Cassie smiled and uttered, "Thank you."

"How in tarnation is them fellers gonna git that thar six leg monstrous critter all the way down in this here hole?" Gert asked.

"Rope wrap down good," Hatch replied.

Gert looked up thirty feet to the opening.

"Oh yeah," Gert said, "I sees it now." He laid a hand on Hatch's shoulder. "You always had the smarts in the family."

Hatch patted his brother's hand and smiled.

Jake, Victor and Carl remained topside to ready the ellack for its downward journey. As the three men wove ropes in and around the doomed animal's legs, Jake had a thought.

"Stop," he announced. "There may be another way." He dropped the rope he held in his hands. "The way we've chosen to go about this is all wrong. I'm afraid we'll end up with nothing more than a splattered ellack and damaged weapons with no way to haul the ones that work."

"So," Victor said, "what do you suggest?"

"I'm going down," Jake said. He picked up the rope he held earlier and unwound it from around the ellack. He handed one end to Victor. "Here, tie this off, to what, I don't care." Victor searched around, unable to locate the ring they had driven into the ground to lower each person.

Jake was growing impatient, the notion evident in his voice. "Right there. Wrap it around the saddle horn and lower me."

Victor nodded, mounted the ellack and wrapped the rope one full turn around the protrusion.

"Ready on this end."

Jake wrapped the rope around his waist, then pulled the tagline down, binding it over the main line.

"I'm off."

This setup allowed Jake to loosen the tagline to lower himself or tighten the tagline to slow or stop his descent. Victor was the anchor. If Jake needed more line or became tangled, Victor could lower him the rest of the way.

Jake hit the ground running."Clay, follow me!"

Jake paid little attention to the mound of calladium shimmering in the artificial light. It tinkled as its macro movement, already degrading to micro movement, would soon become such a fine powder that gravity no longer bound it to the ground.

How ironic, a material that exists within itself; yet, remove it from that environment, and its own touch is enough to destroy itself completely.

Noticing several white coats amidst the rubble, Jake came to an abrupt halt. He dug through the debris until he found the tech's ID badge. He yanked, and with a "click," the badge was freed from the lab coat's lapel.

Jake stood. "Everyone, search through the rubble for any hint of white. Dig if you have to, but I need every ID badge you can find."

Soon he had four more badges. Having already discarded the first one, he perused the ones handed him.

"No!" he barked, as the last four badges hit the ground. "Is this all you found?"

Several heads nodded up and down.

Jake shook his head and thought of another way, but there was none. Some things are just cut and dried.

Cassie's voice rang out. "I have another one, but I can't get to it." She paused a moment. "Come here, I'll need help."

Everyone moved toward the young lady's voice to a scene so surreal it was almost comical. The upper quarter (including half of the thing's head) from one of the Azurians was flailing about on the floor, grasping a badge in what presumably was its hand.

"See what I mean?" Cassie said.

"Land o' Goshen," Gert said. "Taint never in all my born put-togethers seen such a thang."

Clay pulled his pistol, stepped up and placed a boot on the end of the Azurian's arm, covering the ID.

"How does it feel to be the guinea pig?" Clay shot once, shattering the partial thorax and head. The second shot disintegrated the arm, leaving but a small portion under the large man's boot. Clay reached down, picked up the badge and handed it to Jake.

"Hope this is more in line of what you're looking for."

Jake noticed it before he ever touched the badge. A senior technician's seal that would allow him access to any part of the building, using the badge. The name on the card caught Jake's eye.

"Raymond Petimore," Jake said. "He's got to be older than dirt. He was working here when Baine was a one ellack town." Something hit Jake; he found himself swimming in familiarity.

"Wait a minute; Baine *is* a one ellack town." Jake looked at the card one more time.

"I hope Ray's all right; he was a decent enough guy." He pushed Petimore from his mind and held the card up as if displaying spoils from the battlefield.

"Clay," Jake said, "now we can go." Before the two set out, Clay stopped and turned.

"Make sure your weapons are loaded and ready to go. Set up a perimeter around the lab area and all connecting hallways. Remember—nothing in and let's hope there's nothing already in that wants to get out."

"You heard the man," Clive said, "spread out."

"I'll stay right here," Lynch said. "This hallway will be easier for an older fella to guard."

"Suit yourself," Clive said.

Lynch looked to his left at his retreating comrades spreading out to play army, and to his right to watch Clay and Jake disappear.

A curious smile crossed the thin man's face.

Lynch hurried down the hall about ten minutes behind Clay and Jake.

"Looks like the right amount of time behind our two heroes. If any of my comrades miss me, you can bet they won't stray far looking for me."

Lynch began a quick paced yet methodical search for a splitter platform that would allow him to transfer out.

* * *

Jake slid to a halt. Clay, being several paces behind, pulled up beside his friend.

"Find something?" Clay asked.

"This is it," Jake said. He removed his hat and walked around the small, round room, slowing to peer into each hallway before moving to the next.

"This is what?"

"The cases, the weapons, the gas," Jake said. He opened his arms, turning a quarter turn to the left and then to the right. "This is the hub where the lost forty-five seconds afforded me a glimpse at an alien weapon and busted me back to the mailroom." He grabbed Clay by his upper arms. "What I now believe to be weapons created for the core beings, by man to destroy man."

"Slow down a minute," Clay said. "How do you know this?"

Jake released his grip and scanned each hallway. "Here, this is it, this is the one."

Clay started to protest.

"You've got to trust me on this one," Jake said. "I can show you better than tell you."

"Lead the way."

Jake nodded, and both men moved down the hallway. As they neared the halfway mark, Jake pointed at a mound jutting through a doorway.

"Petimore," Jake said. The sliding door hit the body mid-thorax before recoiling, readying itself for another cycle.

"So that's the good doctor?" Clay asked.

Jake swiped Petimore's card. The door stopped and retracted into the wall.

"Yep, that's him." Jake knelt down over the body.

"What's over his face?" Clay asked.

"A respirator," Jake said, "Something we should have on because of these." He picked up a dark, molded object six feet long.

"I'll skip the obvious and just let you tell me what it is," Clay said.

Jake motioned for Clay to join him inside the room.

"Well, we're both still standing, so I guess it means the ventilation system is still working."

Clay's expression exhibited utter confusion. "I'm all yours."

"Those stacked cases," Jake said, "they are literally thousands deep."

Clay looked at the open case on the floor and the weapon in Jake's hands

"And each case contains the same thing you're holding?"

Jake nodded.

"A little surprise for anyone trying to open one, if they were not the intended recipient."

Clay furrowed his eyebrows and looked at Petimore.

"Let me guess—the respirator." Clay knelt down and rubbed the edge of the open case. He stood. "It's a Xanlock seal." He stared at Jake. "We're talking heavy-duty. What kind of toxins are they using that require such extreme measures?"

"Not sure," Jake said. "It's a cocktail of several compounds, one of which is Nicaspac."

Clay shook his head. "If you're right about the number of cases, that by itself is enough to wipe out half the planet, not taking into consideration what else it may be mixed with."

"Kind of gives the impression who or what claims this planet's calladium plans to sterilize whatever's left."

"It would appear so," Clay said, "but back to the thing you're holding. Look around the room. The blast marks I'm guessing are from that weapon. And I'm willing to bet Petimore did the firing." Clay paused for a moment. "What we don't know is, at what was he shooting, and is this mystery creature what killed him?"

"I think it best we assume it was," Jake said. "An indestructible race bent on acquiring thousands of weapons. Weapons able to kill by removing them from their carrying cases. What's one more entity trying to annihilate us from the inside?"

"You haven't lost that endearing sense of humor," Clay said.

"No," Jake said, "but for now we need to lock this room down and get to the livestock transport elevator."

They moved Petimore's body to the next room down, sealing the door shut with one swipe of the dead man's card.

"In case you're wondering," Jake said, "those rooms are hermetically sealed when shut. Kinda like a modern day tomb."

"The chunk of Azurian found holding Petimore's card—" Clay said, "Could it have had anything to do with Petimore's death?"

Jake shook his head. "I don't think so. You saw the way the Azurian was scooting around on the floor. Whatever Petimore was shooting at, was running on the walls and ceiling or flying around the room."

Jake slid the access card into his shirt pocket and buttoned the flap. "As many impact marks were in that room, he had to be shooting as fast as he could, hoping for a lucky shot."

Clay nodded. "It's gonna eat at me until I know what it is."

Jake checked the room one more time, knowing there was nothing else to see.

He pushed the red button which would make the room impossible to enter except by someone with the security level five badge, and that being dependent on conventional means. There was no telling what surprises their blue friends had in store. He watched the door close and listened for the telltale hiss before leaving.

* * *

The blue vortex dissipated one quarter mile from its origin. Lynch dropped to one knee. Transferring always brought about vertigo and he knew this soon would pass, but that didn't make the bile in the back of his throat any easier to force back down. In fact, this time he would lose. The acrid yellow fluid spewed out his mouth and trickled from his nose.

Lynch grunted to clear his throat and then spat. He blew the remaining bile from his nose and rose to his feet. He straightened and found he was surrounded by large blue creatures. One moved menacingly toward him.

* * *

"Everyone all right?" Clay shouted. His voice bounced off the steel walls and reached down the necessary thirty feet.

"Fair to middling," came the reply.

"That was Ruben, I think," Jake said.

Clay shook his head and shrugged.

Jake cupped both hands around his mouth. "We'll be down with the ellack in a few."

They heard several voices yelling a garbled message. Jake and Clay, assuming it was just a response, left the opening on their way to the splitter at the rear of the building.

* * *

"Fair to middling," Ruben shouted.

"Looks like they found a way to get the ellack down to our little slice of heaven," Victor said.

"Cassie," Zachariah exclaimed, "behind you."

Before Cassie could turn, Katie took three steps, the first on the floor, the next two against the wall behind Cassie. Katie extended her staff and flipped the twelve legged arachnid off the wall and onto the floor in an upside down position.

Cassie moved to squash the bug underfoot. She raised her leg and brought it down hard.

"No!" Ruben exclaimed. But it was too late.

"Crunch!" The sickening sound echoed throughout the room.

"Ah!" Cassie moaned. She hit the floor beside the arachnid who was still trying to right itself.

A single strike through the thing's head by Hatch's cane sword ended the bug's attempt to regain its upright stature. Its legs now tapped the ground furiously until all motion came to an end.

Hatch placed his foot on the dead bug and removed his sword. A cloud exploded off the sword's surface.

"What is zat?" Katie asked, waving her hand through the dust cloud as it made its way up and down the room.

No one heard the child's question, all their attention now focused on Cassie.

Ruben knelt down over the injured woman.

"Somebody help me up, instead of standing over me gawking," Cassie said.

"You're not going anywhere, young lady," Ruben said. "Not until I have time to look at that leg."

"There's nothing wrong with my leg," Cassie complained.

Ruben began his examination at Cassie's ankle.

"Now this may hurt a little." He rotated her ankle, expecting a painful response as he did so. No response at all.

She's not injured, he thought. He continued up her leg. Once he reached the knee, Cassie seized. She clamped her mouth shut, and beads of sweat broke out on her forehead.

"Sweetheart," Ruben said, "your kneecap is on the side of your leg. I'm going to count to three and reposition it." He paused a moment, having Zachariah and Victor step in to steady her.

"Ready?"

Cassie nodded.

"Remember—on three."

"One . . . Two . . ."

Ruben jerked the kneecap back into place.

"That's not fair," Cassie complained, "but I'm glad you did it."

"That will be sore for a while," Ruben said. "Maybe next time you'll listen when I say no."

Ruben signaled to Jason and Jason complied.

"Anything I can do to help?" Jason inquired.

"Would you find something—preferably two pieces of wood I can use to splint her knee?"

Ruben tore strips of cloth from each person who had extra clothing to donate.

Cassie gave Ruben a curious gaze."What do you mean when you say 'no'?"

"As you were beginning your jump to plow your foot into the bug, I screamed 'no' for fear of you hurting yourself."

"When the young girl—"

"Katie," Cassie interrupted.

"Yeah, that's the one. When she knocked the bug off the wall I expected it to splatter all over the room. When it didn't and instead slammed into the floor like a boulder, I knew we had a problem."

Cassie looked toward Hatch. "Shouldn't have Hatch's sword only worked once? If you notice the calladium in the large room, what used to be an Azurian fighting force is now a pile of dust. So what gives?"

"When we were converting the ammo from lead to calladium we accidentally dumped double the amount of gas into the mixture. Since we were stuck with the solution we searched for a way to use it."

Jason returned with two pieces of wood.

"Perfect," Ruben said. "Where did you find them?"

"If you dig around long enough, you can find almost anything." Jason smiled and handed the wood to Ruben.

Ruben touched the wood, and for an instant felt something radiate from Jason. Not merely anything, but something good, possibly goodness itself. Ruben took the wood and wrapped Cassie's knee.

"This is going to hurt," Ruben said, "but it's got to be tight so the kneecap doesn't slip."

The pain in her knee had eased. She looked at Ruben. "Go ahead."

"Don't worry, I'll be as easy as possible. And if you're good, I'll finish my story."

Cassie smiled nervously. Somehow the thought of a story didn't ease the pain she knew she was about to endure.

"Now if I remember, we were trying to find a use for the diluted calladium solution. Come to find out, Hatch had the same idea." Ruben paused the story and wrapping Cassie's leg and then chuckled. After a few good yucks bordering laughter, he resumed both. "We turned to find that little mush-mouthed man dipping his sword into the solution, removing it for a second before dipping it again."

Ruben split the bandage down the middle, ending with two pieces.

"Hang tough," Ruben reassured her, "the worst is almost over."

Cassie displayed a halfhearted smile."Do it!"

He wrapped one of the tag lines to the right over the knee and the other to the left. Crossing the two under the leg and bringing both around to meet, below the kneecap, his eyes caught Cassie's.

"Ready?"

Cassie bit her bottom lip and nodded.

He looped the two ends and pulled the knot snug. Looping the ends another time, he jerked the second knot taut, locking both knots firmly together.

"Awh!" Cassie squalled.

"Good girl," Ruben said. "Now for the splint, and you're ready to go."

Cassie wiped her sweat-soaked locks from her face. "Don't forget you still owe me a story."

"Stick good, calladium layers many," Hatch said.

* * *

Lynch quickly shoved his hand into his front pocket and pulled out his blue stone that immediately began to pulsate. The advancing creature slowed to a stop in front of Lynch. The Azurian gazed at the stone, lolling its head from side to side.

Lynch smiled, "You like that, don't you, big boy?"

"Very much so," the creature replied.

Lynch looked at the Azurian and then at the stone in the palm of his hand.

"I heard you speak, but it didn't come from you, it came from this blue rock."

"I am Batook, and you are correct. The stone (as I'm sure you know) can do many wondrous things. Even now, it affords us a way to communicate by acting as translator."

Lynch removed his hat and dropped the stone inside. He ran a hand through his graying, but full head of hair. He tipped his hat, allowing the stone to fall into his hand. Only then did he replace his cover.

Lynch tossed the stone into the air, catching it before it hit the ground. This seemed to annoy Batook. Lynch held the stone in the palm of his hand.

"I just might have some info that you and your boys could be interested in."

"Tell me," Batook inched closer.

Lynch made calming motions with his hands

"I'll tell you everything, including a little story about a substance called gasoline used to extract calladium."

"What do you wish?" Batook said. "Ask and it will be yours."

"Well, it seems to me that these here little blue balls are worth a fortune, and I believe I can carry about thirty of 'em easy enough."

Batook returned to his five waiting comrades. They stood in a tight circle for quite some time. Eventually Batook rejoined Lynch.

He extended a hand that was more like a shallow bowl, full of blue stones.

"For you, per your request."

Lynch began to take them by the handful and filled his pockets.

"Hee, hee, hee. I'm rich; I'm rich, rich, rich, rich."

"Now tell me," Batook demanded.

Lynch revealed the little he understood about the entire project. As Batook was more interested in the here and now, he pressed Lynch to this end.

"About a quarter mile to the west," Lynch said, "is where you'll find them all."

"You would betray your friends?" Batook asked.

"They're nothing to me," Lynch replied.

"As you are to me." Batook's arm became a massive pyramid-shaped sword. He plunged the weapon into Lynch up to its hilt. Four separate pieces of the one known as Lynch fell to the ground curiously covered with small blue stones.

* * *

"I don't transfer unless I have to," Jake said, "I don't like splitting myself into digital strips and flying who knows where. You never know when you come back together if it will be in the right order."

Jake scratched the ellack under its muzzle. "Heard about one guy; he flew through a flock of thrush backs."Jake shook his head. "That man had so many beaks and feathers poking out of him, I understand he took off and hasn't been seen since."

"Take the stairs," Clay said.

"On my way. Meet you at the bottom."

"Don't worry about him," Clay whispered into the ellack's ear. "We'll be fine."

Clay positioned himself beside the ellack on the splitter pad. After thirty seconds, the transfer would automatically engage. It began with a low hum which grew in intensity followed by a vortex wrapping around each occupant. The one transferring would be dissected into quarter inch digital strips. Upon reaching their destination, the digital pieces would be reassembled, usually in the same configuration as they were before the process began.

In less than two minutes, Clay met Jake on the lower floor.

"I expected an ellack body with human arms and your head," Jake said.

"Not this time," Clay said. He guided the ellack off the splitter pad. "Let's get back to the others; we've been gone too long."

"Sounds like they are having a party," Jake said.

Clay squinted and listened carefully. "If the party hasn't already had them."

Clay glanced at Jake. "I'm going on ahead." Clay took off at a jog before Jake could answer.

"Got to watch out for the silent type," Jake said to the ellack, "They'll run off and leave you alone every time." He threw an arm over his companion's neck. "Guess it's just you and me for the next five minutes or so."

* * *

"Looks like I picked the wrong time to leave," Clay said.

"Looks like," Clive replied, "you missed all the fun."

"Where's Jake and the livestock you two went to rescue?" Victor asked.

"They'll be along soon," Clay replied. "What happened here?"

"We had a visit from a multi-legged calladium creature," Victor said. "It slipped up behind Cassie crawling along the wall. The kid jumped in—"

"You mean Katie?" Clay asked.

"Yeah, that's the one," Clive jumped in. "She took that staff she carries, and popped that bug off the wall and onto its back, clean as you please. Before I knew it, Cassie tried to push a foot through the thing's gut, but busted up her own leg."

"Then the little fella that talks so funny . . ." Victor said, finding a place in the story to jump back in. ". . . Hatch, yeah, that's it. He ran that little sword of his through the bug's brain."

By this time Jake had found his way, back to the group with ellack in tow.

"What did I miss?"

"These two will fill you in," Clay said, "I'm going to check out our visitor."

Victor and Clive regaled Jake with what had transpired during Clay and Jake's absence.

Clay tapped the upside down creature with the tip of his boot. Cassie was sitting nearby.

"Yeah, I thought I could kill it with my foot," she said. "Great idea, huh?"

"Is this one of the two that held you and Ruben captive?"

"Identical," she said.

"Then you would think this one would be as vulnerable as the last two you had to deal with."

"Thanks," Cassie said. "Now I feel only half as stupid."

Hatch waddled up to Cassie. "Good leg good?"

Cassie smiled. "Yes, and thank you very much."

Hatch returned the gesture and joined his brother Gert.

"Can you walk on it?" Clay asked.

"One way to find out." She reached up with both arms. "Take hold."

He knelt down and wrapped his arms around her waist. She wrapped hers around his neck. "Better watch out, people will talk."

"Let 'em," Clay said. "It won't be the first time. Now, see if you can put weight on that leg."

She released her grip.

"Don't worry, I've got you."

Gingerly at first, then with more force she transferred weight from the good leg to the bad.

"Look at that." She took short steps. "Let me go."

Clay released his grip. Cassie smiled at him. "A hobble is better than nothing."

Clay nodded in agreement. "Someone did a good job on that leg."

"At your service," Ruben said. "I see you're up and around."

"Thanks to you," Cassie said.

"Let's move our conversation to where this all began," Clay said. "Listen up—everyone to the access area in the large room."

It took little more than a minute for everyone to gather.

"What happened to the pile of caladium?" Jake asked.

"Those blue granules on the floor are all that's left," Carl said.

"The floor seems to be moving," Clay said.

Ruben stepped up.

"As the particles decay, they get to where they're too light to remain grounded. It's almost as if they know where they're going, and the laws of physics no longer apply."

"You kin sure and betcha they is a-goin' sum'ers, I'm a tellin' ya." Gert said. "Elsewise, they wouldn't be a-waitin' on one 'nother. And they is a-waitin'. Take a gander, you be a-seein'."

Unable to resist Gert's challenge, everyone stared at the particles of calladium writhing about on the floor. First one would leave and hover about seven feet in the air. This would happen at seven different points around the calladium dust, which now took on the shape of a heptagon.

"Look at that," Cassie said, "there are six more granules floating up to meet the original seven."

"Seven columns comprising seven particles each? That's 49 total," Ruben said.

"Coincidence? I think not."

"Has anyone seen Lynch?" Clay asked.

As if on cue, four chunks of meat and a round object flew through the opening three floors above and into the calladium dust. A dazzling explosion of blue shot upward. It spun and tightened until it was two inches in diameter.

Zachariah pointed. "The enemy is upon us!"

What was once silent had become a deafening roar.

An Azurian war party, six strong, had lowered themselves, when the spiraling blue mass plowed into the unsuspecting warriors. They were absorbed into its swirling essence, causing what appeared as a worm-like creature to grow.

Seven more parties attempted an assault with similar results. Ruben reckoned the conditions just like being caught in one of the many twisters he had experienced on Earth. Finally, the storm growing too large to occupy the building along with the humans, it ingested the bug and exited the structure through the twelve foot opening.

"What were that thing?" Katie asked. She had pressed herself so deeply into Zachariah's fur clothing she couldn't be seen.

"I cannot say, my child," Zachariah said. "However, I am thankful for its appearance."

Clive cocked his hat back. "Looks like we found Lynch." The neatly trimmed beard, the full head of graying hair and now gray skin to match left no doubt.

"Yep, it's him all right, and I hate to say it, but he's getting a little ripe."

"Clive, Carl, Victor and Ruben," Jake said, "grab a piece and follow me. I've got just the place for him."

"I'm almost afraid to ask if anyone's seen Jason," Clay said, "but has—"

"Right here," Jason said, "I backed down a hallway during all the commotion. I guess a piece of debris caught me in the head. The next thing I remember I was waking up on the floor."

Clay examined the front of Jason's head, just above the hairline. "Your hair's so thick I'm having a hard time finding your scalp."

Clay brushed back the blood matted hair and found a small half inch gash.

"I found the source, but there seems to be something hard just underneath your scalp."

Clay pulled a knife out of his boot.

"Hold tight, this is gonna hurt." He pushed the tip of the knife through the gash and into the underside of the object.

"This is it." Clay patted Jason on the shoulder.

"Do it!"

Clay pried back on the knife, using Jason's forehead as a fulcrum. A sliver of wood popped from underneath Jason's scalp. The slit sealed, weeping a few drops, once the offending object was removed.

"You weren't kidding," Jason said.

Clay removed a rag from his pocket and handed it to Jason. The young man wiped the sweat from his forehead.

"Thanks, and I mean for everything."

"Better get Ruben to take a look at that. He's our unofficial medicine man."

Jason nodded.

"Looks like Jake and the others are back," Clay said. He placed two fingers in his mouth and produced an ear-splitting whistle. "We need to plan our next move. I think it best we get out of this death trap; we may need more room to fight and/or retreat. Jake, what about the cases?"

"If we had explosives, a charge set at the opening into the room would bring down enough material from above to slow their progression. It may conceal the cases entirely."

"What about the gas?" Clay asked. "If too many cases are breached, none of us will make it out of here."

"The room is almost impenetrable; any explosives we could get our hands on would have no effect." Jake stared at Clay. "Are you trying to tell me we have explosives?"

"Grenades," Clay answered, "a limited amount, but enough to bring down the house."

Jake smiled.

Clay returned the gesture.

Ninety-eight

THE ELLACK STEPPED OFF the transfer pad.

"That's it," Ruben said, "Clay and Jake are the only two left in the hole."

"When will we know they're coming?" Cassie asked.

"Yaaaaaa!" was heard from a distance, heading toward the group.

"I can assume that the two banshees moving in our direction are Clay and Jake," Victor said.

Before anyone could answer, the two men came into sight.

"Get ready!" Clay screamed, and Jake repeated.

Ruben placed his hand over the activation switch.

"Now," both men shouted, stepping onto the pad and slamming into the back wall.

Ruben hit the button, but nothing happened. He drove his fist hard into the switch, again nothing.

A muffled "boom" shook the building.

"Everyone out of here, now," Ruben shouted. "Clay, make sure the safety closed board switch is engaged."

Jake saw a ball of fire following the same tract he and Clay had traversed moments earlier.

Clay closed the open switch sending power to the upper controls. His mind blurred as his world filled with orange, yellow and the sense of heat.

Seconds later he was jerked into a bright light and then pushed to the ground by an explosive force. As his head cleared, someone was beating on him, but he sensed no malice.

"Stop," Clay yelled. He rolled over and sat up on his haunches. It was then he recognized why the beating had been necessary. He looked at Ruben.

"Thanks."

"You're welcome. It's rare I get to put out a flaming friend."

A hand touched Clay's shoulder."You all right?"Jake asked.

"I've been better; but all in all, not too bad."

"Looks like you got the worst of it," Jake said. "If Victor hadn't stayed behind and put me out while Ruben was working on you, I'd be a pile of ash by now."

"I didn't realize when we tossed the grenades that there was an incendiary device in the mix."

"No way you could have known; they all looked the same except for the writing on the casing, which we both noticed after it was too late."

 Jake helped Clay to his feet.

"Where is everybody?" Clay asked.

"About a hundred yards that way," Victor answered, pointing his finger southwest.

Clay looked in that direction and observed the ellack and a group of people spread out in a single line. A sense of concern emanated from the gathering. He waved to quell any anxiety.

"We best be joining them," Victor said.

Just a little over halfway, Clay's body tensed, his senses honed to a fine edge. A flash of blue, and he quickened his pace to a fast jog, removing two sawed-off shotguns from their holsters on his back.

"Turn!" Clay shouted.

Jake, Ruben and Victor, weapons drawn, followed Clay.

Two fast slashes and Carl fell to the ground in four pieces, a smile still on his face.

Clive, understanding Clay's single command was in position to obliterate the creature with four shots from each of his sidearms.

Hatch had climbed up the back of an Azurian, lopping off his head and splitting the body lengthwise as he journeyed back to the ground.

Katie used her staff to upset a beast until it toppled, allowing one of the men to finish the creature with gunfire.

Just before Clay and his three followers reached the foray, another contingency of Azurians cut them off.

Clay removed two with shotgun blasts. Jake and Victor downed three more. The last of the six pierced Ruben's shoulder through. A barrage of gunfire reduced the Azurian to shards, save for the calladium blade which remained in place.

"Jake," Clay shouted, "over here."

Jake complied and joined his friend.

"We need to move Ruben out of harm's way until this skirmish is over."

Jake spied an indentation amidst the rubble. They rolled Ruben onto his side, the afflicted arm against the ground. Pushing him into the depression, they covered him with loose pieces of debris and rejoined the fight.

Zachariah used something that resembled a bolo with calladium weights. He would throw the weapon at the Azurian's legs. Once the weights became entangled as they circled around, they would take chunks of calladium from the combatant's legs, causing it to tumble.

Gert bounced back and forth from blue head to blue head, inflicting mortal wounds with something that looked like a small sledge hammer. It was coated with layers of calladium and carried by rope that extended from its short handle. Gert swung the object as he skipped from Azurian to Azurian leaving a path of destruction in his wake.

Jason slammed one Azurian into another, causing devastating injuries.

Random gunfire continued until nothing but blue shards and dust covered the ground.

"Sing out if you need help," Clay said, "and check each other for injuries. After such a battle you may not feel any pain until it's too late."

"From what I can tell," Jason said, "everyone's okay except for Carl and Ruben."

"I'll check on Ruben," Clay said, "Jason, you're with me. Jake, gather everyone together and make ready to leave, not Baine, but this area. Construct a sled for Ruben to travel and hitch the sled to the ellack."

"We'll be back soon, make sure we're ready to go."

"Arghh!" Ruben shrieked, as Clay withdrew the calladium arm from Ruben's shoulder.

Jason stood by with a handful of torn pieces of clothing, ready to stem the flow of blood. As the blue object cleared Ruben's skin, nothing happened.

Clay couldn't believe what he was seeing.

"Not the first drop."He ran his fingers over the wound. "It cauterized as the Azurian arm was removed."

A blue aura, the size and shape of the wound hovered over the area, front and back, just above the skin.

"How are you doing?" Jason asked.

Ruben grabbed his shoulder and rotated it at the same time. "Not too bad, considering."

"No need in hanging out here," Clay said. "Jake should have everything ready."

Clay paused, looking at Ruben. "I guess you won't need that sled, but for the life of me, I can't figure out why." Clay shook his head. "What do you think, Jason?"

"Things seem to be going rather well," Jason hesitated for effect. This left Clay with his mouth and his mind wide open.

"A greater power than you or me and even the Azurians is at work here." Jason smiled. "It would do you well to embrace new ideas, yet follow what you know to be true. For a wayward mind looking for an easy way out will attain that which it so diligently searches."

Clay pondered for a moment and nodded. "Good words; yeah, good words."

"You good to walk?" Clay asked Ruben.

"One way to find out." Ruben rolled from his fanny to his knees. Clay grabbed one arm and Jason the other. Ruben worked one foot underneath.

"Okay, boys, let's go."

As Clay and Jason pulled, Ruben pushed. "A little wobbly, but not too bad. You two can let go now, and thanks for your help."

Ruben took a few steps, then turned and looked at his comrades. "Well, if we're going, let's go."

"It's good to see everyone made it," Zachariah said. "We must see that our fallen are given a proper burial."

After a short ceremony, the group moved deeper into Baine.

"If the death squads procure the weapons," Jake said, "then that doubles our adversaries."

"Yeah," Clay nodded, "but that gives us an advantage, in that the general Azurian population has not been acclimated to this climate. This means they have five minutes above ground before they have to return."

"Can we take that many of them out? We don't even know how the weapons they'll be using operate, and we can expect a massive rush instead of the few that make up each death squad."

"In the first place," Clay said, "I'm more interested in preventing them from returning to their lair than I am blasting them to pieces. That's something they'll take care of themselves if we can keep them topside longer than they can withstand this environment."

Clive volunteered to lead the ellack for a while. This allowed him easy access to his whiskey stash, which was growing dangerously low. He finished two bottles and left the remaining two until he could restock his inventory. This he would do, whether by purchase or by what he liked to call, *replacement with intent to purchase.* At any rate, it would have to be done under the cover of darkness; he couldn't afford to be seen by the others in his altered state.

Clay raised his hand into the air. "I'm calling it. We need downtime and something to eat." He looked at Clive. "And a drink would be nice if our benefactor would see fit to supply us with a bottle."

"You betcha," Clive said. "In fact, I'll throw in another bottle; I'm feeling unusually generous today."

The necessity of a much-needed respite became evident to the warriors with the first drink. By the time the sun was at its lowest, most of the group was asleep with the rest soon to follow.

Perimeter alarms were placed in a semicircle with the group backed up to what remained of a seven story building. This would keep predators out, but also keep Clive in. He looked at each person. When satisfied that all were asleep, he turned the alarm off, led one of the ellacks through, then restarted the perimeter defense.

"Ellack on the outside, little ol' me stuck on the inside." He smiled. "No problem sneaking out if you've got the equipment." Hard claws coated with thin layers of calladium took the place of his fingernails. He scaled the wall in seconds, dropped onto his ellack and headed hell bent for leather to new Baine.

NINETY-NINE

"EVERYONE UP," Clive said. "We've got too much to do to sleep all day."

Cassie tended to Ruben.

"Kin I help?" Katie asked.

"Sure," Cassie said. She pulled back Ruben's shirt. "What have we here?"

"It's real purty," Katie said. "Why is it movin' so funny?"

Cassie ran her hand over where the wound used to be. In its place was a swirling blue aura the same size and shape of the former puncture.

"How are you, Ruben?"

"Good." Ruben ran his hand through the aura. "The shoulder feels fine, but my fingers tingle when I run them over the spot. It's kind of like a mild electrical shock."

"Let's roll you over," Cassie said, "I want to check the exit wound."

Ruben nodded and turned over, exposing his back.

"Looks much the same back here." She ran her hand through the blue fog, experiencing the same electrical charge Ruben had described.

"Since you're doing all right, there's not much else I can help you with. My best advice is eat breakfast and stop whining." Cassie chuckled as she stood.

"Is we gonna eat yet?" Katie asked.

"I'm gettin' powerful hungry."

"I believe we can rustle you up something to gnaw on."

By now, everyone was milling around, breaking their fast with dried meats of various types, bread and lots of coffee.

"How's Ruben?" Clay asked.

"Fine, I guess," Cassie replied. "The wound has healed or, moreover, seems to have never happened. In its place is a blue cloud the same size and shape as the wound hovering where the penetration occurred."

"Any thoughts on why he healed so quickly or what the blue thing you described could be?"

"I couldn't begin to guess, but I'll keep an eye on him."

Clay raised his eyebrows and looked past Cassie. "It looks like your sidekick has traded you for a chunk of meat."

"I think I'll join her." On her way to a cup of coffee, Cassie was delayed by Zachariah, Victor, Jake, Clive and Gert, each inquiring about Ruben's condition.

Finally, she held a warm cup in her hands.

Jason walked her way.

"Stop right there," Cassie barked. "If you ask me how Ruben is doing, I'll throw this cup at you."

"Well, good morning to you, too," Jason said, "and please have a nice day."

Cassie reached for a piece of dried meat, then found herself on the ground. *Groundslide,* she thought.

The answer came in the form of another blast and shock wave. This threw Cassie to the ground a second time, after she had just scrambled to her knees.

"It's the cases," Jake bellowed. "They've breached the room."

Clay stood and braced himself against smaller aftershocks.

"Everyone arm yourselves and get ready for a rush of blue many times greater than the last."

Once again, the ground shook. This time it was a steady beat of footfalls. It grew, as did the sensation of dread. As the first Azurians came into view, a hail of gunfire cut them to shreds.

"They can't stay topside much longer," Clay screamed above the thunderous noise. A sudden uproar of being sucked inside of oneself and blown out the other side, unable to move, overcame each member of the group except for Hatch.

Clay, still able to see from his prostate position, saw the ground open and swallow the hundreds of Azurians who had mounted the attack.

It took several minutes for the paralyzed humans to regain movement.

"You can bet they'll make sure they're above ground the full five minutes next time," Clay said. "That was a dry run."

"How long will they have to stay underground to recover?" Victor asked.

"After the next attack I'll let you know," Clay said. "Gert, you and Hatch come here a minute."

"What it is we kin do fer ya?"

"Can you tell me why Hatch was impervious to the weapons the Azurian's used earlier today?"

"If'n you mean by mpervus, that he were able to move, wince we weren't, I can't agin to tell ya, but Hatch here reckons he might have a sloo-shun." Gert stepped behind and to the right of his brother. "G'head Hatch tell 'em whatcha thunk."

"Is much same small small, zap," Hatch began, "many doodles—"

"Hold on there, wild man," Clay said, waving his hands. "I don't speak gibberish. Gert, step up here and tell me what he's saying before I lose my mind."

Gert pushed past his brother. "I fer sure can't be a knowin' why it is that no one in this here gaggle o people can't understood ol' Hatch," Gert fumed. "He's a-talkin' plain as kin be."

Clay closed his eyes and shook his head. "Gert, humor me, and explain why Hatch wasn't affected by the pulse of energy that paralyzed us all."

Gert and Hatch conversed.

Jake smiled, as several of the group gathered around the two gibbering small fries.

"If I didn't know better, I'd swear they were laying a cussing on each other."

Clay raised his eyebrows and waited for the conversation to conclude.

Gert turned to face Clay. "Now, here 'tis, and pay 'tension, cuz I don't chew my cud twice. Seems that Hatch come in ta this here world witout them thar whatchamacallit's we all gots to hear with."

"Ears?" Victor questioned. "They're right there on each side of his head."

"No, no, no," Gert protested. "It's the workin's up inside he ain't got. They tweren't nary even a hole to hear out of."

"That means it's a sound generator," Jake said.

"Earplugs?" Clay asked.

"Don't know if we can come up with a material that will seal tight enough," Jake said. "Any other suggestions?"

"Maybe so," Clay replied, "are the barrels in the back of the wagon still full?"

"As far as I know, we've had no need to open one," Jake said.

"Good, here's what we need to do. Get the barrels off the wagon. They won't touch the barrels themselves, that puts them too close to the gas, but they may be tempted to move them if they're still on the buckboard."

Before the process could begin, a six strong death squad took the group by surprise.

A sharp blue arm pierced Victor's chest, exiting through his spine. The Azurian threw his arm to the side, allowing Victor's body to slide free and twitch several times after hitting the ground.

Clay turned the creature to shreds and stopped to check on Victor. He barely missed becoming a kabob himself. He raised his head in time to turn his gun and fire, hitting the arm inches before it pierced his head.

A second death squad joined the assault.

"The barrels; dump one of the barrels," Clay barked.

Hatch and Gert unloaded the wagon before the attack.

"You heered the man," Gert said.

Hatch plunged the tip of his sword into the top of a barrel, careful not to let it contact the gas. He cut a slice down the middle of the top and with a tap of his fist the wood gave way.

"Any time now," Clay said.

The gasoline flowed over the edge of the barrel, a moment later a sixty gallon wave inundated the compact battle area, leaving a puddle six inches deep.

The Azurians melted, forming blobs of calladium as the gasoline soaked into the ground.

Zachariah along with Jake, Clive and Jason buried Victor. Everyone gathered, and Jason said a few words over the grave before planning for the next attack.

"Who's he talking to?" Jake asked.

"Not a clue," Clay said. "You know how the people on this planet are."

"Yeah, yeah," Jake said, "If you've said it once, you've said it a thousand times. People on Aon will worship everything from the sun to an ellack turd." Jake looked at Jason.

"There's something different about him."

Clay nodded. "As much as I hate to admit it, I know what you mean."

Before Jake could answer, a familiar low rumble was heard in the distance, growing in volume.

"Everyone follow me," Clay bellowed, "and now!"

What remained of the group set out behind Clay. Gert drove the buckboard and Hatch rode shotgun. Everyone else was borne by ellack.

Five minutes, Clay thought, *five more minutes.*

An Azurian stepped in front of Clive and removed the head and forelegs of his ellack. This caused the animal to drop, dig in and throw Clive forward.

The Azurian raised its deadly arm, primed to strike Clive mid-thorax. Clive's clothes, except for his briefs, ripped and flew from his body. Underneath, a sleek four-legged animal appeared. Its muscular rear legs pushed it past the downward moving Azurian arm.

Clive twisted, turned and extended its forepaw, tearing the creature's shoulder to shreds. The articulate animal Clive had become was three times the size of a man. It resembled a large cat. Its close-cropped fur was green with small black dots circled in yellow and a black mane that flowed from its eyebrows to the tip of its six foot long tail.

Clive's yellow eyes focused on its enemy. It circled and pounced, pulverizing the creature to dust.

Clive's alter ego would have been much more intimidating had it not been wearing a pair of tightie whities and one destroyed boot still clinging, to its left rear foot.

The thundering footfalls sounded as though they would soon overtake the weary fighters. The rear of the buckboard faced the onslaught. Hatch stood behind one of the full barrels, the top scored, but so far, unopened.

Four stood to the left of the wagon and four to the right, weapons drawn, awaiting the blue wave.

The Azurians were seen moving through the ruins of Baine about one hundred yards away. The column advanced another fifty yards and disappeared below the ground.

"Gert," Clay said, "how fast can you run?"

"Twouldn't b'leeve me if'n I teld ya."

"Did you see where the Azurians dropped underground?"

"Had my eyeball right on top of 'er."

"Good. How about the place where you and Hatch dumped the gasoline?"

"You mean wherein we had that thar last fight with them blue critters?"

"Exactly," Clay said.

"I kin find 'er slick as a whistle," Gert replied, smiling.

"Gert, this is what I want you to do. I need you to run, beginning where the Azurians disappeared to where our last battle took place and count your steps. After that, do the same thing in reverse to double check yourself." Clay took Gert by the shoulders. "You understand me?"

"Ever word of it. Now, lemme go so's I's kin get back."

Before Clay said another word, Gert was almost out of sight. In under a minute, a small dust cloud could be seen heading back toward the group.

"Fast enuff fer ya?"

For the moment Clay could do nothing more than nod.

"I need you to do the same thing one more time, but in a different direction."

"Jest point the way."

"Backtrack the fifty yards where we saw the Azurians go underground. Starting there, I want you to run the same amount of steps in the same direction we're moving now and stay there."

Once again Gert sped to the starting point and began his trek passing Clay and the rest.

"Whoa," Jake exclaimed as Gert flew by. Each man had to hold down his hat to keep it from blowing off his head.

Gert stopped and waved.

The wagon and ellacks pulled up to where Gert stood still waving.

"Where did you learn to run like that?" Clay asked.

"No wheres pa'ticular. Most o' my folks is faster'n me."

"Amazing," Ruben said, shaking his head.

"If we're attacked like last time," Clay said, "this should be close to the spot where they head back underground to recover."

"Ingenious," Cassie said.

"I hope it works." Clay replied. "There's nothing that says they won't exit the ground right where we stand." Clay scanned the area he expected the attack to come from. "I guess we'll worry about that when it happens."

"What's the plan, boss man?" Jake asked.

"We know they can stay above ground five minutes at a time and it seems to take around thirty minutes of recovery time underground. The plan is to cut off their doorway so they have to stay above ground."

"Makes sense," Jake said. "We can take a lot more of them out that way than we can with our weapons."

"What about the effect their weapons have on us?" Cassie asked. "Earplugs are still the only defense I can see."

For the first time, everyone noticed Clive standing in his underwear and one boot.

"Nice look you have going on there," Jake said. "Come here. Between the men we should find enough clothes to at least make you respectable."

"As far as earplugs," Clay said, "any ideas on the best material to use?"

"What if we soften a small piece of calladium," Ruben said, "and let that harden in our ear canals?"

Clay thought a moment. "Since that's the only suggestion, and there's no real way to test it except in battle, do it."

Before long, pieces of calladium with the texture of taffy were being passed to each person in the group.

Clive turned his down in favor of his alter ego reappearing again.

"Make it fast," Clay said. "It won't stay soft long."

"I hope we can get this stuff out after it hardens," Cassie said. She pressed the malleable material into her ear canals and helped Katie with hers.

Clay, along with everyone else, felt the calladium harden and expand. As it did so, rendering each person all but deaf.

Once again the massive footfalls fell as shock waves moving closer.

Clay looked for Jason but saw him nowhere. *Surely he wouldn't leave us when we needed him the most!* A stabbing thought traveled through Clay's brain and into his being. He sighed.

"I'd sure feel better if he was here."

ONE HUNDRED

"I TRUST WE ARE BEGINNING TO SEE a return on our investment in the form of calladium on the Aon project?" Gaithor asked Criton.

Criton stood meekly in front of his superior.

"There are inconsistencies as far as communication." Criton said. "I am unable to reach our operatives on the ground, our main contact being President Gaylen. It is as though they have vanished."

"Perhaps it is time to reach out to one of a different sort."

"I do not understand," Criton said. "I've been unable to communicate with anyone. please explain to me different sort."

Gaithor reached inside himself and removed one of the all too familiar blue stones. He handed it to Criton.

"This will tell you who to contact, when to make that contact and anything else you may need to know concerning said contact. Nothing more need be said. Please keep me apprised."

Criton looked at the stone, at Gaithor, and then disappeared into the fog.

ONE HUNDRED ONE

"HAVE I MISSED SOMETHING?" Jason asked Clay.

Between the calladium earplugs and the advancing Azurians, Clay was oblivious to Jason's presence.

Jason laid a hand on Clay's back, causing the big man to whirl around, nearly firing his weapon.

"Didn't mean to startle you," Jason said. "I couldn't be sure with all this distraction if you would be open for conversation, although I should have known you would be."

Clay dropped his arm, the relief evident on his face, and with the other clutched Jason by the shoulder.

"It's good to see you. Where have you been?"

"Just some business to attend to," Jason said. "But you have more important things to concern yourself."

Clay turned his attention toward the enemy at hand. *Wait a minute; I can't hear myself think, so how?* He turned around. Jason smiled and gave a nod. Later, Clay surmised. In fact, much later.

In an instant, the blue army was on top of them. Ruben manned the Gatling gun from the back of the buckboard, making sure it's placement left ample room to accommodate the width of a barrel.

A constant barrage of gunfire disintegrated blue warrior after warrior. Once Ruben cranked the handle, a massive explosion of blue cut a swath through the middle of the Azurian ranks fifteen or more deep.

Clay and Jake ripped holes through their opponents with a stack of sawed-off shotguns, reloading, courtesy of Cassie.

Katie ran in between the legs of the Azurians, dodging their attacks and causing them to slice through their neighbors or their own legs.

Gert and Hatch followed her path from above, leaving a headless carnage in their wake.

Clive destroyed entire beings with one swipe from his massive paws.

The ground was covered a foot or more deep in vibrating shards of calladium.

The action had slowed so much that Jake attempted to remove his earplugs. They popped out much easier than he expected. He held the earplug in the air to encourage everyone else to follow suit. The group complied, happy to join the ranks of the hearing again.

"Look," Jake said, "something's wrong with our blue buddies. You think they're tired and want to go home?"

"That's where they want to go." Clay scanned the ground. "Where are you? You've got to show yourself sooner than later. Gert, Hatch, Jake—in the buckboard now," Clay shouted. "Jake, you're driving. Ruben, back up and keep your eyes peeled. There are still death squads out there, so nail anything that tries to get close to the wagon."

Ruben cocked the slide lever back, readying the gun to fire.

Clay saw the shards of calladium about four feet behind the buckboard bulge and then sink.

"That's it! That's their doorway. Jake, move the wagon back four feet."

Jake jerked hard on the reins, and the buckboard rolled backward the distance.

"Dump the first barrel," Clay ordered.

The gas flowed into the depression, turning it into a thick sludge that acted as a plug sealing the hole.

Azurian after Azurian attempted to enter the closed doorway. As they piled on top of one another, the slow, abrasive process tore the blue warriors apart.

The doorway attempted to widen itself to the right and to the left of the original.

"Right there," Clay said.

Gert and Hatch emptied the second barrel into what would be the last depression.

"THAT'S GOOD COFFEE," Ruben said.

"Ground tree bark would taste good after what we've been through," Clay replied.

Jake sat sipping his coffee, staring at Clive.

"Being certain I'm not the only one curious about your, 'mean and green' status. I feel comfortable speaking for everyone when I ask this question. What in the hell are you?"

Clive chuckled. "I'm surprised you waited this long to ask." He set his bottle on the ground, rolled a smoke and lit it with a branch from the fire. Clive reclaimed his bottle, emptied its contents and took several drags from his cigarette.

"Methodical, huh? That's the way my head works." He finished his smoke and tossed the butt into the fire. "If you're wondering about the big green fuzzy thing, all I can tell you is his name." Clive grabbed a bottle and rolled another cigarette. He emptied half the bottle, and mixed within the smoke exiting his mouth came the answer. "Clive. His name is Clive."

"Okay, so everybody's name is Clive," Clay said. "That still doesn't tell us what you are or why you change."

"I change when the situation deems it necessary," Clive said. "It's not all my doing. When I sense life-threatening danger, that's where I stop and it begins."

"That makes no sense at all," Clay said. "Can you hear yourself?"

"I hear myself fine. What you don't understand is that the process is twofold. Once I see or sense something dangerous, my voluntary senses relinquish all control to the involuntary part of my body. I suppose this encourages my transformation by taking me out of the equation."

Clay stared at Jake and shook his head."I don't understand what you said, but I'll go with it all the same. If for no other reason, you saved a lot of lives out there today."

"Good enough," Clive said. "But since we're on the subject, I need to level with you. I told you earlier that I'm methodical, and that's with most everything of any importance in my life. Now for something I haven't told you. The story I relayed when I was a kid with my friend, Skank, was true, but I didn't quite finish the tale. After Skank was killed, and the man left the alley with the blue stone, I fought with myself. It was an internal battle, and this was the first time the change took place. Over the years, it evolved into what it is now. I learned that large quantities of alcohol gave me more control, but I never forgot that night in the alley. I've been searching for the man who killed my friend, and that's the real reason I came to Aon."

Mesmerized by the story, it took a minute or more for anyone to speak.

"Do you know who you're tracking?" Jake asked.

"*Was* tracking," Clive said. "The man turned out to be Lynch, and the Azurians got to him before I did."

"Always thought there was something strange about that man," Clay said.

"So you have no idea what race you come from?" Cassie asked.

"Astonian," Zachariah said.

Everyone, including Clive, looked at Zachariah.

"How do you know this?" Clive asked.

Zachariah stepped back and grew into a large, winged reptile.

"Well," Clive said, "I guess he would."

Greyshod raised his wings, and with one mighty downward push, lifted off the ground moving away until he was out of sight.

"He goes to gather reconnaissance," Jason said. "The storm is upon us."

"You know," Clay said, "the Azurians seem to be dumb as a stump, but that doesn't click."

"Same ol' Clay," a voice from the past said. "Smart one minute and stupid the next."

"I thought I took care of you a while back, you belligerent, ball of snot."

"Nah, you multiplied your trouble times two."

Clay turned around. Sal Ricky and what looked like his twin, stood beside him. Behind them, eight death squads, numbering almost fifty combatants stood at the ready.

"So it's getting to where you can't kill a stack of slime like you even if I blow you in half."

"It's a good thing you didn't splatter me all over the wall." Sal Ricky laughed and lit a cigarette. "Every piece, no matter how small, grows another me."

"Well, that's about the best news I've gotten in a while. It's not every day I get a chance to kill you multiple times."

"Tsk, tsk, tsk," Sal Ricky said, waving a slimy finger left to right and back again. "Believe me—you don't want to deal with more than one of me at a time."

"Oh, I don't know," Clay said. "As long as you do it the correct way, it could be fun."

Clay spun around and dropped to one knee. Out of his hand flew one shard of calladium. It hit Sal Ricky's clone in the midsection and disappeared. The twin vibrated wildly and disappeared inside himself with a loud sucking sound. A second later, the shard of calladium hit the ground causing a slight *tink, tink* sound.

"Well, snot ball, what do you think of that?"

Sal Ricky said nothing, the Azurians closed around him offering protection.

"You can't run, you fat tub of phlegm, and you sure can't hide behind these blue goons, so hold on, I'm on my way."

Three more death squads moved in from the side, severing the group. Jason, Clay, Jake, Gert and Hatch were together on one side, while Ruben, Cassie and Katie remained in the buckboard with the furry, green Clive walking alongside on the other.

"Well, somebody do somethin'," Katie said. "I ain't gonna stand around with my thumb stuck in my ear." With that, she vaulted into the crowd of blue soldiers dodging blow after self-destructive blow.

Ruben was firing from the back of the buckboard. He kept his shots low so as not to endanger any humans he couldn't see.

Cassie stood behind Ruben among a pile of loaded shotguns, taking out the occasional straggler trying to sneak around and attack Ruben from behind.

Gert and Hatch once again took the high road, but found the death squad not as easily conquered as the typical Azurian had been. They were dodging as much as they were inflicting damage.

Jason had woven his way through the Azurians, emulating Katie.

"I'm about halfway down on ammo," Clay shouted. His right thumb pushed the lever sideways ,and with an upward jerk of his wrist, the sawed-off double barrel split in two, expelling both shells. He allowed the gun to hang by a leather strap. While he fired his revolver with his left hand, he reloaded the shotgun with his right.

Jake used much the same method, and now the two men fought back to back, rotating in a slow deliberate motion.

Clive was ripping his way through blue soldiers like paper.

"Lemme go, you piece o trash," Katie protested. One of the Azurians held the young girl high in the air by her ankle.

A massive crust slide, triggered by a third rush of Azurians brought all combatants down. The ground jerked thirty feet to the east; a second later, it was back in its original position.

Clive leapt to Katie's aid; the movement of the ground carried him thirty feet past his mark.

The Azurian holding Katie acted as a catapult. The violent shifting ground jerked his feet one way, while throwing his upper body in the opposite direction. Katie slid from his grasp, and after a short flight, used her staff and a well-placed body roll to land safely.

The fighting continued. Now it resembled a strange no holds barred wrestling match.

The back and forth motion subsided, with each movement growing shorter than the last until standing was possible again. Before the fighting could continue, a thundering roar like no other caught the attention of man and Azurian alike.

"They're back," Clay said, "and this is by far the biggest wave yet." *No ear plugs,* he thought, and the fighting resumed.

The pulse from the weapons the Azurians carried could be heard, but were not close enough to affect human ears.

"They'll be here soon," Clay said, "and we'll be on our backs with calladium poking out of every inch of our bodies." He fired two rounds with his shotgun, three with his revolver, then reloaded in a never-ending cycle.

"Maybe I can buy us some time," Jason said.

"I'll kiss you right smack on the mouth, for every extra minute you purchase."

Jake, having reloaded his shotgun, pushed the thumb latch on his sidearm and slapped the speed loader over the barrel, pushing it back into place in one smooth motion. He fired twice and paused to reload.

"I'll kiss you twice."

For the first time, both men noticed that Jason had no weapon; instead he waved his hands which repelled any Azurian that approached him.

Not having time to comment on the occurrence, both men accepted what they saw and continued to fight.

A stiff breeze filtered through the crowd, subsided and reappeared a hundred yards away. The source of the wind was soon evident.

Greyshod descended with a ground-shaking thud. Facing the thousands of new arrivals, he flapped his wings. The Azurians' forward progress began to slow. They lowered their heads and gained several steps.

Greyshod dug his claws into the hard ground and increased the intensity of his airflow. The Azurians slid backward, upended and tumbled out of control.

Six more death squads appeared, four from the north and two from underground.

Jake noticed the reinforcements flowing in to join their brethren. "I'm all but out of ammo, and there's more Azurians coming."

Clay was reduced to firing his dozen gun, one barrel at a time. "Same here," he said. He fired once, decimating a soldier.

Gert and Hatch both dropped in from above.

"Consarn zurns, they done an k-nocked all the clajum off'n our sords."

"They've done a good job of bringing us all together," Clay said.

"Easier to do away with if we're all in one place," Jake said.

They were surrounded now, and the Azurians tightened the circle.

"Speaking of all together," Clay said, "has anyone seen Jason?"

Clive backed away from the fighting to attack from behind. With two swipes of his mighty forepaws, he dispatched twelve Azurians before paying the ultimate price.

Ruben and Cassie enjoyed a lull in the fighting as the focus was on the other four.

Jason startled the pair. "Here, take Katie and leave for new Baine now."

The child ran to Cassie.

Ruben opened his mouth to protest.

"It's not up for discussion, now go!"

Katie jumped into the back, Cassie rode shotgun and Ruben drove the team.

"Miss me?" Jason asked.

"Where ya been?" Clay replied.

"Had an errand to run."

"How did you get here?" Jake asked.

"I don't believe we have the time right now to discuss the different modes of locomotion," Jason said, "but get with me later."

Clay chuckled sarcastically. "You actually see a later in our future?"

"I see a lot of things." With that, Jason raised his foot and stomped twice on the ground.

The vibration told Greyshod to take off; the Azurians now back underground. The vibration also told the ellacks pulling the buckboard, full speed for the next three miles. In conclusion, the ground would collapse taking humans, Azurians and the entire city of Baine with it.

One Hundred Three

"YOU HAVE ENTERED MY DOMAIN without being summoned," Gaithor said. "This act may be your last."

"It is for that reason I have come," Criton said.

"Enter and speak."

Criton pushed through a wall cloud and entered the room.

"I trust you made contact," Gaithor said.

"Yes, and with surprising results." Criton tossed the blue stone back to Gaithor.

Gaithor caught the stone and looked at Criton.

Starting with a blue point passing through the wall cloud, a large blue creature entered the room.

"What is the meaning of this?" Gaithor demanded.

"The stone you hold in your hand is a wealth of information," Criton said. "Even though the very essence of calladium is evil, it is so much so it will seek to destroy evil."

Criton and the Azurian moved slowly toward Gaithor. "As for good, once it is introduced, it will protect its host until consummation can occur."

Gaithor stopped, unable to move any further.

"Evil, is an altogether different proposition," Criton continued. "In the absence of good, consummation is instantaneous."

"You must remember," Gaithor said, "we are a benevolent society."

"It is not I who would dream of inflicting such pain, but my new friend."

"I believe you know J. Smith." The Azurian plunged his arm through the cloudlike form, Gaithor, who collapsed in upon himself.

J. Smith wobbled and then dropped to his knees.

"I remember now," Criton said, "you can stand no more than five minutes out of your element or you will cease to be. I suppose my implication of a calladium chamber to provide you with a much-needed respite from this atmosphere must have been misconstrued."

J. Smith took a feeble swipe at Criton. The cloud creature stepped out of the way while J. Smith hit the ground.

"Take care with whom you ally yourself," Criton said, "Gaithor could not be trusted. Me? I'm just a victim of circumstance. My world will starve while I shall feast for the rest of my existence."

Criton broke a small piece from the body of J. Smith, tossed it into his mouth and began to chew.

One Hundred Four

THE WAGON HAD REACHED A CRUISING SPEED of nearly sixty miles an hour. They were more than able to keep up with the ever-increasing sinkhole.

Ruben more or less held onto the reins; the two ellacks seemed to be on cruise control.

Ruben rubbed his shoulder, the one injured by the Azurian. He jerked suddenly and pulled hard on the reins. It took several moments, but he brought the team to a halt.

"What are you doing," Cassie demanded. "We'll be swallowed up if you don't get this wagon moving again."

Ruben said nothing, but wrapped his hands around Cassie's neck and began to shake it.

Katie stood up in the back.

"You leave her be!" She brought her staff down hard on Ruben's arms causing him to loosen his grip. She swept the weapon into his throat and upward, catching his chin. Then, with a full two arm swing, she struck the bridge of his nose, knocking him backwards off of the buckboard.

Cassie grabbed the reins and shook them, sending the ellacks into motion again.

"What's wrong?" Katie said. "We're not movin'!"

The collapsing ground was catching up with the two women, causing the buckboard to drop at an pitch leading to the sinkhole waiting to swallow them.

Cassie snapped hard on the reins. Both ellacks instinctively dropped their extra pair of legs. The wagon began to climb up the incline and back on flat ground just as the sink hole arrived.

Within minutes, they were back up to speed.

Katie stepped over the back of the driver's seat and sat beside Cassie. They looked at each other and smiled.

Cassie's face dropped in terror as Ruben, running faster than the wagon, caught up with the ellacks. He dug his heels into the ground, bringing the wagon to a halt.

He stomped toward the women with one grizzly purpose. Katie and Cassie were both off of opposite sides of the wagon with a different purpose. Katie went to work with her staff, and Cassie pulled two sawed-off shotguns from the back of the wagon.

"Out of the way!" Cassie screamed.

Katie pushed the staff into one of Ruben's eyes and flipped out of the way.

Cassie unloaded one of the guns into Ruben's chest. The impact caused him to jerk, but he kept coming. Cassie's next shot was to the head, removing everything from the nose up, and he still kept coming.

Her third shot removed most of his left shoulder, causing his arm to dangle. Cassie noticed a blue glow emanating from the shoulder wound. She ran back to the wagon, removed one more shotgun and pulled both triggers, disintegrating most of his left side and turning the piece of calladium to dust. With this, Ruben hit the ground and began to decompose as if he had been dead for days.

"On the wagon," Cassie yelled. She brought the team back up to speed, and before long, arrived in Baine.

ONE HUNDRED FIVE

CASSIE AND KATIE AWOKE as the sun reached its highest point in the sky. They left Cassie's modest apartment and looked toward old Baine.

"It's gone," Cassie said. "The ruins, everything, is gone."

"Kin we git somethin' to et?" Katie asked.

"Sure thing," Cassie said.

Cassie watched as Katie finished her second plate of flapjacks. She took a sip of coffee.

"Think that'll hold you?"

Her cheeks puffed out to the point of being unable to talk, Katie nodded.

Cassie finished her coffee."I want you to stay here; I'm going back to Baine."

"Don't reckon you are, leastwise by yerself." Katie pounded her staff on the wooden floor.

"I will not put you in danger," Cassie said.

"I ain't spectin' to get in no danger, but I'm here to tell ya, you ain't goin' with'n out me."

Cassie sighed. "Guess it can't be any worse than what you've been through already."

Cassie saddled two ellacks and set out for the last place Baine was seen. As they moved closer, it seemed as though all the vegetation was removed and replaced with smooth, flat sand.

"Well, ain't this somethin'" Katie said. "Taint no sign of that big hole that were swallower'n' up every thin in sight."

Cassie stopped. She couldn't tell if it was a mirage from the heat waves rising from the sand or a group of people sitting under a huge shade tree. She picked up the pace until she was at a steady gallop.

"Well, looky there, Miss Cassie," Katie said, "I'm a thinkin' that they is people and not one of them thar rages."

"You may be right," Cassie said. "And what's with the *Miss Cassie*?"

"Jest tryin' to show my respect, that's all."

"Well, stop it!" Cassie smiled.

As they drew near to the tree, Cassie made out Clay, Jake, Gert and Hatch. Four ellacks were tied on the opposite side of the tree. The men were finishing breakfast.

"I must say, you four are a sight for sore eyes."

"Right back at ya, missy," Jake said, "Oh, excuse me. I didn't mean to leave you out, Katie."

Katie shrugged.

"What happened?" Cassie asked. "After last night, I didn't expect to see any of you alive."

"I wish I could tell you," Clay said, "but after the ground collapsed, everything's a blur. Everyone woke up this morning on bed rolls, four ellacks and provisions to boot." Clay looked at Cassie and then at Katie.

"What about Ruben?"

Cassie shook her head. It was her turn to look around.

"Where is Jason?"

"Can't figure it out. Whatever happened last night contained his image in every instance. After that, it's just what you see here."

Gert and Hatch rose and walked thirty feet from the rest of the group. Facing the sun, they knelt down, bowed their heads and closed their eyes.

"What are they doing?" Cassie asked.

"Looks like we've got ourselves a couple of sun worshippers."

Everyone joined Gert and Hatch. The two stood.

"Do you really think talking to that big yellow ball will help?"

"Big yeller ball?" Gert questioned.

"Yeah," Jake said, "You know, the sun." He pointed to the ball of fire in the sky.

"You sure not understandin'," Gert said. "We don't worship that there sun, ya consarn idgit. Why, that'd be plumb loco."

Hatch pointed to a set of footprints that seemed to begin from nowhere and head off into the distance.

"We worship the Son of God."

About the Author

 **Lynn Kevin Steigleder** was born in Richmond, Virginia. He spent most of his young adult life as a supervisor in the field of construction and fabrication. When Lynn's department was outsourced within two months of his diagnosis of multiple sclerosis, he realized the need to transition into a new career path.

During a fishing trip, his son suggested that he consider writing as a career, having enjoyed short stories written by his father in years past. His first two novels, *Rising Tide* and *Eden's Wake*, are part of the *Rising Tide Series*. *Terminal Core* is a standalone science fiction novel.

Mr. Steigleder's website is: www.lynnsteigleder.com

Other books by Lynn Steigleder

The Rising Tide Series

Rising Tide

Rising Tide depicts a world in which land is at a premium due to the advancing sea, where man's attempt to adapt has led to a decay of morals into survival of the fittest. In the midst of the ocean, a crew of racketeers rescues a stranded diver, Ben Adams. Is the rescue just a fortunate coincidence for Ben, or has he been led to this rendezvous with fate for a common goal? A mysterious island inhabited by a primitive yet advanced race of people. A devious ship captain's metamorphosis into the essence of evil and a ship's container discovered by itself in a billion square miles of ocean all play a role in this tale of rebirth for a world corrupted by the collapse of morality.

Eden's Wake

Ben's best friend is killed in an underwater implosion on a dying world. Living to die again, the two men reunite and battle for an ancient artifact, a relic which will ensure this planet's survival. Ben crosses a threshold. The world he leaves—doomed; the world he enters—reborn. His wife, Eve, and their bumbling charge, Eleazor, follow Ben through the doorway and blindly into the void. This is Book Two in the *Rising Tide* series.

Available online
and at fine bookstores
and at Soul Fire Press
http://soulfirepress.com